Outstanding praise for Tessa Harris and her Dr. Thomas Silkstone Mysteries!

The Dead Shall Not Rest

"Outstanding . . . well-rounded characters, cleverly concealed evidence and an assured prose style point to a long run for this historical series."
—*Publishers Weekly* (starred review)

"Populated with real historical characters and admirably researched, Harris's novel features a complex and engrossing plot. A touch of romance makes this sophomore outing even more enticing. Savvy readers will also recall Hilary Mantel's *The Giant, O'Brien*."
—*Library Journal*

The Anatomist's Apprentice

"Densely plotted . . . We await—indeed, demand—the sequel."
—*The New York Times Book Review*

"An absorbing debut . . . Harris has more than a few tricks up her sleeve and even veteran armchair puzzle solvers are likely to be surprised."
—*Publishers Weekly*

"Smart misdirection and time-period-appropriate medical details make for a promising start to a new series. A strong choice for readers of Ariana Franklin and Caleb Carr."
—*Library Journal*

Books by Tessa Harris

THE ANATOMIST'S APPRENTICE
THE DEAD SHALL NOT REST
THE DEVIL'S BREATH

Published by Kensington Publishing Corporation

For John and Mary, with love

Is it a time to wrangle, when the props
And pillars of our planet seem to fail,
And nature, with a dim and sickly eye,
To wait the close of all?

—"The Timepiece," by William Cowper (1731–1800)

THE
DEVIL'S BREATH

Chapter 1

Oxfordshire, England,
in the Year of Our Lord 1783

At first the horror of it stayed the bury man's tongue. Staggering out of his cottage as dawn broke he did not shout or scream, but grunted like a half-wit, his arms paddling in the filmy light of the deserted street. As he zigzagged across the road the good people of Brandwick could be forgiven for thinking he was in the grip of strong liquor. He had certainly been full of it the last anyone had seen of him after the casting out.

It was only when the baker, rising early to fire his oven, saw him and went over to him that Joseph Makepeace began to cry out. The sounds he made were unformed, staccato. His arms jabbed at the air, pointing toward his home. His tongue may have been stopped but his eyes spoke; to anyone who looked into them they told of an unutterable terror—too awful for words. His body began to shake violently as his chest, loaded with breath, heaved and pitched like a storm-tossed barque.

Hearing the commotion, some of the villagers lifted their latches and opened their windows. Some came to their doors. Some of them wondered if the devil himself had entered Joseph Makepeace. After the events of the previous evening, there were many who thought the prospect not just possible, but likely. They had gathered in the marketplace to watch the laying on of hands. Evil was abroad, living in his fiendish children, and needed to be banished. There they had witnessed the boy and girl judder and jerk and scream in front of the clergyman. Foul oaths spewed from the girl's mouth. She had lifted her shift, opened her legs. But the Reverend Lightfoot had called upon the Lord. Hymns were sung, prayers were said and he had seen to it that Beelzebub was cast out of Joseph Makepeace's children. Could it be that the devil had now taken refuge in the father? they asked themselves.

Talk of such unaccountable happenings was becoming commonplace. The world was growing a more fearful place by the day. For the past two months, the village and the surrounding area had been held in the grip of a great fog that had blanketed the earth one night and poisoned people and plants alike. What any of them would not give to see a cloud, white and billowing, or a chink of blue sky, just a square the size of a shepherd's smock. That would be enough to reassure them that all would soon return to the usual pattern of things. Yet still this great mysterium covered the countryside and the rivers, infecting everything that it touched just as surely as the devil spread his spore. With the strange haze came the signs; the bloodred sun from dawn to dusk, the raging storms and the balls of fire in the firmament. And with the signs and portents came a mounting sense of impending doom.

The times tested every man's mettle. At first neighbors had helped each other, sharing bread and duties. Then, as more men doubled over in the fields and as more children began to cough and wheeze, some began to question. They all knew their Bible. They all knew that God sent the Ten Plagues to the Egyptians: He changed the water of the Nile into blood—were the rivers not now running with poison? He sent swarms of flies—there were flies that tormented both beast and man. He destroyed crops. Was the corn not withered and brown in the harvest fields? Worst of all, He killed the firstborn. Were not all the fine young men dropping like stones as they labored? The signs were there for anyone to read. These were times not seen since Moses himself walked the land and each day brought a new terror.

The baker put his hand on Joseph Makepeace's shoulder, but

it only served to agitate. He was soon joined by the blacksmith and the watchman and together they tried to steady him.

"Be calm, Joseph!"

"What ails you?"

"Best fetch the vicar."

But Joseph Makepeace just stared at the men, too shocked to speak, so they led him back to his cottage to see whether some terrible fate had befallen his household. Inside they saw an up-turned flagon of gin on the rush mat and a blanket by the hearth. They exchanged knowing glances. He had been too drunk to take to his own bed that night. But it was only when they opened the door into the back room that they saw the children. The baker turned away and retched and the blacksmith stood transfixed. It was the watchman, stout and worldly, who steeled himself to stoop for a closer look.

The girl was lying facedown across her pallet. Her long hair was streaked dark red. Her brother was by her side; his skull smashed like a marrow. Nearby lay their father's shovel, its blade smeared with blood.

The others could see that the watchman's arm was trembling as he stretched forward to turn the girl over. They flinched when she flopped to one side, her eyes wide open and her skin as white as milk. The watchman closed his own eyes, as if trying to blink away the sight, but when he opened them again a second later, he saw faces peering in at the window. A woman shrieked and ran off. The men, three of them, merely gawped.

"Away with you," he shouted. "Be gone!"

"Who could do such a thing?" asked the baker, fighting back the tears. He turned to see Joseph Makepeace, crouched in the corner of the room, whimpering, with his arms cradling his head. "Who did this, Joseph? Tell me it were not you!" He marched over to him and aimed a fist at his face, but Make-peace's arms flew up just in time and took the blow.

"Leave him be!" shouted the watchman. "He's not done this. He was too far in his cups last night to stir."

" 'Tis the work of the devil," the blacksmith reflected, his eyes fixed on the bloody flagstones.

The watchman clicked his tongue and shook his head. "Stop your foolish talk, will ye? We need to do something."

"What?" the other two chorused.

"Go and fetch Dr. Silkstone."

"The doctor from the Colonies?" asked the baker.

The watchman nodded. "He'll find out who killed these two. God rest their souls."

Chapter 2

It had all begun when the first portent came, two months earlier. It happened just after the church bells had tolled noon in the county of Lincolnshire, one hundred and fifty miles to the northeast of Brandwick as the crow flies. The sound carried over the gentle wold, mingling with the song of the skylarks above. It signified to the laborers in the surrounding harvest fields it was time to break. A small platoon of men, armed with scythes, had advanced across three acres of barley, leaving a carpet of jagged stalks in their wake. Behind them came the women, sickles in hand, gathering up the fallen sun-ripe stems.

At the sound of the bells, they put down their tools and walked over to the field gate where one of the women was opening a keg of small beer. Filled jugs in hand, the men settled themselves down in the shade of the stooks they had cut that morning. The June sun was strong and their throats were corn-dust dry.

The knife-grinder collected the scythes to sharpen as they rested. While some of the reapers used a whetstone to hone their dull blades, others relied on his skill to peen out the edges. The young man, his dark head swathed in a bright red scarf tied at the nape of his neck, had driven his anvil into the top of a fence post by the wooden gate and had been doing a brisk trade since the early morning. His mule stood patiently nearby in the hedgerow's dense shade, whisking away with his tail the black harvest flies that dotted the air.

The men drank so long and hard that it was the women who noticed first. One of them, younger than the others, had climbed on the wagon at the top end of the field to hand down hunks of bread and cheese. She was gathering up the baskets when she happened to glance beyond the wold toward the salt marshes. A great flat expanse of open country lay before her, stretching as far as the coast, and the sight of it barely registered at first. She had even continued to busy herself with the task in hand before she realized what she had seen. She looked up again a few seconds later and there it was—a thin bank of gray mist lying low across the horizon. A frown settled on her freckled brow.

"Sea fret's coming in," she called down to the other women below.

They all knew it was bad news. At least a day's work would be lost once the heavy fog that rolled in from the coast had settled on the ripe barley crop.

An older woman hitched up her skirts. "Let's see," she said, holding out her arm to be helped up. She, too, now looked out across the flatlands toward the marshes from the wagon's vantage point. After a moment's deliberation she was satisfied the girl was right.

"Best tell Mr. Bullimore," she said, adding: "He'll not be pleased."

The younger woman hastily clambered down and broke into a trot as she headed toward the cluster of men who sat around drinking.

"Where's our grub then, wench?" shouted one of them. "We're hungry as hawks." The others cheered and whistled, but she ignored their childish taunts and walked straight up to the foreman who sat with his back against a stook, swatting away the harvest flies.

"Mr. Bullimore, sir," she began breathlessly.

The foreman looked up at her, shielding his eyes from the sun's glare.

"What is it, Hester?"

"There's a sea fret coming, sir."

Bullimore, a broad man in his middle years, rolled his eyes and scrambled to his feet. He turned to the east. The heat made the barley fields shimmer like burnished gold. He strained his eyes, squinting in the bright light.

"I see no fret, woman," he chided.

"I saw it from the cart, sir, as God is my witness, and so did Mistress Pickwell."

He eyed her skeptically. "Show me."

She led him to the wagon a few yards up the slope and he climbed onto it for a better view. There was no mistaking what he saw.

"By the . . ."

The young woman clambered up to join him. There it was: a silvery ribbon that clung to the horizon, only now the clouds were more clearly defined than before. The fret was moving inland fast.

" 'Tis a thick one all right," conceded the foreman, then, cupping his hands around his mouth, he called out to the men below: "Get back to work, lads. Fret's coming in!"

The reapers rose quickly and picked up their honed scythes with a renewed urgency. They understood that if there was no barley harvested, there would be lower pay.

"Put your backs into it," shouted Bullimore, striding down the slope toward them. "I reckon we've an hour at the most."

And so they began again, cutting the crack-dry stems of corn with great sweeps of their new-sharpened scythes. The women fell in behind, gathering the cut barley up in their arms in a wide embrace, before evening out the ears neatly to be twined by the boys.

As the men advanced through the crop, so the rabbits and hares scattered before them, running hither and thither. The harvest flies, too, rose in black columns above the barley and flew off. From out on the marsh, a curlew's plaintive cry sounded.

"Hurry, men," called Bullimore. He took off the kerchief he wore and mopped the sweat from his brow.

They made good progress. An hour later several dozen more stooks were standing sentinel. The boys had worked well, binding the stems tight, their young hands protected against the cutting twine by thick leather gauntlets. The barley heads sat drying in the sun, only by now it was losing its heat. The foreman had already noticed a change in the sky. He could read the clouds as if they were words on a page; wispy mares' tails signified fine weather, while mackerel scales warned of a storm, but this sky was quite alien to him. It was as if the words were written in a foreign language. There was something strange; something unsettling about this sky.

It was then that he suddenly felt a cool breeze pique the hairs at the back of his neck. The wind was changing direction. He shivered and saw the goose bumps rise on his arms. The wind was coming about, turning northwest. It could hasten the arrival of the fret. He estimated it would take another two hours at least to finish the field, but he suspected they had half an hour at the most before the fog reached them. He walked up the slope once more to check on its progress. Climbing onto the wagon again, he looked out toward the marsh. The sea of shimmering corn had been dulled by the change in the light, smudging the horizon, making it hard to differentiate between the two. He narrowed his eyes, focusing into the distance, but to his surprise it appeared that the advancing bank of mist had disappeared. He frowned. Were his eyes playing tricks on him? He looked away, then looked back. No, he could see no fret, just an odd haze. It seemed that the fog had been dissipated by the heat, or perhaps by the change in the wind direction. Either way, he breathed a deep sigh of relief. But wait. Now he sniffed the air. What was that smell? Instead of the musk-sweet scent of new-mown corn, he sensed something else; something acrid and bitter. It reminded him of the saltpeter they used to cure the pork mingled with charcoal from the smithy's forge, or perhaps even rotten eggs. He looked over to where the knife-grinder stood by the anvil. He'd heard tell of sparks from the clash of steel on stone setting light to stubble over at Fulstow last week, but he could see no smoke.

Jumping down from the wagon he turned his thoughts back to the men. He decided he would not tell them that the fret had lifted. He did not want to break their rhythm. It was amazing how quickly they could work when they put their minds, as well as their backs, into it.

Striding toward them again Bullimore saw the knife-grinder by the field gate. He was packing up his anvil and whetstone.

"And where might you be going?" he snapped as he drew near.

The young man cocked his head. "I be going the same way as the hares and the rabbits and the flies and the skylarks," he replied.

"But there's plenty more blades to sharpen afore we're through here," insisted Bullimore.

The grinder gave him an odd look. Then, realizing that he was the only person to know that the sea fret had now receded, the foreman softened his tone. Leaning toward the young man, he said quietly: "All's well, now." He reinforced this with a re-assuring nod. "Fret's gone." But the grinder seemed unmoved and instead of gratefully receiving this information, lifted the corner of his fulsome lips in a smirk.

"The sea fret may be gone, but something much worse is on its way," he countered.

"What do you mean?" asked Bullimore, puzzled, but the young man turned his back on him and mounted his mule.

"There are signs, sir," he replied, settling himself in the sad-dle. "Smell the wind. Listen to the birds," he said, and he lifted his black eyes heavenward. The foreman listened.

"I hear nothing," he concluded after a moment.

The young man smiled. "Just so," he said, and he touched his forehead with his finger and kicked his mule. "Good luck to you, sir," he called as he headed off inland, away from the coast.

Bullimore looked grave. That smell was lingering in his nos-trils. It was true, too, that the skylarks were no longer singing and the harvest flies that were such a plague to both man and beast seemed to have flown. But what of it? The threat of the sea fret had subsided. They could work until sundown—another seven hours. The cooler air was welcome. The breeze was picking up now. They would easily finish the field that day; perhaps even start on the next. He shrugged his broad shoulders, dabbed the cold sweat from his brow and began to walk toward his own scythe, which was propped against a sheaf nearby.

He looked up to the heavens once more, shaking his head. Where had the skylarks gone? Why had they flown? And what was that faint acrid whiff that clung to the air? Perhaps he should go and check, just once more. Another look to err on the side of caution. He tramped back up the slope again, his pace quickening with every step. Shaking his head he told himself that he never did like travelers: they'd put a curse on you as soon as look at you; make a man doubt his own judgment. They took pleasure in putting dread into the hearts of God-fearing folk.

Taking a deep breath, he heaved himself up onto the wagon once more. Looking down, he could see the men were making good progress. The women and boys, too. They were gathering and twining as quickly as he had ever beheld them. Needs must when the devil drives, as the saying went, but now the devil was gone. . . . Or was he? First a look of puzzlement, then of shock, then of fear scudded across Bullimore's face. The fret was gone, true, but what was that looming over the horizon? Not mist, but a bank of billowing cloud, its great curves and sweeps and pillows of vapor easily visible, like the full sails of a galleon. It was heading straight toward them. Spread out across the entire skyline, it seemed to be traveling at speed, like an enormous wave blown by the gathering wind. It was rising high, above the skylark's domain, and would soon block out the sun.

It was then that he felt something settle on his arm. Whereas an hour or so ago he had been swatting away the flies that plagued him about his eyes and nose, drops of water now fell on his skin. He looked up and saw the rain falling, mingled with flakes, settling like gray snow on the ground.

Rooted to the spot, Bullimore watched the approaching cloud roll in. He had never seen such a sight before, not in all his years in the wolds. His thoughts turned to the men and women below. He began to call to them, but when he opened his mouth, the sound did not come. There was a harshness on the air; the acrid stench had intensified and clawed at his tongue and inside his nostrils. The rain made his eyes smart and soon tears were streaming down his cheeks. The drops pricked his skin, too, stinging with a painful intensity. His breath no longer came easily. Gasping and spluttering, he staggered back toward the reapers. By now they, too, had seen the ominous cloud looming up over the fields and smelled the stifling vapors. The rain, mingled with the gray snow, was falling heavily, drenching the stubble and making it harder to see.

"Run!" one cried. "Run!" As panic took hold, they dropped their scythes and sickles and leather gauntlets where they stood.

"To the barn," cried Bullimore above the din.

The threshing barn lay in a hollow, just beyond the field gate, and every man, woman, and child headed toward it as fast as they could. The vast bank of cloud seemed to be gathering pace, churning within itself, belching out a foul miasma.

One of the women stumbled. A man picked her up and carried her. Another remained transfixed with fear. Her eyes filled with tears as she watched the thick gray veil draw itself across the sun, blocking out the light.

Now many of the women were screaming, and those who were not screaming were choking and coughing. The men, too, found themselves fighting for breath as they staggered toward the barn in the mysterious half light. One of them, in his teen years, doubled over coughing and dropped to his knees before he reached the gate. But the cloud was almost upon them and no one stopped to help.

By this time Bullimore had reached the barn and, joined by two or three of the men, he managed to prize open the huge wooden doors, herding everyone in like sheep.

"Hurry, for God's sake," he gasped, pulling women and boys inside.

He could still see some fighting their way through the narrow field gate, jostling and pushing each other, but he feared it was too late. The young man he had seen fall was already swallowed up and he knew there were half a dozen others who would not make it to the barn before the noxious fog enveloped them, too. He had to think of those who were already inside.

"Close the doors," he ordered. The men hesitated for a moment, and in that split second Bullimore looked out to see the terrified face of Hester, arms outstretched, groping her way toward them. He saw her body jerk backward, as if the very devil himself had gripped her for an instant, only to spew her out with such force a second later that she fell flat on the ground not twenty yards in front of them. Another second and she had disappeared, smothered by the advancing smog.

"Close them, I say!" cried Bullimore and in a trice they pushed the great doors to and let down the bolt with a thud just as the deadly vapors began to lick at the timbers outside.

"May God save us!" cried Mistress Pickwell before clutching her chest. They were the last words she uttered.

On a ridge half a mile or so away, above the hollow, the knife-grinder stopped his mule and watched with a morbid fascination as he saw the valley and the land below the escarpment disappear under the thick blanket of cloud. Licking his finger, he held it aloft to gauge the direction of the wind. A northwesterly. Next, taking his scarf from around his head, he covered his nose and mouth and secured it at the back with a knot. The hollow had slowed down the march of this monster, but he knew it would soon rise up the scarp and continue its relentless progress inland. He kicked his mule hard in the ribs and took one last look back at the scene below. The threshing barn had disappeared completely now, swathed in a mantle of deadly vapor. The dense fog muffled the cries of those trapped inside. He headed south.

Chapter 3

Even before the first deaths, even before the fog, Dr. Thomas Silkstone detected a certain strangeness in the air. It was a strangeness barely perceptible to most; indeed it was only felt by those who knew the signs, men rooted in the ways of the land or of science. Some might call it a sixth sense or clairvoyance, others perception or intuition. The Delaware Indians of his native Pennsylvania even had a symbol for it—the bat. It helped their shamans see through illusion or ambiguity and go straight to the truth of matters. But, whatever the truth behind the small, and to most, insignificant, happenings that the young anatomist noticed on that bright June morning, he felt an acute disquiet.

The following day he would leave London for Boughton Hall, the Oxfordshire country home of Lady Lydia Farrell, the woman with whom he planned to spend the rest of his life. Theirs was not a straightforward relationship. He would be the first to acknowledge that. Lydia's husband, Captain Michael Farrell, had been charged with her brother's murder, but the captain had been found hanged as he awaited trial. A string of deaths followed and conspired to lead Lydia to attempt to take her own life. But it was only recently that she had revealed the real reason for attempting suicide. When she discovered she was pregnant with Michael's child before their marriage, he had made her submit to John Hunter, an anatomist favored by ladies who found themselves in an undesirable predicament. But the barbarous bid to kill the child in her womb had failed. The son she bore, however, was left with a crippled arm. Then, shortly after the birth, Michael told her that the babe had died in its sleep and no more was said. That was six years ago. In the past few months, however, documents had come to light that gave Lydia hope that her son may still be alive. This was the mission that Thomas had promised to undertake; to track down Lydia's long-lost child. That was why his excitement at the prospect of seeing his beloved once more was tempered with apprehension.

He had slept fitfully the previous night. The air in his room hung hot and humid. He had pulled down the sash in the vain hope that a cool breeze would waft through the opening, but all that permeated from the street was the stench of rotting rubbish and the cries of restless babes and stray dogs. It was only when he managed to turn his thoughts to Lydia's loving smile, her gentle voice and her tender touch, that he felt a sense of calm wash over him and he finally drifted off in the early hours.

His sleep was short-lived, however. He rose at dawn to pack. Pulling out a large valise from under his bed, he began to muster a change of clothes and some toiletries. He hoped he would be able to stay at the hall for at least a month, possibly longer. The events of the past few weeks had left him drained, both physically and mentally, and he relished the idea of spending time with his beloved, away from the stinking dissecting rooms of London.

An hour later the sky was lightening over the rooftops to reveal yet another cloudless day. Thomas walked across the courtyard and down the short flight of steps to his laboratory. Inside it was pleasantly cool. The rising morning heat was kept at bay by the absence of large windows. There was only one, high up in the wall, facing the street. Even so, a shaft of strong light was already warming the stone flags. Thomas was grateful there was no cadaver awaiting dissection. For the last three or four days the city heat had been so stifling as to make any teaching, or indeed study, out of the question. Even he, with his cast-iron stomach and trusty clay pipe that was so often called upon to mask unpleasant odors, was inclined to feel nauseous in such circumstances. When the mercury on his wall thermometer rose higher than eighty degrees, even he found the reek of death intolerable.

Yet there were others who suffered a great deal more than he. The Thames, from which so many of the common people drew their water, was turning into an even more deadly stew of detritus and disease. Horse troughs were running dry and remained unreplenished and small beer was becoming scarce. At noon even the costermongers and hawkers around Covent Garden sought the shade of the Piazza's cloisters and ladies with corsets laced too tight were regularly fainting in the street.

Closer to home, Mistress Finesilver, the housekeeper, complained that her pantry had been invaded by an army of red ants that had taken refuge from the scorching heat outside. Worse still, the milk was lasting no longer than three hours before it soured.

Thomas wondered how Franklin, his white rat, had fared in the stifling night. He walked over to his cage in the corner of the room, unfastened the door, and held out a length of bacon rind he had purloined from his own breakfast plate. Yet instead of the usual greeting from the rat that always jumped into his master's hand, the creature darted out of his cage like a thing possessed and headed straight toward the closed door.

Strange, thought Thomas to himself, forlornly holding out the bacon as he approached him. But the rat ignored his master and simply scratched at the door, making loud squeaking sounds as he did so.

"What's wrong?" Thomas asked out loud, frowning. "What ails you?" Bending down he cupped his hands and picked up the rodent by the scruff of its neck, but it squirmed round and promptly bit him, so that Thomas let out a cry and dropped him the short distance onto the flags. The rat scurried back to the door but, undeterred, the young doctor scooped him up once more and quickly placed him back in his cage, securing the door firmly.

"I shall have to tell Mistress Finesilver to keep an extra eye on you while I'm away," he scolded, pointing accusingly at the rat as it scratched frantically at its cage door. As he did so,

Thomas noticed a droplet of blood on his finger. It was the first time Franklin had ever bitten him. Something had, indeed, unsettled the creature. But he could not let the rat's unpredictable behavior trouble him. His coach left in two hours and he had not begun to pack his medical bag.

He had just put the case on his workbench when, from somewhere in the deep recesses of the laboratory, a solitary bluebottle headed straight for him and began to buzz about his head. He swatted it away and it withdrew, but not upward toward the window as Thomas expected. This was where the flies usually gathered, attracted by the light. No matter how careful he was with his specimens, there would always be flies that laid their eggs in the tiniest of cracks and crevices. And yet . . . It was strange, he mused, that they seemed to be hiding away from the heat, preening themselves in the darkest, coolest corners. There was a constant hum and yet they were not flying. It was as if even they wanted to conserve their energy.

Thomas glanced up at the window once more, his eyes tracing the strong beam of sunlight up to the square of clear blue sky above. The flies were still droning in the background but from somewhere outside he could hear another, much shriller sound that seemed to be growing louder. He stopped what he was doing to listen. Within a few seconds the noise had become a discordance; a squawking, shrieking cacophony that was coming nearer and nearer. Then he saw it; a great, gray wave rolling over the rooftops, completely blocking the light, plunging the room into semidarkness.

Rushing through the door he ran up the steps into the courtyard. Even outside the sky was darkened. The sun, still low over the chimneys and spires, was eclipsed from view by the huge cackling silver cloud that came from the north.

"My God," mouthed Thomas in awe as he stood transfixed.

Hundreds upon hundreds of geese were flying overhead; wave upon wave of them, relentlessly heading south, their silver wings beating in unison. Thomas had never seen anything like it; not even as a child when, together with his father, he had watched excitedly as the annual bird migrations skirted along the eastern seaboard on the long journey south for winter.

From somewhere in the house he could hear Mistress Finesilver shriek.

"What's the ballyhoo?" called out Dr. Carruthers. The old anatomist appeared at the back door, his long stick flailing in his hand. "Silkstone? Silkstone? Are you there?"

The last legion of honking geese had just disappeared over the roof of the next-door building and the light had returned. But it made little difference to Dr. Carruthers, who was almost completely blind.

"Yes, sir. I am here," Thomas reassured him. "Do not trouble yourself. They were geese, sir. As big a flock of Canada geese as I ever laid eyes on."

"Geese?" repeated the old doctor, tapping his way toward the young doctor across the courtyard. "What the deuce were they playing at?"

Thomas knew exactly what his mentor meant. "Yes, odd that they should be flying south in early June," he agreed.

"Most peculiar, if you ask me," replied Carruthers, mopping his brow.

Now that the flock had passed, the sun's rays became even more unforgiving and Thomas saw that the old doctor was suffering.

"Would you not be more comfortable in the shade, sir?" he suggested.

Together they walked into the cooler laboratory and Dr. Carruthers sat himself down on a chair by the workbench.

"So, I daresay you shall not miss the smells of piss and rotting cabbage and dead cats," he chortled, tapping his stick on the stone flags.

Thomas smiled as he began to gather basic medicaments, smelling salts and arnica, from the shelves for his medical bag.

"I have to admit that even I find myself retching within half a mile of Smithfield in this heat," he said, reaching for a bottle of iodine.

The old doctor nodded thoughtfully. "Yes, you deserve a few days in the country, young fellow, especially after all that has passed."

Thomas did not argue. The ghastly episode that had seen the acclaimed Irish giant, Charles Byrne, so humiliated at the hands of the infamous John Hunter had left him feeling deeply wounded. Thomas regarded the giant not only as his patient but also his friend, and his fate had left lasting scars, yet he could not share his pain with Lydia. It was simply another secret he would have to keep from his beloved for fear of plunging her into yet a further bout of melancholia.

Over the past three years she had endured so much; the deaths of her brother Edward, husband Michael, cousin Francis, and mother—plus a forced marriage, but, most terrible of all, the reawakening of the deep-rooted and painful memories of losing a child. Yet in among this gloom, there was a glimmer of hope. There was just the very slightest chance that Lydia's lost son was still alive. Thomas had promised that if that were so he would do all in his power to find him and reunite him with his mother. In the coming weeks this would be his quest, although it, too, would have to remain a secret, between only them.

Dr. Carruthers cocked his head to one side, his mouth curling in a smile. "I am sure your heart will be gladdened when you see Lady Lydia."

Thomas was thankful the old doctor could not see the color rise in his cheeks. Lydia was the first woman in all his twenty-eight years who had ever held his heart so entirely in her hands. "Indeed, it will."

"Excellent, then I wish you a safe journey and a relaxing sojourn at Boughton Hall, young fellow." He mopped the sweat from his brow once more. "Let us hope the weather becomes more temperate. I am not sure I can stand this heat much longer."

Thomas looked up from his bag. His mentor's words reminded him that he had not checked the barometer that day. He walked over to the long glass case on the wall. As he expected the mercury was high, indicating a period of settled weather, but when he tapped its face, he did not anticipate the result.

"Strange," he said.

"What does your barometer say?" queried Carruthers.

"The mercury has risen again," replied Thomas.

"So no end to this insufferable heat?" bemoaned the old doctor.

"It seems not," replied Thomas. Such unusually high air pressure, coupled with the seemingly minor, yet unnatural happenings he had witnessed that morning, did not signify anything in themselves. And yet he felt a worm of anxiety burrowing into his subconscious. It was as if nature and science were colluding together to try to tell him something urgent and important. He only wished he knew what.

Chapter 4

L ady Lydia Farrell sat at her late husband's desk in what used to be his study and sighed heavily. For the past two days she had been poring over the home-farm accounts and her head was swimming with columns of numbers relating to the yields and income of the last three years. Her eyes were sore and her back ached. What was more, she felt totally out of place surrounded by notebooks and ledgers and the paraphernalia of estate management. To make matters worse, it was unseasonably hot and even though the study was relatively cool, she was forced, now and again, to reach for her fan and flutter it vigorously in front of her face.

Slowly she rose and turned to look out of the window. The lawns of Boughton Hall, now slightly browned by the sun, stretched out before her, dipping down to the green woodland beyond. June had been her favorite month; the leaves on the trees were fully unfurled, yet still verdant, and the roses were beginning to bloom. There was an exuberance in nature that used to make her happy, but now she simply felt burdened by responsibility.

She recalled her late father, Lord Crick, who had died three years earlier, telling her that he and his heirs were only the stewards of Boughton. God alone could claim it as His. It was the family's task to tend it as best they could, to keep it prosperous and fertile for future generations. Since her brother's death and then her husband's, that task had fallen solely upon her shoulders and she felt overwhelmed by it. That was why, on Thomas's suggestion, she had engaged a steward to take charge of affairs. Gabriel Lawson had worked for two years at the Crick estate in Ireland, where he had performed his duties competently, but his few months at Boughton had not produced the sought-after improvements that Lydia had planned. Income was down and the estate seemed to be floundering.

A knock at the door made her turn away from the view. "Come in," she called.

Gabriel Lawson stood on the threshold, straightening his top-coat. It was clear that he had been outside in the fields when he had received Lydia's summons. His waistcoat buttons were unfastened and there were patches of corn dust on his sleeves. He had the air of a gentleman and yet there was something in his manner that put Lydia on edge.

"Mr. Lawson, please sit down," she told him, gesturing to the chair on the other side of the desk. She studied him as he approached. He was tall and athletic and the sun had given his skin a healthy glow. She had heard from Eliza, her maid, that all the girls below stairs were in love with him and it was not hard to see why.

"How may I help you, your ladyship?" he asked.

She returned to her seat and looked him in the eye. "I have been going through these accounts that you left me," she began. She did not mention the uneven rows or the blotches of ink she had encountered during her inspection of the ledgers. "It seems that we are not doing as well as we should be, Mr. Lawson."

The steward seemed slightly taken aback by Lydia's tone of authority. He had assumed that when she asked to see the accounts it would be for a perfunctory glance. What did women know of numbers and yields, after all? It was clear he had not anticipated that she would actually try to make sense of the figures before her. The look on his tanned face betrayed his surprise and riled Lydia, even though she had been expecting it.

"The market for both grain and livestock is not good. But if your ladyship has any suggestions . . ." he began, his face set in a beguiling smile.

Lydia broke him off. "Oh, I have plenty, Mr. Lawson," she snapped. "My first is that we discover why the lambs are fetching such low prices at market."

He paused for a second, then acknowledged her comment with a nod. "There is the question of breed, your ladyship. There's not much meat . . ."

"Then change the breed, Mr. Lawson. Or improve it. Our income is falling and something must be done."

Lawson dithered. He was not used to such castigation and feigned hurt. "I am at a loss, your ladyship," came the weak reply.

Lydia sat back in her chair, knowing she had the upper hand. "We must find the reason, Mr. Lawson, and then we must find the answer."

The steward accepted her small victory. "Yes, your ladyship." He nodded his tousled head sympathetically.

"And I believe the answer could lie in science," she said.

Lawson's eyes widened. "Science?" he repeated.

"Yes. Dr. Thomas Silkstone, an eminent man of science, arrives from London later today. I am sure that he will find ways of improving the sheep breed and even our crop yields with his new methods."

The steward, still unable to hide his surprise, simply nodded. "Then I look forward to meeting this Dr. Silkstone," he said in a voice tinged with insolence.

Lydia picked up her fan and began to waft it in front of her. "That will be all, Mr. Lawson," she said. The steward rose and Lydia noted his bow was just a little more exaggerated than good manners required. The estate manager, it seemed to her, needed a little astute management himself.

Amos Kidd's cottage lay not half a mile away from Boughton Hall, on a side track that led from the main drive. It was small and squat and its thatched roof was green with moss, but it had served the head gardener and his wife well these past ten years.

Kidd, a brawny countryman with gray streaks in his hair, had been up at dawn, as usual, tending to the roses. He liked to water them early each morning when they were coming into bloom and was particularly anxious that they should not suffer in the great heat. The rose garden was his pride and joy. Lady Lydia's father, the late Sir Richard, had designed it, but he had planted it, choosing the varieties with care to produce color, scent, and diversity. There were albas with their milk-white flowers and dusky pink French roses with a mild scent. There were Celsianas in a light pink that faded to blush, and sprays of York and Lancaster, flecked with white and pale cherry.

It was around noon when the gardener arrived home, carrying a fresh-cut bunch of blooms that he hid behind his back. It took a moment or two for his eyes to adjust from the glare of the sun to the cool shade of the cottage. In the half light he could make out his wife sitting in the bentwood chair by the empty hearth embroidering a petticoat. It was a scene that gladdened him. There was a quiet stillness in the room and she was at the heart of it. Her profile was silhouetted against the white wall; her long neck, her pert nose, and her hair swept back from her face, tumbling in curls to the top of her shoulders. She lifted her pretty young face and he approached her eagerly for a kiss. Obligingly she puckered her thick, soft lips and he bent down and felt the fullness of them with his mouth. But she pushed him away playfully, holding her nose.

"You stink, Amos Kidd," she giggled.

He sniffed an armpit indignantly, then, remembering the roses, produced them from behind his back. "These'll set things right," he said, holding them in front of her. She closed her eyes to breathe in the scent.

"They are sweet."

"Her ladyship said I could have them. I'll fetch a jug."

A moment later he returned with the roses in water. He set them in the center of the table and stood back to admire them.

"They don't like this weather and that's for sure," he mused. " 'Tis hot as hell out there." He slipped off his leather jerkin, dropping it on a nearby chair.

"Then you'll be wanting your ale," she said cheerfully, still not bothering to rise. "There's some over there." She gestured to the table, which was laid with a plate, a tankard, and a pitcher. A loaf of bread and a large lump of cheese were on a trencher.

Kidd sat down and poured himself some beer. His throat was dry and he gulped it back so quickly that the liquid spilled down the sides of his mouth. He wiped it away with his sleeve and belched softly. His eyes settled upon his wife once more. She was still sewing and he watched the curve of her breasts, ripe as apricots, as they rose and fell with each pull of the thread. In and out, up and down. A single bead of sweat suddenly appeared like a drop of morning dew on her neck and slipped its way slowly down toward her cleavage.

The gardener turned back to the table and picked up the knife. It sliced through the cheese as if it were new-churned butter. He squinted at the blade curiously, then ran his grimy thumb and forefinger down the shaft.

"You sharpened this today, Susannah?"

His wife suddenly shot him a nervous look and after a moment's hesitation replied lightly: "Yes. A traveler called 'round. My scissors were blunt and I needs finish this for Lady Thorndike tomorrow, so he sharpened a few things while he were here."

Kidd was measured. "But you know 'tis not a trouble for me, my love," he said, thinking of the daily grinding of scythes and shears for the gardens. He tore off a hunk of bread, but before he could put it in his mouth, his elbow caught the handle of the knife, sending it clattering to the floor. The noise shattered the calm and his wife jumped a little in her chair. Kidd bent down to pick up the blade, but as he did so he noticed something strange on the flagstones. A gray powder, like coarsely-milled seeds, dusted the floor in among the rushes. He wiped a little up with his finger, the grains sticking to his sweat, and inspected it. Lifting the grit up to his nose, he sniffed and frowned.

"What you been using saltpeter for?" he asked, then added jokily: " 'Tis too hot to kill the pig. 'Twill roast itself in this heat."

"I ain't used no saltpeter. The knife-grinder must have brought it in on his boots," she replied, seemingly indifferent to her husband's query. But Amos Kidd did not like to be treated so and his expression hardened at her words. His mouth set in a grimace and his brows knitted in a frown. She looked up and saw the all-too-familiar signs.

"I want no strange men in my house! You hear?" he thundered. He darted forward and stood over her, glowering, but she held his gaze. Then, putting down her sewing, she rose.

"Now, Amos," she whispered, cupping his face in her palms. "No need to be so angry with me."

Her husband cocked his head like a puzzled child. She traced a bead of sweat down his forehead with her finger and said softly, "After all, you always say 'tis only when the petals are fully open that a bee can collect the nectar."

At this, his welling anger seemed to recede. A smile returned to his lips and he took her outstretched hand and followed her into the bedroom.

"Besides," she began, as she started to undo the laces on her husband's shirt, "the grinder had a story to tell."

Kidd stilled her hand. "What kind of story?"

Her eyes opened wide with excitement. "One that you need to hear, my darling," she cooed, licking his fingers seductively. "But not until the bee has visited his flower." And with that she lowered her head and began kissing his naked chest.

The town of Hungerford was more than used to its fair share of strangers. Lying on the main road from Bath to London, it played host to peers and paupers alike. Good King William spent the night there in the Black Bear after he landed in Weymouth to take the English Crown in the Glorious Revolution of 1688. Cattle drovers would gather regularly on the common and the market attracted traders from miles around. On a clear day the gibbet at Combe could be seen atop the beacon to the south of the town. Crows circling around a swinging cage always served as a reminder to any who abused the town's hospitality. Even so, the stranger who arrived in Charnham Street on that June afternoon was not the customary drover, trader, or fair pedlar.

Dressed in the dark garb of a cleric or a notary, and walking with the stoop of a man bent over a desk all day, this stranger did not mingle with the crowd of country folk. The cooper spotted him as he alighted from the coach and began to move up Charnham Street, and the milliner remarked on him as he passed by her shop. The baker pointed him out to a customer he was serving as being "not from around these parts," and the haberdasher followed his progress as he went out of sight.

The man stopped outside a modest cottage that overlooked the river. A full-bosomed woman with porcine features and a baby on her hip answered the stranger's knock and words were exchanged on the doorstep. To anyone watching the encounter, and there were one or two who did, it would seem that the man's inquiries were given short shrift. Shaking her head, it was obvious to observers that the woman could not, or would not, help with his inquiry. Yet he, doffing his tricorn, would not be put off and appeared to take out his purse and press her palm with a coin. At this her demeanor was seen to alter and she became more civil. A smile, a nod and a flick of her chubby wrist told the stranger that he would best be taking his inquiry off in the direction of Charnham Street. With a cheery nod she bade her caller "good day" in a courteous manner and he headed off toward where she had pointed.

In less than five minutes he had reached his new destination: a tall, thin house that looked as though it could have been a hostelry. It was, in fact, the Hungerford Workhouse. Lifting the tarnished knocker, he struck three times. After a moment or two, the door creaked open and a nervous-looking woman in a cap and shawl about her slight shoulders stood at the threshold.

"May I help you?" she inquired in a voice so soft yet high in pitch that the stranger had to strain his ear to hear it. He doffed his tricorn once more.

"Good day to you, madam." His tone was officious, but polite. "This is the workhouse, I believe."

An anxious look scudded across the woman's face. "That it is, sir," she squeaked apologetically, as if feeling guilty for all the shameful inadequacies that occurred therein.

"Good." The caller nodded. "Then I would speak with the master," he told her firmly.

"You'd best come in, sir," she said, opening the door fully, then, to the surprise of the caller, she threw back her head and shouted at the top of her voice: "Master! Master!" as if the most calamitous fate had befallen the house.

Taking off his hat to show his face properly for the first time, the stranger entered. His complexion was as gray as the hair in his wig, as if he had not seen the sun for many a long year, and he wore a dull expression to match his generally dull countenance.

The hallway smelled of vinegar and stale sweat, and the woman gestured him into a parlor. It was plainly furnished and cold, even though the temperature outside was uncomfortably hot. The rug was threadbare and on the wall hung an exhortation to all those who entered. *Avoid idleness and intemperance*, it read.

"Will you sit, sir?" the woman entreated him. "The master will be with you presently." But before the stranger could oblige, the workhouse master appeared on the threshold. His wig appeared too small for his large head, as if he had borrowed it. And his head, in turn, was attached to his broad shoulders by a neck as wide as a man's thigh. He eyed the caller suspiciously.

"You would speak with me, sir?" he boomed.

Undeterred, the stranger squared up to him. "Yes, sir. I am seeking one of your charges," he told him.

The master narrowed his eyes. "Been in trouble, have they?"

The stranger shook his head. "Not to my knowledge. I would simply know if the person I seek is in your care."

The master's tone softened a little. "Will you sit then, sir?" he said, gesturing to a chair.

Parting the tails of his frock coat, the stranger seated himself, while the master sat opposite him. On the table between them was a large, leather-bound ledger. The master took out a pair of spectacles from his waistcoat and perched them on his large nose. "What name shall I look for, Mr. er . . . um," he asked, peering over the rim of his glasses.

The stranger leaned forward intently, so that he could look at the leaves of the ledger more closely. The book was as thick as a church Bible and in it, on yellowing pages, were row upon row of names, a litany of misery and woe for the poor and unfortunate. Thrown on the mercy of the parish, they were people without dignity and without hope.

"My name is of no import," replied the stranger. He moistened his thin lips in anticipation. "But the individual I seek is a child. An orphan."

The master's shoulders shrugged, his wig slipping slightly to one side. "We've plenty of those here," he snorted.

The stranger did not share the joke, but continued to peer, leaning even closer.

"And the name?" inquired the master, growing impatient.

"He goes by the name of Farrell," he replied. "Richard Farrell."

Chapter 5

Thomas spent much of the journey to Oxford staring out of the coach window, observing the countryside closely. It was a great relief to leave the steaming stew of London behind as it simmered in the almost intolerable heat, and yet his sense of unease did not leave him. He knew he should be feeling elated at the thought of seeing Lydia once more and spending a few days alone in her company, and yet there was a nagging fear at the back of his mind. The few unnatural incidents that he had experienced in London, coupled with the fact that the air pressure was set to rise even higher, had put him in an agitated humor.

As they left the capital for the cleaner air of the country, the natural surroundings became of even more interest to him than usual. He looked heavenward. The cloudless blue over London, smudged by the smoke of countless furnaces and kilns in so many areas, gave way to a sky dotted with wispy high clouds. They signified calm weather. He found that reassuring. As the road skirted the Thames he checked to see if the willows were whitening, heralding a forthcoming storm. They were not. Were the red kites flying lower than usual over the Chiltern hills? He did not think so. Nature was speaking in its own language. But he could not be sure what it was trying to say.

Many years ago, when he had spent time with the Delaware people near his Pennsylvania home, he had seen how they built sweathouses to purify themselves of their ills; steaming their bodies before cooling down in the creek or rolling in the winter snow. They made infusions of skunk cabbage root to treat whooping cough, or a tea of arnica for back pain. He respected their ways, how they tapped into nature's healing powers without harming their surroundings. Each rustle of a tree or call of a bird was regarded as a voice that imparted a wisdom or a truth. Yes, there was much that science could learn from these native Americans, he told himself, and he wondered what they would make of the murmurings that he could now hear in this small but beautiful corner of the English countryside.

Even though the air seemed a little cooler as the coach made good progress along the dust-dry roads, it was still inordinately warm. Despite this Thomas shivered. The sense of foreboding he felt reminded him of when, as a boy, he had stayed with relatives in Williamsburg. Then the heat had been oppressive, too, and he had known from the great pillars of slate-gray cloud they were in for a storm. But during the night, they had been woken by a sound so terrifying that the women of the house screamed with fright. A great banshee wind from the ocean made landfall to the south and roared up Chesapeake Bay, destroying everything in its path. They spent two days cowering in a cellar until the roaring ceased and the great rains stopped, but many had lost their lives during that time and it was a memory that would never leave him.

As soon as he saw the spires of Oxford, however, he forced himself to banish such maudlin thoughts. Thankfully, Lovelock was waiting for him with the carriage and a flask of lemonade thoughtfully supplied by Mistress Claddingbowl, the cook. He began the last leg of his onward journey in relative comfort, although his aching body still complained with each pothole. Yet the pleasure of breathing in fresh, country air outweighed any physical distress, he told himself. The stench and chaos of London was a world away and he and Lydia would be able to put the past behind them and look to a brighter future together.

The coach journeyed on through a narrow valley, bordered by woodland. About ten miles from Boughton, Thomas spotted a small crowd of men and women in a meadow next to the roadside. They were sprawled out in a long line and seemed to be peering at something on the ground. Some of the women seemed distressed, shaking their heads or turning to their menfolk for comfort.

Thomas put his head out of the carriage window.

"What goes on?" he shouted up to the driver. He wondered if someone might need a physician's services.

The coachman, from his vantage point, shook his head.

"Looks like a woe water's sprung up," he replied, craning his neck to see a ribbon of water spilling out into the grassy hollow of a dry river bed.

"A woe water?" repeated Thomas. It was a term that was unfamiliar to him.

The driver nodded. "A stream that springs up as a warning; an omen, like." He puckered his lips thoughtfully, then added, "Last time it happened in these parts the plague came."

The sense of unease that Thomas felt in London suddenly returned as surely as the water that gurgled out of the ground below. He ordered the driver to move off.

The light was almost gone by the time they turned through the gates of the great house. The dust clouds thrown up by the carriage when it was a good mile away had warned the household of his arrival. Lady Lydia Farrell waited on the steps to greet her visitor. A diminutive woman, she had luxuriant brown hair piled on top of her small head and she wore a gown of azure blue. Thomas remembered he had once told her it was his favorite color. He knew she was wearing it for him.

Howard the butler, Mistress Firebrace the housekeeper, together with several housemaids and Will, the stable boy, made up the welcoming party.

"Your ladyship," Thomas greeted her formally.

Lydia smiled and held out her hand. Thomas kissed it, lingering slightly longer than was perhaps considered good manners.

"You are most welcome as always," she greeted him.

Looking into her eyes, Thomas saw an animation that was unfamiliar to him. The melancholy seemed to have disappeared, replaced by a renewed optimism and even joy. This would be their own precious time together, he told himself. This would be their new beginning. He offered Lydia his arm and together they walked through the great double doors of Boughton Hall.

After washing and settling himself into his room, Thomas joined Lydia on the terrace, where dinner was served. Seated side by side, they watched the full moon rise over the lawns. The air was heavy with the scent of roses and a nightingale serenaded them somewhere in the distance.

Lydia had long dismissed the servants and Thomas poured them each another glass of claret.

"I want to propose a toast," he said. "To us. May our future together be as perfect as this evening."

Lydia smiled and clinked her glass against his.

"I cannot wait to have you all to myself for a whole month," he told her.

She nodded, but he noticed her gaze suddenly drop, as if she had remembered something she would rather forget.

"What is it, Lydia?"

She sighed heavily. "I am afraid we have an engagement to-morrow."

"An engagement?"

Lydia nodded and took his other hand. "It is the Dashwoods' annual garden party at West Wycombe Park." She framed her words carefully. "Circumstances have prevented me from attending for the last two years and I promised faithfully that I would be there."

Thomas nodded. Her *circumstances* had, indeed, been difficult to say the least. "And I am invited?"

"Indeed, yes. Sir John is very anxious to meet you. He has heard so much about you." She laid a hand on his.

The young anatomist rolled his eyes. He knew that he was so often the subject of gossip, particularly among the English aristocracy, much of it unfavorable. They regarded him, for the most part, as a colonial upstart, intent on stirring up trouble within the established way of doing things.

"I am sure he has heard of me and I'll wager none of the hearsay will be flattering," said Thomas, wearily. "You know I am an outcast to these people."

Lydia looked hurt. "But if you are to be the future lord of Boughton, then they will have to welcome you, my love," she pointed out.

Thomas regarded her with a bemused look. In all the months that he had loved Lydia and dreamed of making her his wife, he had never really given any thought to the mantle of responsibility he would be expected to wear. He would become the legal owner of Boughton Hall and the entire estate, with its thousands of acres of farmland, its livestock and its workers' cottages. Dozens of men, women, and children would rely on him for their livelihoods. The prospect did not sit easily with him.

"I am a surgeon, Lydia. The blood in my veins runs red, not blue like your English aristocracy," he blurted.

As soon as he said these words, however, he regretted them. She withdrew her grasp and he could tell he had wounded her.

"Forgive me." He caught her eye. "I should not be so insensitive. Please." He gestured for her hand once more. After a moment she did as he asked.

When she spoke again, after a short pause, her voice was measured. "I know how much you have suffered from English prejudice since you came here, Thomas, but you can only show those pompous prigs that you are better than they are through example."

The young anatomist thought for a moment. Her words reminded him of something his father's friend Benjamin Franklin had said to him during one of their meetings at his home. He had raised a plump finger and declared: "A good example is the best sermon."

"Example, yes." He nodded. "You are so wise, my love," he said, then moving closer he whispered, "And so very beautiful."

She turned to face him, but despite her smile, he could see, for the first time that day, a sadness in her eyes. It was that same deep melancholy that he had noticed when she first told him about her lost son. Thomas was reminded of her pain. Any talk of their future always seemed to be bound to the past and the possibility, however remote, that the child she once bore might still be alive.

"I understand about Richard," he said gently, putting his arm around her shoulder.

"While there is hope I cannot give up, Thomas." Her voice broke as she spoke.

"While there is hope *we* will not give up, my love," he echoed. "I promised you that and I will remain true to my word."

She took a deep breath. "Then we shall search for him together?"

"Of course we shall. Where was the last address you found for him?"

"The house was in Hungerford, about a day's journey from here, but he was sent to the local"—she broke off to compose herself before delivering the rest of the sentence—"to the workhouse when Michael stopped paying for his upkeep."

Thomas nodded. "So Hungerford is where we will begin our search," he told her.

Lydia's eyes lit up at the prospect and her face broke into a smile. "Thank you," she said.

Long before the house dogs had stirred and the scullery maid had risen to light the kitchen fire, Thomas was back in his own bedchamber. His first night with Lydia since she had broken off their betrothal so suddenly and without explanation in London the month before had been a blissful one. Her motives—her shame and guilt at the loss of her child—had all become clear now and their love was even stronger as a result, of that he was sure. Now he longed to close his eyes for a few hours' repose before breakfast. He was just about to slip off his breeches and lie beneath the cool, crisp sheets when he glanced out of the window. His view was of the rose garden. The scent of the blooms had drifted upward through his open window overnight and filled his room with their perfume. He was gazing at the myriad of colors, the waxy creams and deep pinks, when in among them he spotted Amos Kidd. He watched as the gardener, his face shaded under his large-brimmed hat, lovingly watered each plant and inspected leaves for signs of aphids or black rot. There was a care in his manner that denoted a man at ease with his garden, as if it gave him the inner calm that some people find in church.

It was then that it occurred to him. Perhaps he should talk to Kidd and see if he had noticed anything strange in the natural order of things lately. If anyone could tell him if the bees were swarming or the seagulls were flying inland, Thomas guessed it would be Kidd. He slipped on his waistcoat and topcoat and crept downstairs, so as not to waken the rest of the household.

Although it was not yet six o'clock the air outside was already languid. The cloudless sky was as blue as the forget-me-nots that clustered in the neatly trimmed borders below. And yet there was something not quite right. He noticed that what few swallows he could see were flying low. Instead of whooping and diving for insects, they were keeping closer to the ground.

"Good morning, Kidd," he greeted.

The gardener jumped in surprise.

"Good morning, Dr. Silkstone, sir," he returned, raising his hat to his unexpected visitor.

"Another hot day," remarked Thomas.

Kidd nodded, resting both hands on his upright spade. "The roses don't care for it, sir."

Thomas let out a laugh. "Not many of us do," he replied. There was a slightly awkward pause as he looked about him; up at the sky, then back down to the roses, as if something was bothering him. "Can I speak plainly with you, Mr. Kidd, as a man of the country?" he asked earnestly.

Kidd pushed his hat to the back of his head with his thumb, so that Thomas could see his entire face. It was weathered as a slab of sandstone but kindly nonetheless. "I would be glad to oblige you, sir."

"Then tell me this," Thomas began. "Have you noticed anything strange in the nature of things these past two or three days?"

"Strange?" Kidd frowned.

"Any signs or portents among the plants or animals that seem unusual for the season?"

The gardener scratched his graying temple, then began to nod slowly. "Now that you mention it, the butterflies have left the buddleia." He pointed to the purple cones on a bush on the other side of the clipped yew hedge that were usually covered in red admirals and swallowtails.

"Really?" Thomas looked intently at him.

"And the honey bees—" the gardener broke off.

"What of them?"

Kidd gestured around him. "Listen, sir." He paused. Thomas heard the faint cooing of doves and the song of a blackbird in the nearby bushes, but no low hum of bees. "There ain't none," he murmured. "The garden be alive with them, normal like, but, come to think of it, I've seen none since yesterday morning."

The doctor nodded gravely. "Very odd. Well, if you see or hear anything else you think out of the ordinary, please tell me, Mr. Kidd."

The gardener doffed his hat. "That I will, sir."

Thomas turned to walk back to the house, but had taken no more than a few steps when Kidd called him back.

"Dr. Silkstone!"

He wheeled 'round.

"There was something else, come to think of it."

Thomas walked closer. "Yes."

"My wife said she were talking to a tinker or some such yesterday who'd come from up north. Lincoln way, I think she said."

"What of it?"

"He said he'd see'd this great gray cloud roll over the fields from the sea and women and men was running from it, but some of them fell, coughing and choking."

This information seemed to have a profound effect on Thomas. "Good God," he muttered. "And this was north of here, you say?"

"Yes." Spurred on by the doctor's reaction, Kidd added: "Those that could ran into a barn and bolted the doors, but it still covered 'em. The devil's breath he called it."

"The devil's breath," repeated Thomas. Then, shaking his head, he said to the gardener, "Let us hope it is not heading this way."

Chapter 6

Thomas Silkstone and Amos Kidd were not the only early risers on that hot June morning. Gabriel Lawson had been up since dawn, too. It was market day in Brandwick and there were some late lambs to take to the slaughter. Two shepherds, father and son, Seth and Noah Kipps, drove the flock, about fifty of them in all, along the narrow lanes. Lawson followed behind in the wagon, narrowing his eyes against the dust that rose from the track as hundreds of hooves loosened it.

Without their mothers the lambs were disoriented, slipping down the dry gullies and ditches, or straying through broken gateways and gaps in hedgerows. While the dogs did a good job rounding up their stupid charges, progress was slow, compounded by the heat and the flies. Nevertheless, they arrived at the market in Sheep Street before nine o'clock and the livestock were all penned in hurdles within minutes.

As the sun climbed, the air was filled with the bleats of thousands of lambs and the shouts of men. Dogs barked incessantly and flies buzzed drunkenly hither and thither, high on dung. The cobbles were wet with sheep's piss and the reek of it stung men's eyes.

Lawson wiped his brow with his kerchief after the last hurdle had been closed and leant against a nearby wall, licking his parched lips.

"Goodly looking lambs you got there, Mr. Lawson," said one farmer, sidling up to him as he watched the proceedings.

The steward gave a self-satisfied grin. " 'Tis why I get a good price for them," he replied.

Within the next hour all of his lambs had been sold and many of them slaughtered on the spot in the nearby shambles. The stench from the spilled blood and entrails in the heat caught the back of men's throats and made them gag. The porters sluiced down the flagstones and cobbles with buckets of water from the town brook, but the stones were so hot that it quickly rose as steam into the air. Lawson was having none of it. He had settled up as quickly as he could. Each lamb had fetched twenty-five shillings and he was pleased with the takings. He put the bank notes in his leather wallet and the shilling coins into his purse.

"A good morning, men," he said to Seth and Noah as they rested against a nearby wall. "Here's a shilling for some ale."

They both smiled broadly. "Thank you, sir," they said.

Lawson, too, decided he deserved a drink. The Three Tuns lay across the street and was doing a roaring trade. As usual, the Reverend Lightfoot and his wife were standing outside trying to persuade imbibers that St. Swithin's offered more fulfilling succor, but to no avail. Mistress Lightfoot eyed Gabriel Lawson reprovingly as he ducked low through the door of the inn. She had the measure of his sort.

The inn was packed full of farmers and shepherds come to town from the surrounding countryside. Pipe smoke curled in the breathless air, helping to mask the smell of sweat and spilled ale. In the corner a fiddler played. The town women, their faces slashed with scarlet and their breasts straining out of their bodices, were out in force, too, eager to help the shepherds and farmers spend their hard-earned cash. Two of them sallied up to Lawson.

"Well, well, Mr. Lawson! How's our favorite customer?" one said, wrapping her arms around his neck.

The steward smirked and lifted her wandering arm off his torso with disdain. Instead he made straight for the bar.

"A tankard of your finest, landlord," he ordered.

"So you've had a good morning?" persisted one of the painted women.

He downed his beer in large gulps and banged his pot on the counter. "You could say that," he replied, then taking his notebook from his pocket, together with a pencil, he licked the lead and wrote down carefully: *30 lambs . . . 20 shillings each. Total: £30.*

Smirking, Lawson looked up to find that he still had an audience.

"I'm anxious to get at the table, ladies," he told them.

They looked at each other and giggled before following him as he made for the back of the pump room, heading toward thick, floor-length curtains. Finding the edge of one of them he drew it back slightly. Half a dozen men, watched by as many women, were seated around a large wooden table, playing pharo.

There was an empty chair and the punters looked up as if they were expecting him.

"Good day, gentlemen," said Lawson. The self-satisfied grin had not left his face. "Luck is with me today, of that I am certain." And he took his seat at the table with a pocketful of cash.

As their carriage turned east, the great golden ball came into view. It sat atop the church of St. Lawrence on a hill that dominated the countryside for miles around. Thomas put his head out of the window and stared open-mouthed. It was every bit as impressive as he had heard, like the dome of a great mosque in a painting from old Araby. Anchored by three heavy chains that were not visible from afar, it seemed that it was merely floating on top of the tower, hundreds of feet up.

"But it is magnificent!" he exclaimed with childlike wonderment.

Lydia smiled at his reaction. "A copy of the Customs House in Venice, I believe," she informed him, adding: "Wait until you see the house."

The carriage rumbled on through enormous gates and there before them, like some great Roman temple, lay West Wycombe Park. Although he had become quite used to the grandiose buildings of London, Thomas was struck by the theatricality of its columned and pedimented facades set against a backdrop of rolling parkland. He had heard much about the estate from Mr. Franklin, who had spent several sojourns there as the guest of the late Sir Francis Dashwood. Once, as they sat drinking coffee in the Bedford Coffee House, his fellow countryman's eyes had twinkled when he recalled the general mayhem at wild parties held in the nearby Hellfire Caves. Thomas had not pressed him further, but from the high color in the great man's cheeks, he could tell it was an unforgettable experience.

Around a dozen guests were already being directed by liveried footmen to a garden at the rear. Thomas and Lydia duly alighted from their carriage and were ushered through. Their host, the third baronet, Sir John Dashwood-King, was there to greet them.

"My dear Lady Lydia, how wonderful to see you again, and how radiant you look," he exclaimed, taking Lydia's hand in a flamboyant gesture, as if she were a long-lost daughter. He seemed a jocular man, with a round face and an even rounder belly.

"Sir John, thank you so much for your kind invitation," replied Lydia, not at all put off by the exuberant reception. She smiled at Thomas. "May I introduce you to Dr. Thomas Silkstone, who is staying at Boughton for a few days?"

The young doctor stepped forward and gave a shallow bow.

"Ah, Silkstone, eh?" barked the nobleman. "A man of medicine from the Colonies, I believe."

Thomas checked his annoyance, but corrected his host nonetheless. "A *former* colony, I think would be fairer to say, sir." He held the baronet's gaze for a moment, and Lydia held her breath, but then he smiled broadly and Sir John followed suit.

"I'll grant you that, Silkstone, but just remember this tea party is at West Wycombe, not Boston!" he joked, and with that he let out such a loud guffaw that his round face turned bright red. "I've had the pleasure of dining with Mr. Franklin here, when Sir Francis was alive, and I have to say, you chaps can give us a run for our money!" His shoulders heaved with laughter.

Thomas, too, began to laugh. He rather liked this jolly-looking nobleman who obviously did not take himself too seriously. "I promise I shall behave myself this afternoon, your lordship," he replied.

"Oh how very disappointing!" replied Sir John, still chuckling.

At that moment, from out of the corner of his eye, Thomas spied the familiar and unmistakable figure of Sir Theodisius Pettigrew, the Oxfordshire coroner. He was standing at the buffet table, chicken leg in hand, with his wife, Lady Harriet. The young anatomist felt it was time to allow Sir John to compose himself once more and he excused himself and Lydia before moving on.

"Well, well, Silkstone!" greeted Sir Theodisius, his fat face splitting in two. "Her ladyship said you would be honoring us with your presence again soon. How it gladdens my heart to see you."

Thomas wanted to tell his old friend that the feeling was mutual, but he simply shook the coroner's hand warmly. "Her ladyship kindly invited me to stay at Boughton for a few days to escape London," he told him.

"Quite right," replied Sir Theodisius, his chin glistening with a mixture of chicken fat and sweat. "So she is introducing you to the rest of polite society in the vicinity!"

Lydia fluttered her fan awkwardly, knowing such words would irritate Thomas. She flashed a smile. "Indeed, Sir Theodisius."

"Then we shall not hold you up," he said graciously, waving the chicken leg in the air.

Just as she turned, however, Lydia saw another familiar face. "Sir Henry," she greeted, holding out her hand. An elderly gentleman with a kindly face came shuffling up to her, took her hand and kissed it.

"My dear Lady Lydia. But you are looking as delightful as ever. By Jove, yes!" he told her.

Thomas saw great affection in Lydia's eyes. "And you are well?" she inquired.

He made a fist with his hand and thumped his chest lightly.

"Bit short of breath now and again, but I can't complain," he replied.

"I am sorry to hear that," said Lydia.

Sir Henry Thorndike studied Thomas with rheumy eyes. "And you are the physician from the Colonies, I believe, sir." This time the faux pas was allowed to pass unremarked.

"Forgive me, yes. This is Dr. Thomas Silkstone from Philadelphia," said Lydia.

Thomas bowed. In the few seconds he had been given to study the elderly man he had made a preliminary diagnosis. His body had been buffeted and bowed by advancing years and his gait was slightly stooped, but it was his lips that gave away his condition. They were a strange bluish purple, a classic sign of poor circulation, or even possibly heart disease, he thought to himself.

"And you are staying at Boughton for a few days?" Sir Henry inquired.

"I have that pleasure," replied Thomas.

Their pleasantries were beginning to wear a little thin when they were joined by a most striking woman. Thomas noticed a distinct change in Lydia's expression. "Lady Thorndike," she greeted her as all eyes turned to the flame-haired beauty who drew beside them. Dressed à la mode in a robe of yellow silk, she was tall and elegant. Yet she fluttered her fan in agitation as much as to cool herself, while on her face she wore a look of disdain as plain as any beauty patch.

"Ah, Julia dear, here you are," said Sir Henry congenially, but his wife shot him a poisonous look before she noticed the handsome young doctor. Then, just as surely, she rearranged her features into a smile and let out a girlish laugh.

"My husband's great age is no excuse for his absence of manners," she remarked, clapping her eyes on Thomas. Without moving her gaze she told Lydia: "Well, well, my dear, I await a formal introduction." Acting as if she had just spied a dish of sweetmeats, she held out a gloved hand to the doctor.

Thomas introduced himself. "Silkstone. Dr. Thomas Silkstone, your ladyship." She was strikingly handsome, probably around the same age as Lydia, with a flawless complexion, high cheekbones, and a dimple at the center of her chin. From her forceful manner, however, he also sensed she was trouble. Lydia's look of pure loathing reinforced this notion.

"I am sure Lady Lydia has told you that she and I are neighbors. Our estate borders Boughton," Lady Thorndike told Thomas, fixing him with a playful smile. "You really must dine with us," she said, waving her fan coquettishly in front of her face.

Lydia was quick to butt in with a firmness that surprised Thomas. "You are most kind," she replied, forcing a smile, "but I am afraid Dr. Silkstone is only here for a few days and we already have several engagements."

Lady Thorndike's expression was quick to sour, but her words to Thomas remained sweet. "A great pity, but I am sure we will meet again, Dr. Silkstone."

Thomas bowed and Lydia tugged surreptitiously at his sleeve, guiding him away.

"Did I detect a certain friction between you two ladies?" teased Thomas when they were out of earshot.

"That woman is as venomous a creature as one could ever meet," hissed Lydia through clenched teeth. "She is nothing but a harlot," she muttered. He had seldom heard her speak with such approbation.

"Her treatment of her husband was rather embarrassing," agreed Thomas, as they strolled across the lawns.

Lydia stopped in her tracks and looked at Thomas squarely. "Lady Thorndike has a reputation that I do not envy," she told him brusquely. "You saw the way she spoke to poor Sir Henry. His first wife died five years ago and his only son, the year after. He married that woman to produce an heir for him. There is no love lost between them."

Sensing he had touched a raw nerve, he backed off. "I shall bow to your judgment, my love," he replied diplomatically.

They walked on, skirting the large muddy bowl of the lake. Deprived of adequate rainfall, its banks were cracked and dry and it contained no more than a very large puddle. It was so hot that they were glad to see a folly up ahead and made straight for it.

Nestled among tall pines at the top of a gentle slope, the Temple of Daphne, with its classical colonnades, looked cool and inviting. Lydia hurried into its shade, but remained agitated. She threw back her head, sighing. "I am sorry, Thomas. I should never have brought you here," she began.

He looked at the careworn expression that was all too familiar to him. He must bring back a smile to her lips, he told himself.

"I'll not hear of it," he mocked her. "Oh, how charming! Do dine with us," he mimicked. "Do not let them trouble you," he told her, smiling wryly. "You managed well enough without them when you were married to the captain. I suspect he did not ingratiate himself with most of your polite society around here, either."

After a moment she returned his smile. "You are right, as usual," she said. And at this, Thomas bent forward and playfully pecked her on the lips.

"Of course I am right. I am a doctor," he teased her and she rested her head on his shoulder, closing her eyes as she did so.

It was only then that Thomas noticed something most peculiar. As he put his arm around Lydia, he gazed down and saw a large brown rat crouching in the corner of the folly. Instinctively he looked around. Narrowing his eyes, he scanned the dense undergrowth nearby. He could not believe what he saw; not one or two, but at least a dozen rats were scuttling in the bracken. He could even hear them squeak.

"What's that noise?" asked Lydia suddenly.

Thomas held his tongue, remembering her deep-rooted fear of rodents. He knew he must act quickly but calmly. Stroking her hair as her head rested on his shoulder, he turned around, taking her with him, and began walking out of the folly.

"Thomas, what are you doing?" she protested, as he led her down the slope onto the main lawn.

When they were safely away from the undergrowth he told her the truth.

"I spotted a rat in the folly," he said.

She heaved a sigh of relief and gazed up at him. "Thank you," she replied. "You know how I hate rats."

He had no intention of telling her that there was an infestation of the creatures. For some reason—he wished he knew what—they had sought higher ground. Normally they would do that in the case of a flood, but water levels in streams, rivers, and lakes were exceptionally low. There had to be some explanation for such behavior. It was yet another piece in the puzzle that both baffled and worried him.

Chapter 7

Lydia was anxious to reach Hungerford by the late afternoon, so the following day Lovelock made the carriage ready before dawn. As they rumbled down the drive of Boughton Hall and out into the lane, Thomas could sense her nervousness. She said little at first, choosing to stare out of the window as the sun rose over the hills.

They skirted Oxford and in a village toward Abingdon stopped at the inn for refreshment and to water the horses. Choosing a seat in the corner, where prying eyes would find it harder to stare, Thomas reached for Lydia's hand. He could only imagine the mixed emotions she was going through and he knew that the next few hours could bring joy and elation or disappointment and despair.

"May I see the letter again?" he asked.

She fumbled in her reticule and brought out the folded piece of paper with its broken seal. She pushed it along the table to Thomas, still folded, as if she herself could not bear to look at it for the umpteenth time.

The letter was written in uneven script, in a hand that was not well educated. The address at the top of the page was River Cottage, Bridge Street, Hungerford. It was dated June 2, 1781, less than three months after Michael Farrell's death. It read:

> *Dear Capt. Farrell,*
>   *Seeing how several weeks have passed since you*

last payed me in respect of your charge and since I have had no reply to my previous letters, I must assume that no more moneys will be forthcoming. I therefore regret to inform you that the child is now in the care of the parish workhouse and will remain there for as long as you choose him to be there.

I am, sir, your obedient servant,
Dora Pargiter (Widow)

The parish workhouse was no place for a grown man, let alone a small boy with perhaps a disability from where Hunter's needle had stabbed him during the failed abortion, thought Thomas. He understood that the notion of her son in such a hellhole was a terrible burden for Lydia. She turned to him suddenly, her face gripped by a scowl.

"How could any woman do that, Thomas?" she blurted. "How could she turn out a little child whom she had nursed for the past three years?"

The young doctor shook his head. "Money makes people act in strange ways," he replied. "But we do not know the full facts. Let us reserve judgment until we speak with this Widow Pargiter."

Lydia knew his words were wise, and her features relaxed a little, as if she had been thrown a thread of hope.

"Perhaps she did not carry out her threat," she muttered, then louder she added: "Perhaps she kept him after all!" Her eyes were suddenly bright with the thought that the widow might have relented and Thomas did not wish to dull them.

"Perhaps, my love," he told her calmly. He brushed her flushed cheek with his finger. "But we will have to wait and see."

The sun had not yet set, but already Amos Kidd had gone to bed. After downing a bowl of vegetable potage he had taken to his rest. He told his wife he would rise even earlier than usual to tend to his roses. It was something that the young doctor from the Colonies had said, something about nature giving warning signs.

Nothing must happen to his beloved blooms. He must be there to protect them. He was their guardian—against wind, heat, frost, flood, greenfly—he would be there for them. So he would be up early, just to see that nothing could harm them.

The heat still draped itself languidly about every surface and although the cottage was cool, Susannah Kidd had unlaced her corset and taken off her skirt, so that she sat in her shift and petticoat. Easing herself into a chair, she stretched out her legs in front of her, planting her small, bare feet down on the flags. Pressed against the stones, she felt the thrill of the coolness dart up through her whole body. She shivered with delight.

The knife-grinder was standing at the window. He had been watching her sensuous dance through a heady haze of liquor for the past few minutes and hoped that he would not be turned away. After all, she had been so very welcoming at their first meeting. The pout of her lips and the look in her eye had told him he would be well received should he choose to call again.

He bent down, picked up a pebble, and tossed it in through the open casement. It bounced once and landed by Susannah's feet. She let out a muted gasp and sat upright. Turning to the window, she saw a head swathed in a red scarf, teeth pearly white against tanned skin. Flying up from her chair, she hurried over to the man who had sharpened her scissors.

"Be gone with you!" she scolded him. "What do you think you are doing?" Her eyes shot to the bedroom door, but the intruder was pulling her close to him. He began kissing her neck, his beery breath filling her nostrils.

"You alone?" he panted.

"My husband is abed," she whispered hoarsely and she pushed his chest hard. But he grabbed her hand and unfurling her fingers, he kissed her palm softly. The thrill of his lips on her wrist made her close her eyes for a second, but still she resisted.

"Be gone with you," she told him, louder this time.

Sensing that perhaps she meant what she said, the knife-grinder backed off, feigning hurt. "Why so cruel?" he asked, his lips drooping.

"I mean it," she growled.

So, pouting like a wounded child, he touched his red scarf with two of his fingers by way of a farewell, and took his leave. All the same, the look in her eye told him that he should return. And he wove his unsteady way back to his mule, mounted it, and silently stole away like the thief he surely was.

Chapter 8

Thomas and Lydia arrived at the Black Bear tired and sore after a journey that had taken them more than seven hours. Chalk dust from the Downs had found its way into the carriage and now a thin film of it covered the seats and the passengers. Because of the heat, Lovelock had stopped more frequently for the horses to take water, so they had endured the lurching and jouncing of the carriage longer than expected. Their relief at their arrival and the thought of a wash and a good meal was, however, enough to put them in better spirits.

They had agreed to take separate rooms to avoid any possible scandal, and after a change of clothes they were shown into a low-beamed dining room. They sat at a quiet table and Thomas ordered a pitcher of wine and a dish of roast lamb and capers. Now and again they could hear raucous shouts from the bar as recently arrived carriers deposited more weary travelers for the night. There was the constant hubbub of toing and froing, of doors banging and orders being barked to the kitchen.

Lydia remained subdued and Thomas felt it his duty to try and distract her from her anxiety over what the morrow might hold. He spoke of Amos Kidd's beautiful roses and of yesterday's garden party at West Wycombe. Soon she was smiling again, so that by the time their food arrived, her appetite was whetted.

"I am so grateful to you for being here," she told him as they ate.

"And I am grateful you chose me to accompany you," he replied. He grasped his goblet, half full of wine. "Let us drink to our quest."

Lydia nodded and lifted her glass, clinking it against Thomas's. "To Richard," she said. "God grant we find him soon."

An hour or so later, when they had finished their meal, Lydia told Thomas she wished to retire to her room. He settled her down in the small but pleasantly furnished chamber and decided to return to the bar for a nightcap. As he was coming down the stairs, he noticed two men bluster in from the street. One was tall and well-dressed, a merchant perhaps. He was talking animatedly with the other.

"I tell you, after what I've been through, this place is most welcome," the young doctor heard him say as he headed for the bar.

Thomas approached, intrigued. He sat down at a nearby table so that he could eavesdrop, cradling his brandy and feigning to read a discarded newssheet.

"It was like the deepest, darkest winter, my friend," continued the merchant. "The snow was gray as ash, and there was a fog that blackened the leaves and poisoned the water."

The other man called out to the serving girl, snapping his fingers.

"Two brandies and make it quick. My friend here has endured a journey from hell," he cried.

Thomas needed to know more. He rose and walked casually over to the bar. "So, sir," he said. "You have had a bad journey?"

The merchant eyed him. "Aye, sir. I've ridden through a sudden choking fog that blocked out the sun and made it hard for a man to breathe."

Thomas looked grave. "A disturbing experience, I'll wager. And do you have any notion as to what might have caused this fog?" he inquired.

The merchant shrugged. "I did not stop to think, sir. I rode on for my life!"

The young doctor was sympathetic. "It must have been terrifying."

"By heaven, man, it was! I saw laborers in the fields fall, choking." He lifted the brandy to his lips.

"And where was this, sir?" Thomas pressed.

"Just outside Bedford," replied the merchant, before gulping down his liquor in one go.

"And that is north of here?"

"Yes, sir. About eighty miles northeast. I took the road south and I'm pleased to say I was clear of it by Buckingham." He turned to his companion. "I hope I never encounter such a fog again!"

"I hope you never do, either," nodded Thomas. But he had the distinctly uncomfortable feeling that this deadly haze, this mephitic gas, or whatever it was, was moving inexorably closer. Suddenly all the strange phenomena he had encountered over the past three or four days began to make sense. The rise in barometric pressure could explain the arrival of this noxious cloud, the unseasonal flight of the geese, the swarming of rats, the absence of bees, and the low-flying birds. Nature knew instinctively that something extraordinary and potentially deadly was in her midst—and it was heading south. If that was the case, then in the next few days it would threaten the city of Oxford and, of course, the Boughton estate.

From the small viewing room inside the golden orb on top of West Wycombe church, three noblemen were enjoying each other's company over cards.

"Sweet Jesu, this has to be one of the best views in Christendom," cried Sir Montagu Malthus. He was peering out from one of the small windows that offered unparalleled views of the countryside as it flattened out toward the Thames. "Windsor Castle is looking splendid this evening."

"We are indeed high up here," replied Sir John Dashwood-King. "Franklin wanted to affix one of his new-fangled lightning conductors to the roof," he said, pointing upward and giggling at what he clearly considered a fanciful notion.

"Full of ridiculous ideas, these Americans," agreed Sir Montagu.

The lawyer, who had been the late Lord Crick's guardian, was a great raven of a man. His tall stature and brooding presence added to his formidable reputation as a ruthless advocate. He had broken his journey between the Inns of Court in London and his country seat near Banbury at West Wycombe Park. The fact that he could play a winning hand and eulogize about the view at the same time spoke volumes to his friends. Not much escaped his prying eyes.

"Yes, this brings back memories of dear Francis," he told the jocular baronet, who was seated opposite him. "Oh, the times we had in the caves!"

Sir John's broad face beamed. "I can believe that. What was the motto? *Do as you please?*"

Sir Montagu's great shoulders jumped at the thought. "And we did, by Jove! Ay, Henry?"

Sir Henry Thorndike was also at the card table, although he seemed less engaged in the game. He had still not fully recovered from the exertion of climbing the dozens of steps leading from the church tower into the globe. He took out his kerchief and dabbed his forehead.

"Oh, yes. The times we had," he replied weakly, still struggling for breath.

Sir Montagu turned to Sir John. "Wouldn't think so to look at him now," he said under his breath.

"So how does he manage that young wife of his?"

Sir Montagu winked. "He lets others do that for him. I'll wager any money you like that the next heir to Fetcham Manor won't be his," came the whispered reply.

Both men turned to see the old man wiping the sweat from his top lip.

Sir John called for more wine and they drank heartily. The talk turned to women and the price of grain, the health of His Majesty King George and the Whigs at Westminster.

"So you have come straight from London?" queried Sir John of Sir Montagu.

"Indeed. I had business with my associates in the judiciary."

"You hatching some plan?" croaked Sir Henry, his breathing still labored.

A smirk settled on Sir Montagu's lips. "You know me too well, Henry," he replied. "I needed to sound out the legality of a certain proposal I wish to set in motion."

"And from the look on your face, your mission was a success?" ventured Sir John.

"Have you ever known me to fail?" An air of self-satisfaction enveloped the lawyer, just as surely as if he had been wearing a cloak.

"So you will make us privy to your plans?" asked Sir John.

"They involve my charge."

"The lovely Lady Lydia?" asked Sir Henry.

Sir Montagu nodded. "The very same. As you know her father, God rest his soul, wanted me to look after her in the event of his death and I have not discharged my duties lightly."

"So you are still on the hunt for a suitable husband for her?"

Malthus nodded. "Indeed, John. Like Fetcham, Boughton was in need of an heir."

"Was?" reiterated Sir Henry.

Sir Montagu sipped his claret. "Yes, events have taken a most interesting turn, gentlemen."

Sir John arched a brow. "And what might that be?"

The lawyer paused for effect as if he were in a courtroom. "I believe Lydia gave birth to a son and that he may well be alive."

The two other men let out a collective gasp.

Sir John jumped in first. "Born on the right side of the sheets?"

Sir Montagu waved his hand dismissively. "That rake Farrell was the father, of that I am sure, so the boy's legitimacy is a mere technicality."

"And how did you come by this information?" pressed Sir Henry.

"I was an executor of Farrell's will. There were bills, letters. I traced them."

"So you have found the boy?" asked Sir John.

"My man is on the trail as we speak."

Sir Henry breathed deeply and took a gulp of claret. "Well, there's a turn up for the books."

"Indeed." Sir Montagu nodded. "And who could resist a noble-woman with a ready-made son?"

Sir John was not so sure. "And what about that surgeon chap from the Colonies. There's talk, Montagu. You should see the way they look at each other."

"A good point," he replied. "And this is where I need your help."

Both men looked at Sir Montagu, then eyed each other quizzi-cally before leaning forward in unison. "We're all ears, dear fel-low," said Sir John.

Chapter 9

"Yes?" greeted the woman warily, a rosy-cheeked child whimpering on her hip. Her full breasts jumped from the top of her bodice as she bounced it up and down to quiet it.

"Mistress Pargiter?" asked Thomas, removing his hat and bowing politely.

"Yes," she repeated. Only this time more confidently.

"Good day to you. I am Dr. Silkstone and this is Lady Lydia Farrell," he said, gesturing to Lydia, who stood apprehensively at his side.

At the name Farrell, the woman's piggy eyes widened and her snout twitched.

"Farrell, you say?"

Lydia stepped forward anxiously. "Does that name mean anything to you, Mistress Pargiter?"

The dame looked uneasy. Her small eyes darted to the floor and back and she jounced the baby on her hip, even though the child was no longer fretting.

"Mistress Pargiter?" pressed Thomas.

"Yes. Yes, that name does mean something," she replied.

Lydia saw the look of embarrassment on her face and decided to compound it. "Captain Michael Farrell was my husband." Her voice was reedy with emotion. "And that was my son you consigned to the workhouse."

The woman pursed her lips, as if biting her tongue. Then,

looking up and down the street, to see if anyone was watching, she said, "You'd best come in."

She showed Lydia and Thomas into a small, shabbily furnished parlor. A young girl was polishing a card table. Down the hallway another baby cried.

"Take him," the widow instructed, handing over the child on her hip. "And see to Samuel." The girl bobbed a curtsy and left with the young boy in her arms, closing the door behind her.

"How many children do you care for, Mistress Pargiter?" asked Thomas.

"I am wet nursing two at the moment and dry nursing one, sir," she replied, tossing her head indignantly.

"As long as their parents keep paying," hissed Lydia.

The woman's small eyes narrowed. "I am not a charity, Lady Lydia. I've managed since my husband passed, but only just."

Thomas could see that Lydia's well-aimed anger was self-defeating. "I am sure you do an excellent job, Mistress Pargiter," he told her.

She paused and straightened her back, as if digesting the compliment. "I like to think so, sir," she replied, patting the back of her lace cap.

"And you do remember the child, Master Richard?"

The widow looked directly at Lydia, studying her face for a moment. "Yes," she replied. "The image of you, he was."

Lydia's lips trembled and Thomas put his hand on hers to comfort her.

"Her ladyship has not seen her son since he was but a few days old," he explained.

The widow nodded. "He was my nurse-child for more than a year, and then I dry nursed him after that." She gazed into the distance, as if picturing the boy in her mind's eye. "A sickly child, mind. And his arm . . ."

"Withered?" interrupted Thomas.

"Yes," she replied, tetchily. "But it were nothing to do with me. That's how he came."

Thomas was familiar with the reputation of wet nurses.

Babes that died in their care were more often than not buried without any questions being asked. He realized he would have to tread carefully in his inquiries. "How long was he with you, Mistress Pargiter?"

The woman raised a stubby finger to her cheek in thought. "I'd say three years, all told."

Lydia put her hand up to her mouth to stifle a groan. For all that time her son was living only a day's journey away and the thought of it cut her to the quick.

"And you received regular payments from Captain Farrell?" quizzed Thomas.

"First day of the month, regular as clockwork, a messenger would come with the money. Then on the first day in April that year, no one came. So I waited till the first day of May and when still no payment appeared, I . . ." She glanced at Lydia, who was looking at her reproachfully. The widow took a deep breath. "I wrote to the captain, telling him I had received no money and that if I had not been paid by the end of the month, the child would be sent to the workhouse."

At these last words, Lydia sprang up, her fists clenched in anger.

"How could you?" she cried, her face crumpled in disbelief.

Thomas tried to calm her. "Please, let Widow Pargiter speak," he entreated her. She sat down again.

"Pray continue," he urged the woman, her back now stiffened in indignation.

"When no word came in the next two weeks, I assumed that no one would be paying for the child. I could not afford to keep him anymore, and so . . ." She broke off, eyeing Lydia, knowing that no more needed to be said.

"And it did not occur to you that the captain might have been ill or indisposed?" scowled Lydia.

A strange smirk suddenly settled on the widow's face. "Indisposed?" she repeated. "Is that a fancy word for being charged with your brother-in-law's murder and thrown in jail?"

Lydia's eyes widened in horror and, without warning, she

leapt from her chair. Thomas held her gently by the shoulders. "Please, calm yourself," he soothed, as he guided her back to her seat once more.

"Bad news travels, you see," goaded the widow, her piggy eyes fixed upon Lydia. "That's how I knew I'd not be paid what I was due."

"So you sent the child to the workhouse?" Thomas's tone remained even, despite the fact that his voice dripped with contempt. He had come across many such nurses during his years of medical practice and he knew most of them to be honest and trustworthy, but they rarely allowed themselves the luxury of forming a bond with their young charges.

"Yes, I did send him to the workhouse," nodded the woman. There was a certain smugness in her tone.

"In Hungerford?" asked the young doctor.

The widow nodded. "In Charnham Street."

Thomas smiled at Lydia. "That is just around the corner, is it not?"

"It is," confirmed the widow. "But I'm not sure he'll be there now."

Lydia frowned. "What do you mean?"

Widow Pargiter's nose twitched again. "You ain't the only ones who've been asking after the boy."

Thomas darted a glance at Lydia. "How so?"

The widow let out a strangled laugh. "A gentleman was here last week. Asking me the same questions, he was. Wanted to know where the Farrell boy was."

The color suddenly drained from Lydia's cheeks.

"And you told him?" asked Thomas.

" 'Course I did," she smirked. "He gave me a crown for my pains."

Lydia rose quickly to her feet. "Well, you'll get nothing from us," she cried angrily. "We will show ourselves out." And with that, she stormed toward the door.

"Thank you for your help, Mistress Pargiter," said Thomas, also rising. Lydia was already in the hallway when he turned to the widow and said: "This gentleman, did he give his name?"

The dame shook her head. "No name," she said, then reflecting again she added: "but he looked like a clerk or a man of law."

Thomas digested the information. "Thank you, Mistress Pargiter. You have been most helpful." He slipped another crown into her palm.

Halfway down the street he caught up with Lydia. He had never seen her so enraged. She was still seething when he took her by the arm and turned her to face him. Her cheeks were wet with angry tears.

"How could that woman treat my son as if he were just a trinket, a thing to be disposed of when he became an inconvenience?" she cried, before burying her face in Thomas's shoulder.

A passerby turned his head and raised an eyebrow at the scene.

"Let us return to the inn," suggested Thomas. But Lydia balked at the idea.

"The only place I am going is to the workhouse. My son could be only a few yards from here, Thomas. How could you make me wait a moment longer?" The wrath of a scorned mother had returned to her voice once more.

"But you must be prepared for disappointment, my love," Thomas reminded her. "This man, this stranger . . ."

Lydia broke in. "There is only one way to find out," she said and, freeing herself from his arms, she began marching in the direction of the workhouse.

Five minutes later they both found themselves outside the tall, faceless building in Charnham Street. Thomas looked at Lydia as if asking her permission to proceed before grasping the heavy knocker. She nodded her assent and the die was cast. A few seconds elapsed before the door finally creaked open and the same nervous woman who had answered to the notary a few days before scurried into view.

"Good day, ma'am," greeted Thomas. "My name is Dr. Thomas Silkstone and this is Lady Lydia Farrell. We are . . ."

At the mention of Lydia's name, the woman suddenly gasped.

"Oh my word," she squeaked. She clamped her sinewy hand over her mouth, then released it again. "Farrell, you say!"

"Yes, ma'am. Is something wrong?" entreated Thomas.

"You'd best come in," she said, her high voice lowering conspiratorially. "Come in, please."

The woman, her gray hair framing her face like coils of wire, hurried into the hallway, beckoning Thomas and Lydia to follow. She stopped outside a door halfway along the dark corridor and knocked. From inside a voice boomed. She entered and shut the door behind her.

"What can this mean?" Lydia frowned, nervously fingering her fan.

Thomas did not reply, but he knew full well that either Master Richard was indeed at the workhouse or that the mysterious man had reached him before they had. He could hear shouted commands in the distance and a child calling out. There was the clanking of metal on metal and the scraping of chairs being dragged along stone flags.

From behind the closed door, they could hear a man's voice. It was raised in frustration or annoyance rather than anger. A few seconds later the door was flung open by the man Thomas assumed was the workhouse master.

"Lady Lydia Farrell, I believe?" He addressed her with a curious regard in his eye, as if he recognized her from somewhere.

"Yes," she replied. Any previous strength in her voice seemed to have deserted her at the sight of the thickset man with his wide neck and large head.

"Come in, pray," he beckoned.

Thomas and Lydia followed him into the room that, with only one small window, was dingy yet pleasingly cool. The flighty woman remained outside.

Lydia sat on a chair in front of a large desk. Thomas sat behind her. Both of them regarded the master like children about to be chastised. A great book lay open on the desk, its leaves edged in red.

"So, Lady Lydia," began the master brusquely, his wig

perched precariously on top of his head. "You are looking for your son."

"Yes, sir, I am," replied Lydia breathlessly. "Mistress Pargiter, the nurse, said that she sent him here." Her hands were shaking with anticipation. "Just over three years ago," she added.

The master nodded and hooked his spectacles over his ears. Consulting the great book, he pointed to an entry. "Yes, on June 10, 1781," he replied.

Lydia leant forward. "Then he is here!" she exclaimed. In her excitement she reached for Thomas's hand, but the master looked grave and shook his head.

"I am afraid not, your ladyship," he said, removing his spectacles.

Lydia's mouth trembled. "What? Then where is he? Please . . ."

The master lifted his great shovel of a hand up in the air and Lydia bit her lip.

"He was here, your ladyship, but he left almost two years ago."

"Then where did he go?" A note of panic entered her voice and Thomas squeezed her hand.

Again the master consulted the ledger. "A gentleman by the name of Mr. Francis Crick took him."

Lydia looked askance. "Francis," she repeated incredulously. It was a few weeks short of two years ago that her cousin had been hanged.

"He said he was his uncle." The master peered at Lydia over his spectacles. "He bore a remarkable resemblance to you, your ladyship," he observed.

"Indeed," snapped Thomas, annoyed by the master's tone of familiarity. "Did he leave a forwarding address?"

The master peered at the ledger. "Boughton Hall."

Lydia's slight shoulders slumped in disbelief.

"But he is not at Boughton. So where is he?" she wailed. "Where is my son?" The revelation was too much for her and she began to sob, reaching for her handkerchief from her bag. Thomas put a comforting arm around her.

"Thank you for your time, sir. But, as you can see, her ladyship is deeply upset. We must go."

The young doctor felt nausea rising in his own gullet. This was a terrible outcome to their visit. It rendered their whole journey futile and, worse still, it meant they would have to begin all over again in their search for Lydia's lost son. For the time being, however, the most urgent need was to return to the Black Bear as soon as possible. Helping Lydia up, he guided her to the door, but just before the master showed him out, he recalled the stranger who, according to Mistress Pargiter, was on a similar mission.

"Sir, one more thing," said Thomas, pausing at the door. "Has someone else, a clerk perhaps, made inquiries regarding her ladyship's son, too?"

The master raised an eyebrow. For a moment he was caught off guard, but then he let out a hollow laugh.

"Why no, sir. Whatever gave you that notion?"

Thomas flashed a look at Lydia. He hoped she would not protest. Thankfully she did not. The young doctor shrugged: "Oh, 'tis of no consequence," he said, and he ushered Lydia into the corridor, where the nervous old woman was waiting.

"Show this lady and gentleman out, will you?" the master instructed her. Nodding her gray head she gestured to the door, but as soon as she was sure no one else was watching, she beckoned to them both and moved closer.

The woman's breath smelled of bile and her hands were shaking, but there was a curious smile on her lips.

"I knew you was the child's mother as soon as I see'd ya," she said to Lydia in a loud whisper. "Just like you, he was."

Lydia looked deep into her dull eyes. "You know something?" She clung to the possibility as if it were driftwood from a shipwreck.

The old woman's forehead wrinkled into a frown. "I know there was a man here last week, asking about the boy."

Thomas nodded and turned to Lydia. "I knew it."

"He gave the master a crown to keep quiet," squeaked the woman. "I knew you was the child's mother. So I'm going to give you this," she said, fumbling in her apron pocket. To Lydia's surprise, she brought out a single earring. It was gold and embedded with pink topaz stones. Lydia gasped at the sight of it as the woman held it up, like a prize or a trophy.

"Where did you get this?" she asked, holding out her hand to take it.

" 'Twas the boy's foundling token," she replied, dropping the jewel into Lydia's outstretched palm.

Thomas gazed at the earring. "And you have the other one?" he asked Lydia.

"Yes. Yes, I do. I thought it was lost, but Michael must have taken it."

A look of delight had settled on the old crone's face, but the sound of footsteps in the hallway brought her back to reality.

"Good day, your ladyship. Sir," she squeaked politely as the door to the workhouse creaked open once more. "God grant you find the lad, my lady," she said, bending her head low so that her shrill words barely caught the air. Lydia squeezed her thin hand before joining Thomas in the searing heat once more.

Chapter 10

It came upon Boughton in the twilight hours, when most God-fearing men were abed. Only those who were awake, like Amos Kidd, sensed the change in the air as it pressed hard against his chest. His head began to ache. It was a sure sign that a storm was on its way. A few minutes later and there it was: a long roll of thunder.

He had been lying on the lumpy ticking, listening to the sound of his wife's soft breath, into the small hours. His heart was filled with a great sadness and he wondered, as he so often did, whether if had he been able to give her children, mayhap she would have been different with him. Mayhap she would not give other men the eye at every turn. They had only been married a few months before an accident took away any hope of offspring. He wiped away a single tear with his grimy fingers.

Another clap of thunder came, followed by a flash of lightning, then another and another, turning the night inside out, making it bright as day for a second or two. Then blackness. Blackness and silence.

Rising to look out of the window, he noticed something strange in the sky. The waning moon was veiled in a strange haze. He opened the latch to sniff the air and caught a distinctive odor; a pungent, acrid smell like the tang of saltpeter, but not saltpeter. But there was more: it seemed to have been snowing. He could not see very far: a peculiar mist had draped itself, like gossamer, around the cottage, but what he could see—the ground, the blackcurrant bushes, the fence posts—were covered in a light coating of flakes. Snow in June? He frowned and shivered and as he did so he realized he was cold for the first time in several days.

Slipping on his smock and breeches, he ventured out. His warm breath curled into the air like steam rising from a boiling kettle. At this hour he would normally hear a nightingale sing in the woods, or the rustle of badgers or the unearthly wail of a dog fox. But this morn was still as stone, and just as cold.

He looked down on the ground where his feet had left footprints, clear as if he had trodden on virgin snow. Yet this was not snow. He bent down and ran his fingers across the grass. It felt spiky and was covered with a strange, powdery frost. He rubbed it between his fingers; it was coarse and grainy. He lifted it up to his nose and snorted. It was then that he remembered; the smell, the powder, the knife-grinder.

Returning inside he grabbed a coat and scarf and lit a lantern. Dawn should have broken by now, but there was no sign of the sun. Instead this strange haze was thickening. He began to take hurried steps down the track toward the formal gardens; a rising sense of panic taking hold as he saw the powder had settled on the hedgerows and verges, too. His roses. What of his beloved roses? Could this be what the traveling knife-grinder called the devil's breath? Was this what Dr. Silkstone had spoken of? He quickened his pace. His heart beat faster. His lungs worked harder, but he found it more and more difficult to breathe. The smell had rasped his nostrils and seared through into his gullet, so that now it was all he could taste. He clamped his scarf across his face to block it out, but the taint lingered.

Looking left and right, he tried to find his bearings, groping sightlessly. Where was the familiar wall of the potager? The gate? The gate into his rose garden should be there. The blanket of fog was now so thick that he was completely disoriented. He stretched out his arms to the side of the track and felt an enormous sense of relief when his fingers touched the mossy flint of the wall. Blindly his hands skimmed across the top of it as he edged his way along the track; each stone a welcome marker.

Not far now, he told himself; a few more paces and he should reach the rose garden. It was then that he felt it on his skin; one or two pricks at first, as if someone were sticking pins into him, but within a few seconds came more. Little stabs of pain were burning his flesh, stinging his eyes. He looked upward. It was raining, and each droplet scalded his skin like acid.

It was noontide when Lovelock took the carriage carrying Thomas and Lydia over the Thames at Oxford and onward toward Boughton Hall. The young doctor was on edge, his nerves as taut as catgut. The expedition to Hungerford in search of Lydia's lost son had thrown up more questions than it answered and had left her distraught. Yet there was something else; the matter of this impending cloud—this strange phenomenona that seemed to choke the very breath out of anyone unfortunate enough to be in its path.

They had traveled at least thirty miles northeast from Hungerford without seeing anything more than the odd cirrus cloud in the June sky. It was still very warm, although Thomas had checked the temperature before their departure. The mercury had dropped by a full ten degrees, so the heat was much more bearable. Nevertheless, the carriage windows remained down to take advantage of the light breeze that had picked up during the course of their journey. Thomas noted, however, that it was blowing from a northwesterly direction and that, he knew, might not auger well.

His gaze turned back to Lydia. She remained deep in thought, looking out onto a summer landscape that offered her no solace.

"You will be pleased when we reach Boughton?" he ventured.

She lifted her face and managed a muted smile.

"I am sure I shall feel much better once we are home," she replied.

Thomas nodded. "Not long now." He tried to comfort her, resting his hand on hers as Lovelock turned the horses on the road to Brandwick. "We're at the crossroads."

Just as he had spoken, however, she jerked her hand up to her throat and coughed. Thomas whipped his head 'round and saw her swallowing hard. It was then that he first smelled it, the pungent mix of sulfur and metal that stabbed the back of his throat, making him gag. He lunged for the heavy leather curtains and drew them across the window as quickly as he could, then taking the tapping stick he signaled for Lovelock to stop the carriage.

"Stay there," he ordered Lydia as he opened the door and jumped down. Lovelock was also coughing in the choking air. Thomas could make more sense of it now. They were on top of the scarp before they began their descent to the estate and he could see that the whole of the valley below was shrouded in a thick blanket of cloud. Only the spire of the estate chapel pierced through like some great needle.

"What is it, Dr. Silkstone, sir?" wheezed Lovelock. He spat on the ground, trying to gob away the bitter taste in his mouth.

"I cannot be sure," croaked Thomas, but he knew the longer they remained stationary, the longer the poisonous air would have to creep into their lungs. "Put your scarf 'round your mouth, man, and get us back to Boughton as soon as you can."

Lovelock obeyed, although the horses, too, were struggling to breathe. Back inside, Lydia had reached for the flask of lemonade and was drinking freely. She offered it to Thomas, who gulped down two or three mouthfuls to ease the rasping in his throat. The young doctor opened his medical bag and took out the gauze dressing he always carried. "Hold this over your mouth," he told Lydia, handing her a square.

All about them the fog swirled over a landscape that should have been so familiar and yet now seemed alien. The sun was completely hidden and the horizon had disappeared beneath a blackening sky. Walls and hedgerows became dark and brooding lines etched against the roadside. The harvest fields that were only yesterday golden with corn were now charcoal gray, the ears of wheat shriveled and dead. A solitary wagon stood by the roadside, grain spilled across it from an abandoned sack. Scythes and sickles lay in the fields, the laborers having fled.

"What is it? What has happened, Thomas?" pleaded Lydia, her eyes smarting with the fumes.

The young doctor shook his head. " 'Tis worse than I feared," he murmured, watching gray flakes swirl about like snow.

"What is, Thomas? Tell me!" cried Lydia, her words dissolving into a cough as she spoke.

"We must not talk," he told her, holding her tightly. "Not until we are inside." She buried her head in his shoulder. Thomas was thankful she was spared the sight of a dead ewe and her lamb on the verge.

A few moments later they reached the Hall itself, but as Lovelock drove the carriage right up to the front steps, no one was there to greet them as usual. Even the house dogs seemed to have retreated. The place was eerily quiet. Thomas was glad to see that all the servants appeared to have taken refuge inside.

Clamping the gauze over their mouths, he hurried indoors, taking Lydia with him, while Lovelock, his kerchief wrapped securely 'round his mouth, rushed to stable the horses.

"Thank the Lord you are safe!" cried Howard as he walked swiftly toward them in an uncustomary show of emotion.

"What has happened?" asked Lydia.

The butler looked grave. "We awoke this morning to a strange fog, your ladyship. Everyone carried on with their duties as best they could until it seemed to thicken and we began coughing and choking and our eyes began to stream. I ordered everyone inside and all the doors and windows to be shut."

"You acted wisely. Thank you, Howard," said Lydia. "Are all the servants accounted for?"

The butler frowned. "The house maids, the kitchen staff, and the footmen are all safe, your ladyship, but I cannot speak for those in the stables or the gardens."

"Let us hope they have the sense to seek shelter until this fog has lifted," she said.

At that moment Gabriel Lawson appeared in the hallway, gray powder dusting his coat. In his arms he carried a young redheaded boy.

"Help here!" he called.

Thomas dashed toward him. "Will!" he cried as he recognized the freckled face of Jacob and Hannah Lovelock's son. The child was pale and his breathing shallow. His thin limbs dangled limply as a marionette's.

"Lay him on the sofa in the drawing room," ordered Lydia. She and Thomas followed anxiously.

Lawson settled the boy as Lydia put a cushion under his head. Kneeling down beside him, Thomas opened his medical bag and brought out a glass bottle containing a syrupy liquid. He poured a little into a cup and held it to Will's lips.

"Drink this," he coaxed. " 'Twill soothe you." He lifted the boy's head gently so that he could sup. Instantly the child's face screwed up in a grimace. Thomas understood that the Spanish liquorice and salt of tartar were not palatable, but he also knew the ingredients eased asthma attacks. He recalled Will's raw skin when they had first met and how he suffered from eczema that was soothed by his mother's unguents. The two conditions, in his experience, often went hand in hand. The boy's natural susceptibilities must have made him even more vulnerable to this noxious fog.

The sound of footsteps rushing into the room alerted them to the arrival of Hannah Lovelock, the child's mother.

"Oh, my Will!" she cried, heading straight for her son, forgetting all decorum. Rushing to his side, she stroked his carrot-colored hair, then seeing Thomas she fixed him with a pleading gaze. "He will be well, will 'e not, Dr. Silkstone?"

Thomas replied honestly. "The next few hours will tell, Mistress Lovelock," he said.

Hannah nodded, running her hand over her son's clammy forehead. "Thank goodness you found him, Mr. Lawson," she said, looking up at the steward.

"And what of the men in the fields?" asked Lydia.

"All of them fled as the cloud approached, ma'am," Lawson told her. "But I cannot say if they all made it to shelter. I know at least two men are dead on the Thorndike estate."

At the steward's words the young boy opened his eyes wide,

as if he had recalled an event or a situation. He opened his mouth and puffed out an inaudible word.

"Hush now, my love," urged his mother.

"You must conserve your breath, Will," Thomas told him.

"But, sir," the boy wheezed. "Mr. Kidd . . . he . . ." He broke off, coughing.

Thomas darted a glance at Lydia. "Amos Kidd. Has anyone seen him?"

Silence.

The doctor leapt to his feet. "The rose garden," he said. "Mr. Lawson, come with me." He handed the steward a square of gauze from his bag and together they headed for the French windows that led outside.

"Close them behind us immediately," Thomas instructed Howard. Together he and Lawson squeezed through the narrow crack in the opened doors and out into the fog.

The cloud remained the same, still thick but no worse than when Thomas had arrived. Before them was an opaque curtain of fog that obscured their view any farther than the balustrade at the top of the steps that led down to the formal gardens. With the gauze clamped over their noses and mouths, they both edged forward, carefully negotiating the shallow treads until they reached the arch of the clipped yew hedge over the entrance to the rose garden.

Signaling Lawson to go left, Thomas went the opposite way 'round the beds. The bushes at the far end were no longer visible and the pungent scent of the blooms was completely masked by the acrid tang of sulfur. Both men skirted the outside of the garden at first, working their way toward the middle.

It was Thomas who found the gardener, lying facedown on a thin strip of lawn between the rose beds.

"Over here!" he called to Lawson.

He turned Kidd over to find his eyes closed and his pallor gray, with great livid patches around his nose and mouth. Feeling his wrist he detected a pulse, albeit weak.

"Is he alive?" blurted Lawson, removing the gauze from his mouth.

"Yes, but barely," replied Thomas, his words breaking up into a cough. "Help me, will you?"

Between them they managed to lift the gardener, wrapping his limp arms around their necks and dragging him, his feet trailing along the ground, back through the French windows.

Kidd's gray-flecked head lolled backward as they laid him on another settee in the drawing room, but the exertion seemed to stir him and he began to cough. Thomas eased him into an upright position and he came to his senses.

At first it seemed that he could not focus; his eyes were swimming in their sockets, but after a moment or two he appeared to understand where he was. When he opened his mouth to speak, however, his breath deserted him and he began to rasp in great heaving spasms.

Thomas poured some more of the syrup and held it to his lips. The gardener gulped it down and almost instantly his breathing was calmer.

"Do not try to speak," the doctor told him, easing him down on the settee. "You must rest."

Hannah was left in charge of the patients and given instructions to call Thomas if there was any change for the worse in either of their conditions.

Outside in the hallway, Lydia faced Thomas. "What is it that has done this to them?" she asked. "What poison is in this fog?"

The doctor could only shake his head. "I have no answer," he told her earnestly. "But I intend to find one."

Chapter 11

"**D**o you think this might be hell?"

The Reverend George Lightfoot stood by a window in the vicarage at Brandwick, contemplating the view. His long hair was parted in the middle and streaked with silver and his large nose twitched as he sniffed the air.

His wife, who had been writing letters at her escritoire, put down her pen and joined him. It was just past eleven o'clock in the morning and yet she had told the maid to light the candles. She stood at her husband's side, towering over the wiry little man by at least three inches. Now she, too, considered what lay beyond the window, even though there was barely anything to see. The fog had enveloped not only the distant hills, but also the chestnut trees at the bottom of their garden. Strange flecks swirled about in the blackness and the smell of sulfur rankled in her nostrils.

"If this were hell, then we would not be here," she told her husband in a matter-of-fact voice. "The Lord would have taken us up to join him at his right hand."

The Reverend Lightfoot nodded, thoughtfully. "Oh, my dear Margaret. How right you are." He felt embarrassed that he could ever have doubted their own salvation.

"The Lord may be showing his displeasure with those who do not seek him out, but we, the righteous, have nothing to fear," she told him, her gaze remaining on the darkness. She has a fine profile, he thought, and a strong jaw to match. She always spoke with such conviction that he almost envied her steadfastness; her complete and utter submission to God's will.

"Then we should pray for those who have caused him such displeasure, should we not?" he suggested. His eyes were stinging with the fog and he wiped them with his kerchief.

"Indeed, we should," agreed his wife. Lifting her skirts slightly, she knelt down where she stood. The Reverend Lightfoot joined her and together they looked out over the blanket of fumes, and folded their hands in prayer.

"Dear Lord, in your infinite wisdom you have sent this great fog upon us, cloaking both good and evil alike. Let those who have provoked your wrath repent of their sins. Lift this veil of darkness from their eyes so that they may see the error of their ways and lead us all into the divine light of your kingdom. Through Our Lord Jesus Christ. Amen."

"Amen," echoed Mistress Lightfoot.

"There will be many who are afraid," he reflected, rising and holding out a hand to his wife.

"And rightly so," she retorted. "Brandwick may not be like London, but we have plenty of our own ne'er-do-wells." She walked back to her escritoire and took up her pen once more.

" 'Tis true," acknowledged the vicar, "but perhaps . . ."

His wife looked up, irritated that she should be challenged. "Perhaps what?"

"Perhaps this fog, or whatever it is, will bring them back to the Lord," said her husband, gesturing forlornly to the blackness outside.

Mistress Lightfoot smiled sourly, as if the taste of the vapor was tainting her tongue. "If the fog doesn't lift, you'll have an empty church this Sunday, George," she told him, and with that she lowered her head to resume her correspondence.

The library at Boughton Hall was a place where Thomas felt at ease. If he could not be in his laboratory in London, surrounded by his gallipots and guglets and his scientific paraphernalia, then here was a good substitute. Lydia's late father, Sir Richard Crick, had kept a good library and should he need references for his experiments, he would know where to look, while downstairs in the kitchen, Mistress Claddingbowl's store cupboard wanted for nothing.

He had overseen the removal of Amos Kidd and young Will Lovelock into more suitable quarters below stairs. Will had shown a slight improvement. His breathing was easier when he had last seen him; but Amos Kidd still gave him cause for concern. His wife remained by his side. His breathing was labored, his fever high, and he seemed to be in considerable pain. The black sores around his eyes, lips, and hands also appeared to be worsening, despite the fact that Hannah had washed them and smothered them in some of her soothing unguent.

It was late afternoon in a day that had seen no shadows. It had remained as black as night throughout the normal daylight hours, so Thomas was forced to work by the glow of a lantern. Before him, on a saucer, was a small quantity of gray flakes that he had collected from the terrace. Next to the saucer, in a jug he had purloined from the kitchen, were a few teaspoons of rainwater, scooped from a stone trough. He had been swift in the taking of these samples. Wearing a scarf over his mouth, he had dashed out of the patio doors and, in barely a minute, had managed to collect what he needed. Now he sat contemplating the mysteries these granules and this rainwater held within them.

How he wished he had his microscope to analyze the grains, or his retort to evaporate the rainwater. As it was, he was forced to rely on the good nature of Mistress Claddingbowl, who had willingly supplied a set of spoons and custard cups and even a flint and spills. Fortunately—although it could be argued that fortune played no part in Thomas's perpetual state of preparedness—he had packed several relevant utensils in his bag. First and foremost was his magnifying glass. It may have lacked the power of his microscope, having less than a two-hundredth of the former's magnification, but at least its power would enable him to conduct a preliminary examination of the powder.

Next came his test tubes. He had brought four with him and now he carefully poured the murky liquid from the jug into one of them. Quite what he was looking for, he was not entirely sure, although he believed there could be a powerful substance at work. He recalled Amos Kidd's face and hands. Those burns were the result of the scalding rain; yet he was convinced it was not the temperature of the rainwater that had caused such injuries but the elements within it.

He drew the lantern nearer and peered at the granules through the seeing glass. The flakes were sharp and angular, like fragments of broken glass, and there was a strange yellowish hue to them. But it was the smell, the acrid tang, that was most convincing to Thomas.

He reached for the custard cup. Mistress Claddingbowl had been most intrigued when he asked her if she could hammer at the sugarloaf in her store cupboard and give him a few ounces. Taking the test tube of rainwater he emptied its contents onto the sugar and waited. After one or two seconds the white granules turned first yellow, then black. Next it began to hiss, then vapor rose from it, until finally it erupted out of the bowl in a great pillar of carbon.

Thomas stared at the charred mass before him. It was as he suspected, but he needed to be doubly sure. He dipped a spill into the dish holding the gray particles, then using a flint lit another spill. As soon as the powder came into contact with the flame, it changed color from yellow to pale blue.

Engrossed in his experiment, the young doctor did not notice Lydia enter the room. She stopped in surprise. "What are you doing?"

He leaned closer to the flames and blew both of them out in a single breath.

"I have just confirmed what I feared since this morning," said Thomas, propping his elbows on the desk and tenting his fingers.

"What is that?" asked Lydia, drawing nearer.

"I am afraid the rain is poisonous. It contains sulfuric acid. The flakes, too. They are molten sulfur. I believe they are mixed together in this deadly fog and until it lifts, crops, livestock, and people are in danger."

Lydia shook her head as the implications of Thomas's words sank in.

"So this acid killed the men on the Thorndike estate?" she blurted.

Thomas nodded. "They breathed it in and it burned their lungs."

Lydia's hands flew up to her mouth at the thought of it.

"Forgive me. I should not have been so specific," he said, but his thoughts had already turned to Amos Kidd downstairs, the acid slowly but surely gnawing away at the soft tissue of his throat and organs.

Lydia read his mind. "Amos Kidd?" She eased herself down into a chair on the other side of the desk to contemplate the fate of the gardener. After a moment, she raised her head to look at the young doctor, who sat in silence, his hands clasped, as if in prayer. "But surely you must be able to save him, Thomas? You will find a way?"

The absence of the sun during the day made St. Swithin's Church in Brandwick a gloomy place. Normally the light would filter through the magnificent medieval stained glass windows, casting cobalt blue shadows on the paving stones below. But that afternoon, the only light came from the few burning candles on the altar. The nave was dull and cold and Mistress Lightfoot was anxious to finish seeing to the floral arrangements as soon as possible so she could return to the relative warmth of the vicarage.

As she rearranged the hollyhocks in a large vase for one of the side altars, she mused on the effects of the fog. The stems had been picked the day before it had descended and were already looking a little jaded. She wondered how the flowers in her garden had fared, but had not wanted to venture around the beds for fear of breathing in the mist. So these hollyhocks needed to last as long as they could.

She had just finished topping up the other vases with water from a jug when she heard the heavy latch click at the far end of the nave. She glanced down the aisle and watched the door open slightly. Pushing his way through, a man stood briefly in the threshold, coughing, before he turned and heaved the door shut once more.

Mistress Lightfoot walked anxiously toward the stranger as he staggered in the aisle. Drawing nearer she could see he was a peasant sort. His clothes were soiled and torn. It was only when he was within a few feet of her that she noticed his head. It was swathed in a bright red bandana.

Wiping the phlegm from around his mouth with the back of his hand, the traveler gave her a smile.

"Begging pardon, madam," he said. "But I've been out in this fog for two days now and 'tis hurting my chest."

She looked at him warily, but mindful that she was in the house of God, she decided to be charitable. "You need water?"

"God bless you, ma'am," he croaked.

"Please sit," she told him, gesturing to a pew.

She fetched some water from a pail in the vestry and gave it to him in the jug she had used for her flower water. He drank the contents down in one.

"Thank you, ma'am," he said, wiping his mouth again. Yet instead of leaving, as she had hoped he would, he remained seated, his palms planted on his thighs, looking about him as if he had never been inside a church before.

Mistress Lightfoot felt awkward. "You'd best be on your way again," she snapped.

But the traveler smiled and shook his head. "I thought perhaps I could stay here the night," he said, his eyes large and brown. "My lungs need a rest from the fog."

The vicar's wife straightened her back and clasped her hands at her waist. "I am afraid we cannot give shelter in the church," she told him, forcing her mouth into a smile. "Why, all the vagrants of the parish would come," she added.

The traveler eyed her for a moment, then nodded. He did not seem surprised by her reaction and rose to his feet slowly. Mistress Lightfoot was relieved that he did not make a fuss. She did not enjoy dealing with his sort but she was quite satisfied with the way she had handled the situation. He lolloped like a weary hound down the aisle toward the door, but just before he reached it, he stopped and the smirk returned to his handsome features as he faced her.

"I should've known better than to look for a little charity in a church," he told her, his hands crossing over his heart in a mocking gesture.

She struggled to counter his logic. "Yes, but, but you do not belong here. You are a stranger . . . a . . ."

"I am a knife-grinder, lady. I make an honest living and I may be a stranger to you, but I have a name."

Suddenly his face twisted and he was hissing at her through his white teeth. Margaret Lightfoot felt threatened. She crossed her arms defensively, but the stranger turned and walked to the door. Before he left, however, he wheeled 'round once more. "If you will not give me sanctuary, I shall look for it elsewhere," he snarled. And he walked back out of the church and disappeared almost immediately into the fog.

Chapter 12

That night, as Eliza brushed her long chestnut locks, Lydia felt an overwhelming sadness. Each firm but gentle stroke seemed to cut into her flesh. The inconsolable despair she had felt in Hungerford on learning that her son had been taken by her cousin Francis returned, and with it came a sense of vulnerability.

Thomas had given her hope. Even on their journey back to Boughton he tried to buoy her spirits. "We shall find him," he had said. "If he is alive, then we shall find him." How she wished she could believe his well-meaning promises. She loved him so very much, but on this occasion she felt his optimism was misplaced. As an anatomist he, of all people, surely had to accept the inevitable. Just as we are born to die, surely there could be no hope of finding her Richard alive.

She put her hands up to her scalp and raked her fingers through her hair. "Please, Eliza, no more," she snapped, turning to face the girl.

The maid immediately withdrew the brush, giving her mistress a startled look. "I'm sorry, my lady, I hope I didn't . . ."

Lydia instantly felt even more wretched. "No. No, 'tis me, Eliza," she said, waving a hand. "I am out of sorts. I need to rest."

Eliza curtsied, returned the brush to the dressing table, and walked over to the bed.

"Is there anything I can get you, my lady?" she asked, turning down the covers. "A draft from Dr. Silkstone, perhaps?"

Lydia shook her head and in an unguarded moment she said, "Not even Dr. Silkstone has a remedy for a broken heart." The instant she had let slip her deepest feelings, she regretted it. Eliza was unsure how to react. She did not lift her gaze, busying herself with Lydia's pillows, but her mistress knew that it was too late.

"I know I can trust you, Eliza," she said softly.

The maid stood still, clutching a pillow to her breast. "Of course, my lady."

For the past four years she had been faithful. There was the matter of the court case, when she had testified against Captain Farrell, but she had only told the truth. To her mistress she had remained steadfast and loyal.

Lydia eased herself into the bed and patted the coverlet, bidding her maid to sit down in a gesture of intimacy she had never shown before.

"What I am about to tell you must never be repeated. Not to anyone."

Eliza straightened her back, as if preparing herself to take an oath.

"Never. I swear," she pledged.

Lydia took a deep breath. "I have a son." The words cracked from her tongue like a whip. Eliza's eyes widened and her head jutted forward, but she said nothing, waiting instead for her mistress to continue.

She went on: "Yes, Captain Farrell and I had a son. I do not know if he still lives." She paused, as if allowing Eliza to take in the momentousness of what she had just divulged. Then, in a gesture that abandoned all decorum and propriety, she leaned forward and Eliza spontaneously put her arms around her mistress as she began to weep.

"Oh my lady," she murmured, stroking her long chestnut locks once more, only this time with her hand.

After a moment or two, Lydia sat upright once more and

composed herself. "He was born six years ago and we named him Richard, after my father, but I believed that he passed in his sleep a few days later. It was only after my husband died that I found out my son had been given to a wet nurse."

Eliza shook her head in bewilderment. "So 'twas the captain who hid your child from you?" she asked incredulously.

Lydia nodded. "That is what Dr. Silkstone and I were doing yesterday. We were in Hungerford, because that was the last address we had for my son."

"But you didn't find him?" Eliza regarded her mistress mournfully.

Lydia stifled a sob. "No. What we did discover was that Francis Crick had taken custody of him. In my grief at my husband's death I confided in him and he betrayed me. God knows where my Richard is now." She choked back the tears and reached for her handkerchief, not registering the look of shock that had darted across her maid's face at the mention of her dead cousin. The girl froze for a moment, as if adding up the information she had just received.

"Mr. Crick, you say?"

Lydia looked up. There was something in Eliza's voice that told her there was more behind her question. "What is it?" Her maid's mouth was pursed. "You know something. Tell me, Eliza." She put her hands onto the girl's shoulders, looking at her squarely. "Please, what is it?"

The color had drained from the maid's normally rosy complexion. "It may be nothing, your ladyship."

"But it may be something," countered Lydia. "Please."

Eliza's shoulders heaved as she took a deep breath, as if she were about to embark on a long journey. "That time, the time when Captain Farrell was in pr . . ." She could not bring herself to say the word "prison." Lydia waved her hand to show her she recalled the situation. "Well, Mr. Crick came to me one day and asks me if I knowed any good girls in London who were used to children."

Lydia's brows lifted in surprise. "So what did you say?"

The maid looked into the distance, as if recalling the incident in her mind's eye. "I says, as it happened, my sister was not settled in her service in Southwark and may welcome a change."

"And?" pressed Lydia.

"So I gave him her address and he thanked me."

"What happened next?"

"My sister wrote to me a few days later saying that she was engaged by the Right Honorable Francis Crick to look after his London household."

Lydia looked askance. "And have you heard from your sister since?"

Eliza shook her head sadly. "No, your ladyship. 'Tis two years now and I ain't heard nothing."

"But you tried to contact her?"

The maid nodded vigorously. "Mistress Claddingbowl helped me write. I'm not well learned in letters, you see. But she never replied, then when Mr. Crick . . ." Her voice trailed off wanly, but her mistress knew she was thinking of his execution.

Lydia rolled her eyes in frustration. Just when there was another thread of hope it had been broken. But a thought suddenly occurred to her.

"Do you still have your sister's letter?"

Eliza looked at her mistress. "Yes, your ladyship. 'Tis most precious to me." She did not say she slept with it under her pillow.

"And does it give an address?"

The girl's eyes lit up like fires. "Yes. Yes, my lady. I believe it does!" she exclaimed.

Lydia clapped her hands gleefully. "Then that is where we must continue our search," she cried. "We shall go to London, just as soon as this dreadful fog has lifted."

Somewhere, in a cold, dark cellar in London, a boy was crying. He was young, probably no more than six, although he was not sure of his own age. His tousled brown hair was knotted and his breeches and jacket were too small for him, showing his bruised shins and wrists. He had boots on his feet, but there were holes in the soles.

There was no light in the cellar, so he sat huddled in the corner. Apart from his sobs, the only other sound he could hear was the squeaking of rats as they scrambled over each other in the darkness. Hunger pains stabbed at his empty belly and his lips were dry as coal dust. With his one good hand he wiped away the tears from his dirty cheeks.

Chapter 13

On the third day of the great fog Mistress Lightfoot could bear it no longer. For the past two days each knock at the vicarage door had presaged another death. There had been six so far, all fine young men who had been out in the fields when the poison rain fell on that terrible morning. Her husband had been in demand to administer the final sacrament, but prayers at the graveside were foregone; standing outside while the noxious vapor persisted was clearly injurious to health.

Mistress Lightfoot had comforted young widows and informed the parish board of the likely newest occupants of the poorhouse. There was much to be done and more to do in the future as the fog showed little sign of lifting. Many were falling ill. Breadwinners. Men with young mouths to feed. She could not sit idly by and watch the terrible events unfold with a resigned inevitability.

"What are you about, my dear?" asked the Reverend Lightfoot as his wife donned her hat and put her shawl about her broad shoulders. He was in the middle of writing his sermon for Trinity Sunday, though not many would hear it. Most would wisely stay indoors if the fog persisted.

"The Lord helps those who help themselves," she replied enigmatically and, he thought, rather unhelpfully. Her chin was jutting out. It was always a sign that his wife had a plan, the vicar told himself.

"I do know that, my dear," he replied, a mild irritation sounding in his voice. "But where are you going in this fog?"

She looked at him with eyes as bright as brass buttons. "I am going to see Lady Thorndike."

Reverend Lightfoot frowned. He was barely any wiser. He knew there was no love lost between the two women who were as different as chalk and cheese. His wife was a doer, a cog that turned wheels, whereas Lady Thorndike . . . There were many words to describe her ladyship and none of them was charitable. She treated most of those with whom she came into contact just as she treated her servants, with utter disdain. She seemed to be in a permanent state of ennui, except, that is, in the presence of virile young bucks. Her ailing husband, who was at least forty years her senior, seemed oblivious to her flirtations. If he was aware of them—and so blatant were they, how could he not be?—he showed no reprobation at all. Instead he merely humored his wife with yappy dogs and ridiculously fashionable clothes that were more suited to Paris salons than Oxfordshire drawing rooms.

"And why, pray tell, dearest, would you want to see her?" His voice could not hide the contempt he felt.

His wife, struggling to put on stiff gloves, stopped and sighed. Looking her husband squarely in the eye, she said, "Those men who've died, they were workers on the Thorndike estate. I am hoping we can make some sort of provision for their families until the parish hears their cases. There are upward of a dozen children now fatherless, with no one to put bread on their tables."

Reverend Lightfoot nodded thoughtfully. "And you would try and persuade Lady Thorndike to provide for them in the meantime?"

"Exactly so," said his wife, brooking no argument. "They are deserving of our charity," she told him, adding: "not like that wretched vagabond."

The vicar admired his wife, but he worried for her safety. The episode with the knife-grinder the night before had been most unsettling for her and he worried that this varlet, who had been so impudent, was still in the vicinity. He voiced his misgivings.

"I wish you would take more care, my dear. That rascal is still abroad and the fog is simply abominable."

From her desk drawer his wife produced a square of muslin with a flourish and held it up to her face, so that just her eyes showed, like a veiled woman from old Araby. The vicar nodded his silver-streaked head and smiled.

"But you think of everything," he said, with a wry smile. He was not sure whether his wife had heard his last remark. If she had, she did not show it. She simply disappeared out of the door, headed for Lady Thorndike at Fetcham Manor, without another word.

The vicarage lay on the edge of the Thorndikes' estate and it was only a ten-minute walk along the lane to the manor house. Although it was not yet midday, Mistress Lightfoot took a lighted lantern with her. The route was very familiar, but even though she did not admit it to her husband, she was slightly apprehensive about venturing out in this damnable fog.

The temperature had climbed steadily over the past two days and yet the grass appeared blackened, as if by frost. It crunched under her sturdy overshoes. She found it strange walking down the lane in silence. In winter the rooks croaked from high up in the copses and in summer the skylarks trilled and the cuckoos called, but this vapor seemed to have robbed the birds of their voices. The hedgerows, too, only last week bustling with butterflies and bees, were deserted. What was more, many of the hawthorn bushes were shriveled and brown; their leaves turned like claws. Worst of all, however, was the vapor itself. It seemed to inveigle its way into every orifice, so that by the time the silhouette of Fetcham Manor loomed large before her, her eyes were smarting and her throat was irritated. She had never been more pleased to climb the steps to the big house.

Even though Mistress Lightfoot was uninvited, Lady Thorndike consented to see her. The vicar's wife was received in the morning room, where she found her ladyship seated at a card table playing baccarat with only her two small dogs for company. When the butler announced her, the creatures came charging toward her, skittering across the polished floor. Lady Thorndike looked up.

"Come here, darlings," she called. "Here, to Mamma." She patted her skirts and the dogs, no bigger than rabbits, bounded back to her and skidded under the card table.

"What an unexpected pleasure, Mistress Lightfoot," she said laconically, still petting the dogs.

The vicar's wife noted her disinterested hostess was wearing a very low-cut bodice and there was a patch in the shape of a heart on her left cheek.

"It is kind of you to see me, Lady Thorndike," she replied with a hint of irony in her voice.

"Won't you be seated?" Her ladyship motioned to a sofa and Mistress Lightfoot duly obliged. "Shall we take tea?"

The vicar's wife would have loved to take tea. Her mouth was as grainy as if she had eaten sand and the taste of rotten eggs lingered, but she had not come on a social visit, so she declined the offer.

"You are most kind, Lady Thorndike, but I am here on a pressing matter."

"And what might that be?" came the imperious reply.

" 'Tis about the families who have been most grievously affected by this wretched fog."

Her ladyship reached for a plate of morsels on the card table and began to feed the small dogs that pawed at her skirts. "Yes, the fog. So tiresome. I should have gone riding today."

Mistress Lightfoot felt her hackles rise. Men are dying and yet all this woman can complain about is that she has had to forego her ride, she told herself. She forced her lips into a brief smile. "Yes, we are all suffering, your ladyship," she acknowledged. "But some more than others."

Lady Thorndike looked up. Both dogs were on their hind legs in begging positions. "How so?" she inquired.

Mistress Lightfoot shifted uncomfortably on her seat. Surely this woman cannot be unaware that her estate workers are dying, she thought. She watched her drop the morsels into each dog's jaws and smile gleefully as they chomped. There was no polite way of putting it, so she cut straight to the chase. "The fog has killed six of your men, my ladyship, and several more are ill."

A look of vague concern manifested itself on the woman's aristocratic features, but altruism was not its cause. "That is most troubling," she agreed, adding disingenuously: "So who will collect the harvest?"

Mistress Lightfoot felt a wave of mounting despair rise deep within her. Did this woman not possess a shred of humanity? "I was thinking more of the men's families, your ladyship. For their food and shelter they are totally dependent on your estate, and now their men are dead. . . ."

Lady Thorndike lifted her hand, stopping the vicar's wife in mid sentence. "You are right, Mistress Lightfoot," she nodded, as if she had just received a revelation.

"I am so glad you agree," retorted the vicar's wife, relieved that she would no longer have to labor the point.

Lady Thorndike smiled, too. "But I am sure our steward is already out looking for new men to take their place," she added.

In an instant the smile was wiped off Mistress Lightfoot's face. How foolish she was to believe her task so easy. "I was thinking more of helping the men's families, with parcels of food. Just to tide them over," she suggested.

Lady Thorndike's lips curled into a smirk. "Parcels of food?" she repeated. A peevish laugh escaped from her rouged lips. "Oh really, Mistress Lightfoot, that sort of thing is best left to people like you. If those workers are dead, then their families need to vacate their cottages to allow men who can harvest to do so. That is why we pay our parish rates, is it not?"

Feeling as if she had been dealt a punch to her ribs, Mistress Lightfoot rose quickly to her feet. The dogs reacted to her sudden movement and began to yap frantically. "I had hoped you would show a little Christian charity, your ladyship. But I see my faith was misplaced," she said, raising her voice over the yelping.

Ignoring her dogs, Lady Thorndike pulled the cord near the

card table. "Charity begins at home, I believe," she sneered, "so I bid you leave mine." And with that, she signaled to her butler, who had just appeared at the door, to show Mistress Lightfoot out.

"Good day to you," she called as the vicar's wife was led away, then bending down to stroke her dogs, she said to them: "We hope she has a safe journey home, don't we, my loves?"

It was obvious to Thomas that Mistress Claddingbowl felt a little uneasy allowing him into her kitchen. Using her ingredients and mixing them in her bowls was one thing, but rubbing shoulders at the table was an altogether different matter. He knew he would have to tread carefully. He had complimented her on the texture of her pastry the other night and thanked her profusely for the flask of lemonade she had provided for his journey from Oxford. He understood that she felt undervalued. He doubted whether Captain Farrell had ever praised her pies or puddings. Yet he did know one thing about the late captain's tastes from Lydia. He had apparently insisted that the cook try her hand at a dish with strange spices so favored by the Indians. He had developed a liking for the flavors of Madras when he was serving in His Majesty's Dragoon Guards. Mistress Claddingbowl had found a recipe for a chicken curry in a cookery book. Frying the poulets, she added the ground spices, beaten very fine, to the dish. A quarter of an ounce of turmeric, a large spoonful of ginger, and a teaspoon of milled pepper were all mixed together, along with a little salt to taste. She had finished it off with cream and lemon juice and the captain had pronounced it satisfactory—praise indeed for one so sparse with his kind words.

So, when Thomas asked her whether by any chance she might have some turmeric in her spice rack, she was delighted to oblige. He was conscious of her watching him intently as he pounded the seeds in a pestle and mortar, then added the powder to a pint jug of milk.

"The turmeric has antiseptic qualities, Mistress Claddingbowl," he told her. " 'Twill help heal any damage done to Mr. Kidd's mouth and throat."

The cook nodded her head thoughtfully, then puffed out her ample chest. "If that is the outcome, sir, then you are most welcome to work in my kitchen any time you please."

Amos Kidd lay in a room a few doors away from the kitchen down a long corridor. This was where the under gardeners usually slept, but they had vacated it so that their master could be nursed more easily. Thomas found his patient conscious and coughing, and his eyes still glassy with fever. Susannah was by his side.

"How fares he?" he asked, bending low and feeling Kidd's pulse. He noted the burns around his mouth and eyes were crusting over, but there was a general listlessness that troubled Thomas. Kidd's head jerked up in another involuntary spasm.

"He coughs like this for much of the time, sir," said his wife wearily. The vigil was taking its toll on her looks, too. Her eyes were puffy and her face was gray.

"Then let us see if this will ease him," said Thomas, pouring out a cup of orange-colored milk from the jug. He held it to Kidd's lips and the gardener managed to take two or three sips before the coughing resumed. It was the doctor's hope that the milk would neutralize at least some of the acid Kidd had ingested and the turmeric would help heal any of the internal blisters.

"Make him drink a few sips of this every hour," he instructed Mistress Kidd with a smile. He did not wish to cause her more distress. At the very least he hoped his remedy would relieve the constant coughing spasms and delay what Thomas feared was inevitable.

Chapter 14

It was market day in Brandwick, but the streets were strangely quiet. Most of the farmers and drovers had not dared bring their livestock to town for fear the journey would kill either them or their animals. Many of those who did brave the fog were in no mood to buy or barter. They had questions and they wanted answers. By ten o'clock small clusters of men could be found huddled in doorways, under cover in the butter market or in the porch of the church. In fact, anywhere that afforded a little shelter from the clawing fog, laborers were gathering and their mood was as bitter as the air they were breathing.

Gabriel Lawson was resting his body up against the bar of the Three Tuns, a tankard of ale in his hand. He had decided to make the journey because he needed more supplies and could not wait another week. He had considered sending a man in his stead, but then he thought of the pleasurable female company that the inn afforded and decided otherwise. His spirits needed lifting and Molly or Jessie or whoever happened to be hanging around the bar that morning would suffice.

The damnable fog meant that the wheat could not be harvested. Not that there was much wheat left that had not been scorched. He had been unable to count how many acres they would have to simply plough in again, but there were many. The other crops, too, had all fared similar fates: the barley, the turnips, and even the apples in the orchards. Worse still, the men who had been picking and digging had also fallen ill after a few hours' exertion. Four of them now lay in their beds coughing their lungs out, no good to man or beast.

He turned his gaze outside toward the market square. It, too, was wreathed in mist and was almost deserted. He could barely see to the other side of it. The traders had not even bothered to set out their stalls. Three or four women scurried from shop to shop, their mouths and noses swathed in stoles or shawls. One of them caught his eye. Even though her face was covered, he liked the way she moved her hips. He smiled. It was then that he saw them: a group of men, he could not say how many. They were a dark smudge that spread across the square, then suddenly stopped.

Intrigued by the throng, Lawson downed his ale and walked out onto the street. He wrapped his scarf around his mouth and traversed the road toward the din. Now he could see the men were laborers. Although he did not recognize them he knew their sort. They were gathering around a man, his head trussed in a red scarf, who was shouting on the steps of the market cross. He clenched a fist and punched the air and several of his audience made the same gesture. From the corners of the square, from the doorways and the porches, more and more men braved the fog to swell the number, until the count was at least sixty.

Lawson moved closer. He could hear snatches of the man's words, punctuated by choruses of "aye" every now and again.

"And I ask you, how are you going to feed your families if there is no corn? You will starve. We will all starve, while the lords and masters will take what little there is for themselves!" cried the swarthy speaker.

Lawson kept his distance, but listened intently to the man's words. A troublemaker, he thought to himself. He had dealt with many such in Ireland. They'd died in the thousands in the famine not thirty years before, then, quite recently, when the landowners switched to growing grain for export, the men and their families were forced to eat potatoes and groats.

It all gave rise to the Rightboys, the Hearts of Oak, and the Steelboys, the peasant secret societies that would kill and maim livestock and tear down fences to redress their grievances against their landlords.

When the worst had come and the men refused to work, he'd been ordered to call in the King's militia rather than accede to demands for better wages or living conditions, or both. Blood was shed. It was never a pretty sight. It spilled on the very dirt that was being fought over. He hoped it would not come to that, but the longer this wretched cloud hung over the land, spreading its poison and killing the crops and those who harvested them, the more likely it seemed.

Thomas had not seen Dr. Felix Fairweather since their encounter in court more than a year ago. Then he had shown himself to be an arrogant ass, the very epitome of everything he hated about the medical profession. While Thomas did not follow the fashion of prescribing purgatives for every ill, he had sometimes mused that a good purge would work wonders for the likes of Felix Fairweather. Yet when he presented himself in the drawing room at Boughton Hall, the physician's arrogance seemed to have dissipated. In its stead there appeared a genuine concern, even fear.

"How may we help you, Dr. Fairweather?" inquired Lydia as he stood before her, his shoulders hunched.

"I am afraid it is a most grave matter, your ladyship," he replied. Gone was his courtroom conceit. His manner seems almost humble, thought Thomas. "Mistress Lightfoot has taken ill. She has succumbed to the fog and is finding it increasingly difficult to breathe." There was an uncustomary meekness in his tone.

Lydia frowned. "I am so sorry to hear that, Dr. Fairweather, but what is it that you would like us to do?"

The physician looked over to Thomas as he stood by the fireplace. "I would ask you, sir, to see if you can alleviate her distress."

The young doctor could have taken satisfaction from such a request. Instead he saw courage in the statement from a man so previously prejudiced against him and his fellow countrymen. "I am flattered you ask, sir," he replied. "And I will, of course, do anything I can to help."

Stopping off at the larder to collect a flask of milk and turmeric that was already mixed, Thomas climbed into the waiting carriage with the physician. The fog felt less moist than it had the day before and the sun seemed to be trying to break through, but the stench still clung to the hot air.

The ten-minute journey took them along lanes and fields that were empty until they reached St. Swithin's vicarage in Brandwick. It was a solid, square house on the edge of the town, just a few yards from the church. Even though it was only early afternoon, a single lamp that burned in an upstairs window was clearly visible through the gloom.

Dr. Fairweather led Thomas upstairs into a large but sparsely furnished room where Mistress Lightfoot lay in bed. At her side, on a chair, sat her husband. He was holding her limp hand, studying it as if it were a precious object. He raised his head at the sight of the two doctors.

His wife coughed and moaned slightly on hearing the men enter the room and the Reverend Lightfoot rose to his feet. "All's well, my dear," he comforted her. "Dr. Silkstone is come to make you better."

Thomas smiled awkwardly. Such an expectation never sat easily on his shoulders. Now that he knew this deadly fog contained droplets of sulfuric acid, he was uncertain as to the efficacy of any remedy. "I can only do my best to alleviate your wife's discomfort," he told the vicar, sitting down by her side.

The woman wore a lace cap, but Thomas could see that the hair that showed beneath it was plastered to her head by the fever. Her skin was grayish in hue and around her mouth and nose were the telltale acid burns that marked Amos Kidd's face. The blisters looked like yellow-crusted sequins as they scabbed over, but they still needed attention.

"I take it your wife was caught in a rainstorm?" said Thomas, opening his medical bag.

The vicar frowned and sucked deeply, as if recalling a moment with so much concentration that he was actually reliving it. "She went visiting in the fog, Dr. Silkstone," he began. "I asked her not to, yet she insisted. On the way back it began to rain and even though she wore a scarf over her face, the water soaked through and burned her skin." His mouth pursed into a grimace and he turned away, stifling tears.

Mistress Lightfoot began to cough again, in long, fluid notes that concerned Thomas. It was obvious to him that there was already liquid in her lungs. Holding the flask of milk to her lips, he tilted it back and she supped a little.

"She must drink this every hour," he instructed. "It will help heal her burned throat."

Yet, just as soon as the woman swallowed the milk, it returned once more in a single spasm, splaying out across the counterpane. It was then that her coughing resumed, the sound of phlegm and mucus rattling 'round in her lungs like beer swilling in a barrel. Her husband held her upright so that she could breathe better between the coughs, which were now almost incessant. It was then she began to retch. She managed to hold a handkerchief over her mouth the first time, so that Thomas could examine its contents. The mucus was dark brown and smelled vile.

A few seconds later, however, after a brief respite, the coughing began again. This time the spasms were even more violent, so that Mistress Lightfoot's shoulders were heaving in great waves with every ferocious contraction of her diaphragm. Her languid lids now opened wide with fear.

"Can you not do something, doctor. Please?" pleaded her husband, trying to steady his wife as she jolted and lurched on the bed like a woman possessed. But Thomas knew that it was hopeless and he dreaded what would come next. He prayed it would be over sooner rather than later and in another three or four minutes his prayers were answered.

With one final great judder, frothy pink foam spurted from the woman's mouth, spraying out over the coverlet and over Thomas. Her husband cried out in terror, but from his wife there was no further sound. She slumped back on her blood-flecked pillows and closed her eyes as the life ebbed away from her.

The somber journey back to Boughton Hall was spent discussing what, if anything, could be done if the fog persisted much longer.

"Men and women are dying daily from this poison, Dr. Silkstone," said Dr. Fairweather. "I've lost three of my patients in the last two days."

Thomas thought of Amos Kidd and the outcome that awaited him. He nodded gravely. "There is sulfuric acid in the air, doctor."

Fairweather's expression grew even more troubled. "Sulfuric acid?" he repeated. "How so? You did your tests?" He emphasized the word "your" as if Thomas were the only scientist to entertain such examinations.

Thomas's methods were often regarded with suspicion by most of the physicians he had encountered in England so far. Yet, on this occasion at least, Dr. Fairweather seemed curious rather than skeptical.

"Yes, I carried out experiments," he replied. "There is sulfur in the rain and in flakes in the air, but I have no idea how they came to be there."

The physician shook his head and sighed deeply. "Then it seems as though all we can do is pray that this fog lifts soon," he said.

Thomas nodded. He thought of the Reverend Lightfoot, lost and bewildered at his wife's side. With his shortcut to the Almighty and his capacity to conduct funerals, he feared that the services of the recently bereaved vicar would be in fierce demand.

As soon as the carriage drew up in front of Boughton Hall, Thomas saw Lydia open the door and begin to hurry down the front steps.

"No, stay there!" he shouted as he jumped down and ran up

the steps to greet her. "You must not come out here," he scolded, taking her arm and leading her back inside.

She looked up at him anxiously. "Thank God you have returned," she cried breathlessly. "Amos Kidd has taken a turn for the worse."

Thomas hurried through the hallway and down the stairs to the servants' quarters. He could hear the rattle of Amos Kidd's cough a few doors away and arrived in the room to find him convulsing violently, just as Mistress Lightfoot had. His young wife was standing a little way off, wringing her hands anxiously, not knowing what to do.

Rushing in, Thomas sat the gardener upright, so that he could breathe more easily between spasms. Dr. Fairweather had followed behind and now held Kidd as the young doctor reached for the flask of milk in his bag. Just as he did so, however, the final convulsion surged. Kidd's wife screamed as the blood sprayed out of her husband's mouth. It came like a summer rain before thunder, in large droplets. The irony of it was, Thomas noted, it was the same crimson as the fairest roses in his beloved garden.

Chapter 15

Gazing into the fire at Boughton Hall later that evening, Thomas imagined he saw the Reverend George Lightfoot. Flames licked at his anguished face, and his mouth was wide open in a scream. He'd seen that tormented expression so many times after a bereavement and yet never on a person of such great faith. Such people had always displayed an inner calm, their belief in God and the promise of eternal life appearing to offer them comfort. The Reverend Lightfoot's despair at the loss of his wife was so tangible that he seemed beyond consolation.

Sitting in the drawing room, thoughtfully cradling the large glass of brandy that Howard had poured for him, Thomas felt a deep sense of foreboding. Lydia sat on the opposite side of the fireplace, working on some embroidery. The traumatic events of the afternoon meant neither of them was in a mood for light conversation, yet they could not bear the thought of being alone. They took mutual solace from each other.

Over the years, Thomas had tried to desensitize himself to death. He had seen so much of it and in so many guises: in disease and in injury, in suicide and even in murder, and yet dealing with it still affected him. He might feel sadness, or sorrow, or sometimes, when the victim's pain was unbearable, relief, but more often he felt a sense of inadequacy. Such feelings were certainly to the fore that evening as his mind replayed the terrified expressions on the faces of both Mistress Lightfoot and Amos Kidd. What agonies must they both have suffered as the acid gnawed away at the lining of their lungs? He gulped down his brandy and shuddered as he felt the liquid burn his own throat.

Glancing over at Lydia, he could see she had retreated into her own world again, as she so often did. The difference now was that he could read her thoughts. Now he knew why, at times, she seemed so melancholy. Now he understood why her eyes would sometimes mist at the sight of a babe or a young child at play. She was in mourning for lost memories, lost embraces, lost time that should have been spent with her son.

"I have not forgotten our search," he said suddenly, his gaze fixed on her face.

She looked up from her sewing, paused, then smiled wistfully. "I know you would not do that," she replied softly.

" 'Twould take us half a day to reach Oxford in this fog, but I've heard it is clear a little way south of the city." His voice carried a timbre of hope. Lydia nodded, but said no more, returning to the gauze wrap she was embroidering.

Left to his own thoughts once more, Thomas turned to Kidd's wife and the memory of her standing frightened and helpless as she watched her husband in his death throes. What would become of her?

"Did Kidd have any children?" he asked a few moments later.

Lydia put down her needle and thread. "No. I don't believe he and his wife could," she replied thoughtfully. "He used to say his roses were his children."

"And what of his wife?" he asked. "Will she have to leave the cottage?"

A look of disapproval crossed Lydia's face. "Michael would have made her go, but I will not," she said firmly. "I shall not be in the business of turning widows out of their homes."

Thomas was assured. "If only all landowners thought like you, there would be fewer souls in the workhouses."

He rose and walked over to the sideboard to help himself to another glass of brandy from the decanter. On his way back he walked over to Lydia and laid his palm gently on her shoulder. She put her own hand on top of his and tilted her head toward him, so that he kissed the top of her hair gently.

Their moment of intimacy was short-lived. Howard's entrance into the room brought them both back to the present. "I have a message for Dr. Silkstone," he announced formally, holding a silver tray on which lay a letter. He proffered it to Thomas, who glanced at it quickly.

"That will be all, Howard," he said, dismissing the butler and opening the letter.

Lydia was looking at him anxiously. "Not more bad news?"

Thomas shook his head. "No. It is more positive," he replied. Earlier that afternoon, shortly after Kidd's death, Thomas had decided that in order to find out exactly how the noxious fog was killing its victims, he needed to carry out a postmortem on the gardener. He had therefore dispatched a messenger to Oxford with a letter to the coroner, Sir Theodisius Pettigrew. The reply had been immediately forthcoming. Permission was granted.

"Tomorrow I shall be examining Amos Kidd's body," he told her. "It may well hold the key to so many questions about this fog."

The cloud of poison had not yet reached London, but the usual pall of foundry smoke combined with the detritus of humans and animals living cheek by jowl still hung over the capital. The miasma of rotting meat and human waste stewed gently in the summer heat, causing many to gag and retch as they ventured out.

The notary found the whole ambience most unpleasant. His stomach was not used to being assailed in this vile way and he purchased a nosegay from a street seller in an attempt to ward off the stink. He was on his way to an address in the west of the capital, in Seymour Street. It was not a bad area, not for London at any rate. There were many tall, elegant town houses here, newly built in the last decade he would guess. They stood in neat rows with freshly painted doors and windows. The mud on the roads had been hard-baked by several days of sun, making it easier underfoot.

He stopped at a house that looked exactly the same as every

other house in the street, tall and thin with long casements. He mounted the steps up to the door and pulled the bell. A neat-looking, plump-faced woman answered, her cap completely obscuring any hair she might have had. Her apron was starched and pristine and she had a matronly air of authority about her that said she would not stand any nonsense.

"Good day to you, ma'am," greeted the notary, raising his tricorn.

"Good day, sir," she replied guardedly.

"I was hoping you could help me," he began, and he produced a sheet of paper and showed it to her. "I am at the right place?"

"Yes, sir, you are," she confirmed.

"Good," nodded the notary. "Then this must be the former abode of the Right Honorable Francis Crick."

For a moment the woman froze, then grabbed the door and started to shut it. "You have the wrong house, sir," she cried. But the notary was too quick for her and put his foot over the threshold, jamming the door open. He fixed her in the eye and saw that she was afraid. "I want no trouble, sir. I keep a clean house."

The notary could tell by her demeanor she was a simple woman who, through no fault of her own, had happened to take a lodger who turned out to be a murderer. Of course at the time she had no way of knowing his vile inclinations. Francis Crick had presented himself as a student of anatomy at St. George's Hospital, not half a mile away. He seemed a sensible, clean young man of noble birth. He always paid his rent on time and kept civil hours, but, according to his landlady, he had a sorry tale to tell.

"He was a widower, sir," recalled the woman, seated in her spotless parlor. "Lost his young wife in childbirth." She had relented and let the notary into her home. She had even offered him tea, although he declined. "That was why 'twas such a shock when the constables knocked on my door one day and told me Mr. Crick was to be hanged at Tyburn the next day."

She slapped her palms on her skirts. "Near fainted away with the shock of it, I did," she huffed.

The notary listened sympathetically. "I can imagine," he said. Yet while he was grateful that she had recounted her own feelings of disbelief and outrage, the information that he really sought had not been forthcoming, so he tried a different tack.

"You said that Mr. Crick was a widower," he began. "But did you ever see him with anyone else? A child, perhaps?"

The landlady's face immediately creased into a frown. "Yes, indeed, sir," she said, nodding her head. "His son looked just like him, he did. Came to visit with his nursemaid on the floor above for a few days. So clean they were." She pointed upward with her plump finger.

The notary leaned forward, his eyes wide. "And do you know what happened to them?"

The landlady's back stiffened. "I couldn't have them staying here no more after that business." She drew her finger across her throat to signify a noose. "I keep a clean house, I do." She clasped her hands on her lap.

"Do you know where they went?" The notary tried to hide his disappointment.

The woman shook her head slowly, as if she was not entirely certain of her answer.

"There is no more you can tell me?" He knew he was onto something. Delving into his topcoat pocket, he produced his purse and laid it on the little side table next to him. The dame's eyes darted to the bag.

"Mr. Crick did leave something in his room." The landlady had suddenly remembered the small packet she had found in a drawer in the dead man's desk. There had been a few guineas inside and she had taken the liberty of pocketing them, as down payment, or surety against future rent owed, she had told herself. There had been a short note, too. It mentioned words like "upkeep" and "provision" and "allowance," but she had destroyed it, of course. She did not want to incriminate herself, did not want to be accused of pilfering from her lodger. So she put the money in the ginger jar in her parlor. After all, she knew there was no possibility of the young man's return.

"I was checking that Maddie, she's my maid, had cleaned the room to my standards," she told him, "when I came across a paper packet Mr. Crick had left." She rose slowly, her knees creaking as she did so, and walked over to the bureau in the corner of the room. "Here it is," she said, handing it to the notary. On it were written the words: *Miss Agnes Appleton, St. Giles, London.* Inside it was empty.

The notary eyed her knowingly and saw that she seemed flustered as her gaze slid away. "This is most helpful, madam. Most helpful indeed," he said.

Opening the drawstring bag he took out a guinea coin.

"For your pains," he told her.

She thanked him and took it without hesitation. And as soon as he was gone she added it to Mr. Crick's money in the ginger jar. With it, she told herself, she would buy a new copper and her linens would be the cleanest in all London town.

Back at home in her cottage, Susannah Kidd found herself alone with her memories and her guilt. The roses in the jug on the table were already wilted, their petals scattered on the table. The water was smelling rank. Amos had been a good husband. He had always provided for her; he had seldom raised a hand to her and never gone carousing in the alehouses in Brandwick. She had been a good enough wife, too. She had made his meals and kept a clean house, darned his clothes and submitted to his fancies in the marriage bed, but everything she did, she did out of duty, not out of love. And she had longed for more. There had been a few times when other men had paid her compliments and she had enjoyed the feeling that had given her. Sometimes she had even flirted with them, although she had never bedded another, not since her marriage at any rate.

The parcel lay on the table. She took out her scissors to cut the string. They reminded her of the knife-grinder, the handsome traveler who had told her she was the fairest woman in the county. She snipped the twine and unfolded the paper. Inside was Amos's clean smock. It was the one he was wearing when he died. It had been spattered in blood. Mistress Firebrace had seen to it that it had been boiled in the copper and now it was without stain. She laid it on the table and touched the stitching, her own fine stitching, and she began to weep.

She was so lost in her own tears that she did not hear the latch lift and the cottage door open.

"Mistress Kidd," called a voice.

She looked up to see the figure of the Reverend Lightfoot. Under his wide-brimmed hat, most of his face was swathed in a scarf.

Wiping away her tears with the back of her hand, she quickly composed herself. "Come in, please," she said, walking over to greet him.

"I am come to offer my condolences," he told her, unfurling his scarf. "And to talk of the funeral arrangements."

The thought of Amos lying in the ground chilled her and she shivered, even though the air was warm. Nor was she used to company. Since her husband's death she had not swept the floor or beaten the hearth rug, and a thin film of dust from outside had settled on what little furniture she had. She showed her visitor a chair by the cold hearth and watched him sit down.

"I'm afraid I . . ."

The vicar, his own face tired and drawn and his hair now turned almost completely silver, shook his head and waved his cane. "I need nothing, Mistress Kidd," he assured her.

She settled herself opposite. "I am sorry for your loss, sir," she told him, sitting stiff-backed.

"Thank you, but I share my grief with many others," he told her brusquely. Without making eye contact, he took out a notebook and pencil from his pocket in a businesslike manner, as if he were a merchant doing a deal, or a notary taking a brief. "Will tomorrow be amenable to you?"

"Tomorrow?"

"For the burial. Bodies are turning fast in this heat. Joseph Makepeace is working flat out."

She nodded. She had not given much thought to Amos's interment. But there would be roses. She hoped that some of them may have survived the fog, although she could not be sure.

"Lady Lydia has kindly consented to your husband being buried on the estate, in the chapel graveyard," he informed her. Still he did not look at her.

"That is kind."

"Excellent. So, noon on the morrow?"

There was an awkward pause before the vicar closed his notebook with a finality that indicated his work was done. He was a busy man. He needed to move on.

Again Susannah nodded, but as she watched him gathering up his scarf and his silver-topped cane, she wondered at his manner. He rose and she followed suit, both making their way to the cottage door.

"Thank you for coming, sir," she said. She was close to him now and could see the rims of his eyes were red. There was a vulnerability about him that stirred something inside her. He acknowledged her words with a nod, but still did not look at her directly. As she watched him wrap his scarf around his neck once more she felt compelled to ask him whether his wife's ending had been as shocking as her husband's. "Were you there?" she asked suddenly, the words gushing out uncontrollably. "Did you see?"

His silver head jerked up, as if surprised by her question, wondering at her forthrightness. She sensed his unease. "Forgive me, sir. I did not mean . . ."

"No one has asked me that," he replied thoughtfully. He fumbled with his scarf, then, for the first time, he looked her directly in the eye. "Yes. Yes, I was there. I saw her pain; the fear on her face." His voice cracked as he recalled the scene.

Susannah saw his own pain reemerge at the very thought of his wife's death, as if she had put her hand in an open wound. His eyes became glazed. She felt her own tears well up again, too, followed by an overwhelming urge to reach out to someone who shared her sorrow. Stepping forward, she laid her head on the vicar's chest and began to sob. Instead of a comforting arm, however, she felt the Reverend Lightfoot's body stiffen awkwardly. He stepped back quickly as if he had just been landed a body blow. She pulled back, too, wiping her tears away with her hands. "I'm sorry. I . . ."

The vicar looked at her oddly; almost with suspicion. "We must find comfort in the Lord." His tone was verging on a reprimand.

She lifted her head. "Yes, of course," she replied. "Forgive me, sir," she repeated, adding, "I have no one else to turn to."

He nodded awkwardly and managed a flat smile, but his eyes remained cold. Picking up his hat and his cane from the table, he moved toward the door.

"Good day to you, Mistress Kidd," he said. He walked out into the fog, leaving Susannah alone with her sadness and her memories once more.

Chapter 16

The body of Amos Kidd, draped in a sheet, lay on a marble slab in the game larder. He shared the cold, solid space with three brace of pheasant and a hare that had been shot before the fog. Not even the poachers were venturing out now. If they did, they did not need to waste their snares or their shot; the corpses of dead animals were littering the fields.

Thomas had promised that after his work was done, he would deliver the body for burial in the estate's chapel grounds the following day. He had asked for lamps to be lit all around. This, together with the low temperature of the room, made his working conditions favorable. Yet there was a terrible irony in his surroundings. He did not feel comfortable performing a postmortem in a place that was traditionally the butcher's domain. The cleaver and the saw that hung above his head were grim reminders of the fact. The metallic tang of blood was added to the sulfur in the air, and the sawdust on the floor was crawling with maggots.

Folding back the sheet, he studied Kidd's face. It was calm. All the muscles were relaxed. It was a far cry from the contortions that his coughing had caused. Yet the burns were still evident around his eyes, nose, and mouth. The acid had eaten away at the skin, puckering it into low ridges and furrowing it into deep pits. Scabs had formed like snow-capped peaks on this new mountain landscape and pus had oozed in rivulets toward his chin. If the sulfur had done this to the epidermis, then no wonder ingestion into the trachea and lungs caused a hemorrhage, thought Thomas.

He looked at his instruments laid out neatly on a cloth beside the body and took a deep breath. Like a priest, he intoned a few words. They were not prayers; just a simple mantra to reaffirm his purpose and to remind himself that he was dealing with a human body that deserved to be accorded dignity in death. He was steady now; composed and ready to begin.

Bending low, he held Amos Kidd's head in both hands and lifted up the chin, so that the neck was easily accessible. His long fingers took hold of the knife. He did not grasp the hilt, but held it lightly and, like an artist with his brush, he skimmed the canvas of the skin with a single decisive stroke that left a fine line of crimson in its wake. Next came a larger blade and more force was applied until the flesh fell away on either side of the incision to reveal the trachea.

Slicing through the muscular tube at the top half of the neck, Thomas could see that the acid had been at work here, too. It had bubbled and boiled and blistered and corroded away whole areas of soft tissue. And the further he ventured into the tangle of the respiratory system, the greater the carnage he could see. Worst of all was the damage done to the bronchi. The tracks and lanes and roads of this landscape, housed in the thoracic cavity, were almost unrecognizable. The gas had mixed with the moisture in the lungs, producing an acid that had washed away vessels and tubules and veins, as if some great tidal wave had inundated them, destroying everything in its path.

The damage was worse than he feared. Stitching up the great flap of skin to re-cover the chest, Thomas felt a terrible sense of dread. It appeared that both Kidd and Mistress Lightfoot had suffered particularly badly because they had been caught in a rain shower of acid. Yet every man, woman, and child in the area had been exposed to the sulfur particles in the air over the past few days, not to mention the livestock. The cumulative effect of such elements could be just as damaging as the rain. The longer the poisonous cloud remained overhead, the more likely it was that many more would die.

Thomas washed at the pump in the yard. He did not wish Lydia to see his bloodied hands and arms. His back ached from bending over the slab and he felt drained. All he wanted to do was rest, but he soon discovered it was not to be. Howard was waiting with a message for him as soon as he walked into the hallway.

"This was delivered not ten minutes ago, sir. The boy said it was urgent."

Thomas was reading the note when Lydia emerged from the sewing room.

"What is it?" She frowned.

"It is from Fetcham Manor," replied Thomas. "It says Lady Thorndike is ill and needs my immediate attention."

Lydia's back stiffened. "That woman does not deserve anyone's attention," she said sharply. Thomas secretly shared her cynicism, but knew it was his duty to attend her. "Why did she not call upon Dr. Fairweather?"

Thomas shared her suspicions, but he felt it was only fair to grant her request for a visit.

"You know I have to go," he told her.

She nodded and shaped her mouth into a smile. "I do, and that is one of the reasons I love you," she said.

Thomas decided to ride to Fetcham Manor. Even in the fog he estimated it would only take him twenty minutes at the most. The cloud was still hanging low and his visibility remained severely limited. All he could see as he rode along the lane toward Brandwick were the limp-leaved trees that stood eerily by the roadside and the blackened verges. He kept a steady pace and arrived at the grand mansion shortly, passing not a soul on his way.

The young doctor's arrival was obviously eagerly awaited and he was shown straight up to Lady Thorndike's bedchamber by her maid. He found his patient lying in bed, but her eyes were open. Her hair was loose on her pillow, red locks coiling like tendrils, and her lips were painted the same cherry red as he remembered on their first encounter. It was a relief to him to find that she was not coughing.

"Go now," she ordered her maid, waving her hand dismissively.

The girl curtsied and closed the door behind her, leaving Thomas standing at the bedside.

"I believe you feel unwell, your ladyship," he began, retrieving her note from his pocket and laying it on the bedside table. "What seems to ail you?"

She studied him for a moment; her eyes moving languidly up and down his body. "I have a terrible heaviness in my chest," she replied, laying her palm flat against the slope of her bosoms.

Thomas frowned. "Are you able to sit up?"

"With your help I could." She held out her hand.

Thomas clasped it, noting it felt warm and dry, not cold and clammy like Mistress Lightfoot's or Amos Kidd's. Gently, putting his other arm around her back, he eased her up. The exertion did not make her cough. This was a good sign, he thought. He felt her pulse. It was strong and steady. At the same time he could also feel her gaze on him, like a hungry bird on a worm. It made him feel uncomfortable.

"Have you been out in this fog, your ladyship?" he inquired, opening his bag and bringing out his listening tube.

She let out a short, sharp laugh. "I have not, Dr. Silkstone. No one in their right mind ventures out in this weather," she snorted. She was wearing a thin chemise, laced at the neck, and as soon as she saw Thomas approach with his listening tube she began untying the ribbon.

"That will not be necessary, your ladyship," said Thomas firmly, suddenly realizing the situation was becoming awkward. He had dealt with such harridans before, but they were usually much older and, he ventured, uglier. She had already loosened the ribbons and pulled down the shoulders of her nightgown, exposing the top half of her breasts, by the time he was ready to examine her. There was no attempt whatsoever on her part to hide her desire.

"Come, Dr. Silkstone. I need a thorough examination," she pouted.

Thomas refused to allow himself to be flustered. Leaning forward, he put the cone of his device to her chest to listen to her breathing. It was then that he felt her take his hand and cup it around her right breast. The listening tube clattered to the floor. Shocked, Thomas looked at her for a split second. It was then that she lunged at him, hooking her arm around his neck and finding his mouth. He grasped her hand as her lips planted themselves on his and prized it from his neck, but she resisted and brought her other arm up and clamped it around his head. At that moment the door was flung open and Sir Henry, accompanied by the Reverend Lightfoot, appeared on the threshold. They had evidently heard the horn clatter to the floor.

"Good God, Silkstone! What do you think you are doing?" boomed the horrified lord, advancing from the doorway.

At the sound of her husband's voice, Lady Thorndike released her grip. "No, leave me. No!" she cried, like some violated heroine in a novel.

Thomas straightened himself and was left stunned at the bedside, his face covered in great smears of lipstick. Sir Henry marched over to the young doctor.

"What is the meaning of this, sir? I've a good mind to call the constables," he panted.

Lady Thorndike intervened. She rearranged her chemise to cover her chest once more. "No, Henry, that will not be necessary. Just get him out of my sight," she ordered.

Thomas, still reeling from the shock of the incident, reached for his bag. He walked toward the door, watched by the stony-faced vicar and Sir Henry. But before he reached the threshold, he paused to face his accusers.

"I can assure you, sir, the only ailment that plagues your wife is an excessive sexual appetite," he told Sir Henry. And with an indignant tug of his waistcoat he took his leave.

Once out into the fog again, he mounted his horse and started off at a furious gallop down the drive. He was angry, both with Lady Thorndike and himself, for not reading the situation sooner. How could he have allowed himself to walk into such an obvious trap? He should have known better. If word of this ever got out his reputation, and with it his career, would be in tatters.

Chapter 17

Gabriel Lawson recognized the man with the red bandana from two days before in the marketplace. Now he was standing by the foreman, Ned Perkins, looking a little too confident for his liking. The man's eyes were jet black and he had an air of insolence; a direct gaze and a square-set jaw told him he would be trouble. He and Perkins had approached him in the tithe barn as he was checking on feedstuffs. There was no one else in sight.

"We wondered if we might have a word with you, sir," Perkins began diffidently enough. He had the weathered face of a man who lived on and for the land.

Lawson eyed his companion suspiciously. "And who might this be?" he replied brusquely, knowing full well.

The man bowed low. Too low, Lawson felt.

"My name is Joshua Pike, sir, and I speak on behalf of farm workers and tenants."

The steward raised his brow. The young man's insolence surprised him so much that, for once, he was momentarily lost for words, so Pike continued. "This fog is killing many men in the fields, sir, so I plead for those who are left standing."

The knife-grinder waited for a reaction from the steward, but when it came, it was not the one he had anticipated. Lawson simply threw his head back and roared with laughter. "You?" He pointed mockingly. "A spokesman? On whose authority, pray tell?"

Perkins shifted uneasily from one leg to the other, his head bowed, but Pike simply smirked. "Many of your men have asked me, sir," he replied.

Lawson looked beyond the young troublemaker, shading his eyes in an exaggerated gesture, as if scanning the horizon. "Many of my men, you say," he sneered. " 'Tis strange I can only see one." Ned Perkins fingered his hat nervously. "Is this true, Perkins?" barked the steward. "Can you no longer speak for yourselves? Do you need this . . . this"—he sneered at Pike contemptuously—"this troublemaker to speak for you?"

The foreman lowered his eyes. "Some of us got to thinkin' . . ."

Lawson shook his head. "You are not paid to think, Perkins. You are paid to work and this fog means there's more work to be done than usual." He turned his back on them, but the young man silently urged the foreman to press ahead, gesturing the older man to follow his master.

"S-sir," Perkins stuttered nervously.

Lawson turned and sighed theatrically. "Tell this scoundrel to go away and we will forget about this incident." He flapped his hand scornfully at Pike.

"And what if I don't go away, Mr. Lawson?" asked the young man impudently.

The steward stiffened. "Then I shall call the other men, the ones who know who pays their wages, and they'll run you out of the shire!" he shouted, the color rising in his face. He stepped toward Pike and only a few inches now separated them.

The young troublemaker kept his ground. His expression did not change, but he wiped a fleck of Lawson's spittle from his cheek. "Very well, sir. I shall leave for now, but as long as this fog hangs around, then so shall I." He was smiling as he said this, but there was a note of menace in his voice.

His tone made the steward clench his fists, but he resisted the urge to hit out. "Be gone!" he cried.

Joshua Pike walked to his mule in an unhurried fashion, still wearing a smirk on his nut-brown face.

Ned Perkins, on the other hand, was left cowering in the corner of the barn. "I don't want no trouble, Mr. Lawson," he pleaded meekly. "He just came up to me in Brandwick and asked me to name my master."

Lawson nodded. He knew Perkins to be a loyal worker who had farmed Boughton estate land for at least twenty-five years, and his father before him. Now his two sons lay in his home, fighting for their lives. "This fog is making it hard for all of us. Just remember that," he told him. The foreman nodded contritely and planted his hat back on his matted head. "Now get back to work with you."

The driver had questioned whether he really wanted to be taken to St. Giles. Not being *au fait* with this particular London district, however, the notary had taken his query as an impertinence. It was not until they were well into the journey east, and he could see the landscape of the streets changing, that he understood the man's reluctance to take him to such a place. The pleasant boulevards and new brick terraces gave way to the ramshackle old town. Houses and shops of varying heights and sizes in divers states of decay were crammed next to each other like an old crone's teeth.

The carriage pulled up outside a narrow entrance at the mouth of a courtyard. The notary smelled the air as he dismounted, then quickly sniffed his nosegay. He did not relish his task on such a day as this, or on any day for that matter. This area was altogether less agreeable. As well as the stink, there were the shouts of hawkers pacing the alleyways and of urchins ducking and diving through the throng. There were whores, too. Temptation and the clap at every corner. The streets were so constricted that most carriages could not pass and some of the top gables almost joined above his head, blocking out the sunlight.

Most disconcerting of all, he did not know where to begin his search. He was looking for a proverbial needle in a haystack. He headed up the thoroughfare, which quickly narrowed. Wet shirts and petticoats were festooned from rafters and over newel posts drying in the hot air. A cat that was making a meal of a bloodied dead pigeon on one of the treads hissed at him and fled with its prey in its mouth. All around he could hear children crying and women shouting. A man with a tame crow on his shoulder held out a hand for alms, while a stick-thin boy spat on the cobbles as he passed. This was no place for anyone, let alone a young nobleman, to be reared, the notary thought to himself.

There were no street names here, no numbers, either. Sometimes there weren't even doors, just panels of wood that screened entrances. He was afraid he would never find Agnes Appleton and even more afraid for his life in a hellhole such as this. His courage was quickly deserting him. He had turned tail and was halfway down the steps when he heard a voice crackle behind him.

"You lookin' for someone?"

He turned to see an old woman, as gnarled as one of the newel posts, sitting on the stairs on the landing above. She had obviously been watching him in his fruitless efforts. The notary allowed a smile to flicker across his lips. At last there was hope in a place that the Lord himself had abandoned many years ago, he told himself.

"Yes. I seek a woman and a boy."

The crone huffed and held out a grimy hand. "Buy this and I'll think on it." Several strands of dark hair were gathered together and tied with a piece of twine. "Belonged to an Irish giant," she croaked. " 'Twill help you find what you seek."

The notary balked, but decided not to protest too loudly for fear of attracting attention to himself.

"Here's a farthing," he said, throwing a coin into her lap and taking the hair.

The crone seemed satisfied. "Tell me more."

"The woman's name is Agnes Appleton and the boy has a withered arm."

The old woman put her gnarled fingers to her forehead and puckered her face, as if experiencing some sort of vision. "A boy with a withered arm, you say? Yes. 'Tis coming back to me."

The notary stooped low. "You recall them now?"

The crone opened her eyes and chuckled. "Mayhap, but

Grandmother Tooley'll need another farthing to help her," she said, holding out her hand once more.

Another farthing duly crossed her palm. "Yes. Went to Covent Garden, she did. To the Rose and Crown. And the boy, too."

"Why would she go there?" asked the notary in all innocence.

Grandmother Tooley let out a phlegmy cackle. "Why would anyone go there?"

Chapter 18

The Reverend George Lightfoot sat at his desk at the vicarage, his face as worn as a well-rubbed penny. His eyes were fixed on a shoddy copy of Christ in the Garden of Gethsemane on the wall. In the little-known Renaissance painting, Jesus was on his knees, praying on the night before his Passion. Around him were his sleeping disciples, the ones who promised faithfully to keep awake in their master's hour of need.

The vicar sighed deeply and his thoughts turned to his own agony. Watching his wife cough and splutter through the night, he had witnessed her fever rising and her mind wandering. Yet he had kept awake. He had kept awake and he had prayed. He had prayed harder than he had ever prayed in his life that she would be saved. He had asked the Lord to take him in her stead. She was the truly good person; the one who never wavered in her faith; the one who was always there for others. Not him. He was weak and ineffectual. Worthless without her. But to no avail. She had been taken. And now, without her by his side, his own agony was only just beginning.

It had been less than a week since his wife's passing, but the trauma had aged her husband by a decade. Gone was the spring in his step; the litheness of his movements. He had always walked out with a cane, but that was only an affectation. Now, drained of energy, he almost felt that he really did need it to steady his shaky steps.

There had been no time for proper mourning. He had been

kept busy by the steady influx of bodies. There had been four burials on Thursday and four more on Friday. That meant that eight widows had to be comforted and upwards of twenty children were left fatherless. The parish had to be informed and the bereaved cared for in practical as well as spiritual ways. Before this would have been Margaret's domain. She was so well-grounded. Her determination to act had been the reason for the fateful visit to Lady Thorndike that led to her death. She only had thoughts for others and paid the ultimate sacrifice for her selflessness.

Suddenly he was reminded of Amos Kidd's widow. He had only spoken a few words to her at yesterday's funeral. He dare not engage with her more. She was so young. So beautiful. He recalled her head on his shoulder in her cottage. Her musky scent, tinged with roses; her rhythmic sobs; the thrill that ran through his body at her touch. It was a sensation that was new to him. His heart beat faster at the recollection of the moment, but he quickly shook his head. He would banish her from his mind.

A blank sheet of paper lay on his desk. He needed to write his Sunday sermon, but the words did not come. Usually he found it so easy to trot out helpful platitudes; to philosophize and eulogize; to castigate and berate. But now life was changed. Now he knew how the people of Egypt felt as the Angel of Death passed over their land or the vicar of Eyam when the plague had visited upon his community just over a century before. The villagers of Brandwick and beyond felt besieged, trapped in a prison not of their own making and only the Lord Himself knew when he would raise his hand and lift this cruel cloud.

He glanced at another sheet of paper on his desk. On it were written the names of the dead men. He scanned the list. They were all good and honest. Jed Burrows and Gil Herbert drank too much on market days. Seth Kipps was a gambler and none of them was averse to poaching the odd pheasant or rabbit for the pot when times were hard. But they were family men. All they did was toil in the fields only to be struck down by this murderous fog. He seized the paper and crumpled it roughly into a ball, hurling it into the corner of the room. He then clenched his fist and hit the desk. There was no justice in their deaths.

The maid knocked on the door, but did not wait for a reply. "I heard a noise, sir. Can I help you?"

The vicar looked up from his desk. His hands were shaking. "No. No, thank you," he said slowly, as if the girl had woken him from a bad dream.

Once she had gone, he allowed himself to sink back into the morass of despair. It sickened him when he thought of Lady Thorndike. What a contemptible woman she was. Margaret had told him about her refusal to help the sick and bereaved and now this—her disgraceful behavior with Dr. Silkstone. Poor Sir Henry had been most distressed by the incident, but not surprised. He had of course berated the young doctor. "That bastard colonist!" he had called him as they sat and drank sack afterward. But he knew, deep down, that his wife constantly played him for a fool. He had said as much on a number of occasions. "She's a temptress, vicar," he confided once. A temptress.

Fingering his Bible unthinkingly, he recalled the look of disgust on Dr. Silkstone's face. The grotesque smears of bright red lipstick on his cheek looked so like blood. He remembered darting him a disapproving look. In reality, however, he knew very well who would have been to blame for the compromising position in which the young colonist had found himself. If that was the case, then he was sure Dr. Silkstone would be feeling utterly wretched. He would be worried sick for his reputation.

Physicians and priests were in an oddly similar position of trust, he thought to himself. The stories they were told in confidence, the confessions made at moments of anxiety and vulnerability, the secrets they had to keep—they all weighed heavily on their shoulders. The sorrows and woes of others made up the cross their respective callings had to bear. Yet whereas Dr. Silkstone put his faith in science, he had to put his trust in the Lord. He thumbed through the leaves of the Old Testament and opened it at the Book of Job. Yes, Job, he told himself; the man whose righteousness was tested by Satan; the man who lost his livestock, his home, his children, and yet did not reproach the Lord. He read the passage about the fire that fell from the sky. It killed his sheep. He read about the mighty wind that caused houses to collapse. The words gave him a new confidence and he felt a surge of energy. God was testing him and testing his people. And he took up his pen and began to write the first words of his sermon: "The Lord giveth, and the Lord taketh away; blessed be the name of the Lord."

Even if Thomas had been minded not to tell Lydia of Lady Thorndike's attempt to seduce him, she would have sensed something was terribly wrong. The evening before he had stormed into the drawing room with a face like thunder, poured himself a brandy and paced up and down. Within a few seconds, however, he was relating the afternoon's events with a fury that Lydia had not seen before. She listened sympathetically, knowing that the fault lay with Lady Thorndike.

"You must not blame yourself for this, Thomas," she had soothed, walking over to him as he stood in front of the mantelpiece. She stretched out her hand to lay it on his shoulder, but he turned away.

"But I do blame myself, Lydia. How could I have been so blind? I should have seen. I should have known."

"You know now," she countered softly. "You have learned your lesson. No harm has been done."

Thomas, on the other hand, could not be so sure.

The following morning, when Thomas awoke and looked out of his bedroom window, he could see as far as the rose garden for the first time in ten days. The fog had lifted sufficiently for him to make out the blurred colors of the flowers, although not the individual blooms. Looking up at the leaden sky he could also see the sun rising behind the fog. The trees were stirring slightly, too. There was a whisper of a breeze blowing from the west. He suddenly felt that perhaps the cloud was dispersing, or moving; perhaps there was just an inkling of a return to normality; to the rhythm of the seasons and the natural order.

Quickly he dressed, hurried downstairs, and ventured outside. But he returned almost immediately. The sulfur was still in the air, lurking in the mist. It remained unsafe to be outdoors for any length of time. A plan. That was what was needed, he told himself; a logical way of tackling the problems that presented themselves. First and foremost the men's lungs needed to be protected; their mouths and noses needed covering. Next, their skin. It must not be exposed. Gloves should be worn. Sturdy boots, too. And wide-brimmed hats to shield the eyes and mouth should more rain fall. The men must work in shifts. Prolonged exertion in the foggy atmosphere seemed to exacerbate breathing difficulties.

In the study he found Lydia and told her his thoughts. She listened earnestly. She would have to find the money for new hats and gloves, she pointed out, but she could see that in the long term, such financial outlay would be well worth it. They had just begun some calculations when Howard knocked on the door.

"Mr. Lawson wishes to speak with you, your ladyship," he informed his mistress.

"Show him in," replied Lydia, seated at the desk.

Thomas had encountered the steward only once or twice before and had taken an instant dislike to him. There was something about his manner that irritated him. Perhaps it was the way he almost swaggered into a room, or the way he smiled at Lydia. Either way, it seemed to Thomas that he was a little too cocksure.

The steward acknowledged Thomas but spoke directly with Lydia. On this occasion, however, he seemed unusually tense. "Your ladyship, I am come about the men," he began.

"What is the trouble, Mr. Lawson?" asked Lydia, gesturing to the chair. She saw the steward glance at Thomas. "You may speak freely in front of Dr. Silkstone," she added.

"They are growing restless," he began. "There's a trouble-maker, a stranger, who is stirring discontent."

Lydia looked disconcerted. "In what way?"

"They want more money to work in the fields. We've lost four good men and at least a dozen more are struck down and they are afraid, your ladyship."

"And they have every right to be," interjected Thomas. "The more they are exposed to this fog, the greater the chances of them being poisoned."

Lydia shook her head. "Dead men can't spend money," she said wryly.

Lawson looked puzzled. "I do not follow, my lady."

Lydia smiled and pointed to the paper in front of her. "What good would more money be if the fog strikes them first?" She did not wait for a reply. "Dr. Silkstone and I have drawn up a set of proposals to help protect them." She slid the paper across the desk so that Lawson could read it.

The steward scanned it. " 'Tis a list," he said dismissively.

"A list of clothing that, if worn, should reduce the chances of the men contracting the fog sickness," reposted Lydia forcefully.

Now Thomas stepped in. "The fog contains poisonous parti-cles that are damaging their lungs. If they wear scarves over their mouths the effects of the gas should be reduced. Add to this a reduction in the time a man is allowed to work outside, and you should see fewer being affected."

Lawson was silent for a moment, as if digesting all he had just heard.

"So do you think that will help allay the men's fears?" pressed Lydia. "We will send to Oxford for enough new clothes and boots for everyone if we have to."

"It may certainly prove worth it, your ladyship," he said fi-nally, nodding his head approvingly.

"Good," said Lydia, clasping her hands together. "The men must know we have their welfare at heart."

Chapter 19

Feeling distinctly ill at ease, the notary picked his way along Bedford Lane toward the Piazza in Covent Garden. Keeping his sweaty palm firmly on his purse, he threaded through an unsavory assortment of actors and musicians toward the Rose and Crown. In his lawyer's garb he looked completely out of place among the painted Paphians and colorful minstrels who frequented the great Italianate square. This was where he had been informed by the old crone in St. Giles that he would find Agnes Appleton. Such information had naturally raised a great concern. If she worked as a serving wench—for what else could she do in a tavern?—then where was the boy? Did she take him with her? Perhaps he, too, worked at the inn, collecting tankards or sweeping the floor. Now, however, making his way past obvious bordellos and other such places of ill repute, another, more sickening thought occurred to him. He banished the very notion of it from his mind and quickened his step.

Presently he came to the tavern, just off the main Piazza. The windows were low and grimy and he could not see inside. Just as he was about to dip down to negotiate the door, however, something, or more precisely someone, was jettisoned outside. Cussing and swearing, the inebriate picked himself up out of the open sewer and skulked off down the street. Such an incident confirmed his grave misgivings, but he feared there was worse to come.

It took a while for his eyes to adjust to these new surroundings after the brilliant sunlight, but it took longer still for him to fully comprehend the squalor that surrounded him. Women in various states of undress were sprawling and draping themselves over virtually every male in the tavern. Some were straddling knees. Some were whispering. Some were kissing, but they all, without exception, stopped whatever libidinous act that occupied them to look at this strange little man in black who invaded their territory.

Now that his eyes were accustomed to the light, he did not like what he saw. He soon gleaned from the lewd demeanor of the woman halfway upstairs leading a man by the crotch that this was no ordinary inn, and that upstairs the hospitality offered was of a sexual nature.

The notary tried to compose himself and marched to the bar. The bawd greeted him with a wry smile, as if she knew his sort only too well: respectable on the outside and as rotten as a worm-eaten apple on the in.

"What can we do for you, sir?"

The little man's chin jutted out in a show of superciliousness. "I am in search of a young woman," he began.

The bawd, a fat woman with a long scar on her cheek, chortled. "Then you've come to the right place!"

The notary became annoyed. "A particular young woman, by the name of Agnes Appleton."

An eyebrow lifted and the bawd nodded. "Agnes!" she called. A moment later a girl emerged from a back room. She was, the notary estimated, in her early twenties, with a pleasant, open face and a comely figure. "Customer for you," the woman said.

The little man gave an indignant wiggle and his mouth pursed up. "I am not a customer. I merely wish to speak with Miss Appleton."

"That's what all your sort say, with respect," cackled the bawd, jerking her head toward the back. "Go in there," she said, then added: "She'll charge, mind, even if 'tis only a *talk* you want." She emphasized the word "talk" as if it was a euphemism for a sexual act.

Clearly unnerved by the situation, the notary followed the girl into the dingy back room. There was some sort of chaise longue up against a wall that was covered in a soiled sheet. The girl sat at one end and, seeing there were no other chairs in the room, the notary seated himself, as far away as possible, at the other. He cleared his throat.

"You are Agnes Appleton?" She was fresh-faced, with only a trace of rouge on her smooth cheeks. He could see that she had a good set of teeth in her head, too.

"Who wants to know, sir?" she replied warily.

The little man took a deep breath. He was relieved at having found her, but troubled that there was no sign of the child. "It is not you I seek," he told her candidly. "I am looking for a boy whom I believe was in your charge."

At this the girl's expression changed. Her features tightened and she sucked in her cheeks.

"Where is he?" asked the notary, an anxious chord in his voice.

"I know of no boy," she mumbled, her eyes wandering aimlessly around the room.

The notary studied her in her awkwardness for a moment. He realized he would have to approach this cross-examination from another angle. Delving into his bag, he brought out a piece of paper on which was written her former address.

"I have been to St. Giles," he said. "I know he was with you there."

Agnes seemed flustered. "What's he done? He's a good boy." Her pretty brow crumpled into a frown.

So many riddles, so many questions, and still no answers. The notary rolled his eyes. "I am sent to discover the whereabouts of Richard Farrell," he told her forthrightly. "Who you are, or what you do, are of no consequence to me. I know that Francis Crick gave you charge over the boy, so I am here to take him back to where he rightfully belongs."

The girl's head began to shake. "The boy's name was not Farrell, sir, but Crick. Richard Crick. He were Mr. Francis's son."

The little man looked perplexed. He paused for a moment then realized that Francis Crick had not told his accomplice the whole truth. She had no idea that the boy in her charge was the son of Captain Michael and Lady Lydia Farrell. And why should he? For all she knew, the child was the result of an indiscretion on Crick's part. It was, indeed, better that way for all concerned.

"It matters not. All I need to know is where he is now," he persisted in an irritable tone.

The girl looked at him and sighed deeply, her ample bosom rising and falling with the effort. It was then that her eyes misted up and her mouth quivered. From her manner the notary gleaned that the boy was no longer with her.

He lowered his face to meet her gaze. "He is not dead?" There was a hint of panic in his words. She shook her head in a way that told him the child was still alive, but not in good health, or worse. "You must tell me where he is, for his sake," he urged.

Agnes looked at him with doleful eyes. "He is in a terrible place," she said slowly. "And 'tis all my doing."

"Where is he?" The notary found himself wanting to shake this sniveling wench, but he resisted the urge. "Where is he?" he repeated with growing impatience.

Again she took a deep breath, as if trying to find some inner strength. "He is apprenticed to a chimney sweep," she blurted, not daring to look up.

The notary's jaw parted in shock. "What?" He could not hide his disbelief.

Now the girl's head dropped low and she hid her face in her hands in shame. "The money was all gone, sir. I had no choice," she cried. Her shoulders began to rise and fall in gentle sobs.

"So you sold him?"

"He were apprenticed," she cried through her fingers.

Exasperated the notary rose and began to pace the windowless room. "He is six years old!" he exclaimed. His mind flashed to an image of a pipe boy wedged up a chimney, barely able to breathe, scraping the soot off flues.

The girl clamped her hands over her ears, as if to block out his harsh words. "Do you think I wanted to? I loved that boy like he was my own. I couldn't keep him. We had nothing to eat. Nothing," she screamed. "You don't know what it's like. Mr. Francis left us no money. We see'd him in jail and he said he would make it good for the boy, but there was nothing."

The notary paused as he recalled the landlady with her spotlessly clean house in Seymour Street and the sideways look she had given the ginger jar that surely concealed her ill-gotten gains.

"We were in a good place and we had plenty to eat until . . . until they h-hanged him." Agnes stumbled over her words. "We had to leave. The landlady said she didn't want no scandal. Made us go. That's when we went to St. Giles. The rats kept us awake at night and Master Rich would cry himself to sleep with hunger. That's why I decided I'd give him up."

The anger that had welled up inside the notary a moment ago now subsided a little. Taking a deep breath, he composed himself once more. Self-control was always more effective with troublesome clients and it was what was required now, he told himself.

"You have obviously been through a difficult time," he observed, trying to remain dispassionate. "But where might this chimney sweep be?"

The girl's entire face had turned the color of her lightly rouged cheeks. She blinked and a single tear rolled down. "In Bermondsey," she said. "His name is Mr. Faulks."

"Very well," said the notary, rising from the chaise longue. He took out his purse and dropped a few coins onto the small table at her side. "Your pieces of silver," he added, though he doubted she would understand the allusion.

She looked up at him with eyes that did not hide her stricken conscience. "If you find him," she said in a trembling voice, "if you find him, tell him I am sorry."

The notary grimaced as she started to sob once more. He turned his back on her and began to walk out, but before he had reached the door he heard the sound of the coins clattering to the floor. In her grief and her shame she had swept them off the table.

Lady Thorndike did not take luncheon that day. Nor did she avail herself for dinner. She had left the house around noon, telling her maid she intended to go for a walk. She said that the mist was lifting and that she was sick of being indoors. Her maid had thought it most peculiar to go out on foot in the fog, but did not dare question her mistress's decision.

When her ladyship did not return to her bedchamber that evening, the maid had informed Sir Henry. He had not seemed unduly worried. There had been a row. Perhaps not a proper row; a row needs at least two protagonists. It was always one-sided with Julia, he mused. She had told him she could no longer stand being cooped up inside and was to meet with her lover, and that was an end to it. Just who this braggart was and where she went were none of his business. Accustomed to her infidelities, he went to bed and slept soundly.

Chapter 20

The following morning, as Thomas had hoped, the fog had lifted even more, although a mist, and the stench, still persisted. There were reports that all was clear just south of Oxford, so Lovelock made the carriage ready. Eliza had packed all the necessary baggage for a short sojourn in London and was to accompany her mistress. Lydia had told Thomas of Agnes's employment and their search would begin at her last known address in Seymour Street.

Dr. Carruthers could hardly contain his excitement when, twelve hours later, Thomas, Lydia, and Eliza arrived at Hollen Street. Their visit was unannounced and Mistress Finesilver was most vexed. It was after nine o'clock and, with no prior warning of the visit, nothing had been put in place. The housekeeper complained that she would have to make up beds that had not been slept in for at least two years and that, through no fault of her own, the mattresses would not be aired. Worse still, she only had a pie and some broth to offer her guests.

Nevertheless, despite the odd acerbic comment from Mistress Finesilver, they were able to enjoy a passable dinner. Afterward, while Lydia retired upstairs to bed, Thomas remained in the drawing room with his mentor. He filled pipes for both of them and they sat in chairs on either side of an empty hearth.

The old anatomist had heard reports of the great cloud in the newssheets and was fully aware of the havoc it was spreading.

"So, I'm assuming you found a way of analyzing the nature of this fog," said Dr. Carruthers, fingering the bowl of his pipe.

"Indeed," replied Thomas, adding wryly: "I was taught well."

"And?"

"And it contains sulfur, both in acid form and in particles."

Carruthers drew on his pipe. "Interesting," he said slowly. "But you do not know the source?"

"No, sir, I do not, but I have a theory." The idea had come to Thomas when he was in the library at Boughton, thumbing through the many volumes he had consulted in his search for a precedent for the noxious fog. He had uncovered an engraving of the destruction of Pompeii in Ancient Roman times and he recalled a similar story from his youth. He explained: "My father told me about a volcano north of my homeland that unleashed a cloud of poisonous gas. It killed many hundreds of native people in the area."

Dr. Carruthers exhaled and a cloud of smoke billowed from his mouth. "So you think a volcanic eruption has caused this calamity?"

Thomas nodded. "At present that is my inclination."

"But how can you test this theory?"

The exact same question had been puzzling Thomas for the past few days, but the answer had come to him as their carriage passed along Craven Street. It was there, in a modest town house, that his father's dear friend Benjamin Franklin had resided while in London. Now living in Paris, where he was America's first ambassador, Thomas knew that weather conditions were one of his many scientific interests. After all, he had produced treatises on meteorology and ocean currents. He drew heavily on his own pipe. "I shall write to Mr. Franklin," he said.

"Your compatriot?"

"Yes, sir," said Thomas. "He is bound to have some view on the matter."

*   *   *

No one noticed Agnes Appleton slip out of the bawd house that evening. There were too many customers downstairs to see her leaving by the back entrance, heading out into the balmy June night. The bell of St. Martin's tolled ten o'clock. She did not look back.

The air was full of raucous laughter and fiddle music trilling from the taverns. The audience was spilling out of the theater in Drury Lane, where they had just seen a performance by Mr. Garrick.

She pulled her shawl over her head. She was not looking for custom. Instead, her eyes firmly fixed on the gutter, she made her way along the Strand and down Whitehall. A dray cart veered toward her and the driver cursed her for being in the way. A sedan chair swerved to avoid her. Someone tipped a bowl of greasy water onto the street. It narrowly missed her feet. She began to cry, but she kept on going. Up ahead she could hear drunken men; sailors singing snatches of shanties. They meandered along the path, shouting at her and making lewd gestures. She did not look up, but kept her head down. Not long now. She would soon be there, she told herself.

Minutes later she had reached Westminster Bridge. Looking over the parapet she saw the moon reflected like a great silver coin in the choppy water. A cooling breeze blew along the river and made her shiver. A few passengers waited on the stairs below. A half-dozen ferry boats were crisscrossing the Thames, struggling against the turning tide. The rushing water lapped around the piers.

From somewhere in the blackness a man's voice called out. A bell struck the hour; she was not sure which. She did not care. A moment later a woman screamed. Then there came a heavy splash and the chill waters of the river closed over the girl's head.

Chapter 21

The notary had spent a second night in London. His task was not proving as straightforward as he might have hoped and now he found himself having to venture farther into the realms of unspeakable poverty and deprivation to which he was certainly unaccustomed. He had visited Faulks's premises and been told he would find the proprietor and his boys at the dust yard toward the river. Rather than wait for him to return, he decided it was best not to prevaricate. He was fully aware that there could be an unpleasant scene and he wanted to see his business over and done with. The sooner he did, the sooner he could return to Oxfordshire.

The first odd thing he noticed just before he reached the yard was the sight of gulls circling overhead. But these voracious birds were not after fish, as the notary soon discovered. They were attracted by catches of a much less romantic variety—of animal entrails and kitchen scrapings. They dived, picked, and soared overhead, clutching their prizes in their beaks, screeching gleefully as they did so. He was glad that he had invested in a fresh nosegay that morning and he held it under his nose and breathed in deeply.

Piles of discarded rubbish shaped the landscape of the yard with hillocks and cones. As far as he could guess, it was an area of about two hundred feet wide and half as long and opened onto the Thames beyond. Flanking one side of the yard were a dozen or so upturned dustcarts.

Women and girls crawled like ants on two or three of the mounds. Some of them sat holding sieves as large as the top of a small loo table, and were catching huge shovelfuls from a feeder. Others simply raked the rubbish with their bare hands. Some of them sang as they worked, their voices drowning the constant drone of the flies on the heaps.

On the other side of the yard were more mounds. These were different in nature; gray and black and smooth. Even though there was hardly any breeze, as he approached fine ashes floated like snowflakes in the air. As he sniffed at his nosegay, he watched half a dozen men and boys emptying sacks onto the piles. They reminded him of black beetles on a dung heap. Gingerly, he picked his way over to them, zigzagging between pot-holes and pools of stagnant water.

As he drew nearer, he observed that these mounds, too, were particular in their nature. One pile, about the height of two men, consisted of cinders, ashes, and other emptyings from dust-holes and bins, while another by its side was made up of fine dark powder. There were several young boys, again with large sieves, who were working their way through the bulging mound, as if panning for gold. They discarded the chunks and lumps they found and their sievings fell onto another pile. This, he assumed, was refined soot which, he had heard, was much in demand by farmers who would use it to preserve wheat and turnips.

By the mound stood a stocky man in a ragged black coat.

"Mr. Faulks?" called the notary.

The man turned. He seemed to have met with an accident and one eye was covered with an oyster shell through which he had threaded a string that secured it around his head. The notary had been told that this was his distinguishing mark.

"I go by that name, sir," replied the man in a surly fashion.

"Then I am hoping you can help me," replied the notary, a little out of breath. "I am looking for a young boy. I believe he is apprenticed to you." He nodded in the direction of the nearest pile. He could see now that there were about three or four boys emptying sacks of soot, but one of them was much smaller than the rest. He struggled more than the others as they stumbled up the slope, each with a burden on their backs. His right arm seemed to dangle helplessly at his side.

"Got into trouble, eh?" he growled. "I'll flail the . . ."

"No," interrupted the notary. "No, there is no trouble," he soothed. "The boy I seek goes by the name of Richard Farrell, although you may know him as Richard Crick."

Faulks nodded, narrowing the one eye that could be seen.

"Young Crick, yes, that's him," he said, pointing to the small child. "Him with the arm. I should never have taken him on, but his keeper, a pretty lass, persuaded me, if you get my drift." He laughed and nudged the notary, who remained unimpressed. "Anyway, he can get up the flues all right, he's that skinny, but he's slow. Too slow."

The notary allowed a smile to flutter across his face. "Then might you consider letting him go?"

Faulks snorted. "You'd have to make it worth me while."

The little man nodded. "I would be very happy to," he replied.

Back at Hollen Street Lydia was waiting for Thomas in the drawing room, staring out of the window. She was already wearing her hat. On hearing footsteps she turned and smiled. She seemed in good spirits and he took advantage of the fact that they were alone. Slipping his arms around her waist, he kissed her lips.

"I am so very nervous," she whispered.

"I know," he replied. He felt strangely unsettled, too, but he did not let on. "Whatever the outcome, I'll always be here for you," he said softly. He was sounding a note of caution. He knew her hopes of finding Richard were high, but he acknowledged the child was only one of thousands of orphans in the city. The chances of him even being alive were very slim, let alone recovering him in good health.

They set off for the Seymour Street address just as soon as they were able. Eliza accompanied her mistress. For once Thomas was glad to swap the country air of Oxfordshire for the city stench of London. Even though the heat was still too much for most, it was preferable to the noxious miasma and he was glad to see the sun again after almost two weeks of thick fog at Boughton.

Traveling west, the streets became wider and cleaner and soon the carriage stopped outside the neat town house from where Agnes Appleton had sent her last letter to her sister. Lydia craned her neck from the inside of the carriage to look at the tall facade. A faint smile skidded across her features at the thought of her son living in this district. Francis had done well to rescue him from the workhouse and place him here, she told herself. Had he done it for love of her, or because he wanted to use Richard as a sort of bargaining tool to win her hand? She would never know.

Thomas alighted first and went to pull the bell. The door was answered by a cheerful freckled maid. The young doctor bowed.

"Good day, Miss," he began. "I am making inquiries about a gentleman who I believe used to lodge here. His name was the Right Honorable Francis Crick."

Any vestige of a smile quickly disappeared from the girl's face.

"The mistress says she don't want no trouble," she snapped. "I am to tell any others who come calling about the boy to go away." And with that, she began to close the door.

It was immediately clear to Thomas that once again they were following in the footsteps of someone else who was searching for the Crick heir. He knew he had to act quickly.

"Please tell your mistress I am sorry to have troubled her," Thomas said, smiling. "We mean no harm," he insisted. Then, turning toward the carriage, he gestured to Lydia. "We are merely seeking a young woman by the name of Agnes Appleton, who was nursemaid to a small boy."

At the mention of Agnes's name, the maid's scowl softened and her eyes widened. Her gaze set on Thomas. "Agnes?" she repeated.

Just then, however, a harsh voice called from within the house.

"Who's there, Maddie?"

The maid became flustered. "No one," she retorted. "A hawker, ma'am," and she began to close the door once more. But just before it shut completely, she stuck her freckled face over the threshold. "Meet me at the Oxford Chapel tonight. Ten o'clock," she whispered. And with those words she retreated and banged the door shut.

Back in the carriage Thomas related the exchange with the maid. "She knows something," he told Lydia and Eliza. "We are to meet this evening."

"What did she say?" pressed an eager Lydia.

"Very little," replied Thomas. "She had been told to stay silent. What I do know is that, yet again, someone has been here before us and paid for silence."

"But what of the maid, sir?" urged Eliza.

Thomas nodded. " 'Tis clear to me that she knew Agnes. She will be forthcoming, of that I am sure."

Lydia took a deep breath and squeezed Eliza's hand. "So perhaps we can finally start to make progress?" she said excitedly.

"Perhaps," replied Thomas. He did not like to tell her he had a nagging suspicion that what the maid had to relate would not be good news.

The carriage turned down Whitehall and followed the river for a few hundred yards, past Westminster Bridge. Thomas was staring out of the window, looking at the ferries ply their trade across the Thames, when he spotted a small crowd gathered on a landing stage. At first he thought they were merely passengers queuing for a ferry at Whitehall Stairs, but then he noticed some women seemed agitated. Several people were leaning over, looking into a ferry that had just moored up, and a man was shouting and waving his arms excitedly.

Thomas leaned out of the carriage and called for the driver to pull up.

"What is it?" asked Lydia.

"Over there," said Thomas, pointing to the group. "They may need a physician."

As soon as the carriage came to a halt, he jumped out and

hurried along the boardwalk over to where the small crowd was gathered. A dozen or so people were clustered around a ferryman. In his arms lay a young woman. Her body was limp. She was fully clothed and dripping wet and there was green weed in her long, dark hair. It was clear she had just been pulled from the water. A thin trickle of foam seeped from her mouth. Thomas ordered the ferryman to lay her down on the jetty and he felt her neck for a pulse. There was nothing. He pressed on her chest and more foam appeared from her mouth, but it was immediately evident to Thomas she had been dead some hours.

"Does anyone know who she is?" he asked, looking up and into the crowd. No one answered. Instead, they began to disperse with eyes lowered. She was just another girl; a servant or maybe even a harlot from her low-cut bodice. There was at least one most nights, found washed up on the stinking shoreline the next day.

In his concern for the drowned woman, Thomas had forgotten about Lydia and Eliza. He looked up to see them both approaching. Scrambling to his feet once more, he waved Lydia back, but she lifted her skirts and picked her way toward him. The crowd was thinning as she drew closer and she caught a glimpse of the dead girl's face. She grimaced and turned her head away almost immediately. Eliza had been following just a few paces behind. She, too, saw the girl, lying prostrate on the boardwalk, her dark hair pulled back off her forehead by the weight of water. Only she did not grimace and turn away. She stared at her in horror before letting out a terrible wail.

"No!" she screamed, and she flung herself forward. Cradling the girl's head in her hands she cried: "Agnes! No!"

Chapter 22

The Oxford Chapel in de Vere Street was but a five-minute walk from Seymour Street. Shortly before the appointed hour of ten o'clock a carriage carrying Thomas, Lydia, and Eliza drew up outside the church. All three of them remained inside, watching and waiting for the maid, too tense to talk. Now and again a deep sob took hold of Eliza at the memory of her dead sister and she shook like a rag poppet. Lydia placed a comforting arm around her, although she, too, was fighting back her own tears. It had been agreed not to reveal the news of Agnes's death to the maid, Maddie, until she had divulged the information she deemed so important.

The light was almost gone, but the glow of the street lamps illuminated the church steps where three beggars huddled in the Doric porch. A young couple strolled past, followed by an older man with a limp. A landau rattled along and off toward Oxford Street. The clock struck ten, but the thoroughfare was deserted.

"She's not coming," said Lydia.

Thomas remained calm. "She will come," he told her. "We must be patient."

A stray mongrel trotted into view, cocked its leg on the corner of a pillar, and went on its way. It was then that Thomas spotted a rustling in the bushes next to the church. A slight figure, its head bent, emerged from the shadows and mounted the steps.

"There she is," he said softly. "I shall go first, then signal to you both."

Gently, and without wishing to draw attention to his presence, he opened the carriage door and made his way up the steps of the church. He could see the young woman clearly now as she stood in the weak pool of light cast by a lantern in the porch. She wore a brown hooded cape that half covered her face, casting her freckled nose in shadow. She stood her ground as Thomas approached.

"Good evening, miss," said Thomas, touching his tricorn respectfully.

The maid gave a short curtsy. "Sir," she replied.

"There is something you wish to tell me about Agnes Appleton?"

She looked about her in a circumspect manner. "First I need to know why you want to find her."

Thomas understood the maid's wish to protect Agnes from any unwanted attentions. "That is simple," he replied. "I have here Agnes's sister and the mother of the boy in her charge. They are both anxious to know what has become of them." He spun 'round and gave the signal for Lydia and Eliza to approach. The girl also turned to see the coachman helping the two women alight from the carriage.

At the sight of the lady and her maid, Maddie's eyes narrowed as she studied them both closely, her eyes darting from Eliza to Lydia. "She spoke of her sister," she said softly, her look set on Eliza. "There is much likeness, sir," she added, shaking her head.

"So you knew Agnes?" Thomas knew he had to tread carefully with his questions. She was risking her own livelihood by meeting them.

"Yes, sir," replied the maid, watching mistress and maid mount the steps toward them. As they drew level, he could see the girl was scrutinizing their faces closely.

"You have Agnes's mouth," she said, addressing Eliza. But it was to Lydia that she directed her most forthright remarks. "The likeness!" she exclaimed as she studied her.

"Likeness to whom?" intervened Thomas.

"To Master Richard, of course," replied the maid. "The same eyes, the same hair . . ."

At her words Lydia could control her emotions no longer. She rushed forward and grasped the maid's hands. "Do you know where he is? Please tell me."

Thomas put his arms about Lydia's shoulders and gently drew her away from the girl, who was shocked and over-whelmed by her reaction.

"Her ladyship has not seen her son for six years," Thomas explained.

Maddie composed herself. "I was told Mr. Crick was a wid-ower and that Master Rich and his nursemaid, that were Agnes, would be staying with us for a while. All I know is Agnes was a good friend to me, sir, and when my mistress turned her and the boy out the house, it were a bad day."

"How long ago was that?" pressed Thomas.

The maid lifted a finger to her freckled face in thought. "More than a year ago, sir. That's why I was fair taken by sur-prise when she came the other day."

Thomas and Lydia shot glances at each other. "You saw Agnes recently?" asked the doctor.

"Why yes, sir. Came to the house. In a right state she were. Looked all wan, she did."

"Do you know why? Was my son with her?" Lydia was growing more agitated.

The maid shook her head. "No, madam," she replied, delv-ing into the folds of her cape. "But she did leave me this." In her small hand she clutched a folded piece of paper. "Agnes asked me to see that Master Richard got it." She held the letter on the palm of her hand for a moment, tantalizingly close to Lydia. Thomas was afraid she might snatch it, but she did not. Under the boy's name, he could make out an address.

"We will see that it is delivered safely to Master Richard," Thomas assured her. He held out his hand slowly to receive the letter.

For a second the maid paused, shook her head, and withdrew the letter back into the folds of her cape. "Agnes said I was only to give it to him if something bad happened to her."

Thomas stiffened, but his expression gave him away. The maid's eyes darted to Lydia's, then Eliza's.

"She's in trouble, isn't she?" The color was draining away from her dappled cheeks as she spoke.

Thomas nodded. "I am afraid so."

"Dead?"

Although none of them replied immediately, Eliza's tears that suddenly welled up and broke forth, spoke volumes.

The maid shook her head. "Did she . . .?"

"They pulled her body from the river this morning," answered Thomas.

Raising her eyes heavenward, the girl sighed deeply and retrieved the letter. "I was afraid she might do something like that," she murmured, handing Thomas the missive. "Maybe this will tell you why."

As soon as she saw her son's name written on the paper, Lydia's hands had flown to her face. "He's alive," she had exclaimed. "He must be!" But her joy was tempered when next she read the address: *Care of Mr. Benjamin Faulks, Chimney Sweep, Bermondsey.*

The letter remained unopened on Lydia's lap on the journey back to Hollen Street. She stared at it as if it were some talisman that was mesmerizing her. It was not until they were all seated around the table in the dining room that Thomas handed her the paper knife to break the seal.

With a trembling hand, Lydia took the knife, but could not bring herself to slice through the red wax. She fumbled for a moment, then dropped the knife, sending it clattering on the table. Thomas retrieved it and, without ceremony, slit the seal and unfolded the paper to reveal a page of script written in a light hand. He cleared his throat and began to read out loud:

> *My dear Richard,*
>   *If this letter ever reeches you, I will be long gon. I know that I did a terrible thing giving you over to*

Mr. Faulks, but God gave me no choice. We had no food, nowhere to live and so, at least, I thort you might stand a better chance.

Your father, God rest his soul, had promised to give us enough money to live off before he died. But there was none and so I was forced to give you away. I am hoping you can find it in your hart to forgiv me and that you grow to be a helthy and hapy young man.

Always remember me as your loving nurs.
Agnes.

Thomas looked up to see tears rolling down Eliza's cheeks. Her mistress put a comforting arm around her, even though she, too, was close to breaking down.

Lydia gazed expressionless into the distance. "He is a pipe boy," she said softly. "She sold him to a sweep."

Thomas looked up at her. "He is alive," he cried. "Richard is alive." At least for the time being, he thought to himself. So many pipe boys only lasted a few months. If they did not die stuck up a chimney, a fatal respiratory disease or testicular cancer would finish many of them off. Either those ills or a beating from their cruel task masters nearly always cut short their young lives. Master Richard's chances of survival were now severely curtailed in light of Agnes's letter. But he could not let his fears show. He also knew Lydia would have to be convinced that this was good news. He forced a smile, and she responded.

"Yes, he is alive," she conceded. "We must thank God for that."

Thomas obtained special permission from the Westminster coroner, Sir Peregrine Crisp, to handle Agnes Appleton's corpse. Normally a postmortem would not be deemed necessary in such a case. Londoners were as used to seeing bodies dragged out of the Thames as they were teeth in a barber's shop. But Thomas had promised Eliza that her sister would receive a decent burial and would not be consigned to a pauper's grave or, worse still, buried at a crossroads, the fate accorded to most suicides.

As she lay on the marble dissecting slab in his laboratory, he recalled how she had appeared on the landing stage by the stairs. There had been fine foam around her lips and when he had pressed her chest, more had appeared. He knew that if Agnes had been alive when she entered the river, water would have entered her air passages, along with inspired air. It would have been mixed with mucus and churned in the windpipe, like soap produces froth in a copper. He pressed her chest once again. More foam trickled out. There was no doubt she had been alive when she hit the water.

Next he inspected her hands. They had seen work, but they remained young. Turning them over, he examined her fingers. They were wrinkled but her palms were still smooth, suggesting to him that she had been in the water for fewer than twenty-four hours. Moving down her body to her legs, Thomas saw that one, her left, appeared broken. He felt the shin bone. It was fractured just below the knee. He felt the other leg. There was a similar fracture there, too, suggesting that she had cracked both limbs when she hit the water. Furthermore, there was no sign of a struggle or a beating. All the evidence pointed to the fact that she jumped off a bridge. The weight of her clothes pulled her down and the tide had dragged her a few hundred yards downstream. Yet it was not so much how Agnes Appleton died that troubled Thomas, but why. Just what had made her do such a thing?

Reluctantly he decided to conduct an intimate examination. The large round sores confirmed his fears. Agnes was suffering from the early stages of syphilis. She had, in all likelihood, been forced into prostitution, like so many young women who fell on hard times. He folded the cloth back over her face. How like Eliza she was, he thought to himself, but the body was beginning to turn in the heat and there was no time for sentimentality.

It was growing late and he found Lydia sitting alone in the drawing room, staring forlornly at the topaz earring the woman at the workhouse in Hungerford had given her.

"We shall look for this Mr. Faulks first thing tomorrow," he assured her, settling himself beside her. "We *will* find Richard."

Chapter 23

Death was beginning to visit the parish of Brandwick so regularly that the Reverend Lightfoot rarely left the church during what few hours of daylight there were. He found himself either in the vestry, writing up the register of deaths—there were very few baptisms and no marriages at all—or conducting funeral services in the nave. Only yesterday he had buried two more men and a child not four years old. Joseph Makepeace had asked for an extra pair of hands to help him turn the graveyard sods. In fact, the vicar was coming to regard funerals as rather mundane. They were neither celebrations of lives lived well, nor mournful services for those tragically cut short in their prime. They were mere formalities.

He looked at the miniature of Margaret that he kept on his desk in the study. How he missed her guiding hand in everything he did. He still found himself asking for her opinion on matters, then turning to find no one there. So often he had told those recently bereaved that their loved ones had only passed to the other side. They were still present, albeit invisible. Only now he was coming to realize that this was not as simple as it sounded—it may even be a falsehood. When he spoke to her she never replied and soon, he feared, he would forget her voice, the way she walked, even her smile.

The sun's angry face had been screened behind the fog yet again, so he had worked by candlelight. The study door was open and, as he gazed at the little portrait, he heard his maid's footsteps coming along the corridor. There was a knock.

"You have a visitor, sir," she told him. "Mistress Kidd."

For a moment he froze.

"Shall I show her in, sir?"

"Yes. Yes," he said slowly, as if in two minds about receiving her. A moment later, Susannah appeared at the threshold.

"Mistress Kidd. What brings you here?" he asked, rising from his chair. She walked in slowly, carrying a basket.

"I have come to thank you, sir," she replied.

"For what?" His manner was strangely abrupt.

"For the funeral service, sir."

He nodded his head.

"And to say sorry, sir," she continued.

"Sorry?"

She lifted her gaze. "For the way I . . ."

His body grew rigid at the recollection of the moment in the cottage; how a thousand volts of electricity had surged through his frame at this woman's touch, as if he had been struck by lightning.

"Very well," he said, not daring to look at her.

There was an awkward silence until she stepped forward. "I brought you this," she said, removing a cloth from her basket to reveal a pie. " 'Tis apple," she told him with a smile. "From my own orchard." He did not look at it as she placed the pie dish on his desk, but kept his eyes lowered.

"Thank you," he said.

Another difficult pause followed before the widow took her leave.

"I best be on my way, sir," she told him, giving a shallow curtsy.

"Very well," he said. Then he instructed the maid: "Show Mistress Kidd out, if you please."

The girl did as she was told, bade the visitor a good day, and returned to the study. "Is there anything else you need, sir?"

The vicar shook his head. "No, thank you," he replied. But

just as she was heading toward the door again, he called her back. "There is one more thing."

"Yes, sir?"

He pointed to the apple pie on his desk. "Take that and feed it to the pigs."

Gabriel Lawson lived in a comfortable estate house that had once been inhabited by the late, and not-at-all lamented, lawyer James Lavington, who had died at the hands of Francis Crick. It lay overlooking Plover's Lake on the Boughton estate. He had been given a small staff and a reasonable living, even though he found it necessary to supplement his income by other means on occasion. His gambling habits were proving a little costly and he had resorted to what he called "borrowing" a few pounds a month from the estate's accounts to cover his expenses.

That evening he had poured himself a brandy and was sitting by the fire awaiting his supper when there was a knock. A moment later his housekeeper appeared and exhorted him to come to the back door. There stood Ned Perkins in the half light of a murky evening. He was fingering his hat and looking troubled.

"What is it?" asked Lawson.

"Sorry to bother you, sir, but I thought you needed to know he's back."

Lawson sighed. "The knife-grinder?"

The foreman nodded sheepishly. "He be talking to the men now, by the threshing barns. Stirring things, he is."

Without a word, Lawson brushed past Perkins and marched over to the stables. Saddling up his horse, he rode out of the yard. "I'll soon put paid to that troublemaker," he said, galloping off toward the barns about a mile down the track.

The steward found Joshua Pike standing on a bale of hay, addressing at least two score men. The light was dim and a few carried flaming torches. Lawson could see some of their faces in the half glow, men like Jack Budd and Tim Blackwell, men who were good workers. He was disturbed that they had allowed their heads to be turned by this rabble-rouser. Even more worrying was the fact that here were others, too, whom he did not recognize. Strangers, workers from nearby estates, he guessed.

As he approached he could hear some of Pike's words.

"Every day this poison fog lingers you are risking your lives, and for what?" he cried, his arm rising and falling as he spoke.

Some of the men cried "Aye," in response. He was confident, belligerent, confrontational in his manner. If he wanted a fight, Gabriel Lawson told himself, he was ready for one.

Skirting 'round the crowd, he guided his horse up to the bale where Pike was standing and loomed over him. Yet instead of falling silent, the young man, without bothering to look at the steward, pointed at him and cried out: "See, you are not free men. They would keep you in chains!"

Incensed, Lawson nudged his horse closer to the knife-grinder, so that the animal's breath wreathed his head. "You are trespassing, Pike," he snarled. "This is private land."

But the troublemaker ignored Lawson's words. Instead, he carried on addressing the men. "Have you no right to the land you work, brothers?"

The steward felt his blood begin to boil. Such insolence. Such effrontery. He surveyed the men below. Some of them had directed their gaze toward him. Budd and Blackwell and a few others wore worried frowns. They started to retreat into the shadows. Seeing their wavering, Lawson decided to take advantage.

"Have you not been given scarves and gloves to protect you from the fog while you work?" he cried. A few men mumbled in reply. "Have your hours not been lessened?" They were turning. He could see it in their gestures. Some of them muttered to each other. "Go home to your families and no more will be said," he told them.

The workers began to peel off in twos and threes, despite the knife-grinder's exhortations. "We will win, brothers!" he called. "Be strong!" But his appeals were now falling on deaf ears, as more and more turned their backs on him and melted away into the murky darkness, Perkins among them.

Now Lawson bent low from his horse down toward the bale, so that his face was level with Pike's. Finally the young man turned; his tanned features bathed in the glow from a sconce that blazed nearby. He was smiling insolently.

"If I catch you on this land again, I'll see that you swing," hissed Lawson.

Still smiling, Pike shook his red-swathed head. "Your men may give you no choice," he said. "If this fog kills many more, you'll have to up their wages."

Lawson was minded to wipe the brazen smirk from his face with the back of his hand, but he restrained himself. The law was on his side. "Get out of my sight and never come back here again," he growled through clenched teeth.

The knife-grinder nodded, but he knew he had scored another small victory. He jumped down from the bale, strode over to his mule, and mounted it.

"You should never underestimate the power of your men, Mr. Lawson," he called as he turned and headed down the track.

The steward shook his fist at him as he watched the mule carrying this thorn in his side back down the lane. That was the problem, he told himself. He knew only too well the sort of things his men were capable of.

Chapter 24

In the early hours of the next morning the deadly fog rolled into London. It came from the north and curled east up the Thames, so that by seven o'clock not a brig nor a barque could move from the wharfs. The temperature dropped like a stone and all sound was muffled by the pillow of poison that pressed down on the city.

As soon as Thomas woke he knew it had come. He did not need to look out of the window. He could smell it on the air; the dry, clawing stench that was so familiar and so deadly. Dressing hurriedly, he went to wake Lydia.

" 'Tis here. The fog is here," he told her, as she rubbed her sleepy eyes. Walking over to the shutters, he pulled them open to reveal the slate gray mist clinging to the panes. "We need to return to Boughton."

She sat up in bed, her hair tamed by a ribbon. "But Richard! What about Richard?" she protested.

"We cannot continue our search in the fog, my love," he told her, sitting down beside her on the bed. "All London will be paralyzed. We could be stuck here for days, if not weeks, if we do not head back today."

A look of despair scudded across her face. She knew what Thomas said was right, but she still clung to the hope that Richard was alive and close by. "Promise me we will return as soon as we can," she pressed him.

Thomas met her glare. "I give you my word," he said, pulling her toward him.

She nuzzled her head in his shoulder. "I know I am needed on the estate."

Thomas stroked her hair. In such a time of need, her place, he agreed, was at Boughton.

Their carriage made slow progress to Snows Hill, where the regular coach left for Oxford. The fog was not as dense as it had been at Boughton. Nevertheless, the poor visibility made traveling hazardous. When they arrived, however, the porter told them the carrier company was canceling the service until the fog had lifted. By a stroke of good fortune their carriage driver heard of their plight and offered to undertake the journey to Oxford himself. So they set off. In a small and cramped vehicle designed for the streets of London that groaned on its axles over every rut in the road, they headed north through the spreading fog.

Before their departure, Thomas had written a letter to the chimney sweep mentioned in Agnes's last letter and left it in the care of Dr. Carruthers. As soon as the fog allowed men to go about their normal business, his mentor would facilitate its delivery. Just what the sweep's reaction would be was anyone's guess, but Thomas hoped that he would be able to return to the capital very soon to negotiate with Mr. Faulks in person. That was, of course, if he was not too late already. They were still no closer to fathoming the identity of this mysterious clerk who preempted their every move. Always seemingly one step ahead of them, he may well have already approached the sweep.

Thomas looked across at Lydia as her body swayed with the movement of the carriage. She smiled weakly at him. Her skin was pale and her eyes red-rimmed from both the stinging mist and from crying. Now that the fog had hit London, returning to Boughton was the best course of action, he told himself, even though what they might find on their arrival still filled him with dread. In all probability the cloud still lingered and there may well be many more struck down, their lungs burning from the sulfur. Yes, the sooner he could get back to the estate, he assured himself, the better it would be for everyone concerned.

The carriage clattered into Oxford in the early evening. All the way along the road from London the air had been murky but it had only slowed their journey a little. Thomas had never been happier to see the pepper pot dome on the top of Christ Church College. The fog that had previously obscured the haze had been greatly dispersed during their absence.

They spent a reasonable night at The Black Horse and set off for Boughton the next morning in relatively good spirits. The cloud had lifted to the rounded tops of the hills to reveal that everywhere the once-green leaves on the trees were now scorched and withered. The pastureland, too, was brown and parched. They took in the harrowing scene in silence until Lydia spotted something strange.

"What are those men doing?" she said, pointing out of the carriage window. Thomas leaned over to see. A human chain, spaced a few yards apart, was walking in a line from the top of one of the hills. The men's eyes were cast to the ground as they progressed down the slope toward the lane.

"They seem to be looking for something," remarked Thomas. He pushed down the carriage window. The same sulfurous stench still lingered, but it was not as strong.

He signaled to the men as they approached. One of them walked over to the carriage.

"What goes on here?" asked Thomas.

The man pushed his hat to the back of his head and scratched his forehead with his thumb. "We're searching for a missing person, sir," he replied.

Now Lydia leaned out of the window and, obviously recognizing her, the man quickly uncovered his head. "Your ladyship," he said gruffly.

"Who is missing?" she asked.

The man frowned. " 'Tis Lady Thorndike, ma'am," he replied.

A shocked look registered on Lydia's face. "How long has she been missing?"

"Three days now," he replied. "She said she were going for a walk and no one has seen her since."

"We will do all we can to help," Lydia told him. "I will speak with Sir Henry."

The man bowed and Thomas gave the signal to the driver to move off.

"Lady Thorndike has spent a night away from her own bed before," she told Thomas knowingly, "but three days without a word . . . Poor Sir Henry must be sick with worry."

"Will you organize a search party at Boughton?"

She nodded. "Just as soon as I can."

There was more bad news waiting for Thomas and Lydia on their return. Despite the fog lifting slightly, more and more men, women, and children were falling sick. Gabriel Lawson updated them on events in the study.

"I've lost two more workers since you left, your ladyship," he reported. His sunburned face seemed much paler now that it had not seen the sun for almost three weeks, noted Thomas. "They say their families are being hit, too. Tim Blackwell has lost both of his babes. The grave diggers are burying them so quick that the vicar can't keep up with them."

Thomas intervened. "And the scarves? They are wearing them?"

Lawson eyed the doctor with unveiled hostility and addressed his reply to his mistress. "They wear them and they are faring better than those who don't on the Thorndike estate—there's half a dozen dead there—but 'tis the young and the old who seem to be worst off."

Thomas thought of Will Lovelock and his asthma. Thankfully he had been spared, but it was inevitable that those with a weakness would be most affected.

"And what of morale generally?" Lydia tried to be more positive in her tone.

Lawson sighed. "The men are not happy, your ladyship. I cannot lie. The troublemaker returned, stirring things up."

"What do you mean?"

Lawson darted a glance at Thomas. "They want more money to work the fields in the fog," he told her.

Lydia nodded. "I understand," she replied. "But 'tis not possible. Not with our income down."

"This troublemaker. He is not from the estate?" interrupted Thomas.

Again Lawson addressed his reply to Lydia. "He is a traveler, my lady. A knife-grinder. His name is Joshua Pike, and he has been calling the men to action, telling them they should demand higher wages."

"And he has been trespassing on my land?" She suddenly went on the offensive.

"He has, but I told him in no uncertain terms to leave," replied Lawson.

Lydia sighed deeply and looked at Thomas. "I see," she said. "If he returns we shall have to call the constables to deal with the matter."

Lawson nodded. "Yes, your ladyship," he said. He rose to leave, but Lydia stopped him.

"There is another pressing matter, Mr. Lawson," she told him. He frowned. "I am sure you have heard that Lady Thorndike is missing."

At the mention of the name, Thomas noticed Lawson's eyes shot to the floor. "I had heard," he replied.

"We need to organize a search party on the estate," Lydia instructed him. "We must spare at least half a dozen men for the task. They should walk the footpaths, looking for any clues as to her whereabouts."

Lawson nodded his unruly head. "I will see to it right away," he told her. He glanced at Thomas in a vain attempt at deference.

"Keep us informed, Mr. Lawson. That will be all," she said, dismissing the steward.

As soon as he had left the room Thomas walked over to Lydia and put his hands on her shoulders. "He knows something about Lady Thorndike's disappearance."

Without turning 'round Lydia reached for one of his hands and clasped it to her chest. "We shall see," she said. "All I can do is show willing for the sake of poor Sir Henry."

*   *   *

The men worked in four teams of two, each taking a specific area of the estate. Ned Perkins was in charge of the search in Boughton's southeast corner. They had been combing the footpaths for a little over an hour and had found nothing. Visibility was poor, but not so poor that they could not see the hedgerows and the ditches on either side of the uneven tracks. With their staves they prodded gorse bushes and hawthorns, but to no avail.

When they came to a fork in the path, Ned Perkins stopped. A short lane led up to the steward's lodgings.

"You and me shall take Plover's Lake," he said, pointing to Adam Smith, a scrawny youth. "The rest of you go on to the threshing barn and we'll catch you up."

So the men parted ways and Perkins and Smith started off on the five-minute walk to the lake. The path soon became uneven, but was still passable, and it was not long before they were standing on the reed-fringed bank. The stretch of water was long and thin, narrowing to just a few feet in the middle, and curving on the eastern shore. Lord Crick had built a small fishing lodge there, with a jetty jutting out over the water, although it had not been used since his death. Without sunlight, and no wind, the lake looked like a flat piece of slate bedded in among the withered irises and bulrushes. Two geese bolted out of the reeds and cackled off into the fog. A moorhen lay dead in its unkempt nest.

Ned Perkins cupped his grubby hands around his mouth and shouted. "Helloooo! Hellooo!" His rough voice, like the crack of a flintlock, sent another two geese scudding to the far shore. On the other side of the water he could see Adam Smith, using his staff like a scythe, swishing through the head-high weeds. They would soon meet up at the fishing lodge as planned. He could see it clearly now; a strangely ornate thatched building, sitting on the water's edge. He remembered when it used to be filled with the late lord's friends from London during the trout season. Now, however, it looked oddly forlorn, its roof greened over and melding in with the surrounding reeds that were encroaching upon it, inch by inch.

He scanned the shoreline. There was nothing there. He would call to Smith and tell him not to bother to beat a path all the way 'round to the lodge. He was just about to signal to him to return the way he had come when he saw something in the shallows by the jetty. Could it be a sack floating? No, it was plum-colored, voluminous. His mouth went dry as he edged closer. It was then that he saw the red hair swirling on the surface, the long tresses of a woman, and he knew he had found Lady Thorndike.

Chapter 25

Thomas arrived on the scene in under an hour. Perkins and Smith had dragged the body from the water and the younger man had run to call help. The doctor rode over to the lake on horseback after instructing Lovelock to bring a covered cart. He also sent word to Sir Theodisius, the Oxford coroner, who needed to be informed of the death. Lydia was given the unenviable task of telling Sir Henry.

Perkins sat a few feet away from the corpse on the bank, looking out onto the lake. The foreman looked as gray as the flat water.

"You have done well," Thomas reassured him.

The doctor could tell immediately that the woman in the plum-colored dress was indeed Lady Thorndike. She was lying face up. He recognized her striking features; those high cheekbones and the dimple at the center of her chin. Only now her rouged lips were blue and her skin as white as alabaster. Tiny nuggets of gravel pitted her nose and forehead and duckweed flecked her hair. Already the flies were buzzing around her.

Thomas's mind flashed back to the face of Agnes Appleton. She had shared a similar fate in London only two days before. He recalled how a thin line of foam had laced her lips, but on Lady Thorndike's face there was nothing, save for a fly that had landed on her cheek. Bending low he placed his palms on her chest and pressed hard. Nothing. No liquid spurted out from her mouth. Thomas tried again, but with the same result. He straightened himself.

"Where exactly did you find her?" he asked Perkins.

The foreman pointed to the spot, just by the jetty. "There, sir," he said.

Thomas walked over to inspect the area more closely. One or two of the timbers on the jetty were rotting away. Some had splintered and cracked. It certainly did not look safe enough to stand on.

"Her ladyship must have slipped and fallen off," ventured Perkins, cocking his head toward the lake.

Thomas did not reply. He was too preoccupied. Up until last month the sun had been so hot that much of the water had evaporated, leaving the level considerably lower than usual. He could tell from the exposed algae coating the gravel like green slime that the lake was only half full. There were signs on the piers of the jetty, too, where weed clung tenaciously to the wood way above the water line.

"She was facedown?" The gravel embedded in her face told him as much.

Perkins shivered at the recollection. "Yes, sir."

"And how deep was the water, would you say?"

The foreman shrugged. "Less than six inches, sir."

Thomas agreed that the lake at this point was, indeed, shallow. He had heard of grown men drowning in a few inches of water, but they had either been unconscious at the time or their faces had been held down until they could no longer breathe. There was, of course, another and, in his opinion, more likely alternative, but he would need to conduct a postmortem to prove that theory.

Arriving back at Boughton Hall an hour later Thomas found Lydia seated with Sir Henry in the drawing room. She sprang to her feet as soon as he walked in, relieved that he could share the burden of a husband's grief. Sir Henry himself remained seated, his heart condition making it difficult for him to stand.

"Silkstone," he said gruffly. Thomas recalled the last time he had seen him was after the unfortunate incident with his wife.

"Yes, sir," he said, bowing. "Please accept my condolences."

The old man huffed. "Told her maid she was going for a walk. She must've lost her way in the fog and fallen." His dry lips trembled and Lydia reached out to him in a gesture of comfort.

Thomas nodded, managing to keep his features expressionless. If Sir Henry thought his wife had ventured out in the fog simply to go for a walk, then he was even more deluded than he had feared.

At that moment Howard appeared and announced the arrival of the Oxfordshire coroner. Sir Theodisius Pettigrew lumbered grim-faced into the drawing room and went straight over to Sir Henry, his flabby hand extended.

"My dear fellow, this is terrible news," he lamented. "Terrible news. How did it happen?"

Sir Henry lifted his head slowly. "She told her maid she was going for a walk," he repeated. "A walk, in this fog!" He was half laughing as he spoke. "She must have wandered by the lake and lost her footing."

Sir Theodisius settled his large backside onto a chaise longue.

"A tragic accident," he said.

"Indeed," agreed Sir Henry, nodding his bewigged head, his eyes moistening as he spoke.

Switching 'round to Thomas, who had just joined him on the seat, the coroner whispered: "Has he formally identified her yet?" The young doctor shook his head. It was an unpleasant duty that needed to be performed and Sir Theodisius took the lead.

Lydia had thoughtfully ordered Lady Thorndike's body to be laid on a bed in one of the guest rooms upstairs, so that when her husband saw her, it appeared she was merely sleeping. Her hair had been combed, her face washed, and her dress smoothed. Her white hands were clasped on her breast, as if in prayer.

Sir Henry heaved himself upstairs with difficulty and gazed

on his wife's face for the last time. "Yes, that is my Julia." He nodded wistfully.

Sir Theodisius put his hand on his friend's shoulder. "Very well," he said. "You are free to make the funeral arrangements."

Thomas, however, cleared his throat and caught the coroner's eye. He needed a private word.

"I shall leave you alone for a few moments," Sir Theodisius said to the new widower.

Joining Thomas by the door, the coroner pulled an irritated face. "What is it now, Silkstone?" he asked. "Don't tell me you suspect her death wasn't an accident."

Thomas looked apologetic. "I cannot be certain, sir," he replied.

The coroner sighed heavily and rolled his eyes. It was almost time for luncheon and his stomach was beginning to growl, putting him in an irritable mood. "So, you want to perform a postmortem?"

The young doctor nodded. "I am not convinced that her ladyship's death was accidental."

Sir Theodisius arched a brow. "The woman went for a walk, lost her way in this cursed fog, fell into the lake and drowned. End of story, Silkstone."

From the look on the doctor's face, however, the coroner could tell he remained unconvinced. "So, if she didn't drown . . ." He stopped abruptly in mid sentence, suddenly reminded of Thomas's habit of expounding scientific theories that were beyond the ken of most mortals. "Oh, very well. You have my permission to examine the corpse," he said grudgingly. "But put it back as you found it, mind. I do not wish to upset Sir Henry any more than we have to."

Chapter 26

The country residence of Sir Montagu Malthus lay three miles south of Banbury. Built around forty years before, Draycott House was a fine example of early Georgian architecture and had been home to the landowner and lawyer for almost all that time. It had served him and his household well over the years, although had he known that his wife, who had died a decade before, would be without issue, he might have chosen somewhere a little more intimate.

He very often found himself rattling around in rooms that should have been filled with warmth and laughter, or strolling in the grounds without another soul in sight. Now and again he was enveloped by a desperate loneliness. So many of his friends had passed on; Richard Crick, then dear Felicity two years ago. He was himself in his dotage and was beginning to feel the lack of progeny most cruelly. Lydia Farrell was the nearest he had to a family and it pained him to see her making the same mess of her young life that her brother, his godson Edward, had before her. That was why he had sent his notary on a quest.

It had been so remarkably fortuitous, he told himself. One might even say a sign. He had been sitting at Lydia's bedside as she lay as still as a statue in the depths of unconsciousness a few weeks before. Her attempt to take her own life had, thankfully, backfired, and so there she was in her bed at Boughton, in a coffin of her own making; not dead, but then not quite alive. She would go for hours without a single movement or a word passing her beautiful lips and then suddenly, one afternoon, she began to mumble. Her eyes remained closed, but her mind was obviously active. At first she made odd croaking sounds, but they soon grew louder. It was then that her parched lips formed intelligible sounds and her face screwed itself up in terror. "No! No!" she had cried. "My baby!"

Leaning forward, Sir Montagu had stilled her flailing arms. "Hush, my dear. All is well," he soothed. A few seconds later her breathing had steadied and she appeared to fall, once more, into a deep slumber. But the seed had been sown. "A baby," he repeated softly. He recalled he had been helping Lydia go through her late husband's papers shortly after his death. There had been boxes and folders and cases full of ledgers and receipts and bills. Lydia's grief had been so great that her mind was not fully on the task in hand. That was why he had said nothing when he had come across some invoices from a wet nurse in Hungerford for the upkeep of a child by the name of Richard Farrell.

Putting together this written evidence and Lydia's own, albeit involuntary, outburst, he had begun making inquiries the previous month. Could it really be that Boughton had a legitimate heir after all? His own visit prior to her ridiculous suicide attempt had shown her to be unwilling to remarry a suitable peer and produce children. He suspected that she was still besotted with that upstart from the Colonies. But now, no matter. He had received word from the notary, a reliable man, if a little slow in some respects, that his mission had been accomplished. The child was in his custody and would be arriving at Draycott House later on that day.

Such news had certainly put a spring in Sir Montagu's step. He had ordered the principal guest room to be made ready. Pastries and sweetmeats were to be baked and even a pony and trap to be put at the young man's disposal. Yes, it would be wonderful to have some young blood coursing 'round Draycott for the time being. Until, that is, Lydia acceded to his demands.

* * *

The body of Lady Julia Thorndike lay on the marble slab in the game larder ready to be examined. A sickly sweet smell wafted around the corpse and Thomas lit a pipe to mask it as he worked. He had already divested her and covered her in a thin white sheet. Now he rolled up the sides to inspect her feet and hands. Taking her cold fingers, he turned them over so that he could see her palms. They were wrinkled, like parchment. The skin on her feet, too, was creased. Dozens of deep furrows lined the soles and between her toes. She had been in the water for at least two days, he told himself.

Next he pressed down on her chest once more, keeping his eyes on her mouth. Just as before, no liquid dribbled from her lips. If she had drowned, then foam would have appeared. He had seen it so many times before. If victims were alive when they went into the water, as Agnes Appleton had been, then their lungs and, indeed, their whole respiratory passage would be filled with foam— the result of a great churning motion that occurs within the chest cavity when water mixes with mucus before the victim is starved of oxygen. Thomas saw for himself there was none here. He did not even have to use his scalpel to determine that Lady Thorndike had almost certainly not drowned.

Thomas drew heavily on his pipe and straightened his aching back. He knew he did not have long to examine the body. Sir Henry did not even know that he was conducting a postmortem and would be engaging an undertaker within the next few hours. He looked at Lady Thorndike's hands once more and in particular her fingernails. They were completely clean. No struggle was indicated. There were no deposits of gravel or mud from the pond bottom. He would have to start from the top: the head.

Resting his pipe on a nearby stone shelf, he began to feel the skull. His fingers raked through the still-damp hair to the temples, then the crown, but he could feel nothing untoward. It was only when he lifted up the cranium and examined the smooth curve of the occipital lobe that he began to suspect. Quickly he turned Lady Thorndike over onto her face to take a closer look.

Using a comb to part her thick red hair, he could see a deep livid bruise, almost as long as a man's hand, covering the lower half of the cranium. Reaching for a pair of scissors from his bag, he cut away the hair near the scalp, then taking his magnifying glass he studied it more carefully. The contusion was, indeed, long, and there was a small cut of less than an inch. Nevertheless the area was swollen, with a great bulge of fluid protesting underneath.

There was something more, too. He peered at the wound more closely. There were two or three flakes of organic material dotted in the hair. Reaching for his tweezers, he teased them out, one by one, dropping them into a phial. Holding the glass tube up to the light, he examined the contents closely. They were leaves of some kind and definitely not duckweed from the pond. He sniffed at them. There was no perfume. Two days in the water had put paid to any scent they may once have had.

His own back was already aching and he stepped away from the table to straighten his spine for a moment. The movement made the candle by the corpse flicker and as it did, the shaft of light caught something reflective. Thomas reached for his magnifier and, leaning over, inspected the wound once more. And there it was: a tiny flake of shiny material embedded deep in the tissue. Grasping his tweezers he plucked it out and held it to a flame. A piece of glass? A shard of mirror? He dropped the fragment into another phial and stood away from the slab. Picking up his pipe, he sucked on it once more. Lady Thorndike had, he concluded, been hit on the head with a blunt object from behind, causing a swelling of the brain. She had, most definitely and irrefutably, been murdered.

Thomas told Lydia the disturbing news as she sat in the study, going over the accounts.

"Lady Thorndike did not drown."

"Then what . . . ?"

"She was hit on the head from behind before she either fell or was dragged into the water."

Lydia put down her pen. "Murder?"

"I need to return to the lake to look for the weapon that was used," he told her, turning for the door.

She stood up suddenly. "No, wait," she said. "Let me come with you."

Thomas shook his head. "The fog still lingers, my love. It is not safe to be outdoors for long." But she set her gaze on him, and he could tell from her determined expression she would not take no for an answer.

They took the dogcart down to the waterside and arrived just as a fiery sun began to set behind the haze. Thomas helped Lydia climb down and saw to it that she covered her mouth with her shawl. He watched her as she picked her way through the reeds over to the shore, rustling as she went. She paused to gaze out over the water.

"We had happy times in this place," she told him, her voice muffled. "My brother and I used to picnic on these shores when we were children. There was a boat here, once. We used to row to the other side." Thomas joined her and put his arm around her. "It used to be moored up by the jetty," she went on, pointing over to the rickety landing stage.

"What happened?" he asked.

"To the boat?"

He put his face close to hers. "To everything." He was looking at the dilapidated fishing lodge, with its moldy thatch.

She shrugged. "Papa died and Edward wasn't ready for the responsibility."

He slipped his hand in hers and together they began to walk toward the lodge, skirting the water's edge.

"Where did they find Lady Thorndike?" she asked as they approached the jetty.

"Just here," said Thomas, stopping suddenly. He dropped his gaze and began scanning the ground. The sand at the lip of the lake was dry and pitted with gravel and larger pebbles. Lydia looked down, too, but walked on ahead slightly. Thomas noticed she left small footprints in her wake. Now he began scanning more intently. There could still be signs of activity on the shore. There had been no rain for two weeks. Somewhere, in among this patchwork of reeds and water flags, there must be tracks, impressions, or some other clue.

They remained looking intently around the rim of the lake for several minutes, but found nothing. Thomas's back started to ache again and he straightened himself. As he did so, he looked to the opposite shore. A handsome house stood squarely on the other side, its roof swathed in the fog.

"Who lives there?" he asked Lydia.

"Mr. Lawson," she replied, her eyes meeting his.

The same thought darted across both their minds, but they said nothing and turned to go back to the hall.

Chapter 27

"'Tis a terrible state of affairs, Dr. Silkstone, and 'tis growing worse by the day." Dr. Felix Fairweather was not a man prone to exaggeration. He was inclined to arrogance and pomposity, like most of the other medical men Thomas had encountered in England, but a scaremonger he was not.

The country physician was sitting in the drawing room at Boughton Hall drinking tea. He had requested an urgent meeting to discuss the awful situation in Brandwick and the surrounding villages. The fog was claiming more lives each day. True, it had lifted a little over the past week, but the sulfurous stench remained. It was still not safe to venture outside without protection for any length of time.

"I have seen a dozen of my patients die this week alone, Dr. Silkstone," said Fairweather, looking unusually vulnerable. "They are running out of room in the graveyard at St. Swithin's."

Lydia intervened. "But what can we do, doctor? As long as the fog remains, people will die." There was a note of hopelessness in her voice.

Thomas had been listening intently to the doctor's description of his patients' symptoms, but had said very little. Instead he had been looking out of the window, surveying the miserable, murky vista beyond. The sky remained pregnant, loaded with gray flakes; the hills deadened by the fog. Finally he spoke.

"From what you say, sir, it seems that the young and the old are most affected. The fog obviously attacks the respiratory system and those who are already weak are the most vulnerable. Is this so?"

The doctor nodded. "I would say that was a fair summary, yes."

Thomas turned to face them. "If that is the case, then perhaps we could put those most at risk in a place of safety."

Both the older doctor and Lydia looked puzzled. "I am not sure I follow you, sir," said Fairweather.

The young anatomist lifted his hand in thought. "What if we could isolate them in a place where the fog could not reach?"

Fairweather contemplated the proposition. "That would obviously be ideal, but surely no such place exists in this area."

"Yes, it does!" interrupted Lydia. Her eyes gleamed with excitement. "I know of such a place." Both men switched their gaze on her. "The caves at West Wycombe," she said emphatically.

"You mean the Hellfire Caves?" queried Thomas, turning the thought over in his head.

"They have not been used for twenty years, but surely 'tis an idea worth exploring?" insisted Lydia.

Dr. Fairweather remained a little confused. "So you would transport the sick and the vulnerable to the Hellfire Caves until the fog lifts?" he asked Lydia incredulously.

Thomas fixed him with a stern look. To the country doctor they were still associated with the debauchery and wild gatherings of the Hellfire Club that were often held there when Sir Francis Dashwood was alive. "Do you have a better idea?"

Fairweather became flustered. "Well no, but I . . . 'tis a great undertaking, Dr. Silkstone."

"But what alternative is there?" asked Lydia. "As you said, more and more people are dying each day. Can we just sit back and do nothing?"

Fairweather shrugged. "No. No, I suppose we cannot," he replied.

Thomas nodded. "That is settled, then. Her ladyship will contact Sir John and, if he agrees, we will inspect the caves for suitability."

"And then what?" The country doctor was clearly uneasy.

"Then we make arrangements to transport the sick to the caves. I will need a list of all your patients who are to be moved."

What was proposed was a monumental task; to organize and execute what was effectively an evacuation and the establishment of a field hospital was no mean feat. Thomas had heard of it being done in wartime, most recently after the Battle of Trenton on the Delaware, but this, this was unheard of. He felt his stomach knot at the enormity of the task.

"Can you let me have your list by tomorrow, sir?" he said to Fairweather.

The doctor sighed. "Very well," he replied, almost sullenly. He drained his teacup and rose. Then, bowing to Lydia, he said, "I wish you good fortune in your endeavors, your ladyship." Thomas detected a distinct note of skepticism in his voice.

Lydia was about to ring for Howard to show Dr. Fairweather to the door when Thomas recalled another weighty matter that needed to be discussed. Somehow, word was out that Lady Thorndike had been murdered and tongues were already wagging in the village. Some people thought she had just deserts, going out into the fog unescorted. What did she expect? Did she not know there were thieves and vagabonds abroad who'd slit your throat as soon as look at you? Others were more specific. That knife-grinder with the red scarf around his head looked shifty, they said. He had been stirring up trouble among the village men. Where was he? Had anyone seen him since the body was found? So the gossip circulated and the fog became not just responsible for killing the vulnerable with its poison, but contributing to the murder of anyone foolish enough to venture out in it, too.

"One more thing, sir," said Thomas, as he escorted the doctor to the door. "Lady Thorndike." He whispered her name while Lydia remained seated.

Fairweather bowed his head reverentially. "Ah yes, shocking affair."

"Yes, indeed," he acknowledged. "Did her ladyship have any enemies that you know of?"

The doctor raised an eyebrow. "A strange question, Dr. Silk-stone," he replied.

"You were her physician, were you not? I just thought . . ."

"I was indeed her physician," replied Fairweather, lowering his voice, so that Lydia could not hear. "And I must tell you"—he leaned closer, conspiratorially—"it would be difficult to find any friends other than of the male sex."

Thomas took his meaning. "I thought as much." He nodded. "Thank you, doctor."

It had been four weeks since she lost her husband and Susannah Kidd was, at last, feeling a little stronger. She no longer sat for hours in her chair by the empty hearth remembering and regretting. Her appetite was slowly returning and she had even ventured into Brandwick to buy what few provisions she could. Lady Lydia had assured her that there was no danger she would lose the cottage and her skills as a seamstress were still in demand.

Even though the sun had not yet set, the light was so poor that she needed to sew by the light of a candle. That evening she was sitting working on yet another shroud when she heard a tap on the window. Startled, she looked up. Standing there, his nut-brown face pressed against the glass, was the knife-grinder. Quickly she rose, quivering with the shock of seeing her unexpected visitor, and hurried over to the door and opened it.

"What do you think you are doing?" she scolded, her palm pressed flat on her chest. "Gave me a real fright, you did."

The traveler smiled a beguiling smile, showing his white teeth. Under his arm he carried his bindle. "Forgive me, pretty lady," he said, tilting his head. Then, looking beyond her, into the cottage, he asked, "Is your husband in?"

She took a deep breath and steeled herself to utter the dreaded words. "My husband is dead," she told him.

The knife-grinder's smile disappeared. "The fog?" She nodded. "I am sorry for your loss." Another nod was followed by an awkward silence. "So you are alone now?" he ventured.

Susannah snorted in disbelief. "You've a cheek!" she cried

and she began to shut the door in the knife-grinder's face, but he thrust his boot over the threshold, blocking it.

"I mean no harm," he said, gesturing with his hands. "This fog is killing me, too. I've been sleeping in barns and ditches since it came. Please, will you let me in?" He forced a cough, slapped his chest, then smiled at her.

For a moment she studied him. His days and nights out in this fog were taking their toll, she could tell that. His eyes were red and watery and his skin was much paler than before. Was she not a Christian woman? She would show him charity in these straitened times.

"Very well," she said, relenting. "You can sleep on the floor in here," she told him, opening wide the door and letting him pass.

"I'm beholden to you, mistress," he said, adding: "I knew you had a heart of gold the moment I set eyes on you."

The boy was much smaller than he anticipated. He looked no more than four, even though Sir Montagu knew him to be six years of age. He stumbled down the carriage steps and had to be helped up by the notary. But he was thin, too. So painfully thin. And how like his mother he was. No mistaking there: the tousled brown curls; the large doe-like eyes. The late earl would have been proud to see his grandson. But what was wrong with his arm? It dangled limply at his side. Surely the child was not a cripple? Sir Montagu's hooded eyes narrowed even more as he stood on the steps of Draycott House, preparing to meet the boy. Surely not a cripple? It had not been easy tracking down this feral child, first in Hungerford, then in the quagmire of London, but securing the future of Boughton would be worth it, although by the looks of things, the boy would need careful handling.

Holding the notary's hand, the child began to climb up to meet the black-garbed man who stood ahead of him on the steps. Sir Montagu eyed him intently, like a hawk would a mouse. The boy stopped, then shuffled awkwardly, still clutching the notary's hand.

Finally Sir Montagu spoke. "So, this is Boughton's heir?"

The notary wore a smug look. "Indeed, sir. This is Richard Farrell."

The lawyer bent down, bowing his head so that it seemed to shrink into his shoulders. He extended a bony hand. The child pulled back, obviously afraid, but the notary grabbed his scrawny shoulders.

"This is Sir Montagu Malthus. You will be staying with him for a while," he explained, pushing the boy forward.

Again Sir Montagu proffered his hand. This time the child stretched out spindly fingers. His nails were black with grime, and he seemed unsure as to what he should do next. He did not take his hand, much to the lawyer's amusement. "Ha," he snorted. "He has no manners, Fothergill. We shall have to teach him some."

The notary chuckled. "Indeed, sir."

"Come," said Sir Montagu, turning his great black frame toward the front entrance. "You must be hungry, young man. We shall eat and then we shall talk. There is so much you need to know."

Chapter 28

Gabriel Lawson was a worried man. At first light he had ridden out to the farthest acreages and was returning his horse to the stables. What he had seen had not been pretty. The few crops that had not been scorched by the rain or poisoned by the fog were languishing in the fields with no one to harvest them. He had lost three more workers that week and six more had been taken ill, despite following the American doctor's orders. To add to his woes, the men who could work were afraid to. They were reluctant to leave their homes and those who would were surly in their manner. They were easy prey for Joshua Pike and his brand of politics.

Thankfully since he had warned him off the estate a few days ago there had been no sign of the troublemaker. Perhaps he had gone to ground, but somehow he doubted it. He pictured his sullen face, the set of his jaw. There was a contempt for authority in his manner that made him think that he had not seen the last of Joshua Pike.

There was talk, too. He had heard the men when they gathered for their small beer in the threshing barn. One of them sowed the seed; perhaps the knife-grinder had killed Lady Thorndike. Perhaps he had seen her by the lake and tried to take advantage of her. And so the rumors had taken root. He did nothing to quell them. In fact he helped fan the flames. It diverted attention away from him. If anyone suspected that he and Lady Thorndike had been lovers, then the law would, no doubt, be upon him.

He recalled, too, an incident on the evening that Julia had arranged to come to his house. She planned to arrive in secret. She said it would be an amusing diversion for her, so bored was she in the fog. When she was late, he went out to the path. It was then he noticed movement in the reeds. Someone was there. A man. But in the mist, he had not been able to make out any discernible features. He had called to him. He did not know if he had been heard, but within a few seconds the figure had disappeared down the track. After that he had thought little of it. But now, thinking on it again, perhaps he had seen the murderer. Could Joshua Pike have been the man he saw by the lake that evening? As much as he disliked him for his science and the hold he had over Lady Lydia, he would mention it to Dr. Silkstone the next time he saw him.

Returning to the stableyard, he found Will Lovelock stoking the coals of the brazier. The boy hurried over to him to help him dismount. Lawson noted that Will was pale and that he tried to stifle his coughs as he held his horse by the bridle. Would the boy be next? the steward wondered. He had already been ill once and survived, but he was still vulnerable.

"Take the saddle with you, then you can get on with your duties," said Lawson, easing himself down from the horse. "I'll take care of myself."

The boy nodded his carrot-colored head. "Yes, sir," he replied, unbuckling the girth strap. He pulled the saddle off, but the exertion only made him cough even more, and he turned toward the tack room, struggling with the weight of his load.

The yard was now deserted and Lawson patted his horse and looped the reins over her head.

"Come on, girl," he said, leading her into the stable and along to her stall at the farthest end of the block. Her hooves clattered along the cobbles and her tail swished at the flies that droned all around. She bellowed long and low through her nostrils. Another horse in a nearby stall let out a loud whinny, too. The sound masked the footsteps of someone approaching. Gabriel Lawson did not hear anything behind him until it was too late. A few seconds later, all was quiet once more.

Susannah Kidd was busy draping her washing on the bushes and trees that surrounded her cottage. With no sun and barely any breeze, she knew it was an almost futile task. The stench in the air would surely impregnate the shirts and smocks and her petticoat and shift. She sniffed. What was that? A new smell. More like ordinary smoke from a chimney or a bonfire. She shrugged. It mattered not. In the end smoke was smoke and grime was grime, and Amos's clothes had needed to be washed before she sold them at market. As for her own undergarments, she had not washed them for so long that there were lice in the seams. She reached once more into her basket and began singing a lament as she hung her dead husband's breeches on a branch.

She was so engaged in her task that she did not hear the Reverend Lightfoot approach in his dogcart. He parked it at the front of the cottage and walked through the gate 'round to the back, where he stood for a moment.

It had been three weeks since he had last seen her. He had tried to banish her from his thoughts, but he had failed. There was something he found almost mesmerizing in the way she moved. The fluidity of her actions, the sweep of her arms, the curve of her neck, and how she tilted her head slightly as she sang her sad song, all thrilled and disgusted him in equal measure.

Her pannier emptied of laundry, she picked it up and turned 'round. It was then that she saw him, standing, watching. She let out a muffled little yelp—not a cry, just an odd sound that signified surprise.

"Reverend Lightfoot!" she exclaimed. "I did not hear you."

The vicar tipped his wide-brimmed hat. "I did not mean to startle you, Mistress Kidd," he said, walking toward her, his cane in his hand. "I was just passing and thought I would see how you fared."

She looked at him with her almond-shaped eyes. Wisps of blond hair had escaped from beneath her cap. Her complexion was smooth and glowing. "I am as well as I can be, sir," she said, the pannier wedged on her hip.

The last time he had seen her in his study, she had appeared strained and troubled. Now, however, she seemed more at ease. Her step was lighter; her demeanor less somber.

"That is good," he said. "You look well, despite this wretched fog that afflicts us all."

There was an awkward pause as he waited for an invitation into her cottage, but it was not forthcoming. She shifted her legs under the weight of the basket, yet still he did not take his leave.

Her lips are the color of raspberries, he thought. He stretched his mouth into a smile. How could he tell her that he was the one who was lonely and lost? He was the one who should be dispensing wisdom and charity and God's love, but his basket was empty, too. Without Margaret he had nothing; was nothing. And all he did now, day after day, was commit people to their graves.

"I came to see how you fared in the light of Lady Thorndike's unfortunate fate," he told her finally.

"Lady Thorndike?"

The vicar nodded. "You have not heard?"

"I heard she had been taken, sir," she replied. The fog seemed not to care to look at the cut of a man's clothes before it struck, she thought to herself.

But the clergyman lifted his eyes heavenward. "So you did not hear they are saying she was murdered?"

Susannah's hand flew up to her neck in surprise. She had caught idle snatches of gossip in Brandwick, but had not tarried to talk.

"Found by the lake, she was. This was her reward for venturing out in the fog," he told her, adding sagely, "We live in dark and dangerous times. You must keep your door bolted."

She noted his warning with a nod. "Indeed I shall, sir," she replied emphatically. A murderer, she thought to herself. How glad she was of the knife-grinder's presence in her home. He would see to it that she was safe.

There was another awkward pause before the vicar waved

his cane nonchalantly. "I shall bid you good day, then, Mistress Kidd," he said finally.

She nodded. "Good day, sir."

He turned and strode purposefully toward the dogcart. Bothered by the flies, the pony was lifting its legs and swishing its tail in a strange dance. He glanced back to see her gazing at him serenely as he mounted the seat. On reflection it was a relief that she had not invited him inside, he told himself. She had not been able to tempt him. He tugged on the reins and his pony moved off, back toward St. Swithin's and yet another burial.

Chapter 29

Thomas and Lydia were in the library, making plans to transport the sick and elderly to the caves. They had outlined their proposal in a letter to Sir John only the day before and he had responded immediately. He had also lost ten men in as many days and was anxious to do everything in his power to save anyone he could.

Despite the fact that the caves had not been used since Sir Francis Dashwood's death, they were still safe and the temperature inside was ambient. He could supply blankets, food, and drink. There was much to discuss regarding the organization of patients. Lydia was animated. Thomas had rarely seen her so energized. She had looked at the records of all those living in the tithe cottages on the estate and had drawn up a list of twenty-three. Some Thomas had treated in the past so he was familiar with their medical complications; others, who Lydia assured him were particularly vulnerable, were new to him.

"You have worked well," Thomas told her.

She gave a little shrug and sighed. "I only wish I could do more. These are just the people at Boughton," she said, waving her hand at the list. Then, as if a kernel of an idea had suddenly planted itself in her mind, she said after a moment: "I *will* do more."

Thomas perched on the desk, facing her. "What do you mean?"

She looked at him with bright eyes. "I want to look after the patients who go into the caves."

At first Thomas thought she was playing with him and smiled, but she returned a serious enough look and he soon realized his mistake.

"I do not jest," she told him firmly. Seeing the sudden ardor in her eyes, he did not doubt it. "I want to help nurse them. If I cannot care for my son, at least let me care for others."

Thomas understood he had touched a raw nerve. She was still smarting from the disappointment of their London trip. She had said little, but he knew there was a simmering sorrow inside her. He took her hands in his. They were so small and delicate and clean. Those hands had never scrubbed steps, nor laid fires. Then he thought of the caves. They may offer a refuge to those with physical weaknesses, but surely no one would spend their days in the sunless confines there through choice?

"It will be dark. Cold."

Lydia's look hardened. "But you will need people to help care for the sick, women with commitment and compassion."

"Women like you?"

Lydia sensed victory. "Until the poisonous clouds lift, those tunnels and caverns are probably safer than anywhere else in the fog's clutches," she persisted.

The doctor shook his head, then smiled in his defeat. "You will make a fine nurse," he said and he kissed her fingers.

"Yes," she said triumphantly. "I will."

Thomas walked over to the window. The leaden sky remained unchanged and the tops of the hills were still smudges in the distance. But out of the corner of his eye he could see something moving. He turned his head to the left and adjusted his gaze to the outbuildings a few yards away. A column of gray smoke was rising straight up into the still air. It was too thick and too near to be a bonfire. Rushing over to the spiral staircase that led to the upper floor of the library, he climbed up for a better view.

"What is it?" urged Lydia, rising from the desk. "What have you seen?"

Looking out of the top window Thomas surveyed the slate gray rooftops of the granary and the dairy and the game larder. The smoke was darker now. And then he saw the flames.

"The stables are on fire!" he cried.

Running down the stairs he called to Lydia. "Raise the alarm. I must hurry."

As soon as he opened the back door he could hear the bellowing of the horses. The air smelled different; no longer of rotten eggs but of burning timber and straw. He continued to run. Someone rang the fire bell. He was joined by others—Howard and Hannah Lovelock. People began to shout. He could hear the crackle of the flames now. One of the stable lads was trying to steady a terrified mare as she reared and bucked in the yard.

Through the haze of smoke, he could make out Will Lovelock, a beater in his hand, frantically pounding away at a flaming hay bale inside the stable. He rushed in and looked around. Jacob Lovelock was struggling with another terrified horse, trying to throw a sack over its head so that he could lead it to safety.

Flames were licking at the beams overhead. "Get out of there, Lovelock!" screamed Thomas, but still he struggled with the horse until, a second later, he had the sack over its head and tried to drag her out of the door. Thomas grabbed the bridle, pulling frantically, and the mare began to move.

The heat was starting to sting his hands and face. He heard a loud crack and looked up. Overhead the flames had caught hold of a rafter and a flaming shard of wood broke off and fell two or three feet away. The horse jerked, but Thomas kept a firm hold until a moment later both he and Lovelock were out in the yard.

By now four or five men had formed a human chain and were passing buckets of water from the yard pump. Soon they managed to get the fire under control. The flames spluttered and hissed like retreating snakes and in less than half an hour only smoking embers remained.

Thomas drew the back of his hand across his forehead. His face was covered with smuts and his mouth felt as though it was lined with ash. The men gathered around him like soldiers waiting for orders. They, too, were caked in soot and their hair was gray with ash.

"Is everyone accounted for?" asked Thomas. The men glanced around, their eyes red and streaming. Their looks darted from one to another, each making mental notes. It was Jacob Lovelock who was the first to realize.

"Mr. Lawson is not here, Dr. Silkstone."

"Does anyone know where Mr. Lawson is?" asked Thomas. There were garbled voices and muted grunts until Will Lovelock stepped forward.

"I saw him, sir. He was in there earlier." The boy pointed a scrawny finger at the blackened building behind him. "But I shouted out as soon as I saw the smoke and I couldn't see him, sir. There was no one in there, I swear."

Thomas sighed with relief. "Thank God for that. And the horses are safe?"

"Yes, sir," chorused two of the men.

"Then we must be grateful," he said, turning toward the stable door. A beam, as black as coal, had fallen across the threshold and he stepped over it to inspect the damage. The flames had licked at some of the nearest stalls, but as far as he could tell, the furthest ones had escaped relatively unscathed. He looked up at the ceiling. Some of the blackened roof timbers had cracked and splintered and would need replacing, but they seemed sound enough for the time being. He stepped over a pile of charred wood, picking his way toward the far end, inspecting each stall as he went.

Quick thinking on the part of Will Lovelock and his father meant that the damage was far less severe than he feared. Metal bars had blistered and buckled and beams and joists needed repairing, but with the help of a joiner and a farrier, the stable could be serviceable again within the week. Yet he wondered how the fire had started. He glanced into the yard at the brazier, a few feet away. It was glowing white; the coals crumbling and flaky. A spark must have flared and ignited the tinder-dry hay. In fact everything was so parched that anything in this intense heat could have sparked the blaze, he told himself.

Having reached the penultimate stall Thomas was satisfied that the block was empty. He was just about to turn back to the door when he saw what looked like the heel of a leather boot. A wooden crate, blackened but not burned, stood in his way. He kicked it to one side and moved forward. There, lying facedown in the hay, was a man. Reaching down, he felt his neck for a pulse. There was none. It was then that he turned the body over to confirm what he feared. It was Gabriel Lawson.

They carried the corpse to the game larder and laid it on the slab. Lawson's coat was dirty with cinders and ash, but mercifully the fire had not touched him. In medieval times in Europe, Thomas had read that friends of condemned heretics used to bribe the executioner to place a sticky brick of poison in among the faggots near the heels. When ignited, deadly fumes were released that killed on inhalation, saving the prisoner the terror of the fire. Thankfully, it seemed that Lawson had been spared the flames. Smoke inhalation must have killed him, thought Thomas. He would have breathed in fumes which would have caused pulmonary irritation and swelling. His suffering would have been short-lived.

Word would be sent to Sir Theodisius, but he did not anticipate his coming. The Oxfordshire coroner had informed the magistrate of Thomas's findings on Lady Thorndike. The steward's death, however, appeared much more straightforward. The fog had indirectly claimed another victim. There was no need for an autopsy. Thomas would simply give the body a cursory examination then release it for burial.

In the undignified surroundings of the game larder, Thomas stood over Lawson's corpse. He imagined his trachea and bronchial tubes as black, sooty passages. The lungs, stripped of soothing mucus, would be raw and inflamed. Death would have been relatively quick; there would have been a degree of burning in the nostrils and mouth as Lawson gulped for air. This would have been followed by an intense pain in his chest as he struggled to breathe. However, such agony would have lasted only seconds and unconsciousness, due to asphyxiation and possibly poisoning, would have followed. He recalled an ancient form of execution whereby a criminal was shut in a bathing room with smoldering coals. He had not found Lawson an agreeable character, but he would never have wished this death on his worst enemy.

So, he would be spared the knife. Thomas would simply give him a superficial examination, beginning with the head. The unkempt curls were full of ash and soot. With his fingers he probed the skull underneath. The ridges of the temporal and parietal lobes seemed in order, but it was when he turned the corpse over, just as he had done with Lady Thorndike, that he found an anomaly. Once more, there was a large swelling on the occipital lobe. Thomas's heart began to race. He parted the hair. The skin was not broken, but there was a massive contusion. Lawson, it seemed, had been struck a blow to the back of his head.

Taking out his magnifying glass from its case, Thomas inspected the wound more closely. There they were again: those odd flakes around the wound. He retrieved one of them with his tweezers and looked at it closely under his glass. Could it be part of a desiccated leaf? he asked himself. He sniffed it and, to his amazement, he detected the faint whiff of rosemary.

Hurrying out into the yard, Thomas marched over to the burned-out stable. Climbing over the beam by the door he edged his way to the farthest stall once more, stepping over a metal pail and a leather nose bag. A number of tools hung on the end wall—hoof picks, rakes, brooms, and a long-handled shovel with a wide, flat blade. Any one of them could have been the murder weapon and now that they were all covered in a thin film of ash, there was no way he could be sure which, if any, was used to execute Lawson.

From one of the back doorways he heard a noise and looked up to see Lydia standing outside, huddled in her shawl, holding a corner of it over her mouth. She was surveying the devastation. Thomas called to her.

"You should not be here. 'Tis dangerous."

She took no notice and remained rooted to the spot, gazing all around at the blackened beams and charred roof timbers. He made his way back along the cobbles to join her. His eyes were smarting and his throat was dry.

"Lovelock told me about Mr. Lawson," she said, her voice catching in the gritty air.

Thomas climbed over the beam and back out into the yard. "Lovelock does not know the half of it," he muttered, his gaze directed to the stone cobbles.

Lydia frowned. "What is it, Thomas? What are you looking for?"

"This!" he cried, suddenly bending low and picking up a charred branch. What was left of it was about a foot long and was completely blackened at one end. "Now what do you suppose this oak branch was doing lying on the stable floor?" he asked.

She was growing impatient. "I have no idea," she snapped. "What is this all about?"

He lifted his eyes from the piece of wood, but remained holding it, almost triumphantly. "This," he croaked, "is what was used to start the fire. It was ignited in the brazier over there."

Lydia swallowed hard. "You mean to tell me that this fire was no accident? It was started deliberately?"

Thomas nodded slowly, allowing her to digest what she had just been told. "Then, Mr. Lawson . . ." Her voice trailed off.

"I am afraid we are dealing with not only an arsonist, but a murderer, too," said Thomas. "Mr. Lawson was hit from behind. It may not have been a fatal blow, but it rendered him unconscious and led to his death from smoke inhalation."

Just then a cart rattled into the yard carrying a pile of sacks. Three men jumped down. One carried an ax, the other two shovels. They headed toward the stable block door. Ned Perkins was among them. He tipped his hat to Lydia.

"Did Lawson have any enemies among the laborers?" asked Thomas as he watched two of the workers shift the beam that blocked the door. He was recalling the steward's account of the men's reluctance to work in the fields while the fog persisted.

Lydia shook her head. "He was not liked, but . . ." She broke off suddenly, remembering Lawson's words in the study about the troublemaker. Thomas was already ahead of her. She looked at him with wide eyes. "Joshua Pike," she said.

That night the storms began. Thomas had noted earlier in the day that the needle of the barometer had dropped. The air felt even more oppressive. The temperature had risen slightly and there was a moisture in the atmosphere that had not been present for many days.

The first low growl of thunder was heard shortly after eleven o'clock. It rumbled and rolled in the far distance somewhere toward Oxford and less than an hour later it unleashed its full fury on Boughton. The violence of the sudden crash set the house dogs barking and the cockerels crowing in the barnyard. Those in the household who had retired to their beds were woken and the maids who shared a room huddled close to each other, fearing the roof might cave in.

Thomas crept into Lydia's bedchamber, as he did most nights, to find her staring out of the window. She seemed transfixed by the storm, watching the intermittent forks of lightning zigzag across the black sky, illuminating the ground below. The claps of thunder were so loud the glass in the leaded panes rattled. He padded across the floor and put his arms around her waist. She settled her hands on his. Still gazing out she asked, "Could it be that the Day of Judgment is coming?" Her voice was calm.

Thomas shook his head. "No, of course not. 'Tis just a bad storm. It will pass and the world shall remain."

Lydia did not seem entirely reassured. "But the people are afraid," she replied. "Eliza says they are praying in the streets and some have even asked the Reverend Lightfoot to perform exorcisms. They think the devil is in our midst."

Outside the hail began pelting from the sky. Stones the size of musket shot hit the window hard and covered the ground within seconds. And still the thunder crashed overhead, only now it came every few seconds.

Lydia lifted his hand and pressed it to her cheek. "At least if the world does end," she whispered, "we shall die together."

*   *   *

Not a mile away, in Amos Kidd's cottage, another young woman was being kept awake by the violent storm. She tossed and turned in her bed for a while, then rose to stand at the window and watch the lightning tear across the heavens. A few seconds later, the bedroom door creaked open.

"Are you afeared?" a man's voice asked behind her.

She did not turn, but remained facing the window. "No," she replied softly. " 'Tis a wonderful show. Maybe 'tis like the firework displays in London I heard of."

The man sidled over to where she stood and, resting his chin on her shoulder, put his arms around her waist. She tensed and let out a short stab of sound, a convulsion of pleasure, not pain, before relaxing into his embrace. She knew that she would not be spending the rest of the night alone.

Chapter 30

It was the middle of the day, but the flaming torches cast eerie shadows on the walls. Lydia shivered and pulled her shawl around her; Thomas shot her a reassuring smile. They were standing just inside the magnificent Gothic entrance to West Wycombe Caves. Ahead of them lay a brick-lined tunnel leading to the caverns themselves, but all they could see was total darkness. Water dripped from the ceiling and lay in puddles every few feet. A drop landed on Thomas's face and he wiped it away.

Sir John Dashwood-King chuckled. "Sadly we can't simply replace any slates when this roof leaks," he joked. Taking a torch down from the wall sconce he turned to both Thomas and Lydia. "Are we ready for a tour?" His deep voice bounced off the rock.

Both of them nodded, although it was clear to Thomas that Lydia was a little nervous. No doubt her opinion was swayed by the tall tales of debauched masques and devil worship in Sir Francis Dashwood's day. There were even stories of a ghost. Thomas had long been familiar with the caves' reputation. Mr. Franklin had loved the whimsical nature of the subterranean labyrinth. His compatriot had still not replied to his letter. Nevertheless he was sure he would approve of the proposals to turn the caves into a refuge for the sick.

"We are indeed ready, sir," said Thomas. The three of them, accompanied by two servants who also carried flaming torches, began to walk slowly along the passageway.

The temperature was a little cooler than outside, but not uncomfortably so, and the air was undoubtedly fresher. For the first time in days Thomas found himself breathing deeply. The smell of damp suddenly became as sweet as new-mown hay. Lydia, too, inhaled deeply and with each breath her steps became less hesitant.

Within a few seconds they passed a small cave stacked with picks and hammers and crowbars and found themselves at the entrance to the first chamber. Oil lamps hung from hooks drilled into the rock and wax candles were stuck into some of the recesses on the walls. It was a small space, but Lydia saw its potential.

"We could store water and supplies here," she said to Thomas.

They carried on for a few yards down a straight passageway until the path forked. "This is the maze," said Sir John, leading the way. "Woe betide anyone who finds themselves in here without a light! Stay close now."

They all ducked down below a jagged outcrop and then straightened themselves on the other side. The passageway was much narrower here, and Lydia's skirts brushed against the rock, but it was nonetheless passable. There were fewer puddles, too. The corridor soon opened out into a huge chamber. As wide as a good-sized ballroom and higher than three men, its floor was level and smooth. A large hook hung from the ceiling from which a lamp could be suspended.

"This was called the Banqueting Hall," said Sir John, making a grand gesture with his arm. "I am assuming this is where you could put a good many patients."

Lydia turned full circle, looking at the cave from every angle. It was more or less circular in shape, about forty feet in diameter she guessed, and there were four niches in the rock where items could be stored or small cubicles created for privacy.

"This is very serviceable, Sir John," she declared. She proceeded to bring a tape measure and a notebook and pencil from out of a small bag she was carrying.

"Could you hold the other end please, Dr. Silkstone?" she asked in a businesslike manner.

Thomas obliged and was soon calling out to Lydia various measurements, so that after a few minutes she pronounced her conveyance done. "If we allow each mattress five feet of space across, we will be able to accommodate at least ten people in here, five on either side," she told Sir John.

"You are most efficient, Lady Lydia," he replied. "Let me show you what else there is to offer."

He led the way through an arch of rock and into another narrow corridor which broadened out after a few yards into a curious recess. A few feet farther on they came to what was known as the miner's cave, where more tools and wooden scaffolding poles were stored. After another minute or so of picking their way over a bed of fine scree, they could hear the sound of running water and turned to find their path intersected by a large pool, fed by a stream.

"The River Styx," announced Sir John proudly.

Thomas's eyes opened wide in surprise. "The divide between this world and the underworld according to Greek mythology," he said, surveying the water.

"Where the souls of the dead are ferried across the river by the boatman, Charon," continued Lydia, pointing to the ornate rowing boat that was moored at the side of the shallow bank.

"Indeed," nodded Sir John. "But I am sure you will not be ferrying any dead patients across it, your ladyship!" He tried to make light of the analogy, but the thought made Lydia uneasy nonetheless.

They stepped onto a small jetty and the servants assisted them as they lowered themselves into the boat and began the short crossing to the other side. Lydia trailed her hand in the clear water. She could see the bottom and estimated it was only knee deep. Nevertheless, it was icy cold.

"Where does the source rise?" asked Thomas as the boatman progressed into the center of the river.

"About a mile away. Underground," replied Sir John.

"So it is fit to drink?" asked Lydia.

The baronet beamed. "Yes, you have a plentiful supply of fresh water."

They were now three hundred feet beneath the church with its golden orb on top of the hill. Above them were thousands of tons of chalk. The boatmen moored up and they alighted on the other side. The deeper they went, the lower the temperature fell. Lydia tucked her hands into her shawl and stepped out onto terra firma once more. They had crossed the River Styx.

Moving ever deeper into the caves, they skirted a large boulder that lay on the path. "Never fear," said Sir John lightheartedly, "that fell more than a year ago." Lydia shot Thomas a glance. Rock falls were not something with which she wanted to contend.

"Are there any other ways out of the caves, Sir John? In case of an emergency?" she asked.

The baronet nodded. "Yes, the miners hacked some crude steps over there," he said, pointing his torch to a small recess to their right. "It's a steep climb, but it brings one out near the church." Lydia made a mental note of the place, but prayed she would never have to use it.

Walking on a little farther they finally reached the Inner Temple, a large round chamber that marked the end of the cave system. Lydia looked about her.

"This is where the notorious Hellfire Club held some of its meetings," declared Sir John.

Thomas's father had heard firsthand of the club's antics from Mr. Franklin himself; how the ladies wore masks so as to remain anonymous and were required to have "a lively disposition."

"I believe it will serve our purpose well," he replied, looking at Lydia. She had already brought out her tape measure and notebook again. While this chamber was not as big as the other, its shape meant that better use could be made of its space.

"I think a further eight patients might be accommodated here," she announced a few moments later after taking more measurements.

"I am only sorry it cannot be more," lamented Sir John.

Thomas thought of the dozens of sick both he and Dr. Fairweather had seen over the course of the last month. The labyrinth of tunnels and chambers offered the only hope of helping the most vulnerable. At least now he hoped a few more lives could be saved.

Thomas had never seen Lydia so animated. On the return journey she talked of organizing wagons to carry mattresses and bedding. The source of clean water was a real blessing, she said, but food would present a problem. She was throwing all her efforts into the project as if she were trying to block out all else. She had not mentioned the search for her son since she had put forward the idea of evacuating the sick and vulnerable. He knew the plan was helping her put her worries aside until she had heard back from Dr. Carruthers about his continued efforts in London.

She did not have to wait much longer. When they arrived back at Boughton in the early evening, Howard handed her a letter on a tray. She stared at it, then seized it with trembling hands.

"Will you read it for me?" she asked Thomas, offering him the piece of paper.

He took it from her and broke the seal. Opening it he recognized the writing of a secretary Dr. Carruthers often engaged for the dictation of his letters and papers. He took a deep breath and read aloud:

> *Dear Lady Lydia*
>
> *I write to inform you of my inquiries regarding your son. Sir Richard was, indeed, working for Mr. Faulks at Bermondsey, but only two weeks ago a gentleman "purchased" him, freeing him from his apprenticeship for a large fee. This gentleman left no forwarding address. I regret that I can tell you no more.*
>
> *Your obedient servant*
> *Sarah Forbes (Mistress)*
> *Per pro Dr. William Carruthers.*

Even before he had finished reading, Lydia had dissolved into tears. Thomas put his arms around her, but she jerked away angrily. "Who is this man who would deprive me of my son?" she cried.

Thomas followed her as she stormed across the room toward the window. "He is alive, my love. Surely that is cause to rejoice?"

She turned and scowled at him. "I will only rejoice when I can hold Richard in my arms, Thomas."

Realizing he had sounded glib, the young anatomist moved toward her and this time she did not push him away. "As soon as we are able, we shall return to London and track this man down. He must have left some clue as to his identity," he told her, holding her tightly.

She gazed up at him. "I will not give up, Thomas," she said. "I will never give up until my son is here, with me, where he belongs."

Chapter 31

As the days wore on and the fog still lingered, it became apparent to Thomas that this was no extreme weather phenomenon affecting the eastern and southern counties of England. Its influence was much more lingering and malevolent. A malignant fear had taken hold. People were adjusting their daily routines and rhythms of their lives lived under its baleful shadow. Some were terrified, others accepting; all were troubled.

Many of the children had developed nagging coughs; many of the old had taken to their beds. Any woman with child feared for her unborn babe. Sheep in the fields developed sores under their wool and were hemorrhaging and dying where they lay, their carcasses picked over by red kites and crows.

For his part Thomas had been working with Mr. Peabody, Brandwick's apothecary, making up batches of formula to distribute among the many sick. He could not see them all, of course. But he managed to visit upward of a dozen dwellings each day and in every home the story was the same: at least one family member would be suffering from the fog sickness.

In their relationships toward each other Thomas also noted very different reactions among people. Some saw the fog as a trial sent from God. They regarded it as an opportunity to reach out to others and help those afflicted. They reacted with random acts of kindness, giving away what little spare food they had to the families who had been left fatherless or fetching water for widows too weak to walk themselves. Not surprisingly the Reverend Lightfoot, his own wife a victim, had taken it upon himself to visit all those who were suffering, dispensing words of comfort. Lydia, too, had sprung into action in a practical way, organizing the evacuation of the sick and vulnerable to West Wycombe.

Last week she had overseen the transport of eighteen patients to the caves, including six children, each with their own warm bedding. Will Lovelock was among them. He had grown even weaker after the fire in the stable and was considered in real need of rest in the clean air. So now Lydia was spending much of her time supervising the two nurses who were engaged to look after the patients. Some days she would work for up to six hours in what she called "the hospital" before Lovelock brought her home in the evening. Thomas made regular visits there, too, but he also tended to the sick of the wider parish.

Yet there were those, he noticed, who turned in on themselves. Some of the men on the estate refused to harvest what little food remained in the fields and orchards. One was even found stealing from Boughton's dairy the other day, caught redhanded with a sack full of cheese and butter. Those who ventured to sell their produce at market offered less food for sale and prices began to rise rapidly. Men started to mutter. The weavers at nearby Cholsey banded together to protest at the price of flour. There was even talk of some surrounding a merchant's house and forcing him to sell his wheat and oats at the old price.

Even the legal system seemed to have ground to a halt. Thomas had notified Sir Theodisius of his findings regarding the death of Gabriel Lawson immediately. Joshua Pike seemed the most likely suspect, but the coroner had responded saying no constables were available to search for him. The suspect seemed to have gone to ground. The same was true in Lady Thorndike's case. The word was that Joshua Pike was responsible for both deaths. Rumors were rife. A killer was abroad, so now doors were shut not just against the fog, but bolted against a murderer, too.

As he sat in the library that evening, waiting for Lydia to dress for dinner, Thomas became overwhelmed with a sense of hopelessness. As a man of science, he knew there would be some logical explanation for this nauseating cloud; there had to be. The longer the fog lingered, the more convinced he was of his theory that the poisonous gas was emanating from a volcano, although he knew not where. It could be from the south, from the mighty Vesuvius that devastated Pompeii in Roman times, or from the north, from his own homeland even. It was possible the prevailing northwesterly winds had blown the ash cloud across to England. He just did not know.

He wondered if Mr. Franklin, in Paris, had also witnessed the choking fog. It may have spread across Europe, or even across the Atlantic Ocean to America and Canada. Perhaps even his own dear father was suffering in its grip. Very few ships could sail in or out of London, so it was much harder to hear word.

Whatever the source, wherever the source, it seemed that mere mortals could do nothing to stop the fog's relenting and increasingly powerful presence. There had been thunderstorms almost daily for the past ten days. These had brought with them more poisonous rain, although thankfully the sulfur content, according to his measurements, had been diluted by a factor of ten. This meant the rainwater was rendered far less harmful to humans, although still undrinkable and nonetheless damaging to crops.

It was little wonder that ordinary townsfolk and villagers were praying for a sign. An evil presence was hovering over the land. The devil was clapping his hands to make thunder, breathing over the countryside to create this deadly fog. Where was God in all this mayhem, or had He created this catastrophe? There were stories of people filling market squares to pray. The Reverend Lightfoot's congregation had grown so much that last Sunday some had to be turned away from St. Swithin's.

The people craved a light to guide them through the darkness, something tangible, he told himself. It did not matter how distant it was, but the human spirit needed just a glimmer of hope. It was then that he remembered why he had come to the library. On his last visit to Brandwick, a few days before, he had spoken with the Clerk of the Market. The town official, a nervous, bespectacled man, had allowed him to inspect the ledger that recorded livestock prices on market days. Thomas had made a note of the accounts submitted most recently for Boughton's ewes, but had not found the time to check them against the estate's own records. Now that he knew Gabriel Lawson had been murdered, he decided to see if they tallied.

Opening the Boughton ledger, he immediately recognized the dead steward's scrawling, unkempt hand that he had seen Lydia trying to decipher on many occasions. Next he produced his own notebook. He was not surprised by what he found. Boughton's sheep had been fetching several shillings more per head than Lawson had recorded.

Lydia walked into the library a few moments later to find Thomas still at the desk. She was dressed in peacock blue for dinner, but even in the soft glow of the lamps her face was pale.

"I thought I would find you here," she said. "Let us go to dine." Thomas looked up and she knew in an instant that something was wrong. "You've found something?"

"Indeed I have," he informed her. "It appears that Mr. Lawson was swindling you out of several pounds on market days."

Lydia nodded her head knowingly. "I had feared as much," she said. "He had a reputation for cards as well as women. I should've known better than to trust someone hired by my husband." She stared at the ledger from across the desk for a moment. "You don't think that this . . ."

"Could this have anything to do with his murder?" Thomas finished her question. "Perhaps, but we must keep an open mind." He closed the ledger and rose. "But it can wait until tomorrow. I am more than ready to dine with a beautiful woman." He offered her his arm and together they were about to walk to the dining room when there was an incredible flash outside that stopped both of them in their tracks.

"Lightning?" gasped Lydia.

Thomas hurried to the window to look out, his eyes widening at what he saw. "No. No, 'tis not lightning. 'Tis far more extraordinary," he said, gazing in awe at the sky.

Lydia joined him as he opened the door to the terrace. Together they ventured out into the night that seemed not like night at all. Only a few seconds ago the sky had been completely black and so had the countryside below. Now everything was illuminated as if it were day. The hills, the fields, the trees, the gardens, all could be seen clearly. Standing on the terrace, they both raised their eyes to the heavens and there it was, streaking across the sky. A great ball of fire, trailing an enormous tail, was darting through the blackness from north to south. Its luster was equal to the sun, illuminating the whole horizon as it arced over the Chiltern hills.

From somewhere in the house there were shouts and cries. The staff flocked to the windows, or rushed outside to see what was happening.

" 'Tis a sign," shrieked Hannah Lovelock, falling to her knees. Others joined her. Some maids were in tears.

"God forgive us!" wailed another.

The spectacle lasted for a few minutes, transfixing all who saw it. Many clasped their hands to pray the fireball would not land on them. They did not deem their prayers answered until the golden orb disappeared below the horizon, plunging the countryside into darkness once again. For a moment or two there was silence as everyone tried to make sense of what they had just witnessed.

Thomas turned to see about a dozen members of the household, from Howard and Mistress Firebrace to the lowest of the scullery maids, gathered either on the terrace, on the steps, or in the gardens below. He addressed them calmly.

"All is well," he said reassuringly. "It was a meteor; a flaming fragment of rock from the heavens. There is no need to fear."

Lydia now took control. She beckoned to Howard. "Nature blessed us with a magnificent spectacle tonight," she told him, "but now everyone must return to their duties." The butler bowed and went to convey her wishes.

She turned to Thomas, frowning. "They think it was a sign," she said. "A portent. They are afraid."

He shook his head. "It was nothing more than a coincidence," he said, trying to calm her nerves. "They should have no fear." He could not tell her that he, too, was afraid, but that his fear had nothing to do with a flaming celestial missile.

Chapter 32

The following day Thomas rode into Brandwick, headed toward the vicarage on the other side of the town. He intended to see the Reverend Lightfoot to take him the few remaining bottles of milky physick to distribute to any of his parishioners who may have need of it. There was hardly anyone abroad. Many of the shops were shut and the market square was empty, save for a few elderly men huddled in a corner. A gaggle of ragged children ran up to him, holding their hands out for money or food, or both. Thomas noted several had coughs. An old woman chewed her gums as she sagged on the front step of her cottage. A few laborers sat on low walls talking, or crouched in doorways. A dog lolled by the water trough and half a dozen tethered horses swished away the troublesome flies with their tails.

Down the broad main street Thomas rode until he reached the outskirts of the town and the church of St. Swithin's. The doors were shut, but he could hear a man's voice inside. Grabbing the large handle, he slowly and carefully turned it and the door creaked open. So this is where the people of Brandwick are, he thought to himself. Row upon row, pew upon pew, was full of people. But this was not a Sunday, nor a Holy Day, but an ordinary Saturday in August, a time when most men would be in the fields gathering in the harvest. Instead they were to be found in their parish church. It did not surprise him. They were all growing increasingly fearful, and last night's meteor was, for many, the final portent. As far as the common man was concerned, it seemed Judgment Day was imminent, but there was still just enough time to make amends.

Despite his best efforts, the creaking of the church door alerted a number of people to his arrival and many turned their heads to look at the latecomer in their midst. So, too, did the Reverend Lightfoot, ensconced in his pulpit. He had just exhorted the congregation to pray for those afflicted by the fog, but he did not lower his own head and spied Thomas immediately.

Straightening himself and lifting his arms in a gesture of exhortation, the reverend addressed the young doctor directly.

"Brethren," he announced. "Even men of science, with their complicated theories and highfalutin explanations, are turning to the Lord. They are seeing the signs and believing. Witness Dr. Thomas Silkstone." He pointed to the door.

All eyes turned to the back of the church, where the young anatomist stood, rather bemused.

"I see fear written on his face," continued the vicar, looking at Thomas directly. Then, shifting his glare to his wider audience, he went on. "I see fear written on many of your faces. But I tell you fear is for sinners. Last night the heavens were illuminated by a strange and mysterious sight, reminding us of God's infinite power and majesty. It is written in the scriptures that he commands 'even the winds and the water' and, I tell you, those who are righteous have nothing to fear. For we have seen the power of the Lord firsthand and know that we will bask in its glory."

Some of the women in the congregation gasped. A man shouted "Alleluia," and some others answered him with "Amen." The worshippers were enthralled by the vicar's words. Even the crying babes on their mothers' laps remained calm.

"So I say to you," he exhorted them. "We may be living through difficult times; the devil himself may be spewing out his foul breath across the land, but the Lord will protect us if we have faith. Believe in Him and the saving grace of his Son, Our Lord Jesus Christ, and he will deliver us from this evil."

A great calm and sense of well-being had descended on the people. They had flocked to the church in fear of their lives, certain that the Day of Judgment was upon them. Yet this clergyman had allayed their fears. If they did but believe in Jesus Christ and his healing love, then they would be safe. No poisonous fog could suffocate them. No meteors could touch them. Their salvation lay in the pages of the Bible and in prayer. If they put their trust in the Lord, all would be well.

Thomas was glad to leave the church. Reverend Lightfoot had embarrassed him, intentionally or not. He was skirting the crowd, heading toward Mr. Peabody's shop—he had run out of turmeric for his physick and intended to purchase some—when a voice called him back. He turned to see the vicar standing behind him, looking solemn. It was clear to him that the Reverend Lightfoot's devotion to his duties was taking its toll. Thomas noted how exhausted the churchman looked. His skin was sallow and drawn over bones that had been previously been hidden under fleshy cheeks. "Forgive my forthrightness in church, Dr. Silkstone," he said.

Thomas was momentarily taken off guard. "There is no need to apologize, sir," he told him.

"I am glad you feel that way." He paused and it was clear to Thomas that there was something more he wanted to say. "I have heard that you are taking the sick to the caves at West Wycombe."

"That is so."

The vicar nodded. "Then I wondered if I might pay a visit?"

Thomas's mind flashed to the faces in church, to the people lapping up the vicar's words like hungry cats would cream. He would bring spiritual solace to the sick and dying, as surely as his own medicaments brought them physical relief. "You would be most welcome," he told him.

"Excellent," replied the vicar, ordering his features into a reassuring smile before adding, "You and I are alike in so many ways, Dr. Silkstone."

The young doctor paused. "How so, sir?"

The vicar's nostrils flared and he gestured at Thomas with his wiry hand. "You are a physician of the body; I of the soul," he said with a shrug. Thomas let the remark pass.

Chapter 33

"What ails the boy?" Sir Montagu Malthus looked slightly disdainfully at the small child lost in the billowing white pillows on the bed below him. His broad black shoulders were hunched over so that he looked even more like a crow eyeing carrion.

The nursemaid answered him matter-of-factly. "He has the fog sickness, sir, like so many." She was a plain, no-nonsense woman with a frizz of ginger hair, whom he had hired to take care of the boy. Yet he had not anticipated this.

Young Richard Farrell lay half awake, half asleep. His dark-brown hair was plastered to his forehead with sweat and his skin was the bluish gray of marble. Now and again he raised his ruffled head to cough. He had his mother's delicate features—the same nose, the long lashes, mused Sir Montagu. A weak child, but handsome nonetheless. His early years had certainly left their mark on his physique. Regular hot meals and cold baths were surely required to toughen him up.

The nursemaid held a spoon of sugared water to the child's lips and dripped it into his mouth. Half opening his white lids, the boy fixed his gaze on her for a moment. His pink tongue appeared and lapped at the liquid like a cat's, but then his head turned and lolled to one side.

Sir Montagu's lips curled and he sighed. "As much as I loathe the thought, we might need to call a physician to bleed the child, might we not?"

Smoothing the coverlet, the nursemaid nodded. "A good bleeding might purge him of the fever," she said thoughtfully.

The lawyer looked annoyed. This was not what he had bargained on. He should never have let the child roam in the grounds while the fog lingered. He should have kept him indoors. That was his mistake. Still berating himself, he was about to leave the room when he spotted Fothergill hovering in the corridor outside. He found his manner most annoying, but he was nevertheless efficient and had done well in tracking down the boy.

"What is it, man? Have you the papers?" he snapped.

The notary sprang forward. Under his arm he carried a large scroll and in his hand a leather wallet. "They are all here, sir," he said. "They merely await your signature."

Sir Montagu raised his arm like a great wing and motioned to the notary to follow him downstairs to his study. "And a messenger is to take them to Chancery?"

Fothergill scampered after his master as he walked quickly down the stairs. "He is waiting as we speak, sir."

"Good," said Sir Montagu, flying into his study and seating himself behind his desk.

Fothergill laid the rolled parchment out in front of him and held it flat on either end with paperweights. Sir Montagu dipped the nib of his quill into the inkpot. "Your signature here, sir, if you will," said Fothergill, pointing to a blank under the script. "And again, here," to another, smaller piece of parchment. Sir Montagu obliged and Fothergill blotted the writing.

" 'Tis done," concluded the master, with a satisfied grin. "Now all we can do is wait."

Fothergill scooped up the papers from the desk. "I am afraid, sir, the court is notoriously slow, especially in the case of wardships."

Sir Montagu was all too well aware that what his clerk said was true. His hand fluttered in the air. Then he thought of the child upstairs, weak and listless in his bed. What if his condition worsened? There was many a man on his own estate who had dropped dead in the fields from the fog sickness. Yet he still liked to think that his own standing among his profession carried a good deal of weight. His peers would no doubt hurry through the application. Time, he acknowledged, was not on his side. He only hoped the permission he sought would be granted before it was too late.

From Brandwick Thomas rode back toward Boughton Hall. There were calls he needed to make on the estate. Thankfully those in most need, Mother Blackwell and Will Lovelock to name but two, had been transported to the caves and their conditions were, according to Lydia, much improving.

He reached Amos Kidd's cottage shortly after noon and found Susannah stitching at the window. She rose to open the door as soon as she saw him tether his horse.

"Dr. Silkstone," she greeted him. She managed a smile, but it was clear to Thomas that she had been crying. Her lashes were wet with tears and her eyes red and puffy.

"I am come to see how you are faring, Mistress Kidd," he told her.

She let out a little sigh. "As well as any widow, sir," she replied.

He nodded understandingly. He had seen so many young women in her predicament in the past few weeks. "I am also come to warn you to keep your door locked."

"Against the fog, sir, or against the murderer?"

"Or murderers," replied Thomas.

Her eyes widened. "You'd best come in, sir," she said.

Thomas walked into the small, low-ceilinged room. A feeble fire spluttered in the grate. On the table was a pile of sewing; sheets and pillowcases from the hall that needed repairing. Susannah motioned him to a chair by the hearth and he sat.

"You talk of Lady Thorndike, sir? Surely there has not been another murder?" she asked, settling herself down in a chair opposite.

Thomas looked grave. "I am afraid so. Mr. Lawson."

She frowned. "How, sir?"

"A blow to the head," volunteered Thomas. "Then the murderer set fire to the stables."

"Set fire?" she repeated uneasily. "The stables were on fire? When was this?"

Thomas paused to recollect. "Last Thursday. In the morning. Why, Mistress Kidd? Did you see or hear anything suspicious?"

She turned to gaze at her own fire as it flickered weakly. She had only just started to lay the grate again; heat water, cook proper meals. Now that she was no longer alone she took more care. He could see her mind working, but she remained silent.

"They are looking for a traveler, a knife-grinder by the name of Joshua Pike."

Her face suddenly tightened and the color deserted her cheeks. She switched her gaze downward.

"Did you see something, Mistress Kidd?"

She remained staring at the floor. "No. No. Nothing."

"Lady Lydia is offering a ten-guinea reward for any information that will lead to his capture. There are posters up in Brandwick and beyond."

"And why would this Joshua Pike want to kill Mr. Lawson?" There was a tone of indignation in her voice, and she flashed an angry look at Thomas.

"They say he was making trouble among the workers and had threatened him."

The fog seems to have both blinded and deafened any potential witnesses, thought Thomas as Susannah's pent-up anger simmered a little longer. After a moment's reflection she forced an insipid smile. Whatever she had decided in her own mind, she was not about to share her thoughts with him. Instead she simply said: "I shall take care, sir."

He changed the subject. "And how is your health?"

She closed her eyes momentarily. "My head aches, sir, same as everyone's 'round here. Sickness, too. But, mercifully, no cough."

"That is good news," said Thomas, reaching into his bag. "But let me give you this." He handed her a dark-brown glass bottle. "It contains physick. If you begin to cough, take two or three gulps and it should ease your breathing."

She reached out her hand, her seamstress's thimble still on her finger. He saw she was shaking.

"You must get lonely out here," he said.

She shrugged. "Sometimes," she replied, shifting nervously in her chair.

"But you are receiving visitors?" He worried about her isolation.

"The Reverend Lightfoot came the other day."

"Ah, yes, the Reverend Lightfoot." Thomas nodded. "He is working all the hours that God gives him." He pictured the vicar rushing from parishioner to parishioner in his dogcart, comforting the bereaved and burying their dead. His eyes were constantly streaming from the fog, his large nose running, yet he exuded a reassuring calm, despite his own personal tragedy.

Susannah gathered a smile. "He is a good man," she said.

"Yes, indeed," replied Thomas.

She looked at him with doleful eyes and bobbed her head. Thomas wished her well and rose to leave.

"And remember, do not open your door to any strangers."

She nodded. "I will remember," she said. She watched the young doctor mount his horse and ride off down the track.

In the bedroom Joshua Pike had been listening. He walked back into the main room wearing an anxious expression. He seemed both troubled and vulnerable. "I swear I didn't kill no one," he told her. "I'm no murderer."

For a moment she stood still, just looking at him, studying his features: the dark eyes, the nut-brown skin, his strong jaw, and the mouth that, when it widened, opened into the most beguiling smile she had ever seen in a man.

"I know you are not," she told him, walking toward him with her arms outstretched.

Chapter 34

Lydia woke to reality that morning after a dream that was both beautiful and terrible. In it she had been with her son. They were walking, hand in hand, in the sunny orchard at Boughton, talking and laughing. She had bent down and kissed him on the forehead. His eyes were large and brown and his hair tumbled in curls around his moon face. He was just looking up at her when a great shadow blocked out the sun and when they both lifted their gaze a man was standing there, dressed in black. She did not recognize him, but he opened his arms and snatched Richard away. The child screamed. She screamed, too, and her screams woke her. She sat up suddenly and realized that she was in her own bedchamber. Eliza rushed in to find her mistress panting and distressed.

"Your ladyship!" she cried, hurrying over to the bed.

Lydia waved her hand. "A dream, Eliza. A nightmare. All is well."

The maid looked at her mistress knowingly, aware she had endured the same nightmare at least once every week since her return from London. Although Lydia had not confided in Eliza, she was sure the dream involved Richard. The maid, too, had been suffering since finding her sister dead by the Thames. The image of Agnes lying drowned in Thomas's arms would remain with her forever. It was another thread of tragedy that seemed to be drawing the two women closer together.

Remembering that Reverend Lightfoot was due to visit the caves that day, Lydia dressed hurriedly. These days she kept her garb as simple as possible. She dispensed with panniers in favor of just a simple underskirt, stays, and a chemise. On her feet she wore her overshoes. The caves were slippery as lard underfoot and her heels could easily get caught in the cracks and crevices in the rock. She had also taken to carrying a fabric bag with a drawstring around its neck. In it she kept items she found essential for her work: a flint for lighting candles, a phial of smelling salts, and sundry other items that were proving so useful to have at hand when caring for the sick.

She found Thomas waiting for her in the hallway and together they walked outside where Lovelock was ready with the carriage. The sun was still blocked out by the veil of fog that hung over the hills and valleys. The fields were now all brown and the carcasses of dead sheep were dotted around. The grain had withered on the stalks and the fruit on the bough.

Lydia frowned. "When will this cloud lift?" she asked, not expecting a reply. "It has been almost seven weeks now."

"We need the wind to change direction," replied Thomas. "We need an easterly to blow the fog clear of Europe and out over the Atlantic."

Half an hour later they arrived at the mouth of the caves. The Reverend Lightfoot was already waiting for them. Cordial greetings were exchanged and after each of them had been given their own lantern, Thomas led the party—Lydia and the vicar, together with two servants—into the rocky passageway. The air was cool but fresh, and they all found themselves eager to fill their lungs.

"Watch your step now," advised Thomas. "There is an outcrop here." The vicar was carrying his cane as usual, which was of great service to him, but he failed to duck quickly in time and scraped his head on the rock. He let out a stifled cry.

"I hope you are not hurt, sir?" asked Lydia, rushing to his side.

He managed a dazed smile. "Oh no, indeed. Just a bump," he replied, rubbing his temple, but Lydia could see his skin had been grazed. His forehead was flecked with blood. "It is indeed narrow in parts," he remarked, rubbing his forehead. "What if, God forbid, there was a rockfall? There must be another way out in such an event?" There was a note of anxiety in his question.

"There is an escape route," Thomas replied. "Just beyond the river, on the farther shore. There are steps that lead up to the surface there."

The Reverend Lightfoot looked satisfied with the answer. "That is good to know," he said.

They continued to pick their way along the passage, stepping over puddles and loose boulders, until they came to the first chamber. Several oil lamps burned brightly in recesses in the rock, green moss springing up in the pools of light they cast. Wooden screens had been erected across two of the recesses to afford a degree of privacy and a narrow set of shelves contained various medicaments and potions for use by the nurses.

Around the walls, ranged on two neat rows of mattresses, lay a dozen women and children. Most were propped up on pillows or sacks to help their breathing. They were all swathed in thick blankets. A baby was crying in its mother's arms. An old woman in the middle of a coughing spasm struggled for breath. In the corner a plump nurse was administering physick to a young girl. The constant sound of wheezing and sniffling, punctuated by rasping coughs, filled the chamber.

The clergyman surveyed the scene. "These poor souls must take great comfort from your care, your ladyship," he told Lydia. "How long do they stay?"

"Until their coughs are sufficiently diminished, sir," she replied. She did not tell him that only three women and a boy had been discharged so far, even though she knew they should have remained. The truth was that there was not enough space to take all those in need of a refuge from the fog. Only when there was a death could another patient be admitted.

They progressed to the farthest chamber, crossing the water in the rowing boat.

"As you see, sir, there is a constant supply of fresh water,"

Thomas pointed out, as the boatman rowed them to the opposite bank.

From there it was just a few more yards to the final chamber, the Inner Temple. The visitor seemed equally impressed with the space that accommodated the men and boys. Here the hacking coughs of the patients reverberated around the smaller space. Another nurse was rubbing an unguent into a man's chest.

"Oil of camphor," explained Lydia. "The vapors soothe the airways."

An elderly man lay groaning in a far corner and a young boy rose from his own palliasse and went over to comfort him. Thomas recognized him immediately by his carrot-colored hair. He smiled at the sight of Will Lovelock, looking much stronger than before.

"You are to be commended, your ladyship," said the Reverend Lightfoot.

Lydia acknowledged his praise. "It has not been an easy task, but it has certainly saved lives, sir."

The party returned the way they had come. The Reverend Lightfoot had seemed a little nervous about entering the caves at first, inquiring as he did about procedures in the event of a rockfall. Thomas suspected that he suffered from some sort of phobia when confined in an enclosed space. He had read of such conditions before. Yet as they made their way toward the light at the end of the tunnel, he appeared much more relaxed.

The reverend extended his hand to Thomas. "A most enlightening tour, Dr. Silkstone," he said.

"I am glad you found it of interest, sir," replied Thomas.

Lydia, too, received great praise. "The Lord will surely reward you for your good works, your ladyship," he told her. Perhaps he might even hold a service when he next visited, he suggested. She agreed it would lift spirits and they all parted on amicable terms.

The clergyman returned to his dogcart and Thomas and Lydia watched him drive off.

"You have worked wonders here," Thomas told Lydia.

She smiled. "It is good to be of use to others."

He knew that her service to the sick helped her forget her own pain and longing for her missing son, as well as alleviate his own burden. As well as caring for the sick, he had other work to do. Two murders had been committed and, at the moment, it seemed he was the only person in authority anxious to discover the perpetrator.

Chapter 35

The Reverend Lightfoot knelt in silent prayer in front of the altar at St. Swithin's. Hands clasped, he stared at the plain wooden cross and contemplated the nature of suffering. How simple an object it was, this cruciform shape. In the Roman Church a plaster statue of Christ would be nailed to it. His face would be contorted in agony. There would be marks from the pricking of thorns around his head and blood where the nails entered his hands and feet. It would be visceral and real. Supplicants could almost put their hand in his side. But this unadorned cross seemed so far removed from humanity. It transcended all suffering and agony. Just as God seemed to. What did he care for the injustices endured by mere mortals? Why should he care? Perhaps, just perhaps there was no God. The voice of Satan filled his head again. He kept hearing it at times like these; when he was alone with his grief.

He bowed his head in prayer, trying to block out the nagging whispers, and from out of the blackness came his beloved Margaret. His heart was aching with the loneliness of loss. He saw her face: serene and sublimely beautiful. She was surely in a better place now, free from the petty machinations of being a country vicar's wife. How she had borne her own suffering with so much fortitude. Their first child had died at two days, their second at two weeks, their third had been stillborn, and their fourth lived but six months. That had been twenty years ago and after that they had slept in separate rooms. They had never come together as man and wife again; yet they had still loved each other with an intensity that rose above any base physical need. She turned her own suffering into something positive: helping the sick and needy of the parish. Her charity was boundless. That was how she had died, in the service of others, trying to organize assistance for those who had lost their loved ones to the fog. He must not be deflected from carrying on what she began. He knew it was what she would have wanted. It would break her heart if she knew that he was losing his faith.

Along with the doubt there came temptation. It had reared its lascivious head. He had loved Margaret, truly and deeply. But a man has needs and now that she was no longer by his side, the urge to give way to his own passions and desires was growing. An image darted into his mind. He banished it quickly, fixing his eyes again on the cross.

"Be gone!" he mouthed. He returned to his prayers to a God who seemed to have deserted him.

The townspeople were greatly afeared after the appearance of the meteor. Many believed Judgment Day was upon them and wished to repent of their sins.

"Oh Lord, bless all those sick and weak I have seen today and all those who care for them," intoned the minister, his hands clasped in front of the altar. "Keep them safe in the knowledge of Your love. Through our Lord Jesus Christ. Amen."

For a few more moments his head remained bowed in contemplation until, in the darkness behind him, he heard slow footsteps coming up the aisle. At first he imagined they were Margaret's. She would come up behind him and place her hands on his shoulders. He would breathe in her lavender smell and feel her touch. Only now it would be cold from the grave. He shivered and turned to see, coming out of the gloom, Susannah Kidd. Quickly he rose to his feet.

"What are you doing here?" he snapped.

The widow was shocked by his tone. The corners of her plump mouth drooped. "I am come for comfort and guidance, sir," she replied. The rims of her large eyes were red.

He softened his tone. "I am sorry. You took me by surprise."

She was wearing a woolen shawl that she drew tightly across her chest. "I need to talk to someone, reverend." Her voice was quivering.

A memory flashed across his mind of how she had turned to him before in her cottage. He recalled her scent: a whiff of roses that spilled from between her breasts. A stab of pleasure shot through his body. "What is it that troubles you?" He looked at her suspiciously, but motioned to a pew. She was not welcome. Could she not see that? She settled herself, keeping her head bowed, until she was ready to speak.

"I am afraid, sir," she began. She was so close to him that he could smell her breath. He dared not look into her eyes.

"All God-fearing Christians are, Mistress Kidd," he replied stiffly. "These are strange times, so we must repent and put our trust in the Lord."

She nodded and pulled at her shawl so that he could see the outline of her breasts underneath. "It is about trust that I need to talk, sir," she said. Her voice was low, almost a whisper, and when her lips parted they reminded him of a blooming rose. For a second he pictured what it might be like to put his lips on hers, to feel their warmth and their sweet moisture.

"Go on."

"If you love someone and you trust them, but you hear they have done bad things, really bad things, what path should you take? What does the Bible say?"

Narrowing his eyes, he studied her for a moment. She was talking in riddles; keeping a secret. What did she know, this Eve who sat before him? She had knowledge and that, in a woman with her attributes, was a dangerous thing. She was hiding something that troubled her deeply. He had seen the signs so many times before: the clammy hands, the licking of the lips, the eyes that looked everywhere apart from at him. Between her forefinger and thumb she twisted a piece of lace on her cuff.

After a few seconds he said, "You should pray, Mistress Kidd. Pray and the Lord will speak to you in your heart. It is written in Psalms: 'And they that know thy name will put their trust in thee: for thou, Lord, hast not forsaken them that seek thee.' "

There was a look of disappointment on her face. She had come in the hope of more. "So if I ask God what to do, he will tell me?" He found her childlike simplicity quite touching, but he knew it was all a mask.

"Yes, Mistress Kidd. And do it soon, for the day is approaching fast when all secrets will be uncovered. A light will be shone into the darkest recesses of your soul and all evil will be uncovered." He was almost glaring at her now. His rhetoric was making her anxious, all right. Those sensuous hands of hers, as delicate as the silk thread she sewed, were trembling. Would she open up to him? There was definitely fear in her eyes. Did she know something about the murders? "Might it help you to confess your sins?" he asked.

Now she looked shocked, like a frightened rabbit. Her head jerked up, sending a strand of long blond hair tumbling down to the top of her shoulder. He had said too much, but he had given her food for thought. Slowly she nodded her head.

"I will think on it, sir," she replied, her voice quivering. "Thank you for your guidance."

She rose, curtsied, and walked to the door with a wavering step, as if she bore a heavy burden. Even in her sorrow he found her exquisitely beautiful.

Chapter 36

A rider brought word to Boughton first thing the following morning. Sir Montagu Malthus was coming that very day. He planned to arrive shortly after noon. Lydia and Thomas were already dressed and about to leave for the caves, so changed their plans accordingly. Lydia had to notify Mistress Firebrace, who notified Mistress Claddingbowl, and the whole household was sent into a frenzy of activity.

"What can he want?" asked Thomas when Lydia was satisfied that all had been made ready. They were waiting the arrival in the drawing room.

"You know very well," replied Lydia abruptly, opening her fan. "He wants me to marry. He has probably found me a perfect suitor."

Thomas knew what she said was true. He sat down opposite her. "And what will you say?"

She paused and looked up at him, resting her fan on her knee. Her shoulders heaved in a deep sigh. "I shall tell him that I shall marry when I am ready, to a man of my own choosing," she said, before fanning herself once more.

It was as Thomas had feared. She did not have the courage to stand up to Sir Montagu. Her words cut him like a knife. "But you would not tell him that you have already made your choice?"

She closed her fan and glared at Thomas. "You do not know

what he is like. He is cold and cruel and vindictive. He hated
Michael and he hates you." She stood up and walked 'round to
Thomas's side. Touching his shoulder she said, "I just need a lit-
tle more time. Please."

He took her hand in his and kissed it. "Of course. I am sorry.
You English do not like to be rushed. I must remember that."
He regretted the sarcasm in his tone, but said no more. Patience
was the virtue that Lydia required of him and he would display
it, for the time being at least.

A few minutes later the carriage bearing Sir Montagu
Malthus pulled up in front of Boughton Hall. Lydia stood on
the steps to greet her guest. The fog still clung to the hills and
treetops, but the sun was discernible as a fierce red globe behind
it. The lawyer swooped down from the carriage and began to
mount the steps. Fothergill followed closely behind, carrying a
leather satchel and a large scroll under his arm.

"Sir, what an unexpected pleasure." Lydia welcomed him as
he came level with her.

Sir Montagu's thick brows knitted as he took her hand and
pecked it with his lips. "I am afraid you will not find what I
have to say pleasant, my dear Lydia," he warned ominously.

The smile that she had managed to gather to greet her
brother's guardian suddenly deserted her and she found herself
momentarily lost for words.

"You must be tired after your journey. Please." She gestured
him into the hall. "We shall see to your luggage."

The lawyer stopped in his tracks. "I have none, my dear. I do
not intend to stay. We have taken rooms at the inn at Brandwick."

Lydia looked puzzled. "So be it," she replied. "But I am sure
you would like some tea."

She led the way to the drawing room and Sir Montagu and
Fothergill followed. Thomas was already standing by the mantelpiece. He bowed stiffly when the men entered.

"You know Dr. Silkstone, Sir Montagu," she said politely.

The lawyer eyed Thomas suspiciously and did not even feign a smile. "Indeed I do," he sneered.

Lydia bade her guests sit in an atmosphere that was far from congenial. Fothergill perched himself on a stool behind his master, laying the large scroll down on the floor while she went to pull the rope to call for tea. Just as she did so, however, Sir Montagu lifted his large hand.

"I would prefer if we talked alone, my dear," he announced. "What I have to say is of a very personal nature."

Thomas shot a glance at Lydia. Would she really let this man dictate to her what she did in her own home? He willed her to be strong. She took her hand away from the bellpull.

"I count Dr. Silkstone not only as my physician, but as a confidant, Sir Montagu," she began. "Whatever you say to me, you can say it freely in front of him."

The lawyer's lips curled in a smirk. "So you have some newfound courage?" he jibed. " 'Twill be interesting to see how brave you feel when I put to you my proposition."

Lydia took a deep breath. "And what might that be, sir?"

Sir Montagu snapped his fingers. Fothergill picked up the scroll from the floor and the two men moved over to the table near the window. "I suggest you come and see this, my dear." He beckoned to her.

Lydia walked slowly, composing herself as she went. She had no intention of betraying the utter dread she felt. Thomas followed closely behind until they were both level with the table and could see the large scroll laid out before them. Fothergill, his pince-nez now hooked safely over his nose, had smoothed out the parchment and weighed it down at either end. At the bottom was a large, red wax seal. Thomas pored over it and recognized the insignia. It was something he had come across three or four months earlier when he was asked to testify in a case involving a young ward. It was the seal of the Court of Chancery. His forehead buckled into a frown.

Sir Montagu leered at Lydia. "I see Dr. Silkstone understands the gravity of this document, my dear, but do you?"

Lydia stared blankly at the parchment and the closely written script. There were so many letters, so many words, all written in Latin. They meant little to her and a rising sense of panic caught hold as she scanned the scroll for something familiar, something she could understand. That something came near the end of the document. She saw the name, written in this bold, confident hand, and she shuddered. "Richard Michael Farrell," she mouthed. Her head shot up. "What does this mean?"

Sir Montagu threw back his head and let out a muted laugh. "It means, my dear, that your long-lost son, the son you thought was your secret, has been found safe and well and is in my custody."

Thomas lurched forward. "It was you. I thought as much!" He jabbed an accusing finger at Fothergill, who took a step back.

"Yes." Sir Montagu nodded. "Fothergill, here, tracked down the boy and brought him safely to me."

Lydia looked at the lawyer in disbelief, not sure whether she should laugh or cry. "You have Richard?"

"Indeed I do."

"Then where is he? I must see him." She rushed forward and grabbed Malthus's frock coat, begging for an answer. "Where is he?" she cried.

Sir Montagu prized her fingers from his garment. "Calm yourself, my dear," he urged her, straightening his coat.

Thomas put his arm 'round her and pulled her away. "Let us talk about this rationally," he said, glaring at Sir Montagu. Unlike Lydia, he had been able to read snatches of the Latin text. He knew what the lawyer had done.

"Ah, the voice of reason," boomed Sir Montagu, flapping his hands in an exaggerated gesture as he pointed at Thomas.

"I believe, sir, you have made her ladyship's son a ward of court."

Sir Montagu gave a shallow bow and skewed his head. "How right you are, Dr. Silkstone."

"A ward of court," echoed Lydia. "What does that mean?"

"It means, my dear, that Richard remains under the legal protection of the court until certain conditions are met." Sir Montagu's face split into a broad grin.

"I want him here, now!" She struggled to free herself from Thomas's hold. "I want to see my son!" Her voice was quivering with emotion, yet still the lawyer wore a self-satisfied, pious look that infuriated her.

"As I said, he is quite safe, but there are certain"—he paused for effect—"certain conditions that must legally be met before I can allow you to see him."

"What conditions?" barked Thomas.

Sir Montagu deliberately turned his shoulder to Thomas and focused on Lydia. Bending low he told her: "The Court of Chancery has ruled that you may have custody of your son on condition that you do not marry a foreigner."

Lydia dropped like a stone onto the settee behind her. Thomas joined her and took her hand in his. She clasped it tightly. Staring ahead blankly she muttered: "How can that be?"

Sir Montagu shook his head. "The court was of the view that an estate such as Boughton must not be allowed to fall into the hands of a citizen of an enemy territory."

Thomas shot up and fixed Sir Montagu with an accusing look. "But the war is over," he protested.

Again the lawyer shook his large head. "No treaty has yet been signed, Dr. Silkstone, so technically hostilities have not yet ceased between Great Britain and America."

Thomas felt his blood boil. Bile flooded his throat. He balled his fists but told himself he needed to remain calm. "This is all your doing, Malthus," he said bitterly.

The lawyer laid his palm on his chest. "Me, Dr. Silkstone? I am merely an instrument of the court," he replied.

Thomas wanted to wipe the smirk off the lawyer's face with his fist, but he contained himself. He knew he was beaten, for the moment at least. He could not allow Lydia to be so tortured. Her features could not have been more pained had she been on the rack with Sir Montagu turning the wheel. Watching her suffer was torture for him, too. Leaping up, he brought his face close to the lawyer's and looked him straight in the eye. "Her ladyship accepts the terms," he said through clenched teeth.

Lydia looked up, but remained silent. There were no words of protest or pleas for justice; just an acceptance of the cruel inevitability that she now faced.

Fothergill delved into his satchel and produced another, smaller sheet of paper which he laid on top of the scroll. He dipped his quill into the inkpot and offered it to Lydia.

"If you please," said Sir Montagu, gesturing to the document.

Slowly Lydia rose and Thomas escorted her over to the table. She looked at him with eyes watery with tears. "I am sorry," she whispered, before she signed her name.

As Fothergill blotted the ink, Sir Montagu gloated. "You give up too easily, Silkstone," he sneered when the deed was done. Lydia was walking back to the settee, out of earshot.

"Believe me I have not given up, but I cannot see the woman I love forced to make such a brutal choice."

The lawyer sniggered. "How very noble of you. And they said chivalry was dead in the Colonies."

Halfway across the room, Lydia turned abruptly. "I have done what you asked, now where is my son?" There was a renewed strength in her voice that had been barely audible a few moments ago. Her uncharacteristic forcefulness momentarily disarmed the lawyer.

"We can take you to him this instant, my dear," he replied, his head bobbing in a bow.

Lydia crossed the room and Thomas followed. The notary held the door open for them, as Sir Montagu watched, but as soon as the young doctor was about to pass, he lifted his great arm and barred his way. Lydia turned sharply and looked at Malthus.

"May I remind you, sir, that Dr. Silkstone is a physician? I wish him to examine my son to see that no harm has come to him." Her words were delivered with such conviction that any objection the lawyer could have raised dissipated.

Thus disarmed, he simply replied: "But of course," and the party walked down the steps to the waiting carriage that would take them to Brandwick and to Richard Farrell, heir apparent to the Boughton estate.

Chapter 37

Lydia's heart was pounding as she climbed the rickety stairs at the Three Tuns. Fothergill led the way and opened a low door that led off the first-floor landing. The moment she had dreamed of for so many years was almost upon her. Feeling she would almost burst with emotion, she took a deep breath and walked into the room. Standing by the window, next to his nursemaid, was a small boy with brown curly hair and large eyes. His head was swathed in a halo of light from the glowing candles and he was dressed in silk breeches and a smart coat. He was unmistakably hers. Arms outstretched, she rushed forward and tried to enfold the child, but he balked at her embrace and pulled away. Nestling his face in his nursemaid's skirts, he turned his back on Lydia. Stunned, she straightened herself and backed off a little distance.

"Do not be frightened. I . . . I will not hurt you," she told the boy falteringly, then turning to Sir Montagu she asked, "You have told him?"

The lawyer smirked. "Richard, you must greet your mamma," he instructed the child, as if he were a schoolmaster telling a pupil to open a book. He turned to Lydia. "I took the liberty of asking the court to change his name. From henceforth he shall be known as Richard Crick, not Farrell. Much better that way. I'm sure you'll agree, my dear," he said.

Lydia did not respond, but merely stood looking at the child as he clung to the nursemaid. Smiling gently, she bent low once more and offered her hand.

Sir Montagu looked down his hooked nose. "The boy has certain feral tendencies," he said disdainfully. "They need to be stamped out."

Thoughts of what her son must have suffered scudded through Lydia's mind: the harshness of the workhouse and the inevitable beatings by the chimney sweep as he forced him to shin up flues. He must have endured so much in his six short years. There would be brutal memories that would be hard to erase.

Suddenly she remembered the earring that the woman at the workhouse had given her. Delving into her bag, she brought it out. "Do you recognize this, Richard?" she asked, holding it up to the light so that the precious stones twinkled.

The child turned his head and wheeled 'round at the sight of the jewel. His eyes lit up and he charged over to Lydia, snatching the earring from her hand.

"Richard, no!" boomed Sir Montagu, stepping forward. But Lydia blocked his progress. "Wait!" she cried, as the child cradled the earring in his hand and his face broke into a smile. "You remember, don't you, Richard?" she said, her voice trembling. "It was your token."

The child looked up at her with his large eyes, which were suddenly sparkling. He ran toward her and she gathered him up in her arms. This time he did not balk, but hooked his arm around her waist. It was then that she noticed the other arm hanging limply by his side. Guilt and sorrow and joy melded into one and she could stifle her tears no more. She kissed her son and held him tight.

Thomas remained watching the reunion in silence. He, too, felt choked with the emotion of the occasion. There was a tenderness so pure between Lydia and her son and a bond so natural, that he knew no earthly thing could come between them.

"You are safe now, my darling," she cried. "I will never let you go," she muttered, holding back the tears.

Thomas knew what she said was true. She would never again allow herself to be parted from her son, even if that meant they could never be man and wife. He looked at Sir Montagu hovering nearby, relishing the touching scene that he had so cleverly engineered. It was very clear that the forging of the bond between mother and son meant that he, Thomas, may never be able to marry the woman he loved.

Lydia was still holding Richard when he began to cough. She loosened her hold and frowned. "How long has he had this?" she asked the nursemaid.

"He has been ill with the fog sickness, your ladyship," she volunteered.

Lydia shot a glance at Thomas. "How long has he had this cough?" she repeated.

Sir Montagu spoke up. "The child is sickly. He has been ill for the past few days."

It was true, noted Thomas, that Richard was painfully thin and his skin was as white as chalk dust. That cough was certainly a cause for concern.

"I will need to examine his lordship," said the doctor.

The lawyer looked at him contemptuously. "Very well, but be quick about it."

Thomas walked over to the child, who remained holding Lydia's hand. "Sir," he said softly with a smile. "I am a friend of your mamma's and I want to help you. Will you let me do that?" His tone was gentle and the boy did not shift his gaze from him. "Perhaps you could lie down," he said, gesturing to the bed.

Richard eyed his mother, as if seeking permission. "Dr. Silkstone will make you feel better, my darling," she assured the boy.

Taking his hand, Thomas guided the child over to the bed and took off his topcoat. He then bade the boy lie down and from out of his bag he produced his listening tube. Laying it flat against the child's chest, he listened to the rhythm of the lungs as they bellowed in and out. They were struggling, he could tell, as they wheezed and blustered within the tiny cavity. Resting the palm of his hand flat on the child's forehead, he detected a fever. His skin was as hot as burning coals and his eyes were red-rimmed and sore.

"Does your head ache?" he asked. The child nodded. "And do you feel nausea?" The boy looked at him blankly. "A sickness just here?" Thomas pointed to his stomach. Again he nodded. "Thank you." Thomas smiled. He did not wish to make his young patient feel any more anxious than he already was. "You may rejoin your mamma."

He watched the child lift himself from the mattress and walk toward Lydia once more, only this time, there was a slowness in his step, as if his previous exertions had tired him out. He started to zigzag across the room, before dropping to the floor.

Lydia rushed forward. Thomas, too, hurried over to where the child lay. Supporting his head in his hands, he looked at his face. His eyes were still open, but it was clear he had difficulty focusing.

"I am afraid he has the classic symptoms of the fog sickness," said Thomas. "We need to get him to bed straightaway."

Sir Montagu loomed over them. "Very well. You may take him back to Boughton," he conceded. "I shall give him into your custody," he told Lydia. "But remember your pledge."

Lydia looked up at him as he glowered at her, cradling her son in her arms. "You can be sure that I would do nothing to risk losing Richard again," she told him. Thomas knew her words to be true.

Chapter 38

Back at Boughton, they settled the boy into bed. The room had not been occupied for some months and the air was hot and stuffy. Since the windows could not be opened because of the fog, the room smelled fusty and damp. The exertion and excitement seemed to have triggered the child's cough once more. His breath came in short wheezes. Thomas had given his small patient a more thorough examination. He suspected his time as a chimney sweep, shinning up soot-filled flues, albeit for a short period, had also taken its toll on his respiratory system. Tiny particles of carbon would be embedded in his lung tissue, causing constant irritation.

Lydia sat at her son's bedside, concern etched on her face.

"Tell me he will be well soon, Thomas," she said, dabbing Richard's forehead with a vinegar-soaked pad.

The young doctor watched her slow gestures of maternal love that came so naturally to her. He tried to reassure her. "Now that he is here with you, I am certain he will be fully restored. Rest and good food will give him strength," he told her, adding: "But most of all he needs his mother's love."

"I have longed for this day for so many years," she said, stroking her son's curls. "But I did not picture it would be like this."

Thomas shook his head. "But he is here and he will be well. That is all that matters now." He stroked her arm. "And once he is a little stronger, perhaps he could go with you to the caves for a few days."

Lydia thought for a moment, and then nodded. "Yes. Yes, we will do that."

Thomas returned his listening tube and a phial of physick to his case. "I shall be on my way now," he told her. There were many more new patients to see. She acknowledged his need to leave with a wistful nod of her head, then lifted her hand just as Thomas was about to turn toward the door.

"There is one more thing I would like you to do." She broke off to frame her words carefully. "Just in case . . . he does not . . ."

Thomas put his finger over her lips to still them and spare her the agony of saying what they both feared most. "And what might that be?" he asked.

"I would like him baptized," she said. "I do not believe he has been and it would please me very much." She bit her lip to stop it from trembling.

"Of course," he replied. "I shall ask the Reverend Lightfoot this afternoon."

Stepping out into the fog once more, Thomas saw Will Love-lock approach from the stables with his horse. "Ah, Will. 'Tis good to see you back," he greeted him. The boy looked pale, but seemed much stronger. His spell at West Wycombe had obviously had the desired effect. He returned the doctor's smile.

"Thank you, sir. I feel much better," he replied with a nod.

Thomas hoped a stay in the cool caves with their plentiful supply of fresh air and untainted drinking water would have the same effect on young Richard. He had just ridden down the drive at Boughton and had turned his horse toward Brandwick, where he planned to meet with Mr. Peabody, when he saw Reverend Lightfoot. His dogcart was jouncing along the lane, headed in the same direction. Thomas spurred his horse to a trot and soon caught up with the vicar.

"Good morning, sir," he greeted him, doffing his tricorn. "The fog seems to have lifted slightly today."

The clergyman did not return his smile. "Good morning, Dr. Silkstone," he said, his lips remaining tight and flat.

The air was thick with small flies and Thomas's horse was slightly skittish, its head flicking erratically, trying to fend them off. "How goes it today, sir?" he inquired.

The vicar waved the flies away from his face. "The Lord calls someone each day," he said gravely.

Thomas had hoped for a better report. The fog was certainly dispersing, albeit gradually. Yet still its legacy lingered. "Then I must delay you no further," he told him.

"Very well, Dr. Silkstone," said the vicar. He was obviously in no mood for pleasantries. Thomas was just about to bid him a good day when he remembered he had been tasked with organizing the young nobleman's baptism. "Lady Lydia would appreciate a call from you, sir," he said, "when you have a moment in the next day or so."

The vicar managed a faint smile. "Very well. I shall go to the hall tomorrow. I am occupied this afternoon."

Seeing the reverend had no wish to engage in further conversation, Thomas tugged gently at his horse's rein and moved off at a steady trot toward the village. Lightfoot followed at a more sedate pace several yards behind him. The doctor needed to see Mr. Peabody about concocting some more linctus and to find out from him the latest additions to the list of patients struck down and needing care.

He arrived at the apothecary's shop to find several people milling around outside. In their midst was Mr. Peabody in a state of high anxiety. He had dispensed with his wig and was sweating profusely.

"Please be calm," he called out, but his voice was drowned by the cries of seemingly angry customers.

"My children are sick!" cried one woman. "We need physick now!" exclaimed another.

As soon as they saw Thomas arrive on his horse, the crowd calmed themselves. "Good people," he addressed them from the saddle. "There will be plenty of physick to go 'round and there will be no charge for it." Lydia and Sir Henry had agreed on that.

At his words, a loud cheer volleyed into the hot air. "But Mr. Peabody and I need to be allowed to work undisturbed so that we can make up more linctus. Return when the church bell tolls seven and a new batch will be ready."

Some of the villagers nodded. It was only fair that this physician should be allowed to make the very medicine that could save their families. And to offer it for free, without money changing hands, was indeed a rare gesture. So the crowd dispersed, leaving Thomas to shepherd a shaken Mr. Peabody into his dispensary at the back of the shop.

All afternoon they worked hard in the heat, measuring, pounding, and blending. Thomas had found that the milk in his original formula was souring too soon and had to be substituted with powdered chalk mixed with a little water. He also made up some new remedies he had come across in journals in Boughton's library. Sage juice and honey were supposedly efficacious when the patient spat blood, while syrup of horehound was recommended for an inveterate cough.

Mr. Peabody had also ordered a large quantity of Peruvian bark that, according to him, worked wonders for a dry cough when taken within twenty-four hours of the first spasm. An amount the size of a peppercorn was to be chewed only as long as the spittle remained bitter, then spat out. Thomas questioned its efficacy, but the need to give some sort of hope to his patients was so great that, as long as no harm was done, Thomas felt anything was worth trying.

It was approaching six o'clock. The light, such as it was in the fog, was fading fast when Thomas realized he needed more elixir of vitriol for mixing. He put down his pestle and went to seek out a new bottle from the shelf in the shop. Glancing out of the window that looked onto the street he saw a small crowd beginning to gather in the market square. At first he thought the people were merely eager to be the first in line for the opening of the dispensary at seven o'clock, but when he saw the Reverend Lightfoot mount the steps of the market cross, he realized he was mistaken.

Moving closer to the window for a better view, he could see the vicar more clearly. He was wearing a surplice and around his neck a large cross and chain of gold. A small table had been placed on the steps by his side and on it was a tall candle and an open copy of the Bible.

More and more people gathered 'round, until the number had swelled to at least a hundred. There was a strange air of expectancy about them. They did not appear angry or aggressive as he had seen them earlier, but rather nervous and excited, as if waiting for something or somebody.

Thomas remained transfixed at the window until, a few seconds later, a cart drawn by a pony pulled up alongside the gathering. The driver jumped down and proceeded to demount the side of the vehicle to reveal two people, lying prone.

Half a dozen men came to the driver's aid and carried the passengers—Thomas could now see they were a young girl and a boy a little older—onto the steps. Both were dressed in loose shifts. The girl was crying and she began to kick out, while the boy flailed his arms in the air like a windmill. His tongue lolled from the side of his mouth and his chin was wet with spittle.

A collective murmur rippled through the crowd as they watched the men seat the children on the steps. The girl tried to rise, but she was held down by a burly man on either side, pressing on both her shoulders. The boy seemed more compliant. His head drooped down, but odd staccato noises flew from his mouth from time to time.

Hearing the commotion outside, Mr. Peabody joined Thomas at the window. He dabbed his furrowed brow with his kerchief. "What is going on?"

"I cannot be sure, but I fear for the safety of those children," replied Thomas, still looking intently at the scene.

From out of the crowd came a man with a flaming torch. He walked up the steps, lit the candle, and withdrew. An odd silence descended on the throng. It was then that the Reverend Lightfoot lifted his arms and spoke.

"Beloved in God," he began. "We are here today to pray for these two wretched souls who their father fears are bringing the devil into our midst."

The vicar then laid both his hands on the girl's head. She jerked, trying to free herself, but he persisted, intoning a prayer as he did so. He did the same to the boy, then clasped his hands together. In a loud voice he exhorted his congregation: "Let us sing together the hymn 'Come Sinners to the Gospel Feast.' "

While the congregation raised their voices in song, Thomas ventured out of the shop and walked across the street to get a better view. He saw the driver of the cart clearly now. It was the gravedigger Joseph Makepeace. His wife had died of the fog sickness the week before and he had buried her, just as he had buried dozens before her. Haggard and hunched, he stood on the market steps by his children, whom the doctor recognized from his visit to their dying mother. Both of them suffered from serious conditions; the girl from the falling sickness and the boy from some form of St. Vitus' dance, which rendered him incapable of speech or coordinated movement.

The hymn was coming to its climax, building up in tone and volume, when suddenly the girl began to writhe. Her eyes rolled back in her head and her limbs stiffened, so that the men who had been holding her jumped back in shock. Some of the women in the crowd screamed.

The girl dropped down and began to convulse on the steps, foul words issuing from her mouth. Flecks of foam appeared at her lips and her limbs twitched uncontrollably. Her father rushed forward.

"See, she is cursed!" he cried, pointing at the child as her body juddered beneath him. "The devil is in her. He has brought the fog on us all!"

Dozens of voices now joined in the fray. Thomas could not

hear what they said, but the tension in the air was mounting. He looked at some of the faces. Eyes were narrowing, teeth were flashing. Like a pack of wild dogs, the people were working themselves up into a frenzy. From somewhere in the crowd he heard a taunt of "witch."

"Burn her!" called another.

He had seen enough. He elbowed his way through the throng and bounded up the steps. The girl's body was still juddering wildly and her head kept hitting the stone steps below. Throwing off his topcoat, he folded it into a cushion. The crowd surged forward; some people jeered. They were enjoying the spectacle. They did not want the foreign physician to spoil it.

"Stay where you are!" shouted Thomas, waving his arm at the baying congregation.

Meanwhile, the Reverend Lightfoot's expression had changed from one of serenity to fear. He had unleashed a fury that he could not control. "Get back!" he called. "Get back in the name of the Lord!" When he held a large wooden cross aloft, the crowd quieted a little.

Bending low, Thomas could see that the girl's tongue had rolled back and she was in danger of choking. Quickly he tilted up her chin. A few seconds later her body relaxed and her eyes closed. She lay unconscious on the steps and the multitude fell silent.

Thomas straightened himself. His face was scratched from where the girl's nails had scraped his skin in her frenzy and his shirt was torn. He surveyed the audience as he caught his breath. Some of the faces were familiar. There was Noah Kipps and his brother Luke, their fists raised. And there was Ann Banks, who had buried her husband last month, her features contorted with hatred. They had turned into monsters just as surely as leaves turn in autumn.

"This girl is not possessed by the devil. She is sick," he told them. His voice was raised but he did not have to shout. Calm had been restored, at least for the time being.

"We are living in 1783. We no longer call women witches

and burn them at the stake!" His words hung in the air for a moment, then fell like gentle rain.

The crowd murmured. They seemed less agitated. Nevertheless, the clergyman remained determined. He stepped forward and whispered to Thomas, "I will cast out the children's demons, Dr. Silkstone," and turned his face away from the expectant crowd.

Thomas looked into the reverend's eyes and saw the deep conviction there. He accepted that this was what the crowd expected of him and that to disappoint them could unleash yet more anger. He took a deep breath and sighed. "Very well," he conceded, "but please take heed."

The vicar nodded. "I do the Lord's work," he assured him, and he turned to the crowd with his arms outstretched. "Let us pray."

On the steps below, Thomas could see the young girl was waking. He bent down and stroked her head. Her left cheek was badly bruised from her fall and her knuckles were bleeding. "All will be well," he whispered, as the Reverend Lightfoot began intoning a prayer over her and her brother once more.

As the vicar spoke, the girl's anxiety seemed to lessen. Her features appeared to relax. She even managed to smile weakly at Thomas when she raised her eyes. "There's no need to be afraid," he whispered. "These people want to help you."

The words of the Lord's Prayer drifted up into the twilight air. As one the people were wishing the girl and her brother well, just as only a few minutes before they had wished them dead. The vicar concluded: "And deliver us from evil, for Thine is the kingdom, the power and the glory. For ever and ever."

"Amen," they all said in unison.

The Reverend Lightfoot then descended the steps to where the children sat, the girl quite still, but the boy still drooling and flopping around. Making the sign of the cross with his hand, he cried: "Demons, I cast you out in the name of the Father, Son and Holy Ghost."

The tide of time stood still for a moment, as if the seconds were parting to allow the devil to leave. Then, at last, the girl eased herself up from the step and holding out her own arms and hands in front of her, seemed to wonder at them. She appeared to grow in stature, like a butterfly gently emerging from its chrysalis. She wiggled and cocked her head and the crowd began to murmur, until finally she spoke.

Lifting her arms high into the air she cried, "Praise the Lord!" and the crowd erupted into loud cheers.

"A miracle!" they shrieked. "God is good! The devil is gone!" Women hugged their children. Husbands embraced their wives. Tears of joy and relief flowed freely. It did not seem to matter that the fog still lingered. It was almost forgotten amid the rejoicing.

Thomas surveyed the extraordinary scene and wondered at man's mercurial nature—one moment a frenzied beast, the next a compliant angel. He descended the steps to where the Reverend Lightfoot was being thanked by his grateful parishioners. So many hands reached out to touch him. "Bless you, vicar!" they said.

Joseph Makepeace came forward and hugged his daughter. His eyes were full of tears. Others came to lift his son. Together they made their way back slowly to the cart. This time the children sat upright. It was a sight that gladdened the heart of the whole community and they waved to them as they drove off, heading for their cottage at the far end of the village.

The crowd began to disperse. Many of the women returned to the apothecary shop at the appointed hour to collect their free bottles of physick before wending their ways homeward, giving thanks that their own children were not possessed. Most of the men, however, repaired to the Three Tuns across the way. Over their tankards of tepid ale they, too, would give thanks, although they were a little less certain as to why they should be so thankful. The fog still remained, but perhaps now that they put their trust in the Lord, and the devil had departed from Joseph Makepeace's offspring, fewer people would be taken to the grave.

* * *

Meanwhile, upstairs in the Three Tuns, across the square from where the extraordinary exorcism had taken place that very evening, Sir Montagu Malthus was hatching a plan. He had invited the recently bereaved Sir Henry Thorndike and his old friend Sir John Dashwood-King to dine. They feasted on grouse and pickled cabbage—there was none fresh—and downed several bottles of claret between them. The mood was lively and affable, despite the prevailing gloom caused by the fog. Sir Henry bemoaned the fact that his laborers were dying in their droves and Sir John complained that he would be forced to sell his wheat abroad for a better price. Sir Montagu's complaint was of a more personal nature.

"Tell me, is it true you have found the heir to Boughton?" asked Sir Henry, pitching forward over the Stilton cheese.

The lawyer's lips curled. "How word travels fast," he said, taking another sip of port.

"Farrell kept that one quiet, by Jove!" chuckled Sir John. "And you are sure he's not a bastard?"

Sir Montagu nodded. "For my purposes, gentlemen, the circumstances of his conception suffice." He sat back in his chair and fingered the stem of his glass, clearly unwilling to divulge any more than he saw fit.

"So your worries are over?" chimed in Sir Henry.

"The boy is now a ward of court. His welfare and position are secured," Sir Montagu replied, smugly.

Sir John threw back his head, laughing loudly. "You are a wily old bird, Montagu."

"Indeed, but I need to be sure that the colonist is well and truly out of the picture."

Sir Henry winked. "Ah, yes. He is set on marrying Lydia. I have seen them together. They make a pretty pair."

Sir Montagu took another sip of port and nodded. "Oh yes, he wants to marry her. But the wardship means I have scuppered his plans for the time being. But if I know our tenacious American, he will find a way 'round the problem."

Sir John smirked. "But if I know you, my friend, you will not be so easily put off."

The lawyer's head bobbed. "Indeed, gentlemen, but I will need both of you to support me in my endeavors."

Sir John shrugged, remembering his encounter with Thomas at his home. "He's pleasant enough, but he is a parvenu. You can count on me."

"And you, Sir Henry?" asked Sir Montagu, turning to his old friend. He found him rubbing his left arm and wincing. The lawyer fixed him with a piercing gaze. "I can see you are unwell, my friend," he remarked.

"This accursed pain has returned," he replied. His lips matched the color of the grapes on the table.

"Then you must get some rest. I have heard it is the best remedy for such ills."

The old man nodded compliantly. "Yes."

"But I still need your assistance. Would it help if I told you that with Dr. Silkstone safely removed from the picture, Lady Lydia Farrell will be in need of a suitable husband?"

Suddenly Sir Henry's pain seemed to be forgotten and an expression of interest settled on his jaded face. "If you put it that way . . ." he began, leaning forward.

Sir Montagu nodded. "Just as long as I can count on you both when it comes to the trial."

"Trial? What trial?" echoed Sir John. The two guests looked at each other quizzically, then turned their gaze on Sir Montagu for an explanation.

He obliged immediately. "It really is quite simple. There have been two murders in Brandwick and, by judicious manipulation, Dr. Thomas Silkstone can be implicated in both."

Sir John frowned. "How so?" he queried.

"The detail is of no importance. Let's just say I have friends in the right places and leave it at that, shall we, gentlemen?"

So it was agreed that Sir Montagu Malthus would do all in his considerable power to have Dr. Thomas Silkstone arrested for a double murder. If all went well he would swing for his alleged crimes and Lady Lydia Farrell would be free to marry a more suitable husband and keep blue blood running through the veins of the Crick line.

"Then 'tis settled," squawked Sir Montagu. And with these words he brought down his palm on the dining table, as if concluding a deal or ending a court session. "We shall bid farewell to Dr. Silkstone once and for all."

Chapter 39

The Reverend Lightfoot could not sleep that night. He still felt elated after the triumphant exorcism. The joy he had experienced as he cast out the demons from those wretched children was truly extraordinary. It was as if, for a moment, some mysterious hand had touched his very soul and empowered him. If he had ever wavered—and he was ashamed to say he had—then this miraculous revelation had set him once more on the true path to salvation. He paced up and down the aisle in his church, raising his arms now and again in praise. The Lord had imbued him with the most wonderful gift. Perhaps, he told himself, he should make more use of it.

He was contemplating how he might help other benighted believers. Surely there were many who needed help to overcome their inconsolable fears? Wandering restlessly up and down the aisle once more that evening he stopped in front of a painting in one of the side chapels. It was of Adam and Eve in the Garden of Eden. Naked and unashamed they were portrayed with the serpent, coiled 'round an apple tree. Suddenly he was reminded of Susannah Kidd. He recalled her lascivious lips, the curve of her breasts, her lustrous hair. He remembered how he had seen her picking apples in the orchard earlier that day. And that apple pie! How apt. Was she not sent to tempt men? Had not all his own reason deserted him in her presence? His heart had beaten so fast that he thought it would burst and when she touched him it was as if his whole body turned to molten rock.

Must she not be possessed by Beelzebub, too, to have such an electrifying effect on him?

Turning to the picture once more, seeing Adam and Eve on the edge, about to fall into the abyss of sin, he made up his mind. This was a sign. Hurrying out of the church, he went to the stable and saddled up his mare. The moon was still veiled by the fog, but his trusty horse knew the roads well and soon he had reached the Kidds' cottage.

Tethering his mount at the gate, he walked softly down the path. He was in luck. A lamp was burning in the bedroom. Mistress Kidd would be shocked to see him at such a late hour, but he would reassure her that he only meant to purge her of her sins. He would tell her that he knew the devil had a hold over her and that he could help her. She had tasted of the Tree of Knowledge. She had told him as much when she came to see him in a vexed state the other day. If she would only submit to his will, then he could cast out her demons and she would be free to live a good and pure life once more. All her anxieties would be banished, all her sins forgiven. The secret that was troubling her would be a distant memory. And when Judgment Day came, for surely it was imminent, then she would be able to meet her Maker with a clear conscience and a wholesome heart.

His tread was light. He did not want to frighten her. Drawing closer he could see the shutters were only half closed. A few paces more and he would be able to see into the room. His mouth went dry and his heart hammered as he drew level with the window. Now the bed came into view. It was empty. There was a sound; water being poured. She would wash herself before taking to the sheets. He could not see her, but he imagined her passing the cool, damp cloth around her neck and between her breasts.

Footsteps. His heart leapt as she emerged from behind the shutters. She was wearing leather stays over her shift and a petticoat and her golden hair was loose over her shoulders. Reaching for a brush on her table, she began running it through her hair with long, firm strokes. His breath came in short pants, now. There was no doubt about it, the devil possessed her. No ordinary woman could have this much power over a man.

He watched her stand and reach around the back of her waist to the laces of her stays. But wait. What was that? More footsteps. There was someone with her. He craned his neck and suddenly saw a man's hands, brown and rough, reach for the laces and begin to loosen them. He saw Susannah close her eyes and her lips curl in a delicious smile, as if pleasure was rippling through her body. Now there was a voice, deep and low. The half-closed shutter obscured his view. She let out a short laugh at something, then gave out a sensuous moan as the man began kissing her neck. The vicar's gaze darted to the rough hands once more. They were sun-tanned hands, hardworking hands that bore many scars on them. It was then he realized: They belonged to the knife-grinder.

The hour was late when Thomas finally arrived back at Boughton Hall. He had stayed much later than he intended at Mr. Peabody's dispensary, ensuring that everyone who needed physick was able to take some away with them. His throat was gritty with dust from the road and he felt exhausted.

The house was silent as he made his way up the stairs to Lydia's bedroom. On his return journey from Brandwick his thoughts had turned to her and how easily she had taken on the mantle of motherhood. He recalled the look of love on her face as she stared down at Richard. There was something of the Madonna in her manner; a serenity that surely only came with complete fulfillment. He thought, too, of Sir Montagu and how he had enlisted the law to keep them apart. She had had no choice but to agree to the terms of the wardship. And for his part, how could he have refused to allow Lydia custody of her only son? It would have been morally reprehensible. Not only that, but she would have ended up hating him for forcing her into such a decision. He did not doubt for one second that she still loved him, but now he would have to share her love.

Slowly he opened her bedroom door. The room was warm

and silent and completely dark. Normally Lydia did not snuff out her bedside candle until he was safely beside her. He edged his way in, reaching out for familiar furniture to guide his path toward the bed. His eyes grew gradually accustomed to the darkness as he approached it and he felt the covers. They remained smooth and the pillows cold and crisp. The bed was empty.

Standing for a moment in the darkness, he thought. Then he realized. Making his way out of Lydia's chamber, he walked along the corridor to the nearest guest room. Slowly, and as quietly as possible, he opened the door. And there they were; mother and son in bed together. Both slept peacefully, with Lydia's arm cradling Richard in its crook.

For a few moments he watched them, listening to their breathing: hers steady and familiar, his shallow and erratic. A pang of sadness shot through him. Had he lost his beloved? Suddenly he felt compelled to kiss her and he walked forward and bowed low, brushing her forehead with his lips. Her eyes opened immediately and she smiled.

"I love you," he whispered.

"I love you, too," she replied, closing her eyes once more.

Moving away from the bed he breathed a sigh of relief. He believed her. Silently he made his way to his own room by the light of a lamp that still burned in the corridor. He resolved to tell Lydia that he understood that she and her newfound son needed time together on their own. He would also tell her that when she felt ready, he wanted to be as a father to Richard, if she would allow it.

Once in his own room he flung off his coat, almost disdainfully, as if wanting to slough off the unsettling feeling left by the evening's strange events. He noticed the lining was torn at the seam as a consequence of his exertions. He would ask Mistress Kidd to mend it in due course. He walked over to the pitcher and ewer. Splashing his face with tepid water, he felt a stinging sensation and remembered the scratches on his cheek. He recalled the baying crowd by the market cross. Someone had cried out "witch." Someone—it may even have been Ned Perkins, humble, docile, Ned Perkins—called for the girl to be burned. Young and old alike had put their faith in such a superstitious ritual. The witch trials of Salem may have been held in a far off land, he told himself, but the sentiments and superstitions were as true today in Brandwick as they had been almost one hundred years ago in his homeland.

Chapter 40

The following morning Thomas went early to check on Richard. He found Lydia already dressed and sitting on the bed, holding her son's hand. She smiled as soon as she saw him enter the room.

"Dr. Silkstone has come to see you, Richard," she said softly, then to Thomas she added, "I think his fever has broken."

Thomas felt the boy's forehead with the palm of his hand. He nodded and looked into his eyes. They were still bloodshot but not as glassy as they had been the day before.

"So, you are feeling better, young man?" he asked gently.

The boy nodded his curly head.

"Perhaps you would like to try and eat today. Some porridge maybe, and we may even find some strawberry jam to put on top, eh?"

Lydia let out a girlish giggle. It was a sound Thomas had never heard her make before and it brought a smile to his own face. He could not recall seeing her so happy. Perhaps this is what it would be like; all of them, laughing together, being together, forging a family. It would not matter that he could not call her his wife in law. He had no interest in her title or her estate.

A sudden knock at the door interrupted the mirth. Thomas answered it. Howard stood anxiously at the threshold. "Sir, there are men from the village to see you."

The smile disappeared from the anatomist's face. He could hear voices below. He glanced back at Lydia. "I am needed," he told her.

She nodded. "Of course. There is no need to worry about us."

Thomas grabbed his case and followed Howard downstairs where a motley bunch of men from Brandwick had assembled in the back hallway. Ned Perkins stepped forward, fingering the brim of his hat, and spoke for them.

"Dr. Silkstone, sir, something terrible has happened."

"What?"

"The Makepeace children are dead."

"How? Why?" Thomas was stunned.

Hastily Lovelock made ready the wagon and drove the doctor, and the half-dozen men who had walked out to Boughton, back into the village.

"They're saying the devil came back to collect his own, Dr. Silkstone," said Perkins as the wagon rumbled its way toward Brandwick. "They're saying the demons weren't never cast out and now they've taken their revenge."

Thomas's mind flashed back to the exorcism and the contorted faces of the crowd. After witnessing such primeval behavior he knew the villagers could believe anything if they chose to. They stopped outside Joseph Makepeace's cottage, where a cluster of women had gathered. Some were weeping.

Thomas found Joseph Makepeace inside, being comforted by a neighbor. He was huddled in a blanket on a chair. He lifted his baleful eyes.

"The children," said Thomas. "I . . ."

Makepeace said nothing but the neighbor jerked his head toward another door. Entering the room Thomas confronted the sickening scene. The boy and girl lay dead where they had slumbered a few hours before, their skulls seemingly crushed. A bloodied shovel had been discarded close by on the flagstones.

The boy was lying slumped on top of his sister. Perhaps he had been trying to protect her, thought Thomas as he surveyed the room. A blow had been struck to the boy's forehead, a ferocious blow dealt, most probably, as he rose from sleep. The girl's nightshift was also stained crimson with the blood from a head wound.

Thomas glanced over at the window. It was open. The killer would have entered there, carried out his gruesome deed, then left the same way. Despite a slight breeze wafting through the open casement, the room was already growing warm as the outside temperature rose. The bodies needed removing before they started to turn. There would have to be a postmortem. Dr. Carruthers had always taught him to keep an open mind, but on this occasion, Thomas was finding it hard. These murders were far more brutal than those of Lady Thorndike and Gabriel Lawson. The children were struck in uncontrolled anger rather than cool calculation. Could there be more than one murderer in the village? Or might the adults' killer be the same fiend who bludgeoned these two unfortunate children in their beds? Only science could provide the answer, the anatomist told himself.

After consulting with the watchman, Thomas ordered the bodies to be lifted into the wagon and taken to the game larder at Boughton. Once again he sent word to Sir Theodisius. He did not seek immediate permission to conduct a postmortem. A non-invasive examination would suffice for now. This time, he knew what he was looking for and he did not need to use a scalpel to find it, even if it was only to disprove the same killer might be behind all four murders.

Just as he was leaving the cottage, he saw the Reverend Lightfoot approach, prayer book in hand. He was looking careworn and anxious. "Is it true?" he asked Thomas.

The doctor nodded. "They were both bludgeoned to death."

The vicar's brow crumpled and he shook his gray head. "What monster could do such a thing?"

"At this moment I am not sure, sir, but I intend to find out," replied Thomas.

Reverend Lightfoot nodded. "I will pray that you do, Dr. Silkstone," he said.

Inside, the vicar found Joseph Makepeace still trembling and mumbling incoherently. Ned Perkins had joined him. He sat on a chair next to the baker and the blacksmith by the empty hearth.

"Why would the Lord let this happen, sir?" asked Ned Perkins after a moment.

The reverend sucked in air thoughtfully, then shook his head. " 'Twas not God's work. This has all the hallmarks of the devil," he replied after a moment.

Perkins's head shot up. "Aye, and we know who that devil is," he said through clenched teeth.

All five men looked at each other knowingly, but it was Joseph Makepeace who, suddenly finding his voice, mouthed the name first. "Joshua Pike."

" 'Tis the knife-grinder that killed Lady Thorndike and Gabriel Lawson and now these young 'uns, too," snarled Ned Perkins, balling a fist and punching his palm. "The sooner we find him, the sooner we can put paid to his murderous ways."

"He'll be hiding up somewheres 'round here," said the baker, wiping his hands on his floury apron.

"Fog means he can't go far," added the farrier.

"It certainly does," said Perkins.

It was then that the vicar, who had been keeping his own counsel, listening carefully to what the men were saying, chose to speak. "And I think I know where he can be found," he ventured. All eyes turned on the Reverend Lightfoot. Had they heard him right? He fixed each one with a knowing look, then said, "And, you are correct. 'Tis very near."

Chapter 41

O nce again Thomas found himself in the presence of the dead in the game larder. He never relished his task when a life had been taken cruelly and by another's hand, but when that life was a child's, it was doubly hard. Not only that, but two children lay side by side on the cold marble slab. The nature of their injuries was so repellent that he had to force his own anger down as it welled up inside him.

First he looked at the boy. His large, wide forehead and low set eyes had presented the perfect target to the murderer. It appeared his injuries had been caused by his father's own shovel that Thomas had retrieved from the cottage. Strands of hair clung to the congealed blood on the blade. The spade, he mused, had been brought down with enormous force in a single blow to the frontal lobe.

Lifting the child's unruly fringe, Thomas inspected the wound. The depression in the boy's skull was at least half an inch deep, but it was not the contusion that arrested his attention. He reached for his magnifying glass and peered at the small flakes caught in the victim's hairline. At first he took them for the familiar particles of sulfur in the air, but when he examined them more closely, he could see they were not. Carefully he retrieved a fragment and dropped it into a phial.

Next he turned his attention to the girl. He guessed she was about twelve years of age. She looked so much younger in death than she had on the steps of the market cross. Gone was the strain in her features; the taut skin across her cheekbones had relaxed and the ridge above her nose caused by frowning was smooth. He noted several bruises on her body, but it was hardly surprising that she bore the marks of her uncontrollable fit in the marketplace. There were contusions around her wrists where she had been restrained and on her knees where she had slipped up the steps. There was bruising around her neck, too, which puzzled him. It was clearly she who had borne the brunt of the killer's wrath. She had been struck not once but at least three times on the head and torso. Her brown hair was matted and made darker by the blood and her chemise soaked around her chest and left shoulder.

Thomas took a comb and teased partings around the head wounds to inspect them more closely. He knew what he was looking for. And there they were. Through the lens of his magnifying glass, in among the egg cases of head lice, he spied larger dots of foreign material. Again he plucked three or four such fragments out of the hair with tweezers and dropped them into a separate phial. Could it be that these small particles linked all four killings?

"Most interesting," he said to himself, lowering another piece of potential evidence into a glass tube. If only he had the facilities of a laboratory nearby. As it was, he would have to wait until a return journey to London to identify the source of these odd and various samples. And with the fog still lingering, he had no idea when that would be.

He was contemplating making a trip to Oxford. Perhaps he could ask his old friend Professor Hans Hascher, who had been so helpful in the past in the quest to prove Michael Farrell's innocence, if he could work in his laboratory? Before he had given the idea more thought, however, there came a knock on the door. He glanced at the table. The bodies of the dead children were a most distressing sight.

"Who is it?" he called.

"Will Lovelock, sir," came the reply through the door.

Thomas wiped the blood from his hands. "Yes, Will," he said, opening the door only narrowly so that the boy could not see inside the room.

"Her ladyship says that the vicar is here and she requests that you come now," he panted, the speech memorized by heart.

Returning to the young lord's bedroom a few minutes later Thomas found the Reverend Lightfoot talking with Lydia. After the morning's traumatic events he had not expected to see the vicar. He was sitting by the boy's bedside reading a passage from the Bible to him, the story of Abraham and his son Isaac. Thomas had assumed he would be busy dealing with Joseph Makepeace and the rest of the shocked community, offering words of comfort after the horror of the double murder, but no, here he was imparting an Old Testament story to a young child as if it were a bedtime fairytale.

"I heard about the children," said Lydia, rising to greet Thomas.

"Most shocking," chimed in the clergyman.

"Indeed," replied Thomas, then turning to Lydia he said, "I am afraid that yet again I am obliged to turn your game larder into a mortuary, your ladyship."

Lydia frowned as she digested the full implication of what Thomas had just related. "So be it," she said.

The Reverend Lightfoot, on the other hand, remained practical. "So while the bodies are in your custody, Dr. Silkstone, I thought it would be a good opportunity for me to call on Lady Lydia," he said, closing the Bible. "My time is not my own these days. One never knows when one will be called upon." There was a certain smugness about the vicar that did not endear him to Thomas. He tapped his cane sharply on the floorboards, like an officious court clerk, as if his every second was precious.

Richard was sitting upright in bed. It was clear to the doctor that his fever was gone, though he knew he might relapse at any moment. Indeed, Thomas himself had been asked by many an anxious mother to baptize her sickly newborn if it was thought it was not more than a few hours for this world. He had always willingly obliged. Offering those few grains of comfort was a sweetener to the bitter pill so often swallowed in such circumstances. However, it seemed young Richard was mercifully growing stronger by the hour.

The vicar opened his satchel and began unpacking the small flasks of sacred oil and water required for the baptism. Taking advantage of the distraction, Lydia moved closer to Thomas. "He does not know," she whispered cryptically, looking at Richard. Thomas understood. Lydia wished to keep her son's identity a secret, at least for the time being.

A moment later Reverend Lightfoot wheeled about, his surplice 'round his neck. "And you are to be the godfather?" he asked, looking directly at Thomas.

"That is my honor," replied Thomas, masking his surprise.

"I explained to the Reverend Lightfoot that Richard is the son of friends of mine in Oxford. The fog sickness claimed them both, so I have taken him into my care." Lydia spoke in a strange, slightly exaggerated tone that told Thomas he was not to question or contradict her any further.

He nodded. "Indeed." He could understand why she did not feel ready to announce to the whole world that she had a son. It would take time for them both to adjust to their new relationship.

"Then let us proceed," announced the vicar, handing both Thomas and Lydia lighted candles.

Richard remained slightly bemused by the proceedings, his dark curls resting on the pillow. His skin was still sallow, but his amber eyes were full of life and they followed Lydia around the room wherever she went. During the baptism he only moved when the reverend poured a little holy water over his head to signify spiritual cleansing. His small body jerked up, but his mother held his hand and soothed him. Shortly afterward he was pronounced free from original sin and both Lydia and Thomas rendered a hearty "Amen."

Candles were blown out and young Richard was patted and caressed. Lydia was beaming and Thomas could not remember when he had seen her so full of joy.

"He is a fine young man," remarked the vicar, packing away his flasks and candles. "And yet . . ." He broke off.

"And yet?" queried Thomas.

"There seems to be something wrong with his arm." He turned away from the bed as he said this, so the boy could not hear.

Thomas looked uneasy, but thought quickly. "An accident, I believe. A fall from a pony."

Turning 'round, the vicar looked at the boy. "So he is a cripple?"

The sudden change of tone shocked the doctor and he shot back, "That is a harsh word, sir."

The Reverend Lightfoot, however, seemed unfazed. "Come, come, Dr. Silkstone. In our line of work we deal with such infirmities all the time. There is no need to be precious about them." Then to Lydia he added, "I am sure he has come to a good home and that you will look after him well."

She nodded. "That is why we are going to spend a few days in the caves. Richard will be able to regain his strength there."

The vicar arched his brow. "Ah, yes," he said. "I have heard that many are returning fully restored after a week or so there." Reaching for his hat and his cane, he walked over to the door, but paused at the threshold. "Oh, and when you have examined the bodies of those dead children, will you let me know what you find, Dr. Silkstone? I would be most grateful. I will show myself out." And with that he bid both of them a good day.

Left alone once more, Thomas went over to Lydia.

"I know I did wrong, but I could not face having to tell the reverend the truth just now," she said, shaking her head.

"He will understand when you do decide to. The idea is still strange to you," he told her softly.

From out of the corner of his eye he could see Richard was watching them. "So, young man, you are looking so much better," said Thomas, smiling. He settled himself on the bed and was just beginning to talk to his new godson, when a tap on the door interrupted the conversation.

"Come in," called Lydia.

Howard stood stiffly on the threshold, looking a little uncomfortable. "I am sorry, your ladyship, but there is a messenger downstairs for Dr. Silkstone." Turning to Thomas he added, "He says he has been tasked to deliver his message into your hands, sir."

Following the butler downstairs, Thomas saw the courier waiting in the hallway. The man's coat and hat were covered in dust and he smelled of sweat and leather.

"Dr. Silkstone?"

"I am he."

The messenger held out a rolled piece of parchment. "I am to give you this, sir, and await your reply."

Thomas opened up the scroll. It read:

> *Dear Dr. Silkstone,*
>   *I am afraid to inform you that Dr. Carruthers is seriously ill. Please return to London as soon as possible. God's speed.*
>
> *Sir Peregrine Crisp,*
> *Coroner*
> *Westminster.*

The doctor frowned. It was as if he had been dealt a swift blow in the guts. "Please tell Sir Peregrine that I will be on my way within the hour."

"Very good, sir," replied the courier, bowing low.

Thomas's heart, that only five minutes ago had felt so much at ease, now ached. He thought of his mentor, obviously close to death. Could it be that he, too, had been struck down with the fog sickness? He had heard reports that all London was still in its grip.

As soon as he reappeared at the threshold of the bedroom, Lydia knew he was the bearer of bad news. "What is it?"

" 'Tis Dr. Carruthers. I need to go to him."

"He is sick?"

Thomas nodded. "I fear the worst. I need to leave this afternoon."

She wrapped her arms around his waist. "Take care, my love," she said.

"Have no fear for me," he retorted, kissing the top of her head. " 'Tis Dr. Carruthers who needs our thoughts and prayers."

Still with her arms around him, Lydia nodded. "I shall pray for you both."

He pulled back so that he could look into her eyes. "And you must take care, too," he told her. "Richard should be very much recovered when I return."

Lydia smiled. "Yes, and the Reverend Lightfoot will see to it that no harm comes our way," she assured him.

Thomas returned her smile, but her words reminded him that he was leaving her at a time when a vicious murderer, or murderers, were on the loose, seemingly killing at random. He felt he was deserting her and yet his mentor and the man who had been like a father to him for the past nine years was close to death.

Returning to the game larder, he covered the children's corpses and entrusted Jacob Lovelock with the task of seeing that they were transported for burial. Then he packed his case, making sure that he took with him the four phials of material he had collected from around the wounds of all those murdered. At least in his own laboratory he would be able to carry out tests on them to ascertain their origin. He was convinced they held the key to whoever was behind these heinous acts. For the time being, however, his priorities lay with the man to whom he owed so much. He just hoped his arrival in London would not be too late.

Word had spread like wildfire across dry gorse brush. Joshua Pike was holed up at the Kidds' cottage. He was the murderer. He was the fiend who had killed not only Lady Thorndike and Gabriel Lawson, but two children as they lay in their beds. He was a monster! The devil incarnate! He had caused nothing but trouble since the day he arrived in Brandwick, terrorizing the vicar's wife and stirring resentment among the laborers in the fields. Justice had to be done, and if the law failed them they would take it into their own hands.

The men gathered by the market cross. They had armed themselves with whatever they could lay their hands on: pitchforks and rakes and shovels. The butcher carried his meat cleaver and the farrier his clincher. The master of the hunt gave permission for the hounds to join in the search. The constable, Walter Harker, came as well, carrying chains to restrain the quarry. Abel Cross, the fowler, had brought along his flintlock, too. It had a short range, but it could blow a hole in a man's gut if it was fired close enough.

Ned Perkins took the lead. This time there was none of the reticence he had shown in his dealings with Gabriel Lawson. His jaw was set determinedly and his eyes were on fire. The fog sickness had taken both his sons that week. He had nothing more to lose. Barging through the men, he rushed up the steps of the market cross to address the crowd.

"Today, brothers, two children were slain as they slept. Two more have been murdered. And still the killer is at large. Yet the powers that be in Oxford are sitting on their fat backsides doing nothing. 'Tis time we acted, brothers." He clenched his fist and punched the air. " 'Tis time we meted out our own justice; time we hunted down Joshua Pike!"

The crowd roared their approval and the dogs began to bark in the excitement. Torches were lit even though it was only the early afternoon, and those few who had horses swung up into their saddles.

From a good distance the Reverend Lightfoot watched the proceedings. The Lord had revealed to him Joshua Pike's whereabouts. A look of disgust distorted his features as he recalled the knife-grinder's rough hands on Susannah Kidd's body. There had been no question in his mind. He had acted in the best interests of the villagers. They were feeling threatened. They were the ones who could not sleep soundly in their beds at night. And if the law of the land appeared powerless, then they had every right to rise up and dispense their own form of justice.

He watched them from the saddle of his mare as they came toward him, past St. Swithin's on the road to Boughton. They were three abreast, with Ned Perkins at the front; a column of men as eager for blood as the baying hounds they mustered.

"You joining us, reverend?" asked Perkins as the men passed the church.

"Most certainly," he replied with a slight bow of his silver head. "I will bring up the rear."

And so the angry mob marched on, out of Brandwick toward Boughton, to Susannah Kidd's cottage. Their voices were raised, excited. Now and again a shout went up. The names of Joseph Makepeace's children were invoked, as if their death had turned them into saints. But the name of Joshua Pike was spat out like snake venom above the barking of the hounds.

Susannah Kidd was in her garden, scattering corn for the few chickens that remained. She heard the slathering dogs first, followed by shouts, then the sound of a hundred boots tramping along the track. Panic seized hold of her and, dropping her bowl of corn, she fled toward the cottage.

"They're coming," she screamed. "They're coming."

Like a shot, Joshua Pike ran out and over to his mule that had been grazing in the orchard at the rear. He hurled the saddle onto its back and began fastening the straps. Meanwhile Susannah walked to the front gate as the men drew level. She tried to compose herself, but she could not hide the fact that she was trembling.

"Where is he?" barked Ned Perkins. The men behind were jostling him; jabbing their pitchforks in the air. His voice was almost drowned out by their growls.

"Who?" was all she could ask weakly.

But the men would not wait. The first few jumped over the fence, then another simply hacked at it with an ax, clearing the way for all the rest to spill into the garden.

Susannah screamed. Her hands flew up to her face and she ran after the invading mob as it trampled over Amos Kidd's precious roses and flooded into the back orchard. The men arrived just in time to see Joshua Pike heave himself onto his mule and spur it into a trot.

"After him!" cried Ned Perkins. Some of the younger ones began running through the orchard toward the woodland where the fugitive was headed. Those with snarling hounds unleashed them and set them on his trail, bounding furiously through the long grass. But Abel Cross simply stood still. Cocking his musket he steadied his own arm, aimed, and fired. A shot ripped through the air and the knife-grinder jerked backward, as if pulled by an invisible rope. But his mule, terrified by the loud noise, trotted even faster. The young man slumped forward for a moment, then righted himself. In an instant he had reached the canopy of leaves at the edge of the wood and, in another, the flash of his red bandana had disappeared altogether.

Susannah was left distraught in the garden as the men surged forward toward the woodland's edge. Her sobs came in great waves, overwhelming her slender body. Dropping to the ground, she pummeled the dirt with her fists and let out a fearful wail.

The Reverend Lightfoot studied her from a few yards away. He watched the tears roll down her cheeks and saw the look of utter despair etched on her features. This was her agony as surely as if the soldiers at Calvary had driven nails through her hands and feet. The corners of his mouth curled into a smirk. Susannah Kidd's demons had finally been banished. Even if Joshua Pike was not torn limb from limb by the baying hounds, even if he did escape, he had been shot. His death could be quick or it could be slow: either way it would be agonizing. But as for Mistress Kidd, he had other plans, and they involved a short spell in prison followed by a dance at the end of a very long rope.

Less than a mile away, Thomas's carriage had turned out of the estate and onto the main Oxford road. He would spend the night at the Black Horse before taking the coach to London at first light. The fog was still lying low over hills and treetops, but it no longer deadened sound as it had before. The dry crack of a gun's report could be heard quite clearly. The noise sent the crows, huddling on low branches, scattering across the sky like musket shot. It also made the horses drawing Thomas's carriage jolt suddenly. He put his head out of the window.

"Everything all right?" he inquired of his driver.

"Sounded like a fowler's musket, sir," came the reply.

Satisfied with this explanation, Thomas settled himself back down, staring out of the window once more. The thought of the next few days filled him with dread. He did not know how he would find his dear Dr. Carruthers. The message had said his condition was serious. What if he arrived too late? There was so much he had left unsaid. He sighed deeply. The only hope he did carry with him was that in his own laboratory he could analyze the samples in his bag. At least surrounded by his own paraphernalia he might finally draw closer to finding the murderer, or murderers, stalking Brandwick.

Chapter 42

The men spread out, worming their way 'round trees and bracken. The hounds had the mule's scent and followed it eagerly. There was blood, too. Luke Kipps spotted a splash of it on a boulder. But they soon came to the river and the trail went cold. The dogs circled helplessly, yelping and whining. They were losing the light, too. The dense tree cover made it hard enough to see, but now tracks were difficult to follow.

"No matter, men," called out Ned Perkins. "He's shot. He'll not get far. We'll be back at first light."

So they wended their way back toward the cottage and to Susannah Kidd. They found her sitting quietly on a bench in the orchard with the Reverend Lightfoot at her side. She seemed calmer, almost resigned to her fate. She did not protest when Walter Harker came forward and told her that she was under arrest. She simply looked up and, in a bewildered state, offered her hands to him, so that he could bind her wrists. Then some other men led her from the bench and lifted her into the saddle of the Reverend Lightfoot's mare.

The long procession wound its course down the lane and into Brandwick once more. The mob no longer shouted and waved their weapons. Their thirst for blood seemed to have been quenched thanks to Abel Cross. They slapped him playfully on the back, or shook his hand. He was the hero of the hour. They talked excitedly among themselves, spoke of the blood on the stone that Luke Kipps had spotted, spoke of the brave way they had hacked down the fence and trodden across the garden. Most of them wore expressions of contentment on their faces, as if they had just finished gathering in a good harvest. Some of them gloated. Now and again one would shove Susannah Kidd in the back with a pitchfork handle. Others spat at her from time to time. "Whore!" one shouted. "Traitor!" called another.

Constable Harker allowed such behavior. It was only right that the men should be able to vent their spleen, letting off a little steam after all their efforts to bring justice to Brandwick, when the magistrates in Oxford had clearly failed.

The vicar followed on at the back of the throng. As he watched the young woman ahead of him, her hands shackled, her shoulders slumped forward, her head bowed, he could not help but think there was something almost biblical about the scene. In the fading light there sat Eve. There sat Rahab and Mary Magdalene. There sat all the evil, vile and sluttish women in the world and they were vanquished. In his own small way he had scored a victory for righteousness and it gladdened his heart.

As they entered the village, the women came out of their cottages, some clutching their children. They had not vented their rage in the chase and when they saw Susannah Kidd, they shook their fists at her. Raising their voices, they taunted her with more shouts of "Whore!" and "Harlot!" Some threw rotten tomatoes or plums at her. One of them hit her on the shoulder and it left a round crimson stain like a gunshot wound.

The procession halted outside the lock-up, to one side of the market hall. Constable Harker unhitched the large key from his belt and opened the low door into a space of no more than four feet square.

The mare carrying Mistress Kidd was brought forward and she was shoved and jostled down to the ground. She stumbled and the constable helped her to her feet, then led her to the cell. Teary-eyed she looked at him for a moment, then ducked her head into the space. The door clanked shut and, as Harker locked it with his great key, a cheer went up from the assembled throng.

The only opening in the lock-up was a small grille. A few men and women jostled to catch a glimpse of the accused woman as she sat huddled in the semidarkness. There were more insults and gobs of spittle, but when all the commotion finally died down, the Reverend Lightfoot chose his moment. As soon as the square fell silent once more and the good residents of Brandwick took to their beds knowing they would sleep much more soundly that night, the vicar approached the lock-up. Standing up against the door, he put his face to the grille, so that his nose wedged between the bars. He sniffed. Oddly enough the young woman still smelled of roses, only now the enticing scent was mixed with sweat. And what was that he could detect? He sniffed once more. Could it be fear?

"You are afraid, Mistress Kidd?" Now that his eyes had adjusted to the dark, he could see her crumpled on the floor, her knees clasped to her breasts.

Without looking up she said, " 'Twas what you wanted." Her voice was as brittle as a cut reed.

"I want you to repent, as any man of God would," he replied, looking down on her cowering in the cell.

Suddenly she lifted her gaze and hissed at him. "I have done nothing wrong."

Her response seemed to disappoint the vicar. He let out a bemused laugh and said, "Then let God be your judge."

Surprised that after all he had tried to teach her she still could not see the error of her ways, he backed away from the bars. "So be it," he told her. He would leave her fate to the Almighty, he told himself. In the meantime he had work to do. There was one other woman who needed to be taught a lesson before the Day of Judgment dawned.

Chapter 43

A small crowd of street urchins and apprentice boys had been milling around the lock-up since the early hours. They were lobbing rotten eggs and dog shit through the grille and shouting taunts. No one stopped them. In fact now and again a passing woman would add her voice to the jeers and insults.

Inside the cell, Susannah Kidd sat with her face to the wall. Her legs were doubled over so that she had lost all feeling in them. She had cried so much in the night that she had spent all her tears, too. Now she just waited in the darkness and the stinking filth that had gathered. She waited and she listened.

The hours were marked by the tolling of St. Swithin's bell and shortly after noon a shout rose up from somewhere nearby.

"They're here!" called a man's voice.

There were more shouts. Doors opened and slammed. Feet clattered on cobbles. Words were exchanged. There was a feeling of anticipation in the fetid air. The prison cart was rolling into Brandwick. Two constables came from Oxford, rough men in leather jerkins bearing the court's crest.

Constable Harker unlocked the cell and hauled Susannah Kidd out. The other two manhandled her onto the wagon, tethering her to the side, like some animal being taken to market. She kept her head bowed and her eyes downcast as the crowd hurled abuse at her. Harboring a fugitive was a serious offense. There'd be no escaping the noose, they said, shaking their fists at her.

The urchins and apprentice boys followed the wagon through the village as far as the main road to Oxford. The rest of the throng had tired much sooner. Most of them were happy to watch the wagon trundle off into the distance. The people's justice had been done.

Thomas spent a restless night at the Black Horse before catching the coach to London in the early morning. The fog had been patchy for much of the journey, sometimes thick, sometimes lifting enough to show a blue sky above it. In London, however, it resumed its grip. It mingled with the smoke from the hundreds of kilns and forges and bakers' ovens and thickened into a soup of smog. The stinking air was dry and hot, too; if anything a degree or so warmer than Oxford. Sounds were strangely muffled. Men shouted not to each other, but blindly into the strange void to warn others of their coming. Even the cabs were traveling with their lamps lit.

Thomas hailed one from where the coach set him down to take him to Hollen Street. Soon he was outside his home ringing the bellpull. Mistress Finesilver answered. Her already pinched face tightened with a look of surprise when she saw it was Thomas. She peered beyond him, out onto the foggy street, holding her apron up to her mouth.

"You'd best come in quick, doctor," she muttered.

Thomas eagerly obliged. "I came as soon as I could," he panted. The acrid smell of the fog was cleaving to his nostrils and palate.

"And why should that be, sir? We wasn't expecting you for another month." She took his topcoat and hat, then cocked her head as if waiting for an explanation.

Thomas frowned. "Dr. Carruthers . . . he is ill?"

" 'Tis news to me," she replied, obviously bemused by the question. "This fog's a devil, but he's not been out in it. Not like me, I can tell you. 'Tis no easy matter trying to find your way to the butcher's or the baker's in this." She chuntered on, but as she spoke Thomas noticed the study door was half open.

"Who's there?" came a familiar voice.

Thomas bounded past Mistress Finesilver, who was still in full flow, and found his mentor seated in his usual chair. He appeared to be in good health.

"Sir, but you are well!" Thomas blurted with relief and he rushed over to the old doctor and took him by the hand.

"Thomas, my dear young fellow!" he exclaimed in delight. "What a wonderful surprise!"

Kneeling beside him, Thomas looked at his mentor's face. His complexion was slightly ruddy, but in this heat it was only natural, Thomas told himself. Apart from this observation, he looked perfectly well. "I was told you were gravely ill, sir."

"Tosh!" the old doctor shot back. "Who blabbed such nonsense?"

Thomas withdrew the note from his pocket. "I have the message here. 'Tis from Sir Peregrine Crisp." In his mind's eye Thomas pictured the tall, imposing figure of the Westminster coroner.

Dr. Carruthers turned his bewigged head. "But you know I haven't had dealings with that old codger for at least ten years. Not since I lanced a boil on his arse!"

Thomas shook his head. "Then why . . .?" He broke off. A thought occurred to him. Someone wanted him out of the way. Someone had wanted him to leave Boughton. "No matter," he said cheerfully. "I am just glad to find you in good health."

But his mentor detected the falsity of his words. They did not ring true. "What is it now, young fellow?" he asked.

"Sir?"

Dr. Carruthers shook his head and lifted a finger to his right eye. "I may be blind, but I see with my other senses, remember? I know that something is troubling you."

Thomas paused for a moment, not knowing where to begin.

"I'll tell you what. Let us eat, then you can fill me in on everything over dinner," suggested the old anatomist.

The young doctor smiled. "What an excellent idea."

Mistress Finesilver was still most put out by Thomas's unannounced arrival. All that she could offer for dinner was a cold pie and potatoes, which she served with a dash of sullenness.

As they finished off a stale loaf with their claret, Thomas told Dr. Carruthers about the severity of the fog at Brandwick that had taken so many souls and how the recent murders had added to the sense of fear among the population.

"The general opinion is that the murderer is a traveler, a knife-grinder by the name of Joshua Pike. But I'm not so certain. 'Tis always easier to find fault with a stranger than with those close to you."

The old doctor nodded sagely. "How right you are," he said. "But if I know you, you will have been dispensing your physick and trying to solve the murders at the same time. Am I right, young fellow?"

This time Thomas's laugh was genuine. "I try my hardest, sir."

"And I'll wager you've brought some samples back for testing in the laboratory, so you can uncover this killer."

"Right again."

"I am rarely wrong," the old anatomist chuckled.

They withdrew from the dining room to finish their port in the study, as they always did. Casting his eye over the familiar furniture and objects, the young doctor noted that Mistress Finesilver's usually satisfactory standards seemed to have slipped in his absence. Given the severity of the fog, he accepted that a certain amount of dust on the mantelpiece and sills was inevitable, but it appeared on every surface. There were cobwebs, too, in many a corner.

Yet it was Dr. Carruthers's appearance that shocked him most. Normally immaculate, egg yolk stains were on his waistcoat. Nor had his shoes been polished and their buckles were dull and tarnished. It seemed that Mistress Finesilver had not been taking care of him with proper respect, thought Thomas.

Both men settled themselves in their usual chairs. A fire was not necessary, given the heat. Thomas's eyes drifted to a pile of newspapers that teetered precariously in the corner.

Remembering their custom he asked, "Would you like me to read the newssheet to you, sir?"

The old doctor let out a short laugh. "Ah, you've spotted the pile. I would not allow Mistress Finesilver to throw them out. I was hoping you would read them to me on your return."

Thomas smiled. "I shall make a start this very evening, sir."

Walking over to the newssheets, he withdrew a copy from near the bottom. A great cloud of dust billowed up and a large spider scuttled across the floor. He looked at the date. August 20, two weeks ago.

Settling himself down in his chair opposite his mentor, he began to turn the pages. For the past month the fog had understandably dominated the news pages, and the meteor had caused great consternation wherever it was seen, but elsewhere life went on. The Montgolfier brothers had amazed crowds in France with their first public demonstration of what they called a hot air balloon, and at home the Flax and Cotton Bill was passed in the House of Lords.

Thomas picked out a few choice articles that he thought would be of interest, such as the court ruling that made slavery illegal in Massachusetts, until he finally came to Dr. Carruthers's favorite section: the obituaries.

"So who's lately kicked the bucket?" inquired the old doctor enthusiastically.

Thomas scanned the columns. Given honorable mentions were a former provost of Eton College, a retired military commander, and a bishop who had died aged eighty-seven. He looked up from the newssheet and saw the old doctor's head was beginning to droop. He began reading again, but almost as soon as he did, his eyes widened and his jaw dropped.

"Good God!" he cried.

"What is it?" The old anatomist suddenly perked up in his chair.

For a moment Thomas said nothing. Then, looking up he said incredulously: "Sir Peregrine Crisp is dead."

"No! You are sure? When?"

Thomas focused on the print. "On August 18. He died suddenly at home, it says here."

Both men stopped still for a moment, taking in this information. Thomas thought of the last time he had communicated with the coroner after the suicide of Agnes Appleton.

Dr. Carruthers spoke first. "Then who . . . ?" He was as startled and confused as Thomas.

The moment he knew the coroner had not sent the message that brought him to London, Thomas had already determined to pay him a visit to get to the bottom of the mystery. But this new revelation put a much more sinister complexion on matters. He wondered if it was to do with one of Sir Montagu Malthus's schemes. He rose and walked over to the mantelpiece.

"My presence was obviously not welcome at Boughton," he said gravely.

Dr. Carruthers nodded, stroking his chin. "It seems to me that you should return as soon as you can, young fellow."

He knew his mentor was right. "I will," he replied. "Just as soon as I have identified the specimens that might reveal the identity of the Brandwick murderer."

"Then I best leave you to it," replied Dr. Carruthers, rubbing his stiff legs before rising slowly from his chair.

Thomas appreciated the solitude. There were books he needed to consult, experiments to conduct, and, of course, there was Franklin. It had always worried him leaving the care of his rat to Mistress Finesilver. If she had not been diligent in her duties regarding Dr. Carruthers, then poor Franklin would surely be very low down on her list of priorities.

Walking across the familiar courtyard and down the steps, Thomas arrived at the laboratory. Grasping the door handle he sniffed the air and frowned. As soon as he walked inside the stench of sulfur hit him. He gagged and reached in his pocket for a kerchief. Holding it to his mouth, he rushed into the room. The window had been left drawn down and a shaft of light from a street lamp above illuminated the coils of smog as they drifted in through the open casement. Hurrying over to it, he pushed up the sash, then rushed over to Franklin's cage. It was as he feared. The rat lay on its back, four legs in the air, gassed by the poisonous air. Unlatching the door, Thomas put his hand in the cage and reached for him, expecting the rat to be stiff and cold. But no, his body was still warm and then he saw him twitch.

Thomas carried the rodent across the room. Opening the door he took him out into the fresher air of the corridor. The rodent was struggling now, his legs flailing around, trying to right himself. Thomas helped him and he sat, stunned, for a moment, whiskers twitching. Next his sides heaved, fast as fury, in and out, in and out.

"That's right, boy. Breathe deep," Thomas told him. But the flurry of activity was short-lived and the rat collapsed after a few seconds. His pink eyes remained open but his breathing became labored and all energy seemed to ebb away.

Thomas stroked his back. If Franklin were a human, he asked himself, what would he do? He thought of the caves at West Wycombe, then glanced at the cellar door opposite. Taking a lamp from a nearby shelf, he opened the door and carefully negotiated the steps. It was much cooler below and the smell of damp pervaded the air, but it was infinitely preferable to the sulfur in his laboratory. In among the trunks full of old papers, the cobweb-festooned carboys of acid, and the kegs of ale, Thomas spied an empty wooden crate in the corner. This would be Franklin's home for the next few hours. He laid him down on a piece of rag. A dish on the floor had been used to catch rainwater as it dripped steadily from a leak above. He soaked the corner of the rag in water, then gently opened Franklin's jaws to let in a few drops to moisten his mouth.

"There you go, boy," he whispered, and he shut the lid of the crate and, taking the lamp with him, made his way back up the steps. He paused outside the laboratory door, but decided against opening it. He needed to allow the gas to dissipate and the larger sulfur particles to settle before he reentered the room. Besides, the hour was late and he was tired. Tomorrow, he told himself, he would confine himself to testing the samples that could hold the key to the Brandwick murders and to finding a more effective treatment for the fog sickness. Franklin would be his first patient.

Chapter 44

Lydia had risen early the next morning to supervise Eliza's packing. They were to spend at least four days in the caves at West Wycombe and she wanted to be sure that she took everything for Richard's care and comfort. Mistress Claddingbowl had also packed a hamper for them. She was, she had told her ladyship, especially pleased that the young master was so taken with her strawberry jam and had given him his very own jar.

Looking out of her bedroom window, Lydia could see there was no change in the weather. The sky remained gray and flat and the sun was a poppy-red disc behind the haze. Richard had coughed a good deal in the night, although he seemed well enough in himself. Yet the tang of sulfur still hung in the air and she knew a spell in the caves could only do him good.

She kissed her son gently on the forehead. "We are going to a place where the air is fresher, so that you can breathe more easily," she explained.

Mistress Firebrace had found some of the late Lord Edward's boyhood clothes stashed away in a trunk in the attic. There were two frockcoats and two pairs of breeches that seemed to match young Richard's size, although they were still on the large side.

Lydia helped him into them. The breeches were loose at the waist and she had to secure a sash around them to stop them falling down, but until Mistress Kidd could make him another pair, she told herself, they would have to suffice. Next came the shirt. The child slipped his arm through the first sleeve, but allowed Lydia to take his withered limb and ease it gently into the other.

"Does your arm hurt you, my sweet?" she asked.

The boy shook his curly head. At least she could take comfort that it did not pain him. Even so, the exertion of lifting his arm triggered his cough once more. She let him rest for a moment or two, then slipped his feet into the shoes that Sir Montagu had provided for him.

The frockcoat was blue, edged in white brocade. She pictured her brother wearing it all those years ago. Of course it was far too big for Richard, hanging limply from his shoulders. Nevertheless it would protect him against the chill in the caves. She guided him over to the cheval mirror. He seemed strangely startled at his own reflection, as if he had never seen himself before. His cheeks had colored a little and the corners of his mouth turned up in a faint smile. It was as much as he had managed over the past two days, and Lydia hugged him. He had only spoken a few words to her.

She, on the other hand, had spent hours talking to him, trying to make up for six lost years. She told him about his father and the Crick family and how he would grow to love Boughton, which would one day belong to him. She told him how he would be a custodian of the house and the land and that he would learn to call flowers and trees by their names. He would be able to recognize birds by their song and breeds of sheep by their wool. And when he was stronger, and this cursed fog had lifted, they would go riding into Brandwick on market day or down to Plover's Lake to fish.

"You look so fine, my dearest," she said, gazing at them both reflected in the mirror, and she kissed him once more.

Eliza knocked and entered. "The trunk is packed, your ladyship," she said.

Glancing across at Richard the maid smiled. "What a handsome young man, your ladyship," she said, almost wistfully. Realizing she had spoken out of turn, she grimaced, but Lydia returned her smile.

"Thank you, Eliza," she replied. "Yes, he is very handsome."

Jacob Lovelock had the carriage ready for noon, but just as they were coming down the steps of the hall another vehicle turned up the drive at speed. The horses drawing it were at a trot and it clattered to a halt right by them. Lydia instantly recognized the crest on the carriage door as the liveryman opened it.

"Sir Theodisius!" she cried. "What brings you here?"

The portly Oxford coroner heaved himself out onto the driveway, but barely managed to return her smile. "My dear, I am come on urgent business," he told her earnestly. "Where is Dr. Silkstone?"

Lydia frowned. "In London, sir," she replied. "He received a message that Dr. Carruthers was gravely ill and he went to his side."

The coroner mopped his ruddy face with his kerchief. "I feared I would be too late," he puffed.

"Too late for what, pray?"

He shook his head and his flabby jowls wobbled. "Young Silkstone has walked into a trap. Dr. Carruthers is not ill to my knowledge and this is all an elaborate ruse to, how can I put it, dispense with the doctor."

"Dispense with? Ruse? You talk in riddles, sir." Lydia was growing increasingly impatient with the coroner. "Please tell me what is going on?"

Sir Theodisius's broad shoulders heaved in a great sigh. "Malthus is behind it," he said.

"Sir Montagu? Behind what?"

The coroner shook his head. " 'Tis clear, my dear, that you and Dr. Silkstone have deep feelings for each other, and 'twould seem that your late brother's guardian is not content to keep Dr. Silkstone out of your marriage bed. He wants him out of your life, too."

Lydia's eyes widened. "What has he done?"

Again the coroner balked and shook his head. "I am not entirely sure, but Sir Henry Thorndike called on me this morning. Sir Montagu intends to implicate the doctor in murder and have him arrested. Silkstone is in grave danger and I have to go to London this instant to warn him."

Lydia stepped forward and clasped Sir Theodisius by the arm. "What will happen to him?"

The coroner, however, was not forthcoming. "I have told you as much as I know. I must be away."

"Then may God grant you safe passage, sir," she said, realizing it was no use pressing him further.

Sir Theodisius's thick lips stretched into a smile and he patted her hand. "He will come back safe and sound," he told her, even though he knew he could promise nothing. Lydia watched as he turned to haul his corpulent frame back into the carriage with a little help from his liveryman.

With a crack of the whip he was off once more. But just as the coach rattled off down the drive, Eliza walked down the steps with Richard, who was holding her hand tightly. Hearing footsteps, Lydia turned toward them.

"Who was that big gentleman, Mamma?" asked the little boy, looking up at Lydia.

It was only then that she realized. The man whom she had come to regard as a father-figure over the past few months had been and gone from Boughton Hall without even meeting her long-lost son.

The carriage ride to the caves passed quickly enough. The haze still veiled the rayless sun, but only the very tops of the hills were now obscured. Lydia sat uneasily, remembering Sir Theodisius's words and thinking of Thomas. She feigned an eagerness to point out to her son all the places of interest on the way. They drove through Brandwick and up onto the Wycombe road and all the while the boy peered through a chink in the thick leather curtains, eagerly taking in the sights of the countryside. Even the few sheep that were left to graze the parched grass caused much excitement. But it was toward the end of the journey that an odd-looking creature that was not quite a donkey and not quite a horse caused young Richard the most wonderment. They came upon it as it grazed on a patch of grass near the entrance to the caves. Wearing a saddle and a bridle, it looked up at the sound of the carriage, pricking its ears and chewing slowly, but its rider was nowhere to be seen.

Chapter 45

Thomas was to be joined by Dr. Carruthers in the laboratory early the next morning. The poisonous gas that had almost killed Franklin had dispersed, leaving a light coating of sulfur on all the surfaces. Thomas ran a damp cloth over the tops of sills, ledges, and tables to remove the deposits. He then lit a fire in the grate.

From outside he could hear the telltale tapping of the old doctor's stick as he crossed the courtyard. Within a few moments he had negotiated the threshold and was sniffing the air as he walked in.

"Someone left the window open."

The acrid smell had faded, but Dr. Carruthers's sharp sense of smell could always detect even the slightest whiff of poison in the air.

"Yes, sir. Does it trouble you?"

He shook his head. "No, besides I have this," he said excitedly. "If the fumes are too much for me I simply sniff!" He was holding up a cane that Thomas had not seen before. It had an ivory top. "Look here," ordered the old doctor, and he flicked open the lid to reveal a sweet-smelling potpourri of herbs and petals.

"I was gifted it in the will of an old colleague."

Thomas remembered his own father possessing something similar. "A physician's cane," he remarked. "Useful for preventing contagion."

"Precisely, or just wafting away these unpleasant fumes," replied Dr. Carruthers, smiling and tapping his way across the floor.

"So you are happy to proceed?" asked Thomas, watching the old doctor ease himself onto a stool by him.

"Of course I am. We must proceed. This air is killing scores of people, young fellow! Coachmen are dropping like flies in the streets, I'm told. So, you need to tell me all you know about the properties of this accursed fog and then we shall put our heads together. What say you to that?"

Although Thomas had wanted to deal with the contents of his phials in relation to the murders first, he could hardly argue with Dr. Carruthers, so he recapped his experiments at Boughton that proved the poisonous air was sulfurous.

"It seems that those who have been exposed to it longest suffer most," he told his mentor, adding, "but those who are predisposed to asthma are struck down much quicker."

At the word asthma the old anatomist frowned. "Interesting," he said, stroking his chin. "Have you tried atropa belladonna?"

"Belladonna?" repeated Thomas. He pictured the delicate flower with its purplish-blue petals. The locals called it deadly nightshade. It was a common sight in the Oxfordshire hedgerows, among the cow parsley and the foxgloves, where he had seen it growing himself.

"I know of the plant," he replied. "But I thought it was used to treat gastric ailments."

Dr. Carruthers nodded. "Indeed, it can be, but given in the right dosage, it can also ease breathing in asthmatics. It may help."

Thomas knew that the plant's properties were many and various. Cleopatra had used it to make the pupils of her eyes larger, and therefore more alluring to men. He also knew that merely ingesting a handful of berries from the plant could easily kill a grown man. Yet he was prepared to bow to his mentor's encyclopedic knowledge. After all, since nothing else was having any real effect, there was very little to lose.

"I assume you have some ready prepared?" said Thomas, already on his way to the storeroom, lighted candle in hand.

"Third shelf on the left, I think you'll find."

Sure enough, there it was: a small porcelain jar marked "Ex. Bellad." Thomas picked it up and peered inside at the powdered petals that looked like dried wood chippings.

"May I suggest we mix this with a little turmeric, sir? That seems to ease the breathing, too," ventured Thomas, thinking of his original formula.

"Yes. Yes," came the reply.

So Thomas produced his notebook and pencil and went back and forth to the storeroom fetching jars and vessels. He pounded and ground with the pestle and blended the powder with honey and oil of vitriol until finally he had produced a mixture that was ready to test.

"Now all we need is a willing patient," said Dr. Carruthers.

Thomas smiled. "I know of one very close at hand, sir."

"You do?"

"Franklin."

"That wretched rat of yours?"

Ignoring the jibe, Thomas went to fetch the rodent from the cellar. "I will be back in a moment," he called.

He found Franklin still breathing, but barely alive. Lifting him gently out of the crate, he brought him back into the laboratory and set him down on the table, still lying on top of the rag.

"Now, all we need to do is work out the quantity of the formula appropriate to his weight and then trial the physick on him," he told the old doctor, who seemed distinctly unimpressed.

"I suppose 'tis worth a try," he said with an unconvinced shrug.

Thomas weighed the rodent in his scales, then after making calculations on his notepad, he measured out the relative weights of the ingredients. Within a few minutes, he had reduced the mixture to the required strength.

"Now for the moment of truth," he said, drawing up the liquid into a pipette.

The old anatomist nodded his head. "I've heard the ingredient can work very quickly," he ventured.

Holding the rat's jaws open with one hand, Thomas emptied the contents of the pipette into its mouth, then closed it shut to make sure he swallowed the physick. The creature barely protested. Thomas then laid Franklin down in the cage, on the piece of rag, to wait for the formula to take effect.

"Now, sir," said Thomas, opening up his case. "For our next task."

"The samples?"

"Yes. I need to identify the contents of these phials." He brought out the glass tubes, each holding small flakes of material, none of them bigger than a grain of mustard.

The microscope lay under a small sheet in a nearby cupboard, thankfully protected from the sulfur dust. Thomas handled it with a renewed reverence and set it down gently on the work surface. Carefully withdrawing a flake from the first phial with a pair of tweezers, he placed it on a glass slide and examined it under the lens. It was the sample taken from Lady Thorndike's wound. A network of tiny woody veins appeared before his eyes.

"What do you see, young fellow?" asked Dr. Carruthers eagerly.

" 'Tis as I thought, sir," said Thomas, sitting upright. "A piece of a leaf."

"And this was found in the hair of the first victim?"

"Yes, sir. Lady Thorndike had been underwater for several hours, so its properties may have changed."

"Then let us look at one that may be easier to identify."

Thomas concurred. The samples he retrieved from Gabriel Lawson's wound could have been tainted by the smoke, but those he had taken from the dead children would have remained, to his knowledge, unsullied.

Looking at the specimen from the dead girl's head wound, he saw the familiar cells of a leaf structure under the microscope. "Another type of leaf," he told Dr. Carruthers.

"Children play among trees and plants all the time," he replied, obviously unimpressed.

Thomas nodded. "Yes, sir, but this leaf material appears desiccated."

He brought out his second sample, this time from the boy. Again he put it on a glass slide and examined it under the microscope. Once more he discovered a leaf structure similar to the type found in the girl's hair. It was edged with a dark stain of blood.

"Another leaf, sir," replied Thomas.

"What about its smell?" asked Dr. Carruthers.

Thomas lifted the specimen off the slide with his tweezers and sniffed. "I cannot detect any scent," he replied, but knowing how keenly his mentor's sense of smell had developed, he wafted it under his nose. "Can you?" he asked.

Carruthers's nostrils twitched. He paused for a moment, frowning, then said: "Yes, there is a faint whiff of . . . of rue, if I'm not mistaken." His face broke into a triumphant smile.

"Rue?" repeated Thomas.

"Yes. Also known as the herb of grace." Dr. Carruthers was chuckling now. The young doctor did not, however, share his mentor's enthusiasm. He remained silent. "What is it, young fellow? Have we not identified the leaf?"

Thomas sighed. "If I'm not very much mistaken, rue is an herb used in exorcisms." He had neglected to tell Dr. Carruthers the full story of the children's unhappy last few hours on earth. The presence of the herb proved nothing. He remembered the Reverend Lightfoot sprinkling a handful of it over each child to symbolize repentance.

"And this?" Thomas offered him a sample from Lawson's head wound.

Another sniff. "This is more difficult," said the old doctor, tilting his head to one side, his nose still twitching. "Let me see, now. 'Tis sharp, and unpleasant."

Thomas watched, holding his breath.

"I have it!" exclaimed Dr. Carruthers, clicking his fingers. "Wormwood."

It was an herb that was familiar to Thomas. "I have used it to treat fevers and indigestion," he remarked.

"And in England 'tis sometimes used in beer instead of hops," added the old anatomist.

"So we have a variety of herbs," Thomas said, trying to make sense of their findings so far. He recalled sniffing what may have been rosemary in Lawson's hair, too. "But there does not seem to be any connection between them."

This time he brought out the phial containing what appeared to be a shard of silver, no wider than a woman's fingernail. "I found this fragment of what looks like silver in Lady Thorndike's wound, too. I shall try the magnetic test first," he said, running a magnet over the sample. It was not attracted. "No," he muttered.

"So it is silver?" asked Dr. Carruthers.

"No doubt," repeated Thomas. "But the fragment is so thin, it may well be from a comb or some hair adornment." He leaned forward, pondering until the silence was broken.

The old doctor suddenly turned his head. "What's that sound?" he asked.

Thomas put down the magnet and listened. A strange scratching was coming from the corner.

"Franklin," he cried. He had been so preoccupied testing the samples that he had quite forgotten about the rat. Hurrying over to the cage, he was delighted to see the creature stirring from the makeshift bed.

"He seems much restored," he told Dr. Carruthers, unfastening the lock and bringing out the rat.

Placing Franklin on the work surface by Dr. Carruthers, Thomas began to examine him. Straightaway it was obvious that his labored breathing had returned to normal. He sat up on his back legs and sniffed at the air, bringing a smile to his master's face.

"If the formula helps Franklin, there is a strong chance 'twill work on humans, too," ventured Thomas.

Dr. Carruthers clapped his hands. "Indeed," he agreed enthusiastically. The excitement, however, was short-lived. From somewhere outside came a commotion. Mistress Finesilver was shouting.

"No! What do you think you are doing?" Her shrill voice could be heard in the courtyard, mingling with the sound of heavy footsteps and men's grunts.

"What goes on?" asked Dr. Carruthers, his head wheeling 'round, trying to make sense of the hubbub.

Thomas hurried toward the door just in time to see it flung open, almost catching him in the face. Two thickset men stood on the threshold, one of them trying to fend off Mistress Finesilver's thrashing hands. The other glowered at Thomas. He wore the insignia of a court official on his coat.

"Tell the woman to stop it, or she'll be coming with us, too," he barked.

Thomas could see that the men meant business. "Mistress Finesilver," he called. She turned, her face flushed with exertion. "Please," he said and she stilled her arms and stood aside.

"Dr. Thomas Silkstone?" asked the same man. He was shorter and less brutish than the other.

"I am he," replied Thomas, squaring up to the inquisitor.

"I have a warrant for your arrest for the murder of Lady Julia Thorndike," he informed him.

Thomas's jaw dropped. "On whose authority?" he cried. "Let me see."

The law officer handed him the paper, a smug look on his face. Thomas scanned it. "But this cannot be!" he said, shaking his head incredulously.

Dr. Carruthers tapped his way over to the door and now stood beside the young doctor. "You are accused of murder?" he asked anxiously.

"This is a warrant for my arrest," replied Thomas, snatching the paper from the officer's hand and glancing at it. "And 'tis signed by Rupert Marchant."

"Marchant?" repeated Dr. Carruthers. "Is he not the . . . ?"

Thomas's mind flashed to Sir Theodisius's arrogant nephew, who had not only hoodwinked one of his patients but also sought to seduce Lydia, too.

"Yes, the conniving lawyer who swindled Charles Byrne for a supposed King's Pardon. It would seem he's been made a magistrate." Thomas's eyes widened in disbelief.

"Enough!" cried the official, "or I'll have you for contempt of court, too." At his signal, the burly constable stepped forward with a set of shackles and grabbed hold of Thomas by the wrist.

"There is no need for force," protested the young doctor. "I can prove I am innocent of the charge."

The official let out a sharp laugh. "That's what they all say!"

"What's happening?" pleaded Dr. Carruthers, standing helplessly behind Thomas.

"Have no fear, sir. Everything will be all right," Thomas assured him, glad that he could not see him in chains.

"But if you are taking him to jail, at least allow the man his coat!" wailed the old doctor, stepping forward with it.

The official looked at him, then at Thomas, and shrugged. "Very well," he conceded.

Thomas was a little surprised by his mentor's request, but as soon as he took the coat, he understood. The old man tapped the pocket lightly. At least the new formula would not be lost.

Lydia had settled Richard down on his new bed in the caves as comfortably as possible. The journey had clearly taken its toll on the young boy, but he had managed to eat a little bread softened with milk and was now sleeping.

There were only six other patients left in the caves, so they had all been moved into the banqueting chamber. The others had been returned to their homes, their breathing much improved by their time resting. Three of them had lost their fight. The ones who remained were nearly all elderly and showed few signs of recovery. Lydia feared for them. That is why, later that afternoon, she was so pleased to see the Reverend Lightfoot arrive unannounced.

It was one of the nurses who notified her of his presence as she sat reading by Richard's side. She looked up to see him standing there, smiling benignly.

"Reverend Lightfoot. How kind of you to call," she greeted him.

He bowed his silvery head. "It is my duty to offer words of comfort to the sick and old, Lady Lydia, and I am sure many of them here would welcome such solace." He lifted the prayer book that he held in his hand.

"I am sure they would," she agreed. She guided him over to the three remaining women, who lay limply on their mattresses. At his arrival two of them eased themselves up and were happy to listen to the vicar read prayers to them. Meanwhile Lydia returned to Richard's bedside. Eliza had been watching him for the past five minutes and reported that he had not stirred.

"You look tired," Lydia told her. "Why not take your rest?"

Eliza nodded, bobbed a curtsy, and holding a lamp went to lie down in the far corner of the chamber. Lydia remained with Richard until, half an hour later, she saw the clergyman close his prayer book and bid the elderly women farewell. She rose as he approached her.

"I am sure your visit was appreciated, sir," she told him, smiling.

"I hope so," he replied. "Widow Buttery does not seem long for this world."

Lydia nodded. The old woman was weakening by the day.

"And how is this young man faring?" The reverend switched his attention to Richard as he lay sleeping. He moved closer and stood leaning on his cane.

Lydia looked at her son's curls on his pillow and the bow of his lips. Color had returned to them at long last. She smiled. "He is improving, thank you, sir."

The Reverend Lightfoot smiled, too, as he studied the sleeping child. "He is so like his mother," he said.

The words jolted Lydia. She shot a look of surprise at the vicar. "His mother?" she repeated.

The vicar raised his gaze. "Yes, your ladyship. Your son is the image of you."

Lydia felt a cold shiver run down her spine. For a second tension hung in the air, then she spoke. "I am sorry, sir," she conceded. "You have found me out. I would have told you, when I felt the time was right."

Reverend Lightfoot smiled. "I know that. But there was no need to hide the boy's true identity from me." He wore an expression of mild hurt that made Lydia feel guilty.

"I was not ready to reveal the truth. He has only been with me for four days." She knew her excuse sounded pathetic, but it was true.

The vicar patted her lightly on her arm in a rare show of emotion. "The Lord knows what is in your heart, my dear Lady Lydia." But instead of soothing her, his words had the opposite effect. Perhaps it was the way his mouth curled in a slight sneer at the corner, or the cold sharpness of his look that pricked her conscience. Either way, as he bade her farewell and walked back into the light after the darkness of the caves, Lydia was left with an inexplicable feeling of apprehension.

Chapter 46

The formidable gates of Newgate prison loomed large. The last time Thomas had been through them was to visit Signor Moreno, the Tuscan castrato, who stood wrongly accused of murder. He was finally acquitted and Thomas could only hope he would enjoy similar justice. In the meantime he was not sure if it was a blessing or a curse to know exactly what lay ahead of him.

The familiar stench soon assailed his nostrils and for the first time in weeks he found himself almost craving the smell of sulfur instead of this gut-churning reek. He was marched inside and his charge given over to a man with a familiar face. His topcoat was flung on the table.

"Well, well. If it isn't the physician from the Colonies," sneered the head jailer. Thomas's heart sank when he saw it was the same ugly brute, with the cruel mouth, who had shown so little compassion to Signor Moreno. The man rose from his desk and paced around Thomas as he stood chained and helpless. "Friend to sodomites, if I remember rightly!" he sneered, looking his latest inmate up and down. "And I see you've even brought something to keep you warm." He picked up the coat and rifled through the pockets. Thomas held his breath. A second later the jailer brought out the folded sheet of paper that Dr. Carruthers had managed to secrete in the coat. Thomas bit his tongue as the jailer examined it.

"What's this scribble?" he asked, a look of disdain on his face.

The young doctor thought it best to tell the truth in the hope that it might appeal to the jailer's better nature, if he had one.

" 'Tis the formula for a physick to help ease the fog sickness," he told him.

For a moment the brute appeared quite shocked. He fixed Thomas with a stare. Perhaps there was an ounce of compassion in that pitiless exterior. But no. Suddenly he threw back his head in a gale of mocking laughter.

"So you would save all London from the great fog, would ye?" he cried, banging the desk with his flattened palm. Then, taking the paper, he held it level with Thomas's face and began to tear it, first lengthways, then widthways.

"No!" blurted the doctor, lurching forward. But the jailer continued his cruel stunt until the paper was left in shreds. He tossed the pieces up in the air so they fluttered to the ground like snowflakes.

Jutting his head forward, so that Thomas could smell his stinking breath, he scowled at him. "If I were you, I'd concentrate on saving yourself, Dr. Silkstone." He glanced at the sheet of paper on his desk. "The charge is murder, I see," he said. Sucking in deeply through his clenched teeth, he added: "At least your stay will be a short one, before your appointment with the gallows."

From the corridor behind him Thomas heard footsteps echo and a stocky young man with a flattened nose appeared. "Mr. Dowd here will take care of you, Dr. Silkstone," the head jailer sneered.

Thomas felt the shove of a fist in the small of his back and he moved on down the dingy passageway. It was every bit as gruesome as he remembered. To his left and right were cells each holding six or more inmates, all manacled by chains. Forced to run the gamut of the other prisoners, he was grabbed and pinched by ragged arms that reached out through bars as he passed. Some were covered in dirt, others in sores. There were shouts and jeers and pleas until, after what seemed an age, he finally arrived at his cell.

Thankfully he was alone. At least whoever was behind his

false arrest had shown the decency to see to that. As for any other privileges, they were few and far between. The cell was a tiny room, barely six foot by six foot, just big enough to take a palliasse and a pail for his slops. There was a small slit for a window high up in the outside wall, so that at least he could tell if it was night or day. He was grateful for such small mercies.

His jailer said little. He seemed diffident, almost uncomfortable, with his new prisoner. And he had a cough, too. Not a loose, persistent one, like those who were afflicted by the fog, but an occasional, chafing one. Once inside the cell he told Thomas to lift his wrists so that his irons could be unlocked. Their eyes met as the young man fumbled with the small key.

"Thank you. Mr. Dowd, is it not?" said Thomas, massaging his bruised hands.

"Sir," he acknowledged, looking directly at him. A connection had been made. The doctor could now make progress. The young man had been carrying the coat and, instead of flinging it on the floor, he set it down carefully on the filthy mattress. Another good sign, Thomas noted.

The clank of the cell door and the turn of the key meant that left in solitude, he could begin to think. He picked up the coat and checked the pockets. They were empty; of course they were. The head jailer's probing fingers would not miss a trick. But just as he was about to toss the garment down once more, he felt something lumpy in the lining; a hard object that was quite long and thin. He inspected the split seam. He fumbled for a second or two, then drew out something so precious that he wanted to shout out for joy when he finally held it in his hand. Dr. Carruthers, in his infinite wisdom, had managed to slip into the tear in his lining something far more useful than a file for the prison bars or a pick for the lock. He recalled the bargain he had made more than a year previously with Captain Farrell's jailer, who was suffering from the toothache. On that occasion not only did he extract the man's tooth, but also a promise from him to preserve the captain's corpse in gin. He had used his medical skills to achieve his own aims and he would, no doubt, do the same again. Thanks to his mentor, Thomas had managed to smuggle into Newgate Prison a bottle containing the new formula that could save countless lives. He kissed the glass and placed it carefully back into the inside pocket of his coat. Soon it would be called upon to save his own life as well.

Settling himself on his palliasse, his folded coat under his head, he decided to go through events. He needed to make sense of what was happening to him, to piece together this awful puzzle. He began by recalling his first days at Boughton Hall. He cast his mind back to the garden party at West Wycombe Park. So much had happened—so many had died—since that fateful day in June when he had first encountered Lady Thorndike that it seemed not mere weeks but years ago.

It was then that he heard footsteps along the passageway. They were slow and heavy and accompanied by shorter, lighter ones. A cough. They were coming nearer. He sat upright. They stopped outside his door. The key twisted; the bolt clattered and in walked Dowd, followed by a very welcome visitor.

"Sir Theodisius!" cried Thomas, grabbing the Oxford coroner by the arm. He would have hugged him had it been thought seemly to do so. As it was, they shook each other's hands for several seconds. "I am so very glad to see you, sir," he said, finally pulling himself away from his visitor.

The young jailer obligingly brought a chair for Sir Theodisius and it creaked under his weight as he eased himself down. He was flushed and his forehead was damp with sweat. "My only regret is that I did not arrive here sooner to spare you this," he huffed, gesturing with outstretched arms to the squalid surroundings.

"But you have news?" Thomas leaned forward on the edge of his low palliasse.

"Indeed I do," replied the coroner, dabbing his brow. "Sir Montagu Malthus is behind your arrest."

Thomas leaned back. "I knew it," he snapped. "So Lady Lydia has explained about the wardship and the conditions the court has imposed at his instigation?"

The coroner shook his head. "What wardship?"

In all the mayhem of the last few days, Sir Theodisius had not been informed that Lydia had a lost son who had been found and was now at Boughton. So Thomas had to relate the whole sorry saga of how Sir Montagu had tracked down the boy and now held him almost to ransom. By forbidding their marriage, Thomas and Lydia were the ones who were being forced to pay the heaviest price.

"I see," said Sir Theodisius finally. "So, not content that you two can never marry, he wants you disposed of at the gallows."

Thomas nodded. "Yes. He wants me dead," he said with a chilling decisiveness. There was a pause as both men pondered the thought. "But how did you know I was here?" he asked.

Sir Theodisius eyed him earnestly. "Sir Henry."

Thomas frowned. "How did he . . . ?"

"He was in on Sir Montagu's plan. There was a note."

"A note?"

It took Thomas a mere second to follow. Somehow the cuckold had managed to obtain the crumpled message that Lady Thorndike had written, asking Thomas to call on her. It did not matter that it was as a physician answering a patient's urgent request that he visited Fetcham Manor, the note was incriminating.

Sir Theodisius leaned forward. "Sir Henry is not happy with Sir Montagu's scheme. He is a good man," he told Thomas, nodding his head. "I only wish I could say the same for my nephew."

Thomas thought of the warrant signed by Rupert Marchant. "Yes, it would seem that his new promotion has gone to his head," he said with a wry smile.

The coroner looked sheepishly at his friend. It was clear to both men that the lawyer-turned-magistrate bore a grudge against Thomas and was only too willing to be complicit in his downfall.

There was an awkward pause until Thomas asked, "So, you have your own scheme to free me from this hellhole?" There was a hollow ring to his enthusiasm.

To his great surprise, Sir Theodisius nodded. He stretched out his stubby fingers toward a small satchel and opened it, retrieving a sheaf of papers. "These should do the trick," he told Thomas, shuffling the sheets.

"And they are . . . ?"

"Papers to sanction your release. I am hoping the office of coroner carries some sway down here." There was something rather vague in his manner that did not reassure Thomas. But in his parlous state, the doctor had little choice but to go along with the option. He watched the corpulent coroner haul himself up from the chair and put his face up to the grille in the cell door.

"Jailer! Jailer!" he barked. Dowd came quickly. "I wish to see your master. Jump to it!"

Thomas felt his guts tighten as, moments later, he heard more footsteps approaching. The cell door opened and in walked the head turnkey.

"You wished to see me, sir?" he sneered.

Sir Theodisius drew himself up to his full height but he was still at least two inches shorter than the brute. "Sir, I have papers sanctioning Dr. Silkstone's release," he said officiously, handing over the sheets.

The jailer eyed him suspiciously. "And you be?"

"Sir Theodisius Pettigrew, appointed by His Majesty King George as the coroner of Oxford," he told him, his chest puffed out like a pouter pigeon's.

The jailer appeared to study the documents closely for a few moments, then handed them back to the coroner. "They are in order, sir," he said, a smile suddenly curling his lips.

"Then Dr. Silkstone can leave with me?" The coroner could not disguise his relief.

The jailer nodded. "Yes," he replied, "if this was Oxford."

"You would play games with me?" cried Sir Theodisius indignantly, his face reddening.

The smile had disappeared from the jailer's face. He shot a look of disdain at Thomas. "The only place he is going is to the gallows," he hissed. And he flung the document down to the floor and stamped on it before walking out of the cell, banging the door behind him.

Sir Theodisius slumped back in his chair and put his head in his hands. Thomas tried to comfort him. "Do not despair, sir. You did all you could."

The coroner lifted his gaze. "But 'twas not enough. I shall just have to try a different tack." His jowls wobbled as he spoke. "I shall return as soon as I have another plan."

Thomas rose with the coroner and shook his hand. He was grateful for his efforts, but he knew he would have to rely on his own ingenuity if he was ever to leave the four prison walls a free man.

Dowd was summoned and opened the door. It took less than ten minutes to escort the coroner from the cells and to return to Thomas. This time he brought with him some bread, cheese, and small beer. The doctor eyed the food and drink gleefully, even though there was mold on the cheese. He had neither eaten nor drunk since early that morning. "Thank you, Mr. Dowd," he said as the jailer set down the plate and cup beside him. He let out an odd bark as he did so. There it was again. That troublesome cough.

A flicker of a smile crossed the young man's face. "No one's ever thanked me before, sir."

"Well, I am most heartily grateful," replied Thomas. He needed to keep him on his side.

The jailer shuffled from foot to foot. "Tell you the truth, I ain't locked up no gentleman afore," he said. " 'Tis no place for the likes of you, if I may say, sir."

Thomas seized the chance. "And you?"

"Me, sir?"

"Yes. A young man like you can't want to spend the rest of your life in a place like this. You must have family, a sweetheart . . . ?"

"I have a wife, sir."

"A wife, eh?" Thomas was just about to pry a little deeper

when he heard the clanging of a bell along the passage. It was the end of the day watch, when the guards changed.

" 'Tis time I was finished for the night, sir," said the young man, half apologetically.

Thomas nodded. "Off you go then, Mr. Dowd. I shall still be here in the morning when I hope we can continue our conversation."

The stocky youth saw the humor in his captive's remark. A ghost of a smile touched his lips. He gave a shallow bow and backed out of the cell, locking the door behind him.

Left alone once more, Thomas ate the rest of his meager rations and drank the tepid small beer. He then lay down on his ticking and watched the light fade outside through the narrow slit in the wall. Beyond he could make out the sounds of the city, the clatter of carts on cobbles and the shouts of hawkers. But when the pulse had slowed down and the rhythms of the quotidian were being exchanged for the throb of the night, he heard another voice join the throng. It was low and possibly belonged to an older gentleman. From the clarity of his tone, he guessed he was not far away, probably just outside the prison gates. It was, he told himself, entirely possible that his soliloquy was aimed at the wretched souls inside Newgate. From the variance in the timbre, Thomas suspected he was pacing up and down outside the prison walls. His message was clear and unequivocal as he called loudly: "Repent, for the hour is at hand. The Day of Judgment is upon us. Prepare ye for the coming of the Lord."

Chapter 47

That night the angels came, or so the villagers said. They hammered on the door of the vicarage. "The Lord is coming! He has sent his messengers!" they cried.

The Reverend Lightfoot shook the sleep from his silver head and rose. Opening the sash, he looked down at the gathering from his window. The people were pointing up above, and when he, too, lifted his gaze, he saw the miracle. There were colors in the western sky. From out of the blackness came a light so bright that it could have been the halo of a whole host of angels. Within the light shone a myriad of hues, opalescent green and lilac, then gold fading above to almost white. To the left and right was a greenish yellow glow. Lifting his eyes even higher he beheld an open fan of pastel pink, reaching almost as far as the zenith. The whole vision was framed by the deepest cobalt blue.

He watched transfixed as the panorama developed to its full splendor before him. An enormous sense of joy and amazement welled up inside him until he thought his heart would burst at the wonder of the Lord. The display only lasted a few more seconds, until the brighter hues gave way and began to fade. A few seconds more and they were gone, leaving only blackness once more.

Below on the vicarage lawn, many villagers were on their knees. Others held their arms outstretched, as if begging to be taken up by the angels. The Reverend Lightfoot wiped a tear from his cheek. "Brethren," he called down. "Tonight we have been truly blessed. Tonight we have seen the wonder of God in all His glory."

"Amen!" exclaimed Ned Perkins and the others echoed him.

The vicar surveyed his congregation. There were around three dozen souls; men and women, some holding babes in their arms. By the light of their flickering torches he could see those same familiar faces who had packed the church to hear him preach last week and who had crowded round the market square to watch him cast out demons. All were poor; all were wanting a promise of a better life in the next world, if not in this. They were looking to him for guidance.

Reaching his hands out toward them, he stilled their murmuring. "Tonight, brothers and sisters, we have been given a sign," he told them. "We must go away and repent of our sins, for the hour is at hand!" His voice grew in strength with every phrase. "The other week we witnessed the great dragon thrown down from the sky, the ancient serpent who is called the devil and Satan, the deceiver of the whole world, and now, tonight, we have seen God's angels. Remember the words of St. Peter: that there will be those who come in the last days with scoffing, following their own sinful desires. They will say: 'Where is the promise of His coming? For ever since the fathers fell asleep, all things are continuing as they were from the beginning of creation.' But we know, brothers and sisters. We know, for the angels have told us. Prepare yourselves, for the hour is at hand!"

"Amen!" they shouted as one. Some of them crossed themselves in the Catholic way and others bowed their heads, or lifted them up to the heavens. There were shouts of "Alleluia! The Lord is great!" as they began to move down the drive and out of the vicarage gates.

The Reverend Lightfoot smiled as he watched them go. Despite his exhortations to watchfulness, he had no doubt that they would all go back to their beds and truckles and palliasses and sleep soundly. They would leave their repenting until the morrow. After all it was easier to atone after a good night's sleep.

Before he retired once more to his own bed, he glanced over in the direction of Boughton Hall, hidden amid a cluster of dark trees, and thought of Lady Lydia Farrell. Ensconced in the bowels of the earth at West Wycombe, she would not have seen the skies above her head. If she had, that doctor friend of hers would have explained it away with his science, no doubt, just as he had the meteor. He would have offered her his logic and reason, expounding his theories of light and space and magnetic forces. But he, the Reverend George Lightfoot, knew better. He knew it was time for her ladyship to face up to her past. For the hour was at hand. Yes, it was time for Lady Lydia Farrell to repent of her most grievous sin.

Thomas slept fitfully that night. The man parading up and down outside the prison walls had not stopped his incessant diatribe much before ten o'clock and then the noise of the other prisoners farther down the corridor had become even more evident. All night long they had shouted and moaned. Sometimes there was a scream, sometimes a sob or a wail, a low drone or mumble, but never the silence that he so craved. He was relieved to see the first shaft of light, albeit a measly one, lance through the window slit into his cell, and even more relieved to hear footsteps approaching a few moments later. There was Dowd's cough and there was his face at the grille.

Thomas stood to greet him. "Good morning, Mr. Dowd," he called through the bars. But there was no reply, as expected. Instead the stocky youth looked troubled. He watched him trim his lantern in silence.

"What is it?" asked Thomas. "Something is wrong."

The young jailer looked up, sighed deeply, and made his way over to the cell. " 'Tis my wife, sir," he said, shaking his head.

"What has happened?" asked Thomas, his hands gripping the bars.

"She has the fog sickness, sir, and was taken bad in the night." He looked at the doctor through the grille. "She's very sick."

Thomas stood for a moment in shocked silence. He had thought to offer his phial of physick to his young jailer to alleviate his own cough, even though he knew it was not a symptom of the fog sickness. Now, however, this turn of fate offered up a much more fortuitous opportunity for him. With the help of his formula, he could take advantage of the jailer's wife's misfortune and turn it into a gain for them all.

The turnkey unlocked Thomas's cell. "What can I do, sir? Is there a cure?" he asked forlornly.

Without a word, Thomas reached for his coat and delved into his inside pocket. Now was the time to play his trump card.

"This physick would greatly ease your wife," he said, holding up the glass bottle before Dowd's watery eyes. The dark syrupy liquid was worth more than its weight in gold and the young jailer reached up to touch the glass. Thomas, however, pulled it back. He did not like to play games in such a cruel way, but he knew that he was holding a very precious bargaining tool. "I will give this to you gladly, Mr. Dowd, but there is, in effect, a noose around my neck."

The turnkey's hand dropped and he took a step back. "But my wife may die, sir."

"And so might I," countered Thomas. He knew he was treading on thin ice. One blow to the chin from this stocky young man could easily knock him unconscious, but he had to trust his instincts. In one quick movement, he leaped to the slit in the wall and squeezed through it the hand that held the phial. "I can drop it and let it smash on the stones below, Mr. Dowd, or I can give it to you and your wife will live."

The jailer looked terrified. "No," he pleaded.

"Do we have a deal, Mr. Dowd?" Thomas persisted. "This bottle in exchange for my freedom?"

"But sir. I cannot. My master . . ."

"I will leave you manacled and you can tell your master I hit you over the head with my tankard," Thomas told him. "You will have the physick and your master will be none the wiser. What say you?"

Dowd gulped, raised his eyes heavenward, then nodded. "'Tis a deal, sir," he replied.

Chapter 48

On the morning of her third day spent in the caves, Lydia ventured out. Standing at the entrance in the early morning light, she strained her eyes to survey the valley. To the west she saw the red sun low in the sky. It was still thinly veiled by the strange haze but there was a definite lifting of the fog. She sniffed at the air. The acrid smell lingered, but had lessened.

Taking a few steps forward she felt something by her foot. She looked down. A rabbit lay dead on its back, its legs stiff in the air and its mouth red with blood. She let out a startled cry. It was a stark reminder that the danger remained.

Looking directly south, toward London, her thoughts turned to Thomas. She had heard no word. She prayed that Sir Theodisius had managed to warn him before he had been arrested and carted off to some godforsaken prison. Feeling isolated and anxious, she was just about to head back into the gloom of the caves when she heard the plod of horses' hooves. Turning quickly, she saw a cart trundling up the hillside, a cloud of dust in its wake. It was Jacob Lovelock, bringing provisions from Broughton.

"Jacob! What news?" she called, hurrying down the track toward him.

The groom pulled up the horses close by. His pock-marked face was cratered with chalk and he looked grim.

"Tell me, Jacob. What has happened?"

He tied the reins and jumped down from the driver's seat.

"There's a lot that's happened while you been away, your lady-ship," he said, whipping off his hat.

Lydia frowned. "Go on."

"Susannah Kidd."

Lydia felt the breath ebb away from her. "Not dead?"

Lovelock shook his head. "In Oxford Prison."

"Why?"

"She was hiding the knife-grinder in her cottage, so they went to get them both."

"Who? Who went?" she pressed.

"Men from the village. Upwards of sixty, they say. They shot the knife-grinder and took Mistress Kidd."

Lydia shook her head in disbelief. "They shot Joshua Pike? But there was no trial, no proof that he was a murderer!"

Lovelock eyed his mistress with a look of resignation. "These are strange times, your ladyship. Men are acting like wild ani-mals." He lifted his head and she could tell that there was more to relate.

"You are holding something back, Jacob. What is it? Have you heard from Dr. Silkstone?"

Lovelock shuffled his feet in the powdery dirt. "There is word from London, your ladyship."

Lydia thought of Sir Theodisius and his mission to warn Thomas. She guessed from the look on Lovelock's face he had not been in time to save him. She braced herself for bad news. "Well?"

"Dr. Silkstone is in Newgate."

"On what charge?"

Lovelock had no choice but to tell his mistress bluntly. "For the murder of Lady Thorndike."

What little color there was in Lydia's cheeks ebbed away. "I do not understand. On what grounds?" she asked, not really ex-pecting a reply. But Lovelock had an answer for her.

"They say there was a note from Lady Thorndike to arrange a meeting."

Lydia shook her head, then remembered. A note did, indeed, exist. It was a perfectly legitimate invitation to Fetcham Manor, issued by Lady Thorndike in her own hand, that had now been skewed as evidence against Thomas. Sir Henry must have delivered it up to the relevant authority before he relented. It was a cruel and deceitful move that she would not have believed him capable of had he acted on his own.

"Sir Montagu is behind this," she said angrily. "He would do anything, anything, to keep us apart!"

Lovelock stood awkwardly. His head was bowed, looking at the cracked ground, waiting for his mistress to compose herself. Lydia breathed deeply and drew herself up. There was no question in her mind. She knew what she had to do.

"You can begin unloading," she told him. When he had completed the task in hand she would tell him of her plans. She would require him to return later on in the day with the coach. She would go to London herself.

Making his escape had proved far from straightforward for Thomas. Dowd had cooperated fully, allowing himself to be manacled so that it appeared as though Thomas had attacked him and fled. It was finding the way out of Newgate's tangle of tunnels that had proved such a challenge. Once he had negotiated those, there was the small matter of the guard on the gate. He had bluffed his way out, saying he had been to visit a gentleman prisoner suffering from jail fever, and had been allowed to leave.

The tang of sulfur had never smelled so sweet as he rode out of London. Stopping off at Hollen Street, he had managed to assure Dr. Carruthers he was well and to retrieve his medical bag. In an act of great foresight the old anatomist had even written out from memory the formula for the physick. Fortified with breakfast and armed with his physician's case, Thomas made good progress. After a brief stop at Amersham, he was riding into Brandwick just after three o'clock in the afternoon. His first stop was Mr. Peabody's shop.

"My goodness, Dr. Silkstone!" exclaimed the apothecary at the sight of the young anatomist.

"You look as though you've seen a ghost, Mr. Peabody," Thomas countered.

The little man approached him, looking flustered. "I am most glad to see you, sir," he said. "But I'd heard word that you were in prison."

"How bad news travels fast," retorted Thomas. "I am a fugitive, Mr. Peabody, but I am also on a mission. Perhaps you could make this up?" From his pocket he brought out the formula for the new physick. "This should be much more efficacious than the original. It should greatly alleviate the symptoms," he told him, handing him the folded sheet of paper. "We need to get to work."

Mr. Peabody nodded and straightaway started assembling his apparatus, while Thomas scanned the shelves of jars and bottles for the appropriate ingredients. There was the belladonna—a goodly amount, although more would be needed shortly—and there was the turmeric. But it was while Thomas was searching for a flagon of oil of vitriol that something caught his eye. It was a blue-and-white porcelain jar labeled "Vinegar of the Four Thieves." He retrieved it from the shelf, lifted the lid, and sniffed at the mixture of dried herbs inside. It smelled very pleasant; refreshingly pleasant. He detected lavender and a hint of rosemary, perhaps. And there was definitely mint. He recalled having heard of the concoction before. There was a story to its origin; a tale of how four thieves in France robbed and stole from the dead during an outbreak of plague, yet were not infected themselves. This vinegar had been their secret weapon against disease.

"I see you have this, Mr. Peabody," he said, holding up the jar.

The apothecary looked up. "Yes, 'tis best used by steeping the dried leaves in vinegar, although some swear by the herbs alone as a pomade."

Thomas sniffed again. There was a strange bitter back smell that was vaguely familiar to him, but that he could not put a name to. He was just about to ask Mr. Peabody for a full list of ingredients when Dr. Fairweather charged into the shop, a worried expression on his face. It quickly changed to one of surprise when he saw Thomas.

"Silkstone! What on earth . . . ?"

"My presence seems to be having an extraordinary effect on people," said Thomas wryly.

The country physician could not hide his shock, or his relief. "I am so glad you are come, sir," he said. There was a breathless anxiety in his voice. "Sir Henry has suffered a seizure and I fear he is not long for this world. He has been calling for you."

Thomas looked puzzled. Why should the man who was instrumental in putting him behind bars wish to see him? For all the old knight knew, he was still languishing in Newgate awaiting trial.

"I am here for digitalis to ease his chest pain, Mr. Peabody." Fairweather handed the apothecary a prescription. "Do not wait for me, Silkstone. Sir Henry may not have much time."

Thomas needed little persuasion. Within a few minutes he had ridden to Fetcham Manor and was being ushered into Sir Henry Thorndike's bedchamber. He found him lying in bed, weak but conscious. His leathery lids opened wide when he heard the young doctor's urgent footsteps. His mouth parted and he made an odd sound, while one of his hands juddered upward.

"You must calm yourself, sir," urged Thomas, seating himself at the bedside. "I understand you wanted to see me."

The old man's lips were the strange shade of purplish blue that Thomas had remarked so many times before when the heart was the seat of a patient's dire condition.

"I did not want to die knowing I had sent an innocent man to the gallows," he said, gasping for breath between phrases.

Thomas frowned. There were so many questions that needed answers. Sir Montagu was behind his false arrest, that much he knew. But how had Sir Henry become embroiled in the plot and, more to the point, why? Looking down on this fragile body as the life ebbed away from it, he doubted he would get any satisfaction. Interrogating the dying man would be futile and morally reprehensible, and yet his eyes were still open and there was an alertness in his manner that made Thomas believe he actually wanted to talk.

"Are you comfortable, sir?" he asked, bending low.

"I want you to know why . . ." He licked his dry lips. "I want you to know why I gave Malthus the note." Thomas thought of the crumpled piece of paper at Lady Julia's bedside and listened. " 'Twas because he swore that if I helped him put you in jail"— a deep intake of breath—"I could have Lydia's hand in marriage."

The revelation sent a shock through Thomas's body. He felt the tips of his fingers tingle. "I see," were all the words he could muster for a while, as he thought about the prospect of Lydia marrying the kindly old gentleman she regarded more as a father than a potential husband.

Sir Henry lifted a gnarled hand again and Thomas lowered his head to hear more. "He offered me an heir, you see," he croaked. "The boy."

Thomas sat upright. "So your marriage would have united Boughton and Fetcham and secured the future of both."

"But the more I thought about it, the more anxious I became," the old man explained, his breath rasping as he talked.

Thomas knew he spoke the truth. That acute anxiety and stress had, in all probability, brought on this seizure.

"I could never have gone through with it," he added, his head shaking on the pillow. Thomas held his hand in a gesture of comfort and forgiveness. At least he would die with a clear conscience. But there was more. Instead of resting after his admission, Sir Henry seemed to become more agitated. His lips began to move quickly and his tongue flashed between them now and again.

"You must rest, sir," Thomas urged.

The old man's brow crumpled. "She was a whore," he mumbled.

Thomas put his ear nearer his lips.

"A whore!" he mumbled again, suddenly finding more strength.

Thomas studied his patient's pained expression. The wrinkles on his face were like lines on a map. Each furrow was an emotion, a laugh or a frown. Without warning he grasped Thomas's hand.

"She told me about the steward," he croaked. "She taunted me."

The doctor clasped the dying man's hand. It was icy to the touch, but his eyes were fixed on him as if awaiting a response.

"So your wife was meeting Gabriel Lawson at the lake that day?"

Sir Henry nodded furiously. "Yes." He lay back on his pillow. "And now they're both rotting in hell!" He spat the words out so vehemently that he sowed a seed in Thomas's mind. Was the old man making a confession? Had he murdered his wife and then her lover? Men had killed for much less. His watery stare was still clamped on the doctor's face. Doubt hovered in the air, but he was a physician, not a confessor.

Still Sir Henry's eyes blazed with a new intensity. "The vicar," he rasped. "Lightfoot."

Thomas felt the burden lift a little. The old man needed a clergyman to hear his confession, not a physician. If he were to admit to murder in his last hours, it should be to the reverend and not to him.

"I will fetch him," he reassured him, lifting the hand that was still clutching his cuff. Yet the doubt remained.

At that moment Dr. Fairweather arrived with the physick. "How does he fare?"

Thomas said nothing at first until he had turned his back to the patient so that he could not hear. "His pulse is weak and his breathing erratic. He has asked to see the Reverend Lightfoot."

Fairweather put down his case on a nearby table. "I have just seen him," he replied. "He was heading out on the West Wycombe road. I called to him, but he did not answer. He seemed most preoccupied."

Thomas frowned. "West Wycombe? He must be on his way

to the caves. I am going there myself. I shall ask him to return here immediately."

The older physician nodded, glancing over at the ailing nobleman. "Very good," he replied, adding softly: "I do not think we have too much time."

Chapter 49

Lydia was making plans to leave for London. It pained her to think she would be apart from Richard for a few days, but she knew he would be in Eliza's good care. Her son had rallied in the caves and she believed he would be well enough to return to Boughton in another day or two. He was now up and walking around with her as she tended the few remaining patients. He had even taken to fetching her cups or bowls or anything she needed for their comfort. That is how he came to be with her in a small antechamber when the Reverend Lightfoot suddenly appeared from the shadows.

"There is a gentleman staring at us," the young boy told his mother as she poured away stale water from a jug.

Lydia turned to see the vicar standing motionless at the entrance. His eyes were fixed in a glazed stare and his mouth was set flat.

"Reverend Lightfoot!" she greeted him, a little startled. "How kind of you to call again."

For a moment he simply stood looking at the two of them in silence, leaning on his cane. A long cape was draped about his shoulders. He stepped forward and smiled a taut smile.

"Good day to you both," he greeted, but his presence seemed to trouble the child, who hurried over to his mother and hid behind her skirts.

"Are you come to conduct a service, sir?" she asked.

The vicar stopped a few inches away from her and tipped his head oddly. "I think not," he replied.

"Then you wish to see your parishioners?" Lydia was still smiling politely, but beginning to feel a little uneasy.

The vicar shook his head and clicked his tongue. "Wrong again, I fear." This time his tone was tinged with a strangeness that made her pause.

She shook her head. "I am afraid I do not understand."

"Oh, but I think you do." The flat smile disappeared as soon as it had come and he pointed to Richard's limp arm with his cane. "You see, your ladyship, I know about the boy."

Lydia smiled nervously and squeezed the child's hand. "Yes, I told you. He is my son." For a moment she stood confused, but he shook his head and looked her in the eye.

"I know your darkest secret."

She worked her face into another smile and shrugged. "I do not understand your meaning, sir."

"Oh, but you do," he said, shaking his head and moving slowly toward her. "You see the hour is at hand and it is time everything was revealed. You can no longer hide from the light in your cave. It is time your secret was uncovered."

"Secret?" She felt bile rise in her throat.

"Shall I tell your son how he came to have a withered arm?"

Lydia's eyes opened wide. "How do you know?" she gasped.

There was a strange glint in the vicar's eye and his voice became infused with disdain. "Your husband told me. I was his confessor, remember? I saw him weeping on his knees in that stinking cell of his, vile sinner that he was."

"No! Enough," protested Lydia, putting her hands over Richard's ears to shield them from the vicar's vicious taunts.

"Oh, but I haven't even started!" he said, his lips curled in a sneer as he moved ever closer.

"I will not listen to this," she said, raising her voice. "I think it is time you left, vicar." She stood her ground even though she could feel her whole body shaking, yet still Lightfoot drew closer.

"I am not going anywhere, your ladyship, until I have accomplished what I set out to do."

Lydia lifted her head. "And what might that be?" She was staring into his eyes, but they told her little, only that he seemed intent on her humiliation.

"I want the boy."

Her eyes widened and she grabbed Richard's hand. "What can you mean?"

There was a strange smirk on the vicar's face. "Give me the boy," he said and he lurched forward, reaching out for the child.

"No!" screamed Lydia, grabbing Richard by the wrist. She bolted out of the chamber and into the passageway. The boy screamed and the vicar darted after them. He lunged for the child's limp arm and tried to tug him away from his mother, but Lydia was too quick for him. Together they headed farther into the cave, running down a rocky passageway to a junction. Ducking under a low outcrop, they wound their way through a narrow tunnel that opened out into another small chamber. A flaming sconce had lit their way along the passage, but its arc of sickly light did not reach far and they were plunged into semi-darkness. Lydia stopped for a moment, trying to adjust her eyes to the gloom. She could hear the sound of her own heart thumping wildly in her chest and echoing in her ears.

It was then that she became aware of a presence in the chamber. Narrowing her eyes to focus, she saw a figure silhouetted against a large boulder; a dark, smooth shape slumped, head bowed, lolling against the rock. She looked behind her. Lightfoot had not yet caught up with them. The man, for she assumed it was a man, must be one of her patients who had strayed. Approaching him she saw he wore a red scarf on his head. She called to him softly.

"Sir," she whispered, not wishing to alert the vicar. No reply. "Sir," she said again, only a little louder.

She stepped forward and sniffed a sickly-sweet smell that

wreathed his body. Now she could see more clearly. He was young and muscular. Thinking him asleep, she touched his shoulder. It was enough to move him, but not to wake him. His body lolled to one side and fell to the ground. It was only then she saw that the back of his shirt was caked in blood and the blowflies were already feasting on him.

Chapter 50

Thomas heard Lydia's scream as he reached the entrance of the cave. The blood-curdling cries reverberated down the rocky passageway. He found Eliza confused and agitated in the passage, a lantern in her hand.

"Where is your mistress?"

"She and Master Richard are with the vicar," she replied. "What is happening, sir?"

"Lightfoot!" said Thomas, staring ahead into the darkness. In a split second he realized that Sir Henry had not been confessing to a double murder, he had been accusing the vicar. Snatching Eliza's lantern he told her, "Go and fetch help."

Hurrying to the entrance of the small chamber the Reverend Lightfoot found Lydia petrified by Joshua Pike's corpse. Her son still grasped onto his mother's hand and his face was crumpled with fearful tears.

The vicar blocked their way, and smiled when he saw the terror in Lydia's eyes. "What ails you, your ladyship?" he jibed. "You look as if you have come face-to-face with your past." His arm flew out to block the narrow entrance, but she managed to duck beneath his arm and turned down the tunnel that led ever deeper underground toward the River Styx.

Water dripped from the low ceiling and underfoot the ground grew more and more uneven. It was becoming increasingly difficult to negotiate. Richard stumbled over a loose rock, but Lydia held him firmly and pulled him up. She knew she had to make it to the steps on the other side of the river.

Torches blazed intermittently along the route and candles flickered on ledges above their heads, casting weak pools of light on the rutted floor. The air was colder here and she could see her breath curl like smoke. She glanced behind. There were footsteps, fast and steady, but she could not see her hunter.

"Come," she whispered to Richard. The terrified child had stopped crying, but she could see his small body was exhausted. Bending low she scooped him up in her arms. She was thankful he was as light as feather down.

Up ahead she could see a large boulder that half blocked the tunnel. She quickened her pace toward it. It was then that she heard Thomas's voice. For a second she froze. Was she dreaming? No, there was his voice again and it was drawing nearer. She looked at Richard. "We will be safe, my sweet," she whispered as they ran toward the shelter of the rock.

Another few paces and she managed to squeeze through the narrow gap between the wall and the huge boulder. She willed her heart to stop beating so violently so that she could listen, but it echoed in her ears, deafening her to approaching footsteps. Gently she set Richard down and flattened herself against the cold, damp stone. She signed to him to do the same. From somewhere, she was not sure where, she heard Thomas call her name once more. Only this time he sounded farther away. Then she heard them. Slow footsteps. Hidden behind the rock, she turned her head toward the passageway. As soon as she saw the vicar, she would kick out and make him stumble. She waited. Again the footsteps. Leather on stone, then silence. Ten seconds, twenty, thirty passed. Her heart had risen into her mouth, but there was still no sign of her tormentor.

Thomas called her name again. Biting her lip, she resisted the urge to reply, knowing that, if she did, she would give away her position. So she remained silent, trying to still her quivering body. But what she had not realized was that the tunnel was circular. The vicar crept up from behind.

"So there you are!" he blurted. Both Lydia and Richard

screamed and darted back between the boulder and the wall. "Wait! Please wait, your ladyship! I mean you no harm," the reverend called after them, waving his cane. But Lydia ignored his pleas and headed back along the tunnel toward the River Styx once more.

Richard began to cry again, so she took him in her arms, only this time he seemed much heavier. "Not far now," she told him hoarsely. Only another few paces and she was sure they would reach the river. The steps through the rock and out onto the hillside were just beyond on the other side. Of that she was sure.

With her heart still pounding in her ears, she reached the entrance to the chamber that was dissected by the river. A mist rose from its surface like gathering ghosts in the half light. It was too deep for her to ford on foot. Her skirts would drag her down. A few paces along the bank she saw the boat moored. Climbing onto the jetty, with Richard's good arm hooked 'round her neck, she ventured out over the water and tried lifting the loop of rope from the mooring post. But she could not move it. It was heavy and coarse and hurt her hands. She set the child down on the wooden slats and tried to lift the loop once more. But it was tight against the post and she was not strong enough to shift it. Forced to concede defeat, she grabbed Richard's hand and ran back down the jetty, but it was too late. Reverend Lightfoot had rounded the corner and stood before her. With the water behind them, they were trapped. Now was the time. Another cry would alert Thomas. As the vicar approached, she took a deep breath, filled her lungs, and screamed at the top of her voice. The cry reverberated around the cavern walls.

"Dr. Silkstone is coming," she panted, holding her child to her side. "Do not come any closer."

Yet still Lightfoot advanced, his steely eyes fixed on her.

"You do not understand, your ladyship. I only have your best interests at heart. Believe me," he said. He stretched out a hand toward her. "I am giving you the chance to atone for what you did."

"Atone?" repeated Lydia, gripping Richard's shoulders tightly. "You are mad!" she cried. Angry tears started to fall down her cheeks. She knew she had to play for time. Thomas would appear any minute; she just had to keep this evil lunatic talking, she told herself.

"Mad?" he echoed. He seemed indignant at the very suggestion. "Not mad, your ladyship. I am here to warn you."

"Warn me? About what?"

"Warn you that the Day of Judgment is here. Last night God sent his angels to the righteous, but there is still time for you to be saved."

Lydia clasped Richard tightly; his small body was trembling with terror. "Saved from what?"

"From eternal damnation, of course." He nodded his silver head sympathetically, as if he were speaking to a child.

"What are you talking about?" snapped Lydia, her body tensing.

"Why, after you tried to murder your own son, of course." He pointed to Richard with his cane. "Was not that the reason you tried to take your own life?"

Lydia stared at her tormentor, transfixed. "How did you . . . ?"

The vicar threw his head back and let out an odd laugh. "I was there at your bedside, my dear. I listened to your feverish ranting. Your late husband had confessed to attempting to dispose of your unborn child and your suicidal utterances allowed me to complete the puzzle."

Lydia began to shake and she let out a strangled cry. "So take me," she pleaded. "I am the guilty one, but he is innocent." She wrapped her arm across Richard's shoulder, shielding him from their attacker.

The vicar suddenly stopped a few feet away. This time his voice was softer when he spoke, his gaze fixed on the boy. "He is the key in all this, don't you see? He is the one who can unlock the mystery of God's plan for us all. He is the one I want." At these words, his eyes suddenly widened and he began edging toward them both once more, out over the wooden slats of the jetty.

"Get back," shouted Lydia. "You shall not touch a hair on

his head," and she stepped in front of her son. But Lightfoot took no notice and his pace grew faster. "Get back!" she screamed once more.

Lydia's last cry had come from somewhere deep within the labyrinth. She was in a large chamber—Thomas could tell that by the resonance of the echoes. There was a longer delay between each one. He guessed she was heading for the escape route on the other side of the river and had probably reached the shore. Holding a lantern aloft, he was able to move quickly down the rocky passages. A fragment of torn lace from the hem of Lydia's petticoat had led him down the right route at a junction. Now he could see the opening to the river chamber up ahead, but he still wanted the element of surprise on his side.

Peering 'round a jagged outcrop, he saw the vicar standing at the end of the jetty, looking out into the water. He could hear splashing and cries. Rushing forward, he saw Lydia flailing in the water, the weight of her dress making it impossible for her to climb out. But instead of throwing her a rope, Lightfoot was ignoring her pleas and manhandling Richard. The boy was screaming and kicking, but the vicar shoved him into the waiting boat and jumped in after him.

"Lightfoot!" Thomas called, racing toward the river, where Lydia was still being held fast in the grip of the water.

The vicar's head jerked up. "Stay away, Silkstone," he cried, unhitching the rope. Before Thomas could reach the end of the jetty he had cast off, leaving Lydia still flailing below. Flinging off his coat, Thomas jumped in the water and grabbed hold of her from behind. His feet reached the bottom and he was able to heave her back to the jetty. She waved a limp hand.

"Please," she panted. "Save Richard." Her breath began to come in sobs now as she reached out with desperate arms toward the boat that was carrying her son away from her. Clasping her by the shoulders, the doctor looked her in the eye. This was no time for hysterics. She needed a cool head.

"Go back. Eliza has gone to get help," he panted. "He's heading for the escape route. They can't get far."

Still trying to catch her breath, she nodded. "Go," she muttered, squeezing his hand.

Wheeling 'round, Thomas waded waist-deep into the river. From his previous crossing, he knew the water was not too deep. A few feet away he could see the boat had reached the other side. Lightfoot was heaving the sobbing boy out onto the shore.

A moment later the vicar had disappeared with Richard behind a rocky outcrop. The child's cries grew fainter and the echoes of footsteps disappeared.

Another minute passed before Thomas dragged himself out on the other side. He had been forced to jettison his shoes and he felt exhausted from battling against the current. Taking a deep breath, he set off in pursuit once more. He knew the steep stairway was nearby, but he had left his lantern on the far shore and only a single lamp burned in the passage that led to the Inner Temple. He began feeling his way blindly along the rock face, listening for the slightest sound.

After a few more paces he heard the patter of falling scree. Lightfoot must have reached the stairway. He knew that Richard would be able to climb fast. His days as a pipe boy would stand him in good stead. But the vicar would find it harder to negotiate the steep, narrow flue.

Now he reached a gap in the wall. This was it. With his bare feet he found the first step, a cold ledge of rock, and began to climb. Lightfoot had left a candle burning at the foot of the steps, so at least he could see a little way up. The angle was steep and he had to clutch onto the ragged outcrops that dotted the sides, heaving himself up.

The stairway twisted so that he could only see a few steps at a time. Of Lightfoot and Richard there was no sign until, without warning, a rock the size of a man's fist came hurtling toward him, ricocheting off the sides. He ducked just in time to hear it whistle past his face. At least he knew they were still there, although he had no way of telling just how far away, or if he was closing the gap between them.

He counted another twenty steps before he craned his neck again to see a welcome sight. Up ahead there was a chink of light. It was weak but at least it enabled him to see exactly where he was going. Stopping for a moment to catch his breath, he saw that his hands were bleeding where the rocks had cut into them like so many razors. His knees, too, were grazed from kneeling on ledges as sharp as surgeon's knives. He took a deep breath and hauled himself up another flight.

Soon he could hear grunts and moans from up above and he knew he was edging much nearer his target. Rounding another bend, he saw Lightfoot's dark shape squeezing itself through a narrow hole at the top. He froze for a moment, pressing his body against the side of the tunnel. Instead of cold rock, he felt the dampness of the earth through his shirt. For a second he caught a glimpse of the darkening sky as thunderclouds rolled in. Then there was the scraping sound of stone on stone as Lightfoot dragged a slab across the entrance, plunging the tunnel—and Thomas—into blackness once more.

The vicar was heading for the church, Thomas knew that. But what then? His mind suddenly flashed to Richard's baptism and the passage of scripture the vicar had been reading when he entered the room—the trial of Abraham. He had thought it an odd choice at the time, but now it all fell into place. God had told Abraham to sacrifice his only son Isaac to prove his love for Him. The sickening thought occurred to Thomas: the vicar wanted to take Richard with him to the top of the tower. Summoning all his strength he flattened his palms and pushed up against the slab. It did not budge. He tried again and it shifted a little. Another push and it moved enough for him to reach through the gap with his fingers and lever it open. Grabbing the sides of the entrance, he heaved his body out to find himself halfway up the hillside above the caves.

Looking up the hill he could see the tall flint walls of the Dashwood mausoleum and behind that, the tower of St. Lawrence Church, topped by its great golden ball. Silhouetted on the grass just above him was the figure of Lightfoot dragging the boy behind him. Looking down the hill he saw Lydia, struggling upward. He waved to her, but she signaled for him to go on without her and he turned to begin the steep ascent.

Chapter 51

The clouds above were dark and heavy and the first drops of storm rain began to fall. In no time at all the hillside leading up to the church and the golden ball became slippery underfoot. Thomas clung on to clumps of grass to steady himself as he climbed. All the while he kept Lightfoot and his young captive in his sights until they skirted the Dashwood mausoleum and disappeared from view.

Toward the top the ground began to flatten out and Thomas quickened his pace, until the path became level and he could weave in and out of the gravestones that stood in neat rows around the church. He arrived at the great doors of the nave just in time to hear the bolt clatter across, blocking his entry. He was right. Lightfoot intended to take Richard up to the top of the tower. He skirted the nave. The only other possible entry point would be one of the windows. Looking around, he spotted a large slab of stone that had broken off a memorial. Summoning his strength he picked it up and hurled it through the stained glass, shattering it into a thousand pieces. Hauling himself up over the stone ledge he jumped down. He was inside.

Glancing to his left he could see, through open doors, the narrow stairway that led up to the tower. He headed toward it, but not before he had unbolted the main doors to let Lydia in when she finally reached the church.

Climbing the first flight of stairs he reached the ringing chamber, where the bell ropes hung from the ceiling. There was no sign of Lightfoot. He crossed the floor to another stairway that led up past the belfry.

Pausing to regain his breath, he heard Richard shout, though he could not make out what he said. With every step he was edging closer and with renewed vigor he tackled the stairs that led to the open gallery. He arrived just in time to see the vicar doubled over the thin iron railings that barred the open edges of the landing, gasping with exhaustion. It was an eighty-foot drop to the ground below.

"Lightfoot!" Thomas shouted above the wind that buffeted the platform.

The storm was gathering and the surrounding trees were being whipped by strong squalls. He drew closer to the vicar, who, despite gasping for breath, still clung on to Richard's arm.

"Leave the boy!" called Thomas. "He has done you no harm."

The vicar righted himself and looked directly at Thomas. There was a strangeness in his facial features that was new. The stiff lips were slacker, yet the jaw was more prominent. But it was the eyes that revealed the most about the vicar's mental state, Thomas thought. The lids were fully retracted, making them appear bigger, and the pupils were massively dilated. Reason was no remedy in this case, the doctor told himself.

Richard was sobbing at the vicar's side, but he pulled him closer.

"The boy stays with me," he hissed, waving his cane in the other hand. Thomas told himself there had to be some logical explanation for this behavior. Why should a man of the cloth suddenly turn into this terrible monster, pursuing a helpless mother and child? Perhaps, he told himself, the strain of bereavement and the ceaseless work with the sick and dying had taken their toll on the Reverend Lightfoot. He had seen it in many a patient before. The gaunt face, the pallor, the occasional flashes of ill temper and the pent-up emotion that spilled over until the mind seethed and lost control of reason. Perhaps this was what ailed the clergyman. He decided a soft approach would be best.

Advancing slowly toward him, he stretched out his arm. "I mean you no harm, sir. Just let the boy go. Think of your wife. Surely this is not what she would have wanted?"

The vicar glared at Thomas for a moment and then his features began to soften. "Margaret," he said meekly.

Thomas willed his heart to stop drumming in his chest and the wind to be still so that he could hear what the vicar had to say. At the mention of his late wife's name, his mood seemed to alter. The vicar was looking directly at him, but with unseeing eyes.

"I will tell you something, Dr. Silkstone," he said, reason suddenly shaping his voice. "I am ashamed to say that my faith died along with Margaret." Suddenly he began stroking Richard's dark curls thoughtfully. "But this child, this innocent, will restore it. Of that I am sure."

Thomas frowned. He had made a breakthrough, but he was uncertain about what to do next. All he knew was that the vicar's mind was finely balanced and on the brink of madness. The slightest disturbance could tip him over the edge. "All will be well," he assured him. He began to move slowly toward him.

The rain started to fall heavily. It masked Lydia's footsteps as she dragged herself, exhausted, up the narrow stairs that brought her out onto the landing. Soaked to the skin and barely able to breathe, she clapped eyes on her assailant in the daylight for the first time. Her beloved son was trembling in his grip. All control and all reason deserted her. Instead, a surge of electricity shot through her body like a lightning bolt and, with an unearthly cry, she lunged at Lightfoot.

"Get away from him!" she screamed, rushing forward with outstretched arms.

"No!" shouted Thomas, diving at her and pulling her back. But the vicar's moment of reflection had passed and Lydia's outburst had broken his mood. Tugging at the child once more, he turned and began dragging him up yet another flight of stairs that led to a small enclosed room just below the roof of the tower.

"Stop him!" screamed Lydia, tears streaming down her face. She ran after them. Thomas bounded after her and jerked her back. " 'Tis too dangerous. Let me go." Leaving her aside, he scrambled up to the final room. It was deserted. There was only one more flight of steps to the roof. A narrow ladder brought him up into the open air. The first rumble of thunder growled low in the distance and he turned to his left to see the magnificent golden ball. Anchored by three metal chains, it loomed resplendent against the brooding purple sky.

Lightfoot stood breathless before him. His wiry frame heaved up and down, but still he held the child in a vise-like grip.

"Do not come any closer, Silkstone," he warned. He raised his cane.

"Sir, I am interested only in the boy's safety. I beg you," Thomas pleaded as he took a step toward them from the top of the stairway.

"Stay back, Silkstone. Stay back!" he roared, but Thomas saw his chance and made a dash toward the child. Lightfoot swiped at him with his cane and Thomas darted to one side. The stick struck one of the chains, unhinging its silver top. Suddenly strange particles whirled and flew in the air. They fluttered for a moment, caught by the wind, before swirling to the ground. Thomas watched them fall, small flakes on the lead roof. Soaked by the rain, they remained stuck to the tiles. Thomas peered at them. Lavender and mint. Sage and rosemary. Wormwood and rue. This was the pomade used for the Vinegar of the Four Thieves. These were the leaves that he had found in all the victims' bloody wounds. These were the leaves that had fallen from a silver-topped physician's cane.

He shot a look of horror at Lightfoot. The vicar tensed and his mouth began to tremble. "Oh God, forgive me!" he cried. His face crumpled into a grotesque grimace. Tears welled up in his eyes. "I could not see how He could take my Margaret and leave so many wicked people on this earth."

Thomas edged closer. "People like Lady Thorndike?"

Another clap of thunder sounded, only this time closer. Lightfoot nodded his head. "She killed my Margaret."

"And what of Gabriel Lawson?"

"He saw me by the lake afterward."

"So you killed him, too?"

Another nod, only this time it was accompanied by a sneer. "He cuckolded Sir Henry. He deserved to die, too."

"But what of the children? Why did you have to kill them?"

The vicar shook his head.

"The children?" he asked, appearing bemused.

"The innocents you bludgeoned to death?" Thomas lunged forward, making a grab for the cane. Perhaps he had been mistaken. Perhaps this was the murder weapon and not the shovel. But the vicar sidestepped and, dragging Richard by the hair, turned and headed toward the ladder that led up to the door in the ball.

Thomas ran after them, but slipped on the wet tiles. Scrambling to his feet again, he saw Lydia emerge from the narrow stairway. She started running toward him just as the sky was torn apart by the first fork of lightning. Looking up she saw Lightfoot at the foot of the ladder leading to the golden orb. Richard was standing on its first rung.

"The ball!" she screamed, pointing to the pair of them as they began the steep ascent.

Thomas dashed toward them and tugged at Lightfoot's cloak, but the vicar turned and hit him back with his cane. A blow glanced against Thomas's head and he fell to the floor, momentarily stunned. Richard, meanwhile, had reached the drop-down door in the ball and opened it.

"Get in! Get in!" called the vicar from below as he began to climb the ladder.

Thomas wondered at Lightfoot's stupidity. A churchman, of all people, should recognize the risk of a lightning strike, so often did they occur in storms, toppling towers and spires across the country. He recalled that Mr. Franklin had urged Sir Francis to fit a conductor to the great orb, but had not been taken seriously.

"You fool!" shouted the doctor, steadying himself against the railings. "You'll get both of you killed in this storm."

Lightfoot ignored his pleas. There was another crack of thunder, this time directly overhead. Richard was inside the great ball now, his head and shoulders sticking out from the door, calling to Lydia below. The black figure of the vicar, his cloak billowing about him in the wind, was halfway up the ladder when the lightning struck. A massive fork pitched itself across the sky and hurled itself at one of the chains that secured the great orb. The shock sent the clergyman off balance. He let out a scream and his body juddered, causing him to lose his footing on the rungs. He fell backward and his body crashed onto the platform below.

Thomas rushed to his side, while Lydia ran to the bottom of the ladder toward Richard. He knew he must act quickly. He felt for the vicar's pulse as he lay facedown on the floor. Nothing. He checked again, but this time he detected a slight ripple under his fingers as he pressed against the carotid artery. Sliding his hand under his upper torso, Thomas rolled him over. His eyes were shut and there was the smell of singed flesh. Glancing down he saw that the cloth beneath the vicar's large gold crucifix was burned.

Meanwhile Lydia had hurried to the base of the ladder. "Come down. 'Tis safe, now," she called up to her terrified son. The child was hanging out of the door like a rag poppet. His convulsive sobs had given way to dry fear as he had watched events unfold below. Gingerly he turned his body and began climbing down the ladder. His mother was standing at the bottom and hugged him as he jumped into her arms. "You're safe now," she told him, kissing his head. "That man can do you no more harm," she said, looking at the prostrate vicar.

Thomas was still kneeling beside him, wondering at the sheer power of the lightning strike that had surged from the ladder to the cross and chain on Lightfoot's chest. That the vicar still lived was a miracle in itself. Somehow he would need to carry him down the tower. He was contemplating how to maneuver him toward the steps when suddenly he heard a noise coming from the stairwell. He turned to see Ned Perkins emerge.

"Dr. Silkstone!" he called.

"Perkins. Thank God!" replied Thomas.

The foreman approached, a troubled expression on his weathered face. "I were driving here with supplies when I saw Eliza," he explained. "I heard—" He broke off when he saw the vicar splayed out beneath him and looked at Thomas for an explanation.

"He is not dead, but stunned," said the young doctor. "Here, help me lift him."

Perkins bent low and put his hands under the vicar's arms, then, throwing his head back, began to heave. It was then that Thomas saw them: four deep nail marks on the foreman's neck. They were identical to the scratches he had sustained on his own face when he had tried to calm Joseph Makepeace's daughter. Both men's eyes locked. The instantaneous look of horror on Thomas's face betrayed his realization.

In a split second Ned Perkins knew that his wickedness was uncovered. He dropped the vicar like a sack of corn and shuffled backward.

"You!" cried Thomas, glowering over the foreman as he retreated toward the stairs.

"She asked for it," bleated the foreman. "The way she looked at me. A witch, she were. She put a spell on me!"

Thomas shook his head. "She refused you, didn't she? And when her brother tried to protect her, you killed him, too."

Backing toward the stairs, Perkins nodded his head. "The devil was still in them both!" he protested as he reached the top of the flight. Just as he was about to turn tail, he lost his footing and slipped. Dropping down half a dozen steps, he smacked his face against the treads. The momentum catapulted him head over heels down the remainder of the stairs until he hit the landing.

Thomas rushed to see. Looking down he witnessed the foreman desperately struggling to raise himself, but it was obvious to the doctor from the acute angle of one of his lower legs that it was broken. Ned Perkins could go nowhere for the time being.

Just as he was about to join the suspect below, Thomas heard Lydia's sudden scream. Jerking his head up, he could see that the vicar was regaining consciousness. He ran over to where he lay. Lightfoot's eyes were now opened wide. Without warning he sat bolt upright, sending the doctor off balance. Richard called out and in one swift move the vicar was on his feet again. Towering over Thomas, his expression was one of unbridled glee. "I am alive, Silkstone. And the child was spared." His face was glistening with rain and his hair was whipping around in the wind and yet he was wearing a broad smile. "Do you not see what this means?"

Thomas dragged himself up from the floor. "Why do you not tell me?"

Lightfoot gloated. "It means that God has spoken. I offered him the boy as a sacrifice, as Abraham did Isaac. I took him up the mountain and I would have killed him, but the Lord stayed my hand." He lifted an arm up and pointed to the golden ball. "Do you not see? I am saved!"

Thomas tensed, wondering what might be the madman's next move. Perhaps now he would come to his senses. He held out his hand, willing him to take it. "Then you will come with me?"

Lightfoot paused, as if contemplating the gesture.

"Come," repeated Thomas, extending his arm. But a strange laugh suddenly escaped from the vicar's mouth and he darted toward the railings, climbing onto a rung.

"You put your faith in science, Dr. Silkstone. I put mine in the Lord! Let us see who is right!" he cried. His cloak was billowing behind him in the wind, buffeting him like a black sail. The sky was lit up by another flash of lightning. Yet as he teetered on the railings, more than a hundred feet from the ground below, Reverend Lightfoot showed no fear. He wore the sublime expression of a man who is entirely certain of his own immortality. With his back to Thomas he called out, "Is it not written: 'In their hands they shall bear you up, lest you dash your foot against a stone'?" It was a statement, rather than a question. There was a confidence in his stance as he spread his cloak outward as if he had grown great wings. And in one huge bound he leapt off the parapet.

No angels came to catch the corners of his cloak and bear him up. No visions appeared in the sky. There was no voice from the heavens. And for a moment the only sound that could be heard above the storm was the sickening thud of the vicar's head as it caught a gravestone before he hit the ground.

Chapter 52

The poisonous fog persisted until the beginning of September, when it lifted just as quickly as it had come. Great men pondered on it, churchmen and scientists alike. But those who were most touched by it, the poor and the weak, were not interested in its cause, but in its effect. It left in its wake shriveled corn, withered fruit, and shattered lives.

Thomas stood with Lydia on the terrace at Boughton Hall, looking out over the once-lush gardens that, for so many weeks, had been deprived of shadows. The roses were nipped in their buds, their heads fallen and their petals lying scattered on the ground. Amos Kidd would have been saddened to see such a sight, he told himself. He thought of Kidd's widow, Susannah. She had been freed from jail as soon as he had notified the Oxford magistrate of the Reverend Lightfoot's confession. She was now back at home in her cottage, with the remnants of her own life, a torn patchwork quilt with its stitches unraveled.

The fog had brought with it so many unforeseen consequences. It had opened some people's hearts and minds to each other and it had closed others. It had filled some heads with fantastic notions and others with practical reason. It had turned wicked men to religion and previously good men into murderers. While the Reverend Lightfoot had allowed the Lord to deliver his justice at the foot of a church tower, the verdict on Ned Perkins had come in court. After conducting a full postmortem examination, Thomas was able to prove that the foreman had caused the bruising on the Makepeace girl's neck when she resisted his advances. Her brother had tried to defend her and both had fallen prey to Perkins's frenzied vengeance as he wielded their father's shovel. The enlightened jury was not convinced by the foreman's claim that he had been bewitched, and so he was hanged for the murder of the two children.

In his hand Thomas held a letter that had been delivered a few minutes before. It was from Paris, from Mr. Franklin. The American ambassador to France had confirmed his theory that the sulfurous cloud was, indeed, made up of gas and ash from a volcanic eruption. The volcano was, he believed, in Iceland.

The grass on the lawn in front of them was brown and lifeless. Only the weeds seemed to be growing. Weeds will always grow, thought Thomas. And yet it was the first time in weeks that they were able to breathe freely of the untainted country air. Somewhere in the wood beyond a skylark sang; just one, but to anyone who heard it, its song was as shrill and as sweet and as perfect as any skylark's had ever been.

Richard was wheeling a hoop. He was chasing it, like a puppy chases its tail, as it spun 'round and 'round. He seemed fully recovered from his illness and from his traumas of the last few weeks. Lydia reached for Thomas's hand as they watched the boy at play.

"This is a day I thought I might never see," she said softly, her voice full with emotion.

Thomas nodded. "It is a wonderful sight."

"And you think he might have the use of his arm one day?"

"The exercises I showed him will strengthen it." He turned and looked down on her, small as a bird, yet beaming with a mother's pride.

"Thank you," she said softly.

Thomas was puzzled. "For what?"

"For not making me choose between you and Richard."

He nodded and smiled. "A wise man knows better than to force a mother to choose between him and her child."

There was another silence. They had not spoken about Sir Montagu or his plans to keep them apart. All charges against

Thomas had been dropped, and Sir Henry, although he had recovered from his seizure, had withdrawn any intentions he once had regarding marriage to Lydia. Yet a cloud still hung over them. It may not have contained sulfur dioxide but it was poisonous nonetheless. As long as the court order was in place they could never be married. And yet there was hope.

Thomas brandished Mr. Franklin's letter once more. The final paragraph contained more news. "A treaty has been signed."

Lydia turned. "Between our two countries?"

The young doctor nodded, his face breaking into a smile.

"So you are no longer an enemy?"

Thomas put his arm around her. "Our two nations are at peace."

"Then does that mean . . . ?" She was daring to hope the wardship would be annulled.

Thomas shook his head. "No, the order remains, but we do have grounds to fight it in court."

Lydia looked triumphant. "So that is what we shall do. We shall engage a lawyer . . ."

Thomas butted in. "A trustworthy lawyer."

"Yes." She let out a little laugh, acknowledging her mistakes of the past. "A trustworthy lawyer, who will fight our case." She paused. "How long will it take?"

Thomas knew the wheels of English justice turned so very slowly. "Six months. A year." He thought, in all probability, it could well be two or three.

Lydia stared ahead. "What shall we do in the meantime?" she asked gently.

Thomas sighed. "I shall return to my work."

"So you will go back to London?"

"Yes." The doctor took a deep breath. "Sir Joseph Banks has asked me to catalogue specimens, medicinal plants, that sort of thing, from an expedition to the West Indies."

She gazed out over the gardens once more and nodded. Richard was bobbing up and down behind the low hedge in the rose garden. "It is a great honor for you."

Thomas drew her closer. " 'Twill keep me busy," he told her.

"And it will give you more time to spend with Richard on your own."

She nodded and clasped one of his hands. " 'Tis true I have to make up for six long years without him."

His heart fluttered when he heard she could accept his temporary absence in such a positive light. "And then I shall return and we will be together again," he told her.

"Even though we cannot be man and wife?"

"Maybe not as man and wife for now," he said, glancing over at Richard, who was running toward them. "But perhaps as a family."

Panting, but smiling, the child pulled himself up just short of his mother and held out a rose. It was in bud. Lydia took it and thanked her son. Holding it up to her nose she sniffed its perfume. The little boy turned tail and ran once more to his hoop. It was only after he was back on the lawn again that Thomas realized. Richard had given his mother the bloom with his left hand.

Postscript

Before the year was out the normal death rate in Britain is estimated to have risen by a staggering 16.7 percent, the equivalent to approximately 30,000 extra deaths. Many of these were apparently due to respiratory failure and related conditions. The "Great Fogg," as it was known, was the greatest natural disaster to hit the country in modern times. It took several months, however, before the phenomenon was attributed to continuous eruptions from the Laki fissure in Iceland. But there was worse to come. The remaining volcanic gas and ash in the atmosphere diverted the sun's rays and led to the coldest winter for centuries. Many more were to suffer in the coming months.

Chapter 1

bury man: Old English term for a gravedigger.

barque: A sailing ship with three or more masts.

mysterium: Latin word for mystery that is often used in the phrase "mysterium tremendeum," or overwhelming mystery.

great fog: In 1783 the Hampshire naturalist Gilbert White described it thus: "The peculiar haze or smoky fog that prevailed in this island and even beyond its limits was a most extraordinary appearance, unlike anything known within the memory of man."

bloodred sun: A contemporary account states that at noon the sun was "as blank as a clouded moon, but lurid and blood-colored at rising and setting." The poet William Cowper famously wrote at the time: "He sets with the face of a red-hot salamander, and rises (as I learn from report), with the same complexion."

balls of fire: Contemporary records show there was an unusually high number of recorded sightings of meteors between 1783 and 1784, along with several other natural disasters, leading the period to be dubbed the "annus mirabilis," or year of awe.

Chapter 2

wolds: A range of hills in the county of Lincolnshire that run roughly parallel with the North Sea coast.

stooks: A number of sheaves set upright in a field to dry with their heads together.

small beer: Beer mixed with water.

fret: A sea mist, especially common to England's east coast.

flies: The Hampshire naturalist Gilbert White remarked that: ". . . the flies swarmed so in the lanes and hedges that they rendered the horses half frantic, and riding irksome."

lower pay: Laborers were often hired at harvest and were paid by the day or week.

dense fog: A visitor to Lincoln, the county town of Lincolnshire, reported to the *Gentleman's Magazine* in July 1783: "A thick hot vapour had for several days before filled up the valley, so that both the Sun and the Moon appeared like heated brick-bars."

Chapter 3

Delaware Indians: Also known as the Lenape, the tribe originally lived along the Delaware River in New Jersey.

bat: Some Indian tribes of the northwestern United States regard the bat as a symbol of diligence, while in the Great Plains, the animal is said to impart wisdom.

John Hunter: A renowned anatomist who employed questionable methods to obtain corpses for dissection.

milk: Hampshire naturalist Gilbert White wrote that "the heat was so intense that butchers' meat could hardly be eaten on the day after it was killed."

Canada geese: According to the *Oxford English Dictionary*, the term "Canada Goose" was first used in 1772.

Smithfield: The location of a London livestock market dating back to the tenth century. In 1726 Daniel Defoe described it as "without question, one of the greatest in the world."

Charles Byrne: The man known as "the Irish Giant" is said to have wished to be buried at sea when he died to avoid being dissected.

Chapter 4

Celsianas: A variety of rose dating back to the late eighteenth century.

saltpeter: Also known as potassium nitrate, saltpeter has been used to cure and preserve meat for more than two thousand years.

Combe Gibbet: Erected in 1676, a replica gibbet remains on the same spot. The original was erected to hang George Bromham, a married farm laborer from Combe, and Dorothy Newman, a widow of Inkpen. The pair was found guilty of the murder of George Bromham's wife Martha and their son Robert.

Hungerford Workhouse: In 1782 Edward Sheppard, the owner of an inn called The Three Tuns, let the premises in Charnham Street for use as a workhouse.

cooper: A craftsman who makes barrels.

Chapter 5

sweathouses: Every Delaware Indian settlement would have a steam house where sickness could be "sweated out."

Williamsburg storm: Between September 7 and 8, 1769, one of the worst storms of the eighteenth century devastated the Chesapeake Bay area, leaving Williamsburg almost flattened.

woe water: According to a Chilterns tradition, certain bournes, or streams, only flow at times of tragedy or disaster and are called woe waters. One such recorded instance was during 1665 at the time of the Great Plague.

"A good example is the best sermon." The quote appears in the 1747 issue of Benjamin Franklin's *Poor Richard's Almanack*.

Chapter 6

The Three Tuns: A tun was a barrel.

pharo: The English alternate spelling of faro, a popular card game that originated in France.

great golden ball: The famous landmark was erected on top of the tower of the church of St. Lawrence, West Wycombe, by Sir Francis Dashwood. It is hollow and can seat up to eight people. The Hellfire Club may have met inside. Mirrors may have been used to signal to another nearby tower.

Church of St. Lawrence: Built on an Iron Age fort, the fourteenth-century church was completely remodeled by Sir Francis Dashwood, who added a new tower.

West Wycombe Park: The house, in Buckinghamshire, is one of the finest examples of Italianate architecture in England. Although the structure is owned by the National Trust, it remains the home of the Dashwood family today.

Sir Francis Dashwood: A notorious libertine and bon vivant, he created the infamous Hellfire Club, which sometimes met in the Hellfire Caves.

Bedford Coffee House: A Covent Garden coffeehouse, popular with actors and literary figures.

Hellfire Caves: A series of hand-carved tunnels created by Sir Francis Dashwood, near West Wycombe Park, from the original prehistoric caves. They lie three hundred feet underground and are open to the public.

Boston: On December 16, 1773, a group of colonists threw a large quantity of tea into Boston Harbor to protest against the fact that it was taxed by the British Parliament and not by their own elected representatives. Only much later did the incident come to be labeled the "Boston Tea Party."

Benjamin Franklin: The American polymath was a friend of Sir Francis Dashwood's and a frequent visitor to West Wycombe. After a trip to the Hellfire Caves he wrote: "The exquisite sense of classical design, charmingly reproduced . . . whimsical and puzzling as it may be in its imagery, is as evident below the earth as above it."

Sir John Dashwood-King: The half-brother of the infamous Sir Francis Dashwood, he inherited the title and estates on Francis's death in 1781. He was a member of the Hellfire Club, which his brother had founded.

Temple of Daphne: Designed around 1745, the folly still provides a meeting and resting place in the grounds of West Wycombe Park.

The Black Bear: There was also a White Bear Inn in Hungerford. The word "black" was dropped during the nineteenth century and the Bear remains a hotel in the town today.

Good King William: In 1688 the Protestant Prince William of Orange landed at the head of an army in Devon and met the Commissioners appointed by James II at the Black Bear. He went on to become King of Great Britain.

Chapter 8

Downs: The Berkshire Downs run east-west, with their scarp slope facing north into the Vale of the White Horse and their dip slope bounded by the course of the River Kennet. Geologically they are continuous with the Marlborough Downs.

Inns of Court: Buildings or precincts where barristers traditionally lodged, trained and carried on their profession.

Chapter 9

wet nursing: Women, especially those had given birth to an illegitimate child, sometimes had to give their baby up, temporarily or permanently, to a wet nurse. In other households it was deemed acceptable to place a baby with a wet nurse until it was weaned.

foundling token: An item pinned to a baby's clothing for identification purposes when a mother brought her child to London's Foundling Hospital, established in 1739. It is now known as The Foundling Museum.

Chapter 10

sulfur: It was not until 1777 that sulfur was found to be an element and not a compound.

powdery frost: The Hampshire naturalist Gilbert White reported twenty-eight days of continuous frost.

Spanish liquorice and salt of tartar: According to Wesley's *Primitive Physick* this is a remedy for an asthmatic cough.

Chapter 11

magnifying glass: The origin of the magnifying glass is uncertain, but they were certainly widely in use by the fifteenth century.

sugar: Households bought their white sugar in tall, conical loaves, from which pieces were broken off with special iron sugar-cutters.

great pillar of carbon: A dramatic reaction is caused when sulfuric acid is added to sugar to produce carbon.

Chapter 13

baccarat: A card game enjoyed by gamblers and similar to pharo.

curry: The first documented recipe for "currey" was published in *Art of Cookery* by Hannah Glasse in 1747. This recipe is reflective of a typical Indian curry.

Chapter 14

famine: The Irish Famine of 1740–1741 should not be confused with what became known as the Great Famine of 1845–1852.

Rightboys, the Hearts of Oak, and the Steelboys: Peasant secret societies were formed in eighteenth-century Ireland to oppose brutal landlords.

Chapter 15

Seymour Street: Built around 1769 as London grew to the west.

Oxford Chapel: Now known as St. Peter's, the chapel was built in 1722.

Whitehall Stairs: A public landing place, as opposed to the Privy Stairs a little farther up river, where ferrymen would ply their trade. At this time there were only two bridges across the Thames, London and Westminster.

Tyburn: The place for public executions until 1783, after which time Newgate Prison was used.

Chapter 16

listening tube: The stethoscope was the recognized invention of a Frenchman, Dr. René Laennec, in 1816.

Chapter 17

St. Giles: The area in London most associated with an Irish population during the eighteenth century. It was also one of the most lawless areas of the city.

Covent Garden: An area particularly noted for prostitution. Many young women came to London from the country looking for work in domestic households, but quickly fell prey to the vice trade.

Chapter 18

The Angel of Death: According to the Book of Exodus, in the tenth and final plague, God sent the Angel of Death over the land of Egypt to kill the firstborn of all Egyptian humans and animals.

Vicar of Eyam: William Mompesson persuaded the villagers to close themselves off to the outside world during an outbreak of plague in 1666, thereby preventing its spread.

sack: The drink now known as sherry.

"The Lord giveth . . ." The full quotation can be found in the Book of Job 1:21.

Chapter 19

Piazza: An area of taverns, shops, brothels, and coffeehouses in Covent Garden. By the end of the eighteenth century it had been dubbed "the great square of Venus."

Bermondsey: An area of London to the south of the river in the borough of Southwark.

pipe boy: The colloquial name for a chimney sweep's boy.

Chapter 20

volcano: Canadian Indian legends record a British Columbian eruption of the Tseax Cone around the years 1750 or 1775. It is believed around two thousand of the native Nisga'a people died due to volcanic gases and poisonous smoke.

Craven Street: Benjamin Franklin lodged in a house here between 1757 and 1775, while he was mediating between America and Britain. Today it is open to the public.

treatises on meteorology and ocean currents: Benjamin Franklin wrote several papers on these subjects.

St. Martin's: The church of St. Martin-in-the-Fields, just off Trafalgar Square.

Drury Lane: A notoriously riotous street, known for drunkenness and prostitution.

Garrick: David Garrick was the most famous actor of his day.

Chapter 21

loo table: Originally designed for the card game loo, it was a table with a round or oval top that was hinged to facilitate storage when not in use.

refined soot: In his book *Modern Husbandman* (1750), William Ellis recommended that soot and coal ashes, as well as cows' hooves, hogs' hair, and even pigs' trotters, should be ploughed into the soil to improve its fertility.

Chapter 22

testicular cancer: Also known as soot wort, this was a form of occupational cancer that was initially identified by Percival Pott in 1779.

barber's shop: Barbers also acted as dentists, regularly pulling teeth.

sores: A symptom of primary syphilis. The sores, or chancres, resemble large bug bites and are often hard and painless.

prostitution: An estimated one in five women in London was engaged in the sex trade at this time.

Chapter 23

electricity: A number of scientists were conducting experiments into electric charges at this time, including Benjamin Franklin and the preacher John Wesley.

Chapter 24

brig: A two-masted, square-rigged ship.

pepper pot dome of Christ Church: Sir Christopher Wren designed the famous dome of the Oxford college.

Chapter 26

undertaker: By the middle of the eighteenth century undertaking was an established profession in London and soon spread to the provinces.

Chapter 27

caves at West Wycombe: Impoverished local villagers were paid a daily wage of one shilling to tunnel underground. The caves were all excavated by hand and the chalk was used to make a major road connecting the area to London, Oxford, and Gloucester. They became known as the Hellfire Caves when the eponymous club began to hold meetings in them. Such was the club's reputation for orgies and black magic, however, that it had disbanded by 1763 (according to church records). After this the caves began to fall into disrepair.

Battle of Trenton on the Delaware: Washington ordered a field hospital to be set up near the crossing point in 1776. Today you can visit Thompson Neely House, where many of the troops were treated. It forms part of Washington's Crossing National Historic Landmark.

Chapter 29

bathing room with smoldering coals: An ancient method of execution was to shut the criminal in a bathing room with smoldering coals until he suffocated to death, although the mechanism of death was not understood until the mid-nineteenth century.

storms: Hampshire naturalist Gilbert White wrote of "tremendous thunder-storms that affrighted and distressed the different counties of this kingdom." One correspondent in the *Gentleman's Magazine* (August 1783) proposed that there was "no year upon record when the lightning was so fatal in this island as the present."

firework displays in London: Several parks and pleasure grounds held displays at this time.

praying in the streets: Preacher John Wesley wrote at the time: "Men, women and children flocked out of their houses and kneeled down together in the streets." At Sunday service he reported the church was full—"a sight never seen before."

Chapter 30

Gothic entrance: Built after 1752, the flint entrance was designed to look like a Gothic church to be seen from West Wycombe Park, just across the valley.

River Styx: According to Greek mythology, the river separated the mortal world from Hades. The subterranean position of the Inner Temple directly beneath St. Lawrence's Church was therefore thought to represent the divide between Heaven and Hell.

Chapter 31

developed sores: Eight out of every ten sheep are thought to have died, while half of all horses and cattle perished.

the weavers at nearby Cholsey: Shortages meant grain was being sold at 30 percent more than its pre-fog price, sparking riots. At Halifax in Yorkshire, men from the surrounding weaving villages gathered to force merchants to sell their corn at old prices.

a great ball of fire: On August 18, 1783, what was known as the Great Meteor was seen crossing Britain from the North Sea down to the English Channel. The most notable account of the episode was given by Tiberius Cavallo, an Italian natural philosopher who was a guest at Windsor Castle at the time, in volume 74 of the *Philosophical Transactions.*

a sign: The General Evening Post reported on August 26, 1783, that "a Methodist preacher in his sermon on Sunday, informed his audience that the meteor seen a few evenings ago, and which went over their heads, was a warning gun, but they might resort assured that the next which came would not fly so high, but blow their brains out."

Chapter 32

Judgment Day: On a visit to Witney, Oxfordshire, in 1783, the Methodist preacher John Wesley wrote that during a thunderstorm, "those that were asleep in the town were waked and many thought the day of judgment had come." He went on to record: "Men, women and children flocked out of their houses and kneeled down together in the streets."

Chapter 33

Chancery: The Court of Chancery exercised wardship jurisdiction, but it was notoriously inefficient and was finally abolished in 1875, although the Chancery division remains to this day.

Chapter 34

panniers: Worn under the heavy skirt of a Georgian lady, it was a device designed to support the material.

Chapter 35

many believed Judgment Day was upon them: The Morning
Herald, and Daily Advertiser published an account from Honi-
ton, Devon, on December 21, 1783. It stated: "About three
hours ago we were all struck with a panic too dreadful to be described; a universal terror seized the whole town, and most people believed the world was at an end, for that the moon was
falling from heaven." The Hampshire naturalist Gilbert White
wrote, "There was reason for the most enlightened person to be
apprehensive."

Psalms: "And they that know thy name will put their trust in
thee: for thou, Lord, hast not forsaken them that seek thee."

Chapter 36

a ward of court: A person under twenty-one who was the subject of a wardship order, ensuring the court has custody. As long
as the minor remains a ward of court, all decisions regarding his
or her upbringing must be approved by the court.

an enemy territory: England officially declared an end to hostilities in America on February 4, 1783, but the Treaty of Paris
was not signed until September 3, 1783, and not ratified until
January 14, 1784.

Chapter 38

sage juice and honey: According to John Wesley's Primitive
Physick, these were beneficial to a patient who spat blood.

horehound: An herb used for centuries to alleviate chest conditions.

Peruvian bark: A source of quinine.

exorcism: The most famous exorcism at this time was carried
out in 1778 on George Lukins, a tailor who for eighteen years
had been subject to atypical fits. Seven Methodist ministers per-

formed an exorcism after which he reportedly returned to normal. An article in *The Gentleman's Magazine and Historical Chronicle* criticized the account, stating that Lukins actually suffered from "epilepsy and St. Vitus's dance."

"Come sinners to the gospel feast": The hymn was composed by Charles Wesley in 1747.

St. Vitus' dance: A brain disease that causes involuntary movements or spasms.

Chapter 39

Tree of Knowledge: According to the Book of Genesis, this tree grew in the Garden of Eden.

Salem: The Salem witch trials were a series of hearings and prosecutions of people accused of witchcraft in colonial Massachusetts between February 1692 and May 1693.

Chapter 41

Isaac: According to the Book of Genesis, God commanded Abraham to offer his son Isaac as a sacrifice to prove his loyalty.

fowler: A hunter of birds.

musket: In 1770 British hunters coined the word "sniper" to designate a great marksman—one who could shoot a tricky flying bird such as the snipe with a fowling piece.

Chapter 42

Rahab and Mary Magdalene: According to the Book of Joshua, Rahab was a woman who assisted the Israelites in capturing the city of Jericho. Most English translations describe her as a harlot or prostitute. Mary Magdalene was branded a prostitute by Pope Gregory in his homily on Luke's gospel in 591.

lock-up: A small temporary jail remains in Church Loft, West Wycombe to this day. A whipping post can be seen nearby.

Chapter 43

Montgolfier brothers: The first public flight of their famous balloon was on June 4, 1783, in France.

Flax and Cotton Bill: "An Act for the more effectual Encouragement of the Manufactures of Flax and Cotton in Great Britain" was debated and passed by the House of Lords in July 1783.

Chapter 45

a physician's cane: The head of the cane was perforated and contained certain vinaigrettes and aromatic powders that could be inhaled as a method of preventing contagion while treating patients.

atropa belladonna: Often associated with the treatment of intestinal disorders, the plant was used for centuries as a treatment for asthma and hay fever because of its antispasmodic properties.

rue: As well as its many medicinal purposes, rue is also known as "Herb of Grace" because it has been sprinkled in exorcisms.

wormwood: Also known as absinthe, mugwort, and *Artemisia absinthium,* it comes from the Aster/Daisy family of plants and has hallucinogenic qualities.

magnetic test: silver is not magnetic.

Chapter 46

gates of Newgate: Newgate Prison was badly damaged in the Gordon Riots of 1780, but was rebuilt by 1782. The following year the site of the London gallows was moved from Tyburn to Newgate. Public executions outside the prison—by this time, London's main prison—continued to draw large crowds. The gates dating back to this period can be seen at the Museum of London.

Day of Judgment: John Wesley, writing about his stay in Witney, Oxfordshire, during the period of violent and frequent thunderstorms said, "those that were asleep in the town were waked and many thought the day of judgment had come."

Chapter 47

colors in the western sky: The description is based on writings by Luke Howard, known as the father of meteorology. He witnessed the incredible events of 1783 as a boy and is thought to have been greatly influenced by what he saw. In southern England two weeks after the Great Meteor there are several reports of aurora sightings, described in the *London Chronicle* (September 7, 1783) as "one of the strongest Aurora Borealis ever seen in this country."

great dragon: A report in the *Morning Post And Daily Advertiser* (August 21, 1783) relates that "A Methodist preacher, who saw the aerial phenomenon on Monday night last, described it the following evening in his sermon thus: I saw heaven open, and lo! a prodigy! a revelation! in flames, a huge beast with seven heads and ten horns: seven crowns and ten comets issued; and like a wounded whale, gasped in the vacuum for the period of one hour, till at last the great mystery suddenly fell! Michael prevailed, and hurled the dragon down head-long."

St. Peter: Taken from 2 Peter 3:4.

Chapter 48

Vinegar of the Four Thieves: Legend has it that thieves who robbed from plague victims in a southern French city, usually between the fourteenth and eighteenth centuries, were protected from infection by this combination of herbs. By the nineteenth century its use had spread to America. According to *The Virginia Housewife,* published in 1838, the mixture is "very refreshing in crowded rooms, in the apartments of the sick; and is peculiarly grateful when sprinkled about the house in damp weather."

digitalis: The use of *D. purpurea* extract for the treatment of heart conditions was first described by William Withering in 1785.

Chapter 50

Dashwood Mausoleum: Based on the design of the Constantine Arch in Rome, the mausoleum was the resting place of members of the Dashwood family from 1765.

Chapter 51

lightning conductor: Although there is no evidence that Benjamin Franklin suggested a lightning conductor be affixed to the golden ball, he may well have advocated it. His invention in 1752 met with almost universal disapproval among clergymen, despite the fact that dozens of church towers were regularly damaged by lightning.

"In their hands they shall bear you up, lest you dash your foot against a stone": Luke 4:11.

Chapter 52

Franklin: Benjamin Franklin's treatise on the bizarre atmospheric conditions of 1783–4 were contained in his *Meteorological Imaginations and Conjectures*. Initially he thought the fog might be due to the "vast quantity of smoke, long continuing to issue during the summer from Hecla in Iceland."

treaty: The Treaty of Paris, signed on September 3, 1783, ended the American Revolutionary War between Great Britain and the United States and its allies.

Sir Joseph Banks, 1743–1820: An explorer, botanist, and scientist, he was involved in most British voyages of discovery of his day, including that of *The Bounty* under William Bligh. From 1773 he acted as unofficial director of the Royal Gardens at Kew, organizing expeditions and collecting botanical specimens that arrived from all over the growing British empire.

West Indies: Several wars were fought over these islands in the Caribbean Sea, mainly between the Spanish, French, Dutch, and British. Possession often changed with the outcome of numerous naval battles. In 1783 Britain owned several islands in what was known as the Colony of the Leeward Islands, Jamaica and its dependencies including the Cayman Islands, the Colony of the Bahama Islands, the Colony of Bermuda, and the islands of Barbados, Grenada, St. Vincent, Tobago, and Dominica.

Author's Notes and Acknowledgments

I was first alerted to this most extraordinary, and yet hitherto relatively unknown, episode in modern British history by a fairly recent phenomenon. In April 2010 most of Scotland and England and, indeed, much of northern Europe, found itself at the mercy of a volcanic ash cloud. Thousands of flights were canceled, millions of air passengers were stranded, and the economic fallout was huge. The eruption of the Eyjafjallajokull Volcano in Iceland lasted twenty-three days, and yet this most recent episode pales in comparison to another eruption in Iceland's modern history.

Our twenty-first-century inconveniences and frustrations were as nothing compared with what happened when, on June 8, 1783, another eruption in Iceland, of the Laki fissure, sent 132 tons of toxic gas hurtling into the atmosphere. The effects were devastating, not just for Iceland, where half the livestock died and a quarter of the population was wiped out due to the subsequent famine, but for a large area of northwest Europe, too.

Not only that, but contemporary European observers during that period dubbed it an "annus mirabilis," or year of awe, because of the remarkable concentration of natural disasters. Added to the inexplicable poisonous fogs were violent thunderstorms, huge hailstones that reportedly killed cattle, and even frequent meteor sightings. There is little wonder that many people at the time feared the biblical Day of Judgment was near.

What we now know to be the simultaneous eruption of 130 craters along the huge Laki fissure sent lethal clouds of sulfur dioxide and fluorine into the atmosphere. Some saw the resulting poisonous haze as an act of God, while others, at the dawn of the European Enlightenment, regarded it as a scientific phenomenon, although its cause was not known at the time. (It was Benjamin Franklin who first postulated the theory that a volcanic eruption in Iceland was responsible.)

It seems that until we experienced our own "Great Fogg," the catastrophic effects of Laki seemed to remain largely forgotten because of the equally momentous political events of the time, such as the American War of Independence and the French Revolution. Nevertheless, from the natural disaster there are many lessons to be learned.

This is a work of fiction and, as such, I have taken liberties with the facts to enhance the dramatic tension of the story. Scientists are still debating the full impact of the Laki eruption; the "Great Fogg" may not have been associated with a volcanic ash fall and its arrival would certainly not have been as dramatic as portrayed in the previous pages. Nor could it have been predicted. Yet its study could prove vital to our own future. When Laki does erupt again we need to be more prepared to deal with its deadly fallout. If we are not, then the consequences could be even more serious than they were 230 years ago.

In my research I am indebted to the staff at the Museum of English Rural Life, Reading; Gilbert White's House, Selbourne, Hampshire; the Hellfire Caves and St. Lawrence's Church, West Wycombe; the Museum of Methodism, City Road, London; and Benjamin Franklin's House, Craven Street, London. Thanks also go to Dr. Kate Dyerson; Dr. Richard Payne of Manchester; John and Alicia Makin; my agent, Melissa Jeglinski; and my editor, John Scognamiglio.

—England, 2012

THE
DEVIL'S BREATH

A DR. THOMAS SILKSTONE MYSTERY

TESSA HARRIS

KENSINGTON BOOKS
www.kensingtonbooks.com

KENSINGTON BOOKS are published by

Kensington Publishing Corp.
119 West 40th Street
New York, NY 10018

All Kensington titles, imprints, and distributed lines are available at special quantity discounts for bulk purchases for sales promotion, premiums, fund-raising, and educational or institutional use.

Special book excerpts or customized printings can also be created to fit specific needs. For details, write or phone the office of the Kensington Special Sales Manager: Kensington Publishing Corp., 119 West 40th Street, New York, NY 10018. Attn. Special Sales Department. Phone: 1-800-221-2647.

Kensington and the K logo Reg. U.S. Pat. & TM Off.

ISBN-13: 978-0-7582-6700-9
ISBN-10: 0-7582-6700-2
First Kensington Trade Paperback Printing: January 2014

eISBN-13: 978-1-61773-027-6
eISBN-10: 1-61773-027-0
First Kensington Electronic Edition: January 2014

10 9 8 7 6 5 4 3 2

Printed in the United States of America